Michael B Fletcher is an Australian writer of adult and YA speculative fiction including fantasy, science fiction and horror genres with over 100 short stories published in magazines and anthologies in Australia, USA and the UK, and two collections, *A Taste of Honey* (Double Dragon/Fiction4All 2021) and *Kings of Under-Castle* (IFWG Publishing 2013).

His published novels include a fantasy trilogy, *Masters of Scent* (IFWG 2022-2024) and *Kat,* a co-authored YA scifi (IFWG 2024).

T0288790

Other Michael B Fletcher Titles by IFWG Publishing

Kings of Under-Castle (humorous short fiction collection)

Masters of Scent Trilogy (epic fantasy)
    Masters of Scent (Book 1)
    Tumblers of Rolan (Book 2)
    Shadow Scent (Book 3)

Kat (with Paula Boer) (Young Adult science-fiction)

Masters of Scent Trilogy: Volume 3

Shadow Scent

by
Michael B Fletcher

IFWG Publishing International
Gold Coast

www.ifwgpublishing.com

Acknowledgements

The completion of the *Masters of Scent* trilogy has been an epic but rewarding journey. I have appreciated input from a number of people along the way especially my close writing friends in the Gunnabees writing group that provided suggestions on aspects of the trilogy in a non-critical comfortable environment. Then there was the ongoing development through workshops, courses and masterclasses, all of which helped me hone my craft.

My thanks go to my publisher, Gerry Huntman of IFWG Publishing for having confidence in my writing and bringing *Masters of Scent* into the real world. A special thanks to Sarah Morrison for producing the marvellous covers for the three books and to Noel Osualdini who made editing the final manuscripts an, at times challenging but overall pleasurable journey.

A final mention should go to Kim, my friend, writing critic and wife, without whom *Masters of Scent* would never have been born.

Chapter One

"We have much to consider!" Vitaris' voice echoed in the vast hall. He flexed his rounded shoulders before pushing his shaven head back into the headrest of his carved wooden chair, stretching taut the purple and golden robe he wore. He rested his hands on the dark-wood table as he looked at his sons seated on each side of him.

Faltis, tall and thin, crossed one leg over the other before changing back, lips moving on his pale face, dark eyes looking inward while his fingers tapped the arms of his chair. He started to speak, then lapsed back into silence.

Jakus, a strong, commanding presence, leant forward. "Indeed Father, we do," he agreed. "I take it you are referring to the imminent arrival of my ambitious brother?"

"Hmm." Vitaris looked at Jakus, then across at Faltis. A frown flickered over his lined forehead before he turned back to his oldest son. "He is the catalyst, yes. But that doesn't negate our need to determine what is best for Sutan and our plans to rule more than just this country. You have to some extent facilitated this by your foray into Rolan and the acquisition of the red crystal, although the value of magnesa is yet to be determined. However," he continued as Jakus opened his mouth, "I have no need to go into this now. It is for you to update Brastus at the appropriate time, calmly and, as befits a leader, rationally. He is your ally, not enemy." He looked at his gnarled hands spread on the dark wood before him.

Jakus harrumphed and leant back.

"So," Vitaris continued, "we need to look at the strategy after consolidating Sutan. We need to return Ean to our rule, then conquer Rolan and Tenstria. Reports from Brastus' campaign reveal that Tenstria is all but under our control. Which is more than I can say for Ean." He glanced from under bushy eyebrows at Jakus.

Jakus' eyes glittered and a scent aura flashing deep reds and purple thickened around his head.

"But"—Vitaris held up a placating hand—"that will not be my concern. I have yet to name my successor, and it will be between you and Brastus. Faltis has shown himself to be of inferior character."

Faltis raised his head. "Vitaris—or should I say *dear Father*—you have no idea what I went through. What I have lost. How I fought alongside my brother to achieve *his* goals. What I have learned. Yes"—his eyes turned inward—"what I have learned. Do not discount me, old man!"

Vitaris and Jakus looked sharply at Faltis.

"It will be up to you Jakus to work with Brastus. I have no wish to be involved in more altercations and backstabbing," Vitaris sighed. "Remember what you need, what Sutan needs, what our future is. Sutan is about more than one man. Remember this when you plan.

"Work with your brothers, my son. Make Sutan proud. Leave me a long-lasting legacy."

"Why don't you make use of your tame soothsayer then, Father?" interrupted Faltis. "If you want to know the future, use her!"

"I have no objection, Vitaris," added Jakus reasonably. "Bring her in. Let us see if she says anything of value."

Vitaris slowly nodded, then flicked a hand towards one of the indistinguishable figures standing in the alcoves along the walls. "Fetch Xerina!"

The sound of the guard's boots faded away while the trio waited. Jakus could hear faint creaks from Faltis' chair as his brother fidgeted.

Remembering what happened last time I relied on the old woman, thought Jakus, recalling his brother's attempts to oust him and kill his tame Eanite, Kyel, when he had first returned to Sutan years before. Faltis had interpreted one of Xerina's Knowings as the justification to attack his returning party and attempt to kill the youth.

That, Jakus smirked to himself, *had resulted in his own downfall. Now look at him, twitchy, with no friends, and even his own son, Bilternus, has nothing to do with him.* Faltis looked over as if he knew Jakus was thinking about him, his eyes like dark holes in a skull. Jakus shuddered involuntary. *Something has gone wrong with him since our campaign in Rolan.*

The click of a stick and shuffle of feet coming from the back of the hall broke through his introspection. They could see the bent shape of Xerina hobbling towards them.

"Y…you asked for me, Shada?" puffed Xerina to Vitaris without acknowledging Jakus or Faltis.

"I need to know which of your foretellings may have bearing on the future of Sutan and our expansion?"

"Shada?" The old woman lifted her head, straightening her worn grey robe. "The Knowings that come to me on the scent winds are vague, uncertain things which can't be called to order. If they come and my interpretation is that they'll impact on this country or your plans, then I most certainly will advise you."

"Dispense with the baggage, Father!" growled Faltis. "Anything she says is couched in such vague terms it can be interpreted in any way. Her saying an Eanite would destroy Sutan was just a lie. We all suffered because of it."

"Yes, that was foolish." Jakus looked pointedly at his brother.

"My Shada"—Xerina leant forward on her stick—"Knowings can refer to the here and now or the distant future. Am I to be held responsible for them?"

"Xerina," said Vitaris, "I am asking whether you have had any foretellings or Knowings regarding our future, from the consolidation of Sutan and the achievement of our ambitions. You must have something if your position in our household is to be of any worth."

"My Lord Vitaris, I am but your servant, as I have been for many years now." She bowed her greying head, knuckles gleaming whitely on the head of her stick. For a moment her harsh breathing was the only sound, until she raised her head. "Small or light Knowings have been occurring, taking much to interpret. They have been so vague I haven't reported on them until I could gain a better understanding."

"There, you see, she's been holding out on us!" yelled Faltis. "Useless. Kill her!"

Xerina swivelled her head, eyes pinning Faltis. "Yes, you would like that, wouldn't you?" She paused, taking a few breaths before turning back to Vitaris.

"I will endeavour to do what I can, Shada. But what I can tell you is that the future is uncertain. Dark and uncertain for all of you. But"—Xerina looked at Jakus—"beware of your brothers and what they bring.

"That is all, Shada. I will return to my rooms and continue with my research."

She looked at Vitaris until he nodded, and then turned to begin her slow walk out of the hall.

Faltis stood and pointed a shaking finger at her departing back. "I still say, *kill her.*"

Jakus hardly noticed Faltis' action as he thought on what Xerina had said. *I must know more,* he thought. *My—and Sutan's—future depend on it.*

Jakus hurried as fast as his old Ean war injuries allowed to his rooms on one side of the palace. He entered noticing the cold feel to the air. "Damn," he muttered, "Nefaria hasn't lit the fire."

He shook his head as he remembered that his companion of many years was lying in a forgotten grave in Rolan, on the other side of the world. "Blast you, Nefaria. I never realised how much I relied on you. Another thing the old woman's Knowings didn't foretell." The air coalesced in front of his nose, and he fired a dark scent bolt into the wooden bureau at the end of the room, causing a spurt of splinters to fly into the air. "And here I am again, going to ask that woman for her advice!"

Jakus reached the damaged bureau and carefully inserted a scent probe into two small holes halfway down one side. A quick twist caused a panel to slide away, revealing a woven sack. He pulled off the tie and dipped his finger into the red crystals contained in the sack, then licked the finger as he sat back on his haunches.

"Ahh," he sighed, his face softening, "*you* are worth all the trouble. I look forward to ruling Rolan and controlling the supplies of magnesa." The pain in his side impinged on his enjoyment and he stood with a groan. "Now to confront the old woman in her lair."

Jakus moved through the palace, striding out to push through the strain of his old scars until he reached the corridor leading to the healing areas and the quarters of the soothsayer. He took little notice of the quiet room filled with sunlight and the scent of flowers, nor the waterlilies floating on the rectangular pond as he looked for Xerina. The drug filled his system and he felt ready for anything.

Xerina lifted her head from her contemplation of a parchment on the small table in front of her; other than a slight tensing of her body, she seemed unperturbed to see him.

"Yes, my Shad?" Her thin grey eyebrows rose into a nest of wrinkles.

Jakus stood above her considering her insolence. Unlike Faltis he recognised her value, but like his brother he would be happy to kill her. Something about her drew an off chord. He shook his head and drew upon his scent skills, the magnesa enhancing his abilities. Even if his father was controlled by this old woman, he would not be.

Coils of scent rose around his head, pulling together the motes of odour into a strong blanket, thickening, twisting until he flung it at Xerina. He would smother the old woman to an inch of her life, force her to admit what she had learned, force her to tell the truth.

The scent blanket fell over Xerina but instead of settling on her it slipped, piling to one side like a loose coil of rope.

She gave him a quizzical look.

He pulled and yanked at the blanket, trying to drag it over her and exert his control. It failed again. He drew back, blinking as he saw a greyness outlining her form.

She smiled, one eyebrow raising.

Jakus' hand fell to his dagger. "What are you...doing?"

"Please," she said, "tell me what you want. I will help in any way I can."

Something gave way in Jakus and he slumped, letting go of the scent blanket and his attempts to control Xerina.

"You…" he said, deliberately ignoring the failure of his scent control, "you must tell me what will happen. To return the world to Sutan rule, I need all to assist. You will help me!" Jakus paused, chest heaving, refusing to consider how Xerina, an old woman, could defeat his mastery of scent power with so little effort. He continued to block off that line of thought as he waited for Xerina's response.

"Jakus, I am not a miracle worker. I don't know everything. I can't give you what you want. I can only advise. Are you willing to accept that?" She crossed her arms and sat back in her chair.

Jakus looked around and snagged a chair near him. He sat with a thump. "Go on," he spat, as if the words left a bad taste in his mouth.

"You are on a knife's edge," she smiled sympathetically, "a knife's edge that the world will depend on. What you do from here will determine the fates of Sutan, Ean, Rolan and even Testria. Magnesa is not the answer, even though I know you think it is, but I also suspect you will ignore this advice and fight it, most likely be defeated by it. And, as reflected in the Knowing of years ago there has been no reason to change my interpretation."

"Your interpretation?" snarled Jakus.

"Yes, my dear Shad. It is that the seeds of destruction of Sutan are in the hands of an Eanite."

"Who, damn you!" Jakus stood with a wince knocking over the chair.

"I don't know. Knowings are vague like that." She smiled up at him. "I am only the messenger."

Jakus' hand flexed on the handle of his dagger before he swung around on his heel and left the room.

Xerina slumped back in her chair.

Chapter Two

Faltis looked into the harsh sun through unseeing eyes, his thin face strained, black-covered body twisting. Sounds surrounding him—the clatter of animal hooves over dusty gravel, the hiss of wind through thorny foliage, the croak of lizards on the rocky outcrop bordering the western side of the single-storey building—were ignored. For the physical world didn't impinge on the battle he was fighting; the enemy held an unassailable position, an advantage Faltis couldn't comprehend, couldn't defeat.

He clapped his hands to the sides of his head and screamed his anguish.

Septus was in an unfamiliar place. He knew his previous enemy, had been part of his body and had been prepared to die with his death. But his will to live had forced him from his host's dying body and target the nearest receptive mind. And he had kept his existence, tenuous at best, inside this unfamiliar brain. His moving from a parasitic existence inside the mind of his greatest foe was forced by circumstance during the battle for Mlana Hold in the country of Rolan. His priorities had changed. His first motive, the conquering of the heroic Eanite fighter Targas had now been supplanted by the desire to destroy Jakus, the former leader of the Sutanite occupation of Ean and his competitor. He knew this mind he inhabited was one close to Jakus and would use it ruthlessly, comfortable as he was in that host. The chance to defeat the Sutanite leader and rule through his body became the only reason for his continued existence.

Septus pushed deeper, making his *presence* known, making Faltis subservient to him as the new owner of this brain, this body.

Faltis screamed again, still gripping his head, and stumbled to his knees. People came running from the house in response, but Faltis couldn't speak, couldn't answer, for he was controlled by the essence that was Septus, the dead Septus, who refused to die. And he was unable to tell anyone.

Bilternus stood in the shade of the house watching his father pounding his fists bloody into the gravel. Members of the household gathered around Faltis, all aware of their master's fits and the dangers to any who tried to intervene. Bilternus felt pity more than most for the once proud man brought low by an addling of his brain.

He wasn't the same man who had assisted his brother Jakus in the invasion of Rolan and subsequent rapid withdrawal in the face of the scent power of the defenders. Even though Faltis had been against Jakus and his grand schemes to conquer the country, he had eventually joined forces and lent his power to the attack.

But Bilternus had seen the final assault and the killing of the famous enemy Targas by his father as they fought in the caverns of Mlana Hold. And he had taken part in their force's withdrawal, along with their prize of stocks of the scent-enhancing magnesite. It was then he noticed a change in his father's personality and recognised that something unexplainable had happened.

Their long return sail to Sutan had not improved Faltis. He had become uncommunicative and withdrawn, not even participating in Jakus' celebration of achieving his goal of obtaining large quantities of magnesite, from which to make the crystals of magnesa. Despite Bilternus' repeated attempts to communicate with his father, Faltis had kept to himself.

It was a relief when they returned to their properties in Sutan and were away from the influence of his uncle, Jakus, and Vitaris, his grandfather in the capital, Sutaria.

The years had passed and now the long-awaited return of Brastus was imminent. Correspondence from Brastus in Testria had indicated there would be conflict between him and his brother Jakus over the right to rule Sutan. Meanwhile, Faltis had fallen away as a force to be considered, ignored by the powerful factions jockeying for the leadership. The likelihood of civil war was growing.

Bilternus shook his head and prepared to go back inside.

"Son!" a powerful voice echoed, pulling Bilternus around. His father stood nearby, a dishevelled but commanding figure in his black cloak, beckoning with an imperious hand. "Come here!"

"Damn. What now?" Bilternus grumbled, suspicious at this sudden change in the man.

As he approached, he sought his father's face to see if he was normal, sane, trying to make sure that he had returned to his senses.

Faltis' brow creased, tilting his head to the side as Bilternus approached. *Almost as if he doesn't want me to see into his eyes. Is it him? I wonder.*

"We need to prepare to see my brother and ready for Brastus' return," said Faltis. "Organise it."

"Is it wise, Father? You haven't been yourself lately."

A dark scent aura rose around his head and Bilternus took a step back.

"Why wouldn't I be?" asked Faltis, still avoiding eye contact. "Just do it!"

"If that's your wish." He turned and went back towards the house.

"May I be of assistance, my Lord?" asked a tall, thin young man moving to his side.

Faltis swivelled to look at the leader of his scent masters before shaking his head. "No, Piltarnis, not at this time. I prefer you to not draw undue attention. Maintain the training regime with magnesa; this is a vital task and needs the group's focus."

Bilternus saw Methra, his father's consort, waiting in the shadows just inside the door and immediately felt a pang of sympathy for her. He could at least walk away from Faltis' mood swings, but Methra was always in range. He had ceased trying to assess her scents, as all too frequently she was shielding some hurt.

"Methra, my father wants to go into the city for meetings. Please prepare his best clothing."

He noticed her face whiten before she ducked her head and moved out of sight.

Nothing good will come of this, he thought as he followed her into the house.

Bilternus slipped into the corridor leading away from the palace's great hall and towards the soothsayer's rooms, happy to leave his father with Vitaris and Jakus while they discussed the latest developments regarding Brastus' return. His uncle's fleet was expected in Southern Port, which would mean much toing and froing as the various factions aligned and the inevitable power struggles occurred, something he wanted to avoid.

The air grew softer, calmer, as he neared Xerina's rooms. Somehow the testosterone-filled atmosphere of the palace was negated here.

"Ah, Bilternus, I wondered when I might see you."

He smiled at the spontaneous welcome from Xerina as he entered the scented room. Dappled light reflected off the leafy pond built in a narrow courtyard along one side.

"Please, sit." She waved a hand at a wickerwork seat across the table from her. "I was about to have tea." She clapped her hands and a young woman appeared through a dark doorway. "Empha, would you be so kind as to bring refreshments for my guest and me?"

The woman bowed her head and disappeared back through the doorway.

"Is that the same girl you've had here before—I mean when the Eanite, Kyel, was here?"

"Very observant, Bilternus. She has been a faithful acolyte and shown much promise in scent control, including the 'other', or women's scent."

"'Other' scent, Xerina?"

"Yes, one that your Kyel and I had long discussions about," she smiled across the table. "Did he not tell you of it during your time together on your campaign to Rolan?"

"No. No, he was very close-mouthed about his dealings with you. Are you saying he knew about another form of scent control?"

"I suppose I am," Xerina nodded, "but I am getting ahead of myself. You haven't come here to talk about scent control, have you? I can see your aura is dark and concerned. I take it your father and uncle are involved, perhaps regarding the return of Brastus?"

"You are most knowledgeable, my lady. But that's not my main issue." Bilternus looked up as Empha emerged from the doorway with a tray holding a steaming teapot, cups and a plate of scones.

She smiled, her large bright eyes assessing him, before nodding at Xerina and departing.

"You serve," Xerina said.

The fragrance of peppermint filled the air as he poured the faint green liquid into two cups.

"I suspect your concern is regarding your father and his, er, *affliction*, then?"

Bilternus handed Xerina her cup, took his and sat back. "Yes. I think you may have an inkling as to what it is, what's causing it?"

"I have some thoughts. Tell me what you know."

Bilternus took a sip of the hot liquid before placing it back on the table. "It all started, if I think back on it, during the battle at Mlana Hold in Rolan. That was a horrible time, the last time I saw Kyel in fact, and when so many people were killed. All for that blasted red crystal Jakus is so fixated with. It was when we were retreating, I saw something had changed in my father. There was something different about him. It was as if…someone was looking out of his eyes, not my father, not Faltis.

"Since then it's just gotten worse. Even today he had a fit, out in the yard at home. He went mad, screaming, slapping his head. Then he acted as if nothing had happened, ordering us around. Something is wrong with him."

Xerina took a long drink from her cup and pointed at the scones. "Eat while I think on this."

Bilternus buttered a scone, then took a bite while he waited.

"When I was asked for predictions on the future of Sutan by your grandfather, I mentioned that some of my Knowings were ambiguous, indicating there would be power struggles and much discord ahead. One such area was the uncertainty surrounding your father.

"Something about him that is not him. You were right about a momentous event during the battle, many deaths and much use of scent control, scent magic if you will. I don't claim to know everything, but something beyond my knowledge has been at work. Targas, the hero of the Eanite rebellion, and then your father, Faltis, have had a link. It's evil, but I don't know what it is.

"These are times when I could curse my Knowings and their vagueness. All I know is that this 'link' will impact. It has had and will have a role to play. It's just as well you're aware and ready for this. Do not relax your guard or become complacent for it may be up to you in the end."

"Phew!" Bilternus slumped back in his seat. "You worry me sometimes."

"Of necessity, young Bilternus." She reached over and patted his hand. "Now finish off the scones, please."

"**M**aster Bilternus?"

Bilternus looked up to see Empha standing in the doorway.

"Shad Jakus is calling for you, in the great hall."

"Oh?" He stood, turned to Xerina, and nodded. "Until another time?"

"I'll look forward to it," Xerina said over the rim of her cup. "Now go."

Bilternus brushed past Empha and headed down the corridor.

He entered the hall, hearing the murmur of voices from a group of people seated around the large table in its centre. Aside from his father, Jakus and Vitaris, and army commanders Kast and Dronthis, he saw two women he knew well, Poegna and Sharna.

Poegna looked up as he approached and nodded. He nodded back to the slim, pleasant-faced woman, remembering the role she now played in Jakus' life. She had filled the vacuum left by Nefaria's death, to become the Shad's consort. He had learnt little of how the arrangement was working but assumed it suited both parties. *Not my business,* he thought.

Bilternus smiled at Sharna, the flamboyant redhead and commander of Jakus' ships as he slipped into a spare seat beside her. The Shad grunted.

"Now you're here we can look at how we prepare for my brother's arrival, right Vitaris?" Jakus glanced under his eyebrows at his father.

Vitaris frowned and scanned those sitting at the table. "We need to consider the ramifications of having all my sons in the one place at the one time and how we can work the deployment of our resources to achieve the best results for Sutan. In so saying I don't want anyone taking it on themselves to act without our knowledge." He looked pointedly at Faltis. "It is not in our best interests."

Faltis snatched a quick glance at Jakus, then looked at the parchment in front of him. "You'll need to keep my big, strong brother, Brastus, in line then. I trust your old injuries don't weaken you at all?"

Jakus glared at Faltis, taking a long breath before tapping on the parchment. "You all have copies of the resources we have available for my plans to bring Sutan into its rightful place in the world. The addition of Brastus' troops and equipment, including ships, will make us unstoppable. With my magnesa it is not a matter of if we can rule the known world but when."

"You still have that problem." Faltis' voice was high-pitched and nasal. "Brastus will not agree unless he's in charge. You have your tame soothsayer to thank for warning us about that."

Vitaris cleared his throat. "Enough! We are agreed that we should work together in the interests of Sutan. Further, it is up to you, Jakus, to welcome Brastus and ensure that we are united as a family. Show him your plans, listen to his advice and share your resources, particularly the red crystal, with him. I'm certain the best interests of Sutan and our ruling family will win out in the end.

"I don't want discord. I want you to all work together. Remember I am reaching the end of my life and my dearest wish is to see a successful future for Sutan. Don't"—he stared at Jakus, then Faltis—"disappoint me." His shoulders slumped as he looked down at the parchment, not hearing the faint snigger from Faltis.

Jakus' scent aura darkened as he resumed scanning the words.

Chapter Three

A peal of laugher echoed across the rounded granite boulders, bouncing between the rugged mountainous crags, causing a group of sunbaking lizards to scatter in alarm.

A squat, brown-coated animal lifted a honey-dripping muzzle and looked down at the girl sitting on an overhang at the base of an outcrop of granite that pierced the centre of the clearing like a spear. Her eyes danced in her tanned face as she rocked back, pointing a finger at the animal.

"You…you should see yourself, Vor. Just look at your face. You should be saving some for the poor pria instead of robbing all the hive's honey."

As if in answer, a long pink tongue twisted from the voral's snout and licked at the honey coating its dark face. It gave a grunt towards its mistress and continued to dig into the crevice high on a weathered rock face.

"Come on, Vor. I mean it. Leave some for the rightful owners or they'll have none to last the winter."

The shaggy coat of the voral's rump twitched as if the animal was debating whether to ignore the command.

A huge, banded bee suddenly buzzed loudly into the clearing, making straight for the intruder destroying its hive.

"Look out, Vor!" she shouted.

The voral looked up and swung a clawed paw at the bee.

"No Vor, no. Come."

The animal half rose on its hind legs, watching as the bee circled, before quickly scrabbling backwards down to the rock-strewn floor of the clearing. Other bees buzzed into the clearing joining in the attack, barely avoiding the black claws as the voral backed away.

The buzzing increased in intensity as the bees noticed the second intruder. A number broke off and dived towards the girl.

The voral turned and ran towards his mistress.

"What have you done, Vor?" yelped the girl, focussing on the oncoming, head-sized insects. She slipped to the ground as the animal skidded to a stop at her feet.

"Quick!" She crouched down, a hand on him, a dark scent cloud erupting from her mouth. The voral shimmered and they both disappeared. The bees hovered uncertainly, curved stingers pulsing in and out of their abdomens, searching the rocks and potential hiding places. Their feelers flickered as the creatures buzzed back and forth trying to locate their quarry, missing the blank spot where the intruders had been only moments before.

The bees circled until the scent of their spilled honey drove them to repair their hive high on the rock face.

Silence resumed.

A little time later, the air wavered and the girl and voral reappeared. She watched the industrious bees for a moment before snapping her fingers and getting to her feet. "Come Vor, that was far too close even for you. Those stings could seriously hurt us, you know. We're going back." She headed for a small gap in the towering rocks.

The animal looked up at the hive before scampering after his mistress.

She made her way half running, half walking down the precipitous track, dodging around rocky projections thrusting into her path. She hesitated at a particularly sharp turn and waited amongst some hardy, fragrant-leafed bushes until she heard the sharp claws of her companion clattering across the broken rock.

She smiled, her light eyes gazing at the view from under her fringe of brown hair. "Wait a moment, Vor." The vista from her vantage point was striking.

They stood at the head of a wide valley extending over a vast distance towards the south, large eruptions of rock breaking the ground, showing the influence of the mountains behind them. A scatter of toy-like buildings spread away from the arms of the slope, merging into the surroundings with their grey rock sides and timber tiles or slate roofs; rock walls angled from the side slopes towards the centre of the valley.

They could see figures moving along a paved road leading to a narrow river that rushed away on a straight course into the distance. The lowering sun showed green and brown fields before a slight haze closed off the view.

"I never get tired of it, Vor. Never." She reached down and wound slim fingers into his coarse fur. "Ew, you're still sticky. You better sleep out of the cavern this night."

The dark snout lifted, and his small black eyes seemed to wink at her.

"No use looking like that. You just better clean up, is all. Now come."

She slipped over a precipitous slope and made her sure-footed way down the narrow path.

"Anyar…huff…there you are."

"Just coming, Cathar," she responded to the slim, fair-haired woman dressed in green tunic top and brown trousers making her laborious way up the path.

"The sundown meal is ready and Boidea wants to see you—more lessons, I think."

"I know," Anyar pursed her lips, "more lessons. I just wanted to have some time with Vor. He was getting restless."

"You sure it was only Vor?" smiled Cathar.

The young girl laughed. "That's what I'm telling Boidea and Mother, of course."

They turned, joined their hands, and walked down the path, the voral snuffling along behind.

The path bent towards a low cliff extending a considerable distance across the head of the valley where the river emerged. A wide, dark opening from which spirals of smoke emerged dominated the cliff face. Many figures were moving in the semi-darkness.

Anyar knew they were tending the fires and preparing the tables for the meal from the kitchens deeper in the cavern.

"I don't think Vor needs feeding, Cathar," said Anyar as she swung their joined hands. "He's full of honey."

"I feel sorry for those poor bees. They spend so long collecting nectar from the trees down in the valley and storing the honey safely in the mountains, then along comes Vor."

"I made him leave some, though. But *I'm* hungry."

"I'm certain you are the rate you're growing. Now come, I think I can see Sadir at the entrance. She'll be looking for her wayward daughter, if I make a guess."

The way to the cavern was steep and tortuous. Anyar knew it was built like that to make it harder for an enemy trying to reach the defenders. She briefly thought to the horrendous day, some years before, when a Sutanite army had attempted to do just that. The day her father, Targas, died. It was also the day Alethea, the former Mlana of Rolan, had forced the enemy to retreat, and when Anyar had come into her power.

She shook her head to clear the memory, and kept climbing. Anyar could sense her mother at the head of the path, worried as always. The odours of her concern came clearly through her scent. Sadir had never fully recovered from the loss of her partner, but for Anyar the memory of Targas was already fading as she sought to reconcile her maturing powers with her growth towards womanhood.

"Anyar, my love!" exclaimed her mother, throwing arms around her. "Where have you been? I was worried."

Anyar endured the hug for a moment and then wriggled free. "Just out with Vor." She looked up at Sadir, noting the lines on her face and the beginnings of grey in her wavy brown hair. "You know you shouldn't worry about me. This is all part of what I must do. I must prepare. I must develop my power. I'm not a child anymore."

Sadir took a step back and smiled at her daughter, who stood nearly her height. "No," she sighed, "you're not. You're growing like a weed; whether it's this country's influence or the influence of Alethea's memories in you, Ean rest her soul, I don't know.

"But come and get some food. You must be hungry."

"Yes, Mother." Anyar took the proffered hand.

They sat at a long wooden table, one of a number placed around a series of fires set along the large entrance to the vast cavern. Several people were rushing between the tables from the kitchens with large platters of steaming meat or tubers and root vegetables. A large pot on each table gave off aromas of rich, herb-infused gravy.

"Move along Anyar," came a deep voice. "I missed you at lessons after noon. Where were you?"

Anyar looked at the large woman sliding along the bench seat next to her and smiled. She felt a furry mass at her feet move with her. "I wanted to take Vor for a walk higher in the mountains. He said he wanted to have some honey."

"He did, did he? Are you that in tune with him?"

"Yes, Boidea, I am. I know what he wants, and he knows what I want."

Boidea looked under the table into the voral's eyes. "Yes, he does look like he's interested in what we're saying. Is it part of your awareness now?"

Anyar nodded as her mother placed a plate of food in front of her. "I think it is. The scent notes are subtle, so much so that I'm not really aware of it, but it seems to work."

"Hmm." Boidea rubbed her strong chin. "Maybe it's something we can incorporate it into your lessons?"

"Anyar," interrupted Sadir, "eat your dinner before it gets cold."

"Yes, Mother."

"I'll see you after the meal, if you're not too tired," said Boidea.

Anyar rubbed a sandaled foot on Vor's furry head as she took a mouthful of food.

The fires around her hissed and crackled in a gust of wind, sending a flurry of sparks high into the air to be whipped under the overhang and into the darkness beyond. The stars shone against the cold night sky, a reminder that spring had only just arrived. A shiver prickled down her spine, not just because of the cold but also from a sense of foreboding. *Soon,* she felt her inner voice say. *You must prepare.*

"Anyar?" Sadir leant forward to place a hand on her daughter's shoulder. "I'm fine, Mother," she replied curtly as she took another mouthful of food. Boidea grunted and nodded knowingly at Sadir.

"And how are you, my favourite niece?" Strong arms grabbed Anyar around the waist and lifted her into the air.

"Ky!" she squealed. "Put me down or I'll throw up all over you."

"Sorry." Kyel lowered her carefully to the floor and moved his hand to her shoulder. "Just can't help myself." He grinned at her through his fringe of sandy hair. "I was looking for you earlier, but you had followed that wretched animal up into the mountains. He'll only lead you astray, he will."

"We both wanted to go for a walk, although Vor was more interested in the honey, I think." She smiled sideways at her uncle.

He reached down to her and grasped her hand. "I thought we might like to look at the stars for a moment."

"Uh huh," Anyar nodded. "Do you want Cathar to come too?"

"Cathar?" Kyel looked over to the recesses of the cavern. "Is she nearby?"

"I'm certain we can find her, Uncle Ky," she replied with a lilt in her voice.

"No, not now. I just want to show you some stars I've seen. Come on." He pulled on Anyar's hand, and they walked to the mouth of the cavern. The darkness spread before them with only several flickers of light breaking the black of the valley floor. Overhead the stars were dazzling, and it was almost impossible to make out individual points of light.

"Do you see, Anyar?" Kyel pointed into the night sky. "The large star near two others, almost in a line? No, look further, to the east. One of the smaller two is yellower."

The chill of the night drew goosebumps from her exposed skin, and she snuggled against him. "Yes, I see them. Why?"

"Good," he paused for a moment, "for they're the stars I used to look at when we were at our hometown of Lesslas, in Ean. And they're also the stars I could see in Sutan, the land of our enemy."

"Oh," said Anyar in a small voice, "so if we can see them in Ean as well as Sutan and Rolan, we're all close. Does that mean the stars are a long way away?"

"I believe it does, Anyar. It also means that our three lands are not that far apart and if one wants to affect the other, they haven't far to go to do it. What one does can impact on the other."

"I know what you mean," she said, snuggling closer. "We don't have much time, do we?"

"No, knowing the mind of our enemy as I do, we don't have much time."

They stood for a while looking into the night sky, until Anyar shuddered suddenly.

"It's cold. So cold!" She clutched at Kyel's arm.

"Come inside, Anyar. We need to warm you up." Kyel pulled Anyar against his side and they walked briskly into the warmth of the cavern.

"I need to go to the crystal cave. Now!"

"Mother! Boidea! Anyar's asking for the crystal cave."

The women acted in an instant, snatching Anyar up and leaving Kyel alone near the fire. He watched as they disappeared into the recesses of the cavern.

Kyel shook his head for a moment before slumping down on a seat.

"An ale?" Cathar proffered a tankard to him before sitting down. "You needn't worry. She's in the best of hands."

"I feel I should go with her. And why the crystal cave? I've never even been in there, only women and female trainees are allowed." He pushed a hand through his hair. "It's frustrating to just sit here."

"You know it's to do with Anyar's understanding and the shadow scent. Besides, men can't use shadow scent and have rarely been in the cave."

"No, that's not quite right, Cathar. When I was in Sutan I met with their old soothsayer, Xerina, and she showed me how to see it but she called it an *other* scent."

"Even so, it's best to let Anyar do what she needs to do. We will have to just wait."

"I know." Kyel half turned to look into the pretty woman's sympathetic eyes. "It's just that I fear for the future and how young Anyar is for what she'll have to go through."

"Don't worry," Cathar said, slipping an arm through his, "we'll be with her."

"Hmm, but will it be enough?" He pulled her closer as he lifted the tankard.

Chapter Four

The light was caught and flung around the walls of the cave in infinite points of red, flashing and moving, everything a reddish hue. The darker ceiling, supported by walls of the softer, paler rock, was dotted with innumerable coloured crystals, reflecting the light of their lamps.

Sadir drew in her breath as she, Boidea and Anyar crunched across the gravel-strewn surface to one of the benches scattered around the space. The magnificence of the crystal cave was not lost on her, and nor was the fact that this was the raw material of magnesa, the target of the ruthless Sutanites.

"Over there, Mother," said Anyar quietly.

The scent-minimised clothing, simple shifts that hung from their shoulders, glowed redly as they settled Anyar on the cushioned bench and set a lamp in an alcove, allowing the light to be directed upward.

"Do you need anything, Anyar?" Sadir asked.

"The Knowing is strong. I must allow it to be, to tell me what it may. Leave me, please."

Sadir hesitated but Boidea held out a hand to her. "Come. Anyar is in the grip of a Knowing. I recall the Mlana doing the same on occasion."

"We will be nearby, my daughter."

They stood and moved back to the entrance, Sadir watching the slim figure of her daughter settle back on the bench. The flickering red was thickening as swirls of shadow scent grew, almost obscuring Anyar's form. The very sight brought unpleasant memories of Targas, her dead partner's ordeal in this same room when they had been trying to remove Septus' disembodied influence from his head. But their attempt had failed, even as it nearly destroyed Targas' mind. *Not something to be trifled with.*

Now Anyar! My poor Anyar.

Sadir felt Boidea pull at her shoulder and reluctantly let herself be drawn through the opening. The cloth hanging there fell, closing the interior of the cave to her sight.

"We'll wait here; it's near enough, Sadir. Do not worry."

They sat quietly on a ledge in the dark corridor in the faint glow of their remaining lamp, Sadir biting her lip to stop questions from pouring forth.

"I have sat here at times for Alethea when she was in the thrall of a Knowing," whispered Boidea, resting a hand on Sadir's knee. "Best to let yourself absorb the atmosphere and not allow thoughts to bubble."

Sadir leant forward seeking a glimpse of her daughter, Alethea's heir, as she endured the foretelling that the Knowing would bring. *So young*, she thought. *Too young to be forced to be the next Mlana and lead Rolan in these dangerous times. Why did Alethea have to keep everything so close to her chest and then require my daughter to grow up so fast? Not even a childhood!*

She gulped and buried her head in her hands.

Anyar barely noticed them go as she focussed on the swirling redness around her. She could feel the influence of the cascading scents and the powerful magnesite of the cave's structure. Within it a subtle, thicker scent filtered through, all-encompassing, filling her body, making her mind float on a soft sea. It felt so comfortable, holding her, securing her thoughts so she had no wish to leave.

A tiny push infiltrated her mind so she couldn't get comfortable, an itch she had to scratch. A groan burst from her lips and her body seemed to rise from the comfort of the bench and lift into the air, following the swirling scents. Rock was no impediment and she rose into the night sky, higher and higher. Stars grew in her vision, familiar, recently seen. They seemed to bathe the country below in a scarlet light, highlighting lands and cities. She had no real understanding which cities, but knew they would be important in the future.

She moved across these lands without thought, recognising she was heading to the east, leaving Rolan and its port city of Requist before lifting over the mountain range dividing Rolan from Ean. There she saw Nebleth, Ean's capital and home to many of her mother's friends. She remembered the city, recalled being caught and almost killed with her mother in one of the enemy's traps. But they had been rescued by her father, Targas, and of course Vor. Her hand reached unthinkingly for the absent animal as she thought of his loyalty and continued friendship.

Then her vision shifted, again to the east and over mountains and rugged terrain. Finally, another city came into view, harsher, less joyous, the city of the enemy. She dove closer to see Sutaria for the first time, the city holding danger for her people.

The skeins of scent thinned as she approached, and she instinctively tried to retreat within her body, but something was pulling her and wouldn't let her go. A face filled her vision. A cruel face of sharp lines, beak nose, small eyes and skin spread tightly across a hairless skull. The black robe covering his tall form just failed to disguise his bent body adjusting from a previous hurt. He was shouting, whether in anger or fear she couldn't tell.

Across from him stood another man, almost identical in appearance, the recipient of the first man's attention. Yet this man was less arrogant, harsh lines softened by attitude and dissipation, showing a subservient yet uncaring attitude.

She watched enthralled, careful not to break her concentration while gleaning all she could from the Knowing.

She knew she had seen these men or their like before when younger, and knew they represented danger. They were important to the future of her world, and she needed to keep watching.

Then the shouting stopped. The dominant man stepped away as if satisfied, or…or unable to make headway in the argument.

Anyar leant forward, focussing on the scene in the scudding scents of her Knowing. Something was about to happen. Why the foretelling was occurring might be revealed.

The figures blurred, softened, their outlines superimposing, hard to separate.

Anyar had to force a breath.

A face appeared, emerging from the lesser man, sharpening into focus, a face with the same cast as the others. She noticed it was grinning, stained teeth showing through a bloody tear in a cheek, eyes close together in a white face.

The original figures solidified and were separated by this new entity, yet they seemed unaware of his *presence*.

Maybe it's part of the Knowing, she thought.

Then she knew. For the eyes focussed past the men and directly on her. She shivered and tried to flee her connection.

As the scene began to waver it spoke to her, mind to mind. "I see you, Targas' spawn. I destroyed him. I'll destroy you too!"

Anyar fell backwards onto the bench, her heart racing, breath coming in gasps. "What's happened, Mlana? What did you see?"

Anyar felt concerned hands on her body, a warm wet cloth on her brow, and was thankful she was back amongst friends.

Alethea's rooms, now belonging to Anyar, had been designed to allow small gatherings, places where people could meet, discuss and plan in relative comfort. A large fire crackled and spat against a wall, pushing warmth into the space. Green-dyed perac-wool hangings softened the rock walls while one large table with comfortable armchairs set around it dominated. Several couches were against the wall on either side of a door leading into a sleeping room with two beds.

Sadir was relieved her daughter had recovered from her ordeal and smiled at the untidy-looking figure of Vor wandering out of the opening to the bedroom. He purposefully slumped next to Anyar's chair, letting out a grunt; his mistress' hand dropped onto his ruff.

She could see the scents of honey rising from the mug of warm perac milk Anyar was sipping and hesitated interrupting her to find out more of the Knowing. Instead, she scanned the table noting the concern on everyone's faces as they waited. Boidea was on her opposite side, while Cathar, Drathner, Xaner, Xerrita and Kyel completed the group—all were scent masters, and Drathner and Xaner also commanded Rolan's forces. A formidable group, she thought. The clunk of Anyar's cup against the table attracted everyone's attention.

"I have a question for you all," Anyar said, breaking the silence with a firm, young voice. "I have had a very significant Knowing, a foretelling of danger, a warning for us to be ready, and signalling the intent of our enemies. I recognised Jakus and his brother, Faltis; we have had dealings with them before, here at Mlana Hold, but there was another, same look to him but not there at all. He saw me, knew I saw him and said he was coming for me.

"His face was torn, eyes crazy in a white face, and he knew my father."

"Septus!" hissed Sadir. "How can he still be? He died with Targas. It can't be him, it can't."

"He can't have gotten away, can he?" asked Boidea. "How would it even be possible? Oh, I wish Alethea were here, she would know. Maybe, if he got into Targas' mind he could have done it again when…Targas…you know." Her voice trailed away.

"So, if that were possible," added Drathner, "who would he have gone to? Kyel?"

"There was so much confusion I couldn't tell," Kyel answered. "I was focussed on my sister, especially when Jakus and Faltis were fighting there, in the Hold."

"I…I think," Anyar interrupted, "it was from the lesser of the two in my Knowing."

"Faltis!" snapped Kyel. "It was him. It must have been. He was weak, beaten by Jakus. If Septus could do what you think, it must have been him."

"So Septus is still a threat, a bigger threat than we thought. If he got my husband, he's not getting my daughter!" Sadir let out an explosive puff of air.

"Mother," added Anyar, "he is part of what is coming to us, something we must prepare for. The Sutanites mean to have our magnesite and control us all."

"So, Mlana," said Xerrita, "was that the question you wanted to ask all of us?"

"Please Xerrita, I don't feel worthy to be called Mlana. Alethea is too recently gone for me to take on her title. It needs to be earned. As you have rightly asked, that wasn't my question. I have long considered this and would like your thoughts.

"Why did the Mlana allow the Sutanite invaders to take all the magnesa we had stored at Mlana Hold? Why not hide it away and not give them such a powerful weapon?" Anyar's gaze, light like her father's, held those around the table.

"I was closest to Alethea," said Boidea. "She kept many things near to her chest, always had a reason even if it was not clear to the rest of us. I can't really fathom an answer even if it seemed an oversight at the time."

"An oversight?" said Xaner. "I remember we had to clear the warehouses in Port Requist before the Sutanites attacked, making certain none was available to them. Then they marched towards Mlana Hold; not even Nosta was allowed to have supplies, although they didn't break the siege there and gain access—again Mlana's orders, which we didn't question. So, the supplies were here, waiting for the Sutanites. Of course, they stole them when they retreated from Mlana Hold and took the magnesa back to Sutan. We harried them but didn't retrieve any."

"So, the Mlana was playing a deeper game? What was it?" murmured Boidea.

"That is why I asked you the question," said Anyar. "I don't have an answer, except…"

"Except?" asked Sadir. "I hope that doesn't mean we don't survive; that they win?"

"I could try to explain but I'm still new to all this. I don't have answers. I really wish I did." Anyar's eyes closed briefly, and Sadir could see dark lines under them. "So"—her eyelids snapped open—"I'll try.

"A time is coming where everything will be exposed, where we will have to make decisions which may have significant consequences to us, our lives and all we hold dear. This will be a time of challenge where any advantage may be enough to win, be it us or the enemy. We need to be ready." Anyar slumped in her chair and Vor stood on his hind legs to lean on his mistress.

"That's enough!" Sadir stood and waved everyone away. "Anyar needs rest." She stood and waited while everyone filed out before putting her arms around her daughter and leading her into the bedroom. Vor followed.

They sat around a fire in the cavern eating and drinking while discussing the conversation in the Mlana's quarters.

"Kyel, you were talking earlier about an old soothsayer you met in Sutaria," said Cathar. She was leaning into him as she took a bite of an apple pastry.

"Xerina was her name," he said, placing his arm around Cathar's waist. "It was a calm place when I was having a very rough time, and she knew so much—another foreteller, a Knower. And she was from Rolan."

"What?" asked Boidea. "How could that be?"

"Xerina told me she had left Rolan when young, seeking adventure, but had been captured and sold to Sutan. She had lived as their soothsayer for a long time."

23

"Ah," Boidea nodded knowingly, "there were stories of someone, a sister to Alethea I think, destined to be the Mlana, who disappeared, forcing Alethea to take on her responsibilities. So, she's still alive and in the land of our enemies? How interesting. I wonder if this is prophetic, if this Xerina is important in the journey of our new Mlana and the future of Rolan and our world."

"Boidea, I spent some time with her and, if anything, she's as wise as your Alethea was, is involved in the future and was my friend. Maybe there's hope from that quarter." Kyel looked at Boidea and his sister before sipping on his beer.

Chapter Five

"Nephew, I want you and Sharna to return to Southern Port to watch and report on any activity relating to my brother, Brastus," Jakus said to Bilternus and his fleet commander. He sat at the table in his rooms sipping a red wine while looking over a parchment; Kast, his army commander and Poegna sat either side of him.

"This"—he tapped the parchment with the bottom of his glass—"is the real outline of our resources, not that one I showed to my father and his cronies. I want all of you to be mindful of this and the need for secrecy." His scent aura darkened as his attention focussed on the document. "I'll soon be bringing other allies to Sutaria in preparation for the challenge that will come from Brastus. I have little hope that he'll have foregone his ambitions in favour of what is right, and I have no doubt he seeks knowledge of what he may face when he attempts to usurp my rightful place as leader.

"We must be ready!" A small slop of red wine fell to the parchment. Poegna drew out a cloth from the pocket of her dark robe and wiped it off. "You are lucky"—his hooded gaze swung to Bilternus—"that you have proven your worth. Continue to do so and you'll be in my confidence even more." An audible crunch came when Jakus dropped his hand into the pouch at his waist.

Bilternus caught the flash of red as Jakus slipped crystals into his mouth and saw the Shad's eyes briefly glaze over as he looked to Sharna. "Anything at all that you can glean concerning Brastus or, indeed, my father, from your network in the Port will be invaluable. Remember, I rely on you."

"Certainly, my Shad. Our interests are as one." Sharna pushed a lock of red hair away from her eyes. "Our ships are near full readiness for when needed, even in the event of any clash with Brastus' forces. I have no indication that Vitaris is showing any influence in this area."

"Good. Good." Jakus looked into his wine as if the redness was pulling at him. Bilternus thought for an instant Jakus was affected by what was afflicting his father. Suddenly the man lifted his head and caught Bilternus watching. His eyes refocussed.

"Where's Faltis? I need to have some time with him."

"Back at our home, Uncle. Do you want me to fetch him?"

Jakus shook his head. "Later! My time to confront Vitaris is nearing. Leave me."

They all stood and left Jakus alone with Poegna. Bilternus saw her hand snake across his uncle's shoulders as he went through the door. *I remember Nefaria in her place,* he thought. *I liked her, yet Jakus has just forgotten her. After all she did for him, he's just forgotten her.* He barely stopped himself from slamming the door on his way out.

"Poegna"—Jakus' arm slipped around her waist—"you have been a good friend to me. When all around me are unfeeling, enemies even, you are with me." He pulled her onto his lap. "And I reward my friends."

He reached into his pouch and withdrew a small pinch of magnesa. "You are worthy. I only give this amount if you are worthy." His long fingers slithered over her face, and she opened her mouth. He pushed the red crystals between her lips.

"Take it. Feel it. Feel the power. Feel the control it gives you." He pulled her head around and stared into her dark eyes. "I can see it working. Can't you feel your scent centres expanding and growing with its power?"

Poegna's eyes glazed over, her scent aura reddening and growing around her head, building and merging with Jakus'. Swirls of scarlet joined with the deepest of purples, flashes of bright red clouded around them. She flung her head back, exposing her throat, uttering a high-pitched yell.

Jakus growled into her throat and stood, lifting her with him. He slipped a free hand into the front of her dark robe as he stepped towards a couch against the wall. "Share it with me, Poegna and I'll make you ruler of the world."

He fell with her onto the cushioned surface and began his invasion of her mind and body.

Bilternus, having no wish to return home, see his father and experience his unnerving ways, found his feet taking him towards Xerina's rooms. She was always calm and her rooms peaceful, with none of the power plays. *Besides,* he thought, *she might have news of what is happening elsewhere.* In the few weeks he had known the Eanite, Kyel, he had grown to like him. When the Sutanite army retreated from Rolan, Bilternus hadn't realised Kyel had been left behind.

It wasn't until a while later he found out that his friend had not been killed in the battle but had remained with the Rolanites. He hoped the stigma of being with the enemy had not prevented Kyel from rejoining his family.

Maybe Xerina will know. She's got many hidden talents, perhaps one of her Knowings had told her.

He hurried down the corridor into her area of the palace.

"**Y**ou turn up when I was thinking of you." Xerina was sitting in her seat, sunlight haloing her form; scents filled that halo, pale and ethereal. Bilternus felt like bowing to her, such was his awe. "Sit, please, and enjoy the tranquillity of my space." She motioned to the spare seat at the small table.

He sat and gazed through the slender stone columns at the pond filled with floating plants and the numerous flowers dotting its surface. Insects hummed, dashing through the coils of scent emanating from the blossoms.

"Their fragrance and colour give me much pleasure, Bilternus." Xerina smiled across at him. "As you can see there are two cups, so I would be grateful if you will pour."

He lifted the heavy teapot and began to pour out the fragrant liquid as he considered the foresight of the old woman.

"Can you see the drift of scents surrounding the flowers?"

"Pardon, Xerina?" He glanced at her wizened face before returning his gaze to the pond. "Yes, I can."

"You know I asked your young friend Kyel to do this, sitting on that seat. So, if you would, describe them."

"Kyel? Really? Is he alright? Do you know?"

"Please." She nodded towards the flowers.

Bilternus leant on the stone sill and concentrated. "The flower head scents have the most pastels, mainly greens, blues…pink and yellow.

"Now look to a stronger colour," Xerina urged."

"Uh huh," he said, leaning forward on his elbows. "I'm seeing a blue-green, dark but thinner, almost lost in the paler colours."

"Now concentrate. Do you see anything else, no matter how insignificant?"

Bilternus tried hard, focussing, blocking off the extraneous sound and scent. A bee dashed across his vision, its wake causing flurries of scent to spill across the dark colours drifting in ever-increasing circles. He squinted until he thought the spread of scent was unusual. He slumped back into his seat with a huff. "All I can see that seems to be different is how the scent, the paler components, are spread further, blocking off others, but nothing else."

"Poor Bilternus, I'm being a mite hard on you, but for a reason. More tea?"

"No."

"What I am leading up to is serious." She gave a tight smile. "My job, if you like, is to interpret any foretellings I have for the benefit of the ruling family. Some of these have been used, others not acted upon. You are already aware of the Knowing that foresaw the demise of Sutan at the hands of an Eanite, and the furore it caused some years ago—that hasn't gone away. In fact, it's been slowly reinforced by other insights, by themselves not significant but together of import."

"Yes," He clamped a hand on his knee to stop it jiggling. "Can you tell me what you're getting at?"

"Yes, my point." Xerina leant forward and patted his other hand. "It is about you, young man. You have a significant role to play, where you face danger and may lose everything because of it. If you survive, then the future of the world will be impacted by you."

Bilternus' jaw dropped, the hum of the insects over the pond filling in the silence. He looked back to Xerina. "So, what are you telling me? What am I supposed to do?"

"No, it's what I can do. I must prepare you, if you are willing."

"But you don't really know me. If I'm anything like my father or my uncle I mayn't be worth helping."

"Do you doubt me, Bilternus?"

"No, I suppose not," he sighed, folding his arms across his chest. "So, what's this about?"

"It's about preparing you, warding you against what is coming so you may be able to survive."

"That sounds ominous, Xerina. What do you suggest?"

"Ah." Xerina let out a soft breath. "Remember the little exercise you just did with the scent? That's how."

"You do speak in riddles, Xerina. So, what do you want to do?"

"I have had many Knowings which I've tried to interpret over the years; whether I'm right or wrong it is hard to know but I merely operate with the tools I'm provided. So, I come to the *other* scent, one which I introduced to your friend, Kyel. It is an unknown scent to those in Sutan and because of that has significant value. Even the great Jakus has met his match with it. It is there that I need to protect you."

"Again, how?"

"The *other* scent is usually only seen and used by women, particularly in the country of my birth, Rolan. It is a scent lying behind the normal scent you see or expect to see. But what I can discern and use in different ways is that extra scent."

"So, if what you're saying is true, I wouldn't be able to use it anyway?" he asked.

"I agree, and it is not necessary that you do, Bilternus," continued Xerina. "What I want is to prepare you for when your beliefs and ideology are confronted. There is likely a time when you will be tested, most probably by Jakus, but there is another presence which may also be a danger. Either way you need to be protected. And I am willing to do this if you consent."

The hum of the insects, the creak of stone and timbers reacting to the heat of the day washed over him as he sat and thought through what the old soothsayer had told him. Empha came in and placed a plate of fresh scones on the table but even that didn't rouse him. Did he want Xerina to perform scent 'magic' on him or was he happy to take his chances now he was forewarned?

"Xerina"—he finally focussed on her calm face—"what is it you need me to do?"

"Bilternus, I need you to sit still and allow me to infiltrate your scent centres, let me move within them and protect those parts of your being that would appear dangerous to your enemies, and would cause them, in similar investigations, to doubt your loyalty."

"Phew, Xerina, you really want me to trust you?"

"Of course, that goes without saying," she smiled tiredly. "But I only have your best interests at heart, unlike others, and if there's any way to stop them hurting you then I would like to try. Ultimately, it is your decision."

"Do it, then." He leant forward.

"You will make a wise ruler," she murmured, ignoring his slight jump at the comment. "Lean your head back and relax."

Although Bilternus' eyes were closed, he sensed a darkening of the air in front of him until a tickling began in his nostrils and over his palate. The tickling moved up and into his sinuses. He could feel a pulling, unnerving but not unpleasant, unlike the experience he had had when his uncle had tested his loyalty some time ago. It moved deeper, softly, slippery, smoothing over roughness he didn't know he had, making some of his scent memories more distant and vaguer. He shivered as it seemed to move into the centre of his brain. Bilternus held off the desire to sneeze as long as he could. Then it happened. He sneezed and sat up in the chair.

"Sorry, sorry. I couldn't stop it."

"'Tis done. The best I could do," said Xerina. "As long as you have some control of your will you should be able to hide betraying thoughts from the usual interrogations your leaders may carry out. Please remember what we have done, in time of need, and keep it between us.

"Now, those scones will only go stale if they're not eaten."

Bilternus belatedly noticed the food and his hunger returned.

Chapter Six

"I'm getting too old for this," said Lan, as he slowly walked up the stone steps of the castle. He smiled at the tall, fair-headed man next to him.

"Never, Lan, you haven't changed a bit in all the years I've known you. I think you're ageless." Jelm returned the old scent master's smile. "Though maybe another wrinkle or two, if I look closely."

"Then don't look too closely," Lan laughed, tightening the sash of his worn grey robe. "Still, it's good to finally get to Regulus. The journey from Sanctus to the city doesn't get any shorter, even with a swift perac and good company." He looked to the woman in a flowing grey robe and the two youths on his opposite side.

"My thanks, Lan," said the woman. "Jucial, Eren and myself have appreciated the company of this old veteran of the civil war. The tales he can tell are good to pass the time, even though I've heard most of them before."

"Lethnal, allow me a modicum of mystery. I thought the youngsters were thoroughly enthralled."

"I did appreciate them, Master Lan," said Jucial. "Both you and Scent Master Lethnal are heroes of mine."

"Not sure I believed half of them myself," laughed Eren, his voice breaking, "but my da reckoned I'm lucky to be travelling with you, and he's a good judge."

"Thank you, both. I'll admit Lan and I had significant roles in the defeat of the Sutanites, but not enough to be considered heroes, at least not in my case," responded Lethnal, running a hand through her short grey hair. "Let us get into the castle so we 'olds' can put our feet up."

"Come," encouraged Jelm as they stepped out of the morning sun and through the darkened doorway, "we have refreshments waiting and Regna is nearby, too."

"Regna," murmured Lan, remembering the beautiful wife of Heritis, both of Sutan, and consequently former enemies of Ean. Their subsequent role in working for the new Eanite government by administering the city of Regulus for the past six years had proved their loyalty, although there were still some questions surrounding Heritis. Regna, however, was shown to be a true friend and capable administrator.

"Usual place," said Jelm, as he ushered them into a largish room down a narrow corridor. "Fire's lit and we have mulled wine and pastries."

"Juice, if you have it," said Jucial, as she sat on a lounge facing the fireplace.

"The wine, please," said Lethnal, smoothing her robe beneath her. "Lan, I think, prefers beer."

"Of course," said Jelm. "A favourite of his and our not-forgotten friend, Targas,"

"Yes," said Lan, "we spent some time here having a beer or two." He looked over to Jucial from his seat near the fire. "Now Targas was a real hero. A man who fought long and hard for the rights of the oppressed people in Ean and lost his life in the battle for Rolan." He lowered his eyes and looked into the fire. "As did a great friend of mine, a very dear friend."

Jucial turned and raised her eyebrows to Lethnal. "Alethea," Lethnal whispered, "the Mlana of our neighbouring country, Rolan. The Sutanites have a lot to answer for."

"Welcome, my dear friends," said a tall brunette, sweeping into the room, a colourful scent aura of pinks and yellows around her head. "Forgive me for not meeting you." She held out her arms to Lan and their scents merged.

Lethnal stood and joined their reunion. She had a lot of time for this effervescent woman, noticing immediately the increased development of her scent control.

"Sorry, Jucial, Eren," said Jelm, "they are old friends and have some catching up to do. I'll introduce you. Regna, these are acolytes Jucial and Eren. The youngsters are on their first visits to Regulus, I believe."

"Welcome," said Regna, pulling away from Lethnal and Lan. "I hope Jelm has offered you refreshments?"

"I'm being well looked after," Jucial said shyly.

"So am I," said Eren, "but I would're liked a beer."

"You're hardly old enough but if Lan says so"—she saw a quiet nod—"then I won't be a poor host. Now, let's all sit down and catch up," continued Regna. "We've a lot to talk about, I guess."

The discussions about the state of Ean and any issues concerning Regulus went well into the night, the only negative being the absence of Heritis.

"Why don't you all retire?" suggested Lethnal. "It's been a long day and besides, I'd like to have a brief time with Regna."

"Certainly." Lan stood. "My thanks to you both for your hospitality." He nodded to Regna and Jelm, then, placing his hands on Jucial's and Eren's shoulders, guided the youths out of the room.

The firelight threw reddish gleams through the small glasses of Rolan cordial they each held. Lethnal took a sip and smiled.

"My dear Regna, I certainly appreciate the taste of the cordial. For some reason we don't have it often in Sanctus, even though several traders come through from Rolan nowadays. I suppose it's from the time of scarcity during the civil war. Can't get into the notion of having regular access to our 'women's' drink."

"Yes, it's very nice to have at a quiet time. It takes me back to when Sadir first introduced me to the 'Shadow' scent. We were sitting in the courtyard when she told me she could see it as another scent behind the normal scents. I had difficulty even seeing normal scents then, but with the cordial I have developed my abilities. I can see and manipulate them now."

"I'm pleased, Regna, just as I am happy to catch up again." Lethnal smiled and took another sip from the small glass. "Now you might be a scent master, but I could discern some worry in your aura. Is it about Heritis, by any chance?"

Regna nodded, rolling her glass between both hands. "Even before the Sutanite fleet burnt Port Saltus on their way to attacking Rolan, Heritis was acting weirdly. Although he denied he was involved, he hasn't been the same since. He's much more secretive, often away, and never comes to me anymore. Our consorting is a sham at best."

"Oh, Regna." Lethnal placed a hand on Regna's knee.

"Worse still, Lethnal," she gulped, "he's using that red crystal. I've become much more adept at picking up on that, and his secretive habits can't disguise the aura of magnesa. Where he gets it and why he's using it, I don't know. He won't talk, and I've given up. Maybe Lan...?"

"Maybe, but be prepared, Regna. It may not go the way you want. Part of the reason we're here is to discuss the situation in Sutan and what we and Rolan should do to prepare for it. I have a feeling that Heritis may have an influence here. If so, we may have to react accordingly."

"Do what you have to," said Regna, "for I'm at my wit's end. Ean is my home now and I'll do anything I can to help protect it, even if my consort is involved. But enough of that. Please, have some more cordial," said Regna, filling her glass from a tumbler on the table, "I have plenty."

The moon had risen, high and bright, shining on the broad grey river that was the Great Southern flowing on its inexorable way past the city of Regulus guarding the rift in the Sensory Mountains, through the capital city of Nebleth and on to the Port of Saltus.

A rider, black-clad on a dark steed, followed the road that paralleled the river's course. He passed through the capital and continued towards the port city. Only a few travellers noticed him this late at night, and fewer still gave him more than a cursory glance. None shared the lonely road with him for long.

"Ah!" screamed Regna, sitting up in her bed, her hand flinging out to knock a small, empty glass to the stone floor.

The scream and the smashing of glass brought Lethnal and Jucial running, in their nightgowns, from their nearby sleeping quarters.

"Regna," called Lethnal, "are you alright?"

"Ah, wait," said Regna sleepily, "there's glass on the floor. Just light the lamp near the door."

Lethnal picked up a fire starter next to the lamp, lit the wick and held up the light. She and Jucial saw Regna running her hands through her dark hair, her nightdress askew.

"Can we come in?"

"Please mind where you tread. Just sit on the bed while I collect myself."

They picked their way into the bedroom around the shards of glass and sat on the side of the large, square bed. Regna propped herself up on pillows at the head.

"I…I must have had too much cordial last night," she smiled wanly at Lethnal and Jucial. "I've had the weirdest dreams."

"Dreams?"

"I saw Heritis, riding out of Regulus, down the river road. He was almost halfway to Port Saltus. I tried to call out to him, ask him what he was doing, but he didn't hear…didn't hear."

"Sure it was a dream?" asked Lethnal.

"It must've been, although there's more."

"Regna, why don't we clear up the glass, settle you with some hot milk and talk about what you've been through?

"Stay there while Jucial gets a broom and I'll head to the kitchens. It's too early to wake the staff and I know how to boil milk."

"Thank you."

"Come Jucial."

Lethnal had built up the fire in the stone oven and placed a pan of perac milk on the top when she heard a noise behind her.

"I was woken by the ruckus," said Lan, wearing a soft pale nightshirt with a blanket across his shoulders. "I believe there is more to it?"

"Lan, I think you might be right. Would you like some hot milk? I'm making some for Regna and Jucial."

"Mmm, with honey. Same for Eren, as he's awake."

The five of them were soon sitting on Regna's bed sipping hot milk in the comforting light of the lamp as Regna recounted her dream of Heritis heading to Port Saltus.

"I think you may be reflecting an actual happening, easy to clarify after dawn. That Heritis has left could be easily explained by his wish to avoid my presence, but there's more, Regna, isn't there?"

She studied her mug for a while before looking up at Lan and nodding. "There is, but it's confusing, as if I've gone mad. I didn't want to tell you."

"We'll need to hear, Regna. Right from the beginning, for, if I'm not mistaken you've had a Knowing."

"What? A Knowing. A prophesy? I've never had anything like that."

"Maybe it's opportune," suggested Lethnal. "Us being here and having several glasses of cordial could have triggered one."

"If you think so."

"Please Regna, tell us. From the beginning," said Lan. "We'll decide if there's meaning to your dreams."

"Well, I've already mentioned the first part before you came in, Lan, about Heritis riding to Port Saltus. But the weird thing was I was above him, seeing him riding along as if I was there. It's after that things get even more peculiar."

"Go on."

"The moon. It was so big and clear, almost as if it was directing me, taking me along. I was curious, wanting to get closer to Heritis, seeing his face and hoping for some strange reason to see if he was thinking of me. Silly, I know. But I couldn't, as something was pulling, dragging me towards the mountains, towards the Long Ranges in the east. I struggled but it was like I was a leaf blowing with the wind.

"I flew past, so fast, then the desert, then the sea, always the moon was shining, glittering. Then," she gulped, "I saw a myriad of white points on the sea. I followed them to the land, a large port, big city, familiar from a long time ago. Ships were landing, bustling, but I didn't stop there. I moved inland following a river; not as wide as the Great Southern, more winding. Another city, the biggest I've ever seen, and although I was young when I left Sutan I knew it was Sutaria.

"Then I zoomed in, down towards a huge sandstone building, maybe the palace. I saw a face; an old woman and…and she saw me. She really saw me. She smiled and said…"

"What?" breathed Lethnal.

"She said…'Beware the enemy inside the enemy. Your role is crucial in the end. Be prepared. Your sacrifice will not be in vain.'"

"And…?"

"And I screamed and sat up in my bed. That's it."

"The woman, what did she look like?" asked Lan.

"Grey hair, old, stooped, but her eyes were very bright. And, I've just remembered, she was surrounded by shadow scent."

"Lan, it's Alethea's sister," said Lethnal excitedly. "Has to be."

"Yes," he said, thinking of the very dear friend he had lost. "It must be. I think there is no time to waste. A true Knowing, I believe. And a warning.

"We need to talk to Jelm, begin preparations and send a message to Rolan.

They met with Jelm at the kitchen table and detailed his network of contacts to carry messages to all. The enemy was on the move. Scent messages were to be sent to Port Saltus to try and capture Heritis before he could leave, presumably to Sutan, and to place Ean on a war footing.

"And Jelm, my friend, I fear you'll need to take the arduous journey across the mountains to Rolan. I'm too old and can best serve in Ean. It is my belief that Rolan will be the prime target, and as we need to protect our allies and support the new Mlana's efforts to stop this, we need to work together. Just take several people with you and leave soon. Unfortunately, time is of the essence."

"I concur, Lan, Lethnal, and will endeavour to go as soon as practical," said Jelm. He turned to Regna. "A truly remarkable Knowing, Regna."

She looked at her hands and slowly shook her head. "At least we know where my former consort's loyalties lie."

Chapter Seven

The road remained the dusty, rocky trail he remembered, little greenery apart from the grey non-descript bushes interrupting the barren landscape. The overnight stop at the Grosten River ford had brought the only relief to an unpleasant ride from Sutaria. The remainder of the ride to Southern Port would be much of the same.

Bilternus heaved on the reins of his perac, forcing its long-necked head to turn towards him, its large, dark eyes swivelling in alarm. "Quieten down," he said firmly, patting its woolly brown side while floating a calming scent over the animal. An unpleasant smell drifted over them from the river: a combination of dankness, foul mud from the nearby marshlands covering part of the plains away from the river and the hint of one of the most infamous denizens of Sutan, the scartha. Bilternus glanced across to the ford, hoping not to see one of the large, scaly beasts eying them up for its meal. He noticed Sharna was leading her steed up a long slope towards a clump of bushes and briefly admired the movement of her tight muscles in the bright green of her trousers.

"Will we be safe up there from the scartha?" he called. "From what I remember there are some in the pools around the rapids."

"Done this trip a few times, Bilternus," Sharna responded as she led the perac into the leafy grove of bushes. "They don't tend to come up this slope. Besides, the bushes have a strong masking scent." As if to emphasise her words, a chill wind blew in from the Steppes of Stone far in the north of Sutan, bringing an unpleasant combination of odours to Bilternus' nose.

"Better set up camp though. You cooking, or shall I?"

"Happy to cook, Sharna. The least I can do," he replied as he unsaddled his animal. "Just better water my perac first."

"I'll water them. if you want to start the fire." Sharna took hold of the reins of the long-legged animals and led them back down the slope towards the pool, while Bilternus cleared out an old fireplace ringed by small rocks. He built a pile of twigs and branches, used a fire-starter and had it blazing as Sharna returned.

They had eaten a meal of meat softened in red wine with a mixture of beans and fungi, before they settled back on the mats, pillowed by the saddles. Stars already twinkled as the sky turned from a light blue to a deep purple and then black.

"You are a good cook. I could eat the same tomorrow night, but we'll be in Southern Port by then." Sharna lay back with her arms cradling her head. "It's good to be out here without any responsibilities, no ships to prepare, no people to organise and no schemes to become involved in. Just the two of us to worry about."

"And scartha."

"And scartha, Bilternus. Although I do have something to keep them at bay if they get too friendly."

"What? A big stick?" he laughed.

"No. Magnesa."

"Magnesa? You've got enough magnesa to stop scartha? Did Jakus give you more?"

"Yes. You have a small supply though, don't you?"

"Yes," he replied, "but little enough."

"I suppose it's the responsibility of leadership, particularly once we're in Southern Port." Sharna sat up. "We'll be his eyes and ears in the Port, so I may need to use more of it."

"Fair enough," said Bilternus. "It is interesting that the Shad has a lot of the red crystal but rarely gives it out."

"It can be deadly, Bilternus," said Sharna. "And it will be very influential in the future. Don't wish for it too much. It's not the wonder drug. It has side effects."

"Ah," he said, looking over at his older companion, "I'm aware of that. I've noticed little things. Jakus, and my father too, are different sometimes."

"Don't say anything," said Sharna. "If you use it sparingly, it should be fine."

"Hmm, unlike Jakus…"

"That's his issue and he does have old injuries to counter, too. You mind yourself, Bilternus, if you want to come out of this with your skin intact."

They sank back onto their saddle pillows and watched the sparks from the fire fly high into the star-studded sky until sleep claimed him.

His night was restless, filled with noises, a glow filtering through his eyelids, different smells chasing unusual dreams. Bilternus started, sitting up with a groan and rubbing sleep-filled eyes as the sun struggled to rise above the low hills to the east.

"Sharna?" he growled at a shape standing nearby. "Haven't you been sleeping?"

She turned to look at him, hair tossed and unruly over a pale face. She pulled her thick, ochre-coloured coat tighter, walked to the fire and stirred the cold coals with a stick, then added a bunch of dried leaves and twigs. A coil of smoke began to rise.

"Had a disturbed night," she murmured. "All that talk of scartha must've filtered through to them. That, or the smell of fresh perac, or human. Anyway, I heard a noise and saw at least one moving up the slope. Several scent bolts aided by magnesa crystals kept him and his friends away. Surprised you slept through."

"Sorry, you should're woken me up," he responded.

"Little need," she said. "Now you do the tea and I'll saddle up. I want to get to the Port before dark."

The waft of the sea and the noise of traffic hit them as they rode up the main street of Southern Port. After a relatively quiet trip from Sutaria the scents and bustle of the city came as a shock.1

"I suggest we walk, Sharna. There are too many people and the horns on the draught animals look wider than I remember," said Bilternus.

"Good idea. Our perac need a break anyway. Besides, it's not too far to the compound," she replied.

They dismounted and walked their animals in single file past numerous carts, mostly heading to the wharves. The wide-bobbed horns of the heavily built perac-like animals forced them to keep well to the verge of the highway. Most of the people leading the carts or carrying goods were poorly dressed males of a mixture of races. Others were better dressed, indicating their more genteel professions, including merchants and shop keepers, their coloured clothing standing out amongst the more subdued colours worn by the servants and workers.

They were soon out of the crowd and following a street with regularly spaced wooden poles holding night lanterns. After crossing an intersection and moving into wider tree-lined streets containing low but extensive buildings, they saw Jakus' compound. It was set back across flat bare ground, the long grey-stone building featuring small narrow windows set deep into thick walls.

"We'll stable the animals and find sleeping rooms for ourselves," said Sharna, "then meet in the common room for a meal."

As they led their animals across the stony ground towards the back of the building, Bilternus felt the gaze of several scent masters from within the compound. *Could they see into his thoughts? No. Impossible.* He quickly heightened his scent aura to ensure he would be easily recognised as friendly, noticing that Sharna had done the same.

"Cer?"
Bilternus looked up into wide blue eyes in a pretty face, recognising Sencia's scent even as she placed a plate of meat-filled gravy and greens in front of him.

He smiled as his mind flooded with memories of last seeing her years ago while in the company of Kyel. His then-companion had had a fling with her, and he saw that the years had only improved her looks. He blushed slightly as his groin responded to his thoughts.

"I see you remember me, Cer. It has been a while." She looked down and her cheeks coloured prettily. "I don't suppose you've heard from your Eanite friend, then?"

"Things have changed, Sencia. Kyel stayed behind, in Rolan. I don't think you'll be seeing him again."

"Oh, I had hoped…"

"And what about you now? Are you partnered?"

"Ah, no." Her eyes searched his face. "Most of the people I meet are soldiers or sailors just passing through. I did like Kyel though; he was sweet."

"Am I going to get served or are you going to jaw all day?" asked a gruff voice.

Sencia looked up to a large guardsman sitting further down the long trestle table. "Be with you in a moment.

"Can we meet later?" she whispered to Bilternus. "I want to know more."

Bilternus nodded as Sencia hurried back to the kitchens. He saw the colourful form of Sharna coming into the meal hall and waved to attract her attention.

"**W**ord is that Brastus' fleet is nearing the port. Outrider ships have been sighted— that's just what I've gleaned with a few words—near here. We'll need to go to the docks to get the latest, find a place to best assess what his strengths are, who he's bringing back home." Sharna put another mouthful of food into her mouth.

"So, after we eat?" said Bilternus.

"Nothing else to do till night, have you?" Sharna raised an eyebrow.

"No," Bilternus said without hesitation, shaking his head. "It's opportune to go now since it'll be very busy once his fleet lands."

They walked through the throng of people and animals near the docks, noting that word had got out of the impending arrival of numerous ships. Labourers and carts were already jostling for position to service the unloading of any vessels arriving before nightfall; it was expected that the main body of the fleet would anchor off the port until next day's high tide.

"Keep an eye out for any officials or others of interest, Bilternus. Some will have an idea of what's going on with Brastus' ships. I'll head over to the Harbour Master and see what he has to say. Any significant arrival of ships will impact on the services I can get for my vessels, so it's logical that I raise questions with him." Sharna smiled and hurried off.

Bilternus watched her weaving through the crowd until her slight form was lost from view before he headed along the wharf. An inn, more accurately a lean-to with a few stools and a plank bar, was situated to one side of the bustling throng, so he bought a tankard of a dubious beer and settled back to wait.

When the sun was moving lower over the flat lands towards the west, Bilternus saw a narrow, two-masted vessel being towed to the pier by a tender boat. He wondered whether it held Brastus or merely was preparing for the arrival of the fleet next day. He gulped down the last of the beer and made his way with the throng to where the ship was being tied up. He stood at the back of the excited crowd, hood over his head, and listened.

After hearing that Brastus had remained with the fleet, merely sending the frigate to facilitate preparations for the next day, he watched the captain and first mate head down the wharf to the Harbour Master's office. He moved closer to the crew engaged with activities on the ship to hear what they had to say. That they were re-provisioning the vessel and were ignoring the curious onlookers was interesting, but he carefully scanned the sailors on the deck, looking for anything unusual. Finally, something caught his interest.

The voyage from Tenstria to Sutan was long and arduous, and dependent on the prevailing winds—over fifteen days, according to the gossip on board. Consequently, those aboard should have been keen to disembark, yet they remained busy on the ship. Obviously, they had been ordered to do what they were engaged in. That was significant, yet what caught Bilternus' interest was the man standing unobtrusively at the stern, well away from the dock side of the ship. He watched the man quietly assessing the scents around him, which indicated he was a scent master. It gave an indication of the way Brastus was thinking, in that he was anticipating a reaction to his arrival in Southern Port..

Bilternus stepped back through the crowd and went to find Sharna.

They met back in Jakus' compound that night to discuss what they had learned. Bilternus shared his thoughts on Brastus' preparedness for any confrontation and Sharna confirmed he had brought nearly his entire force back to Sutan, leaving only a token army in Tenstria. It appeared Jakus had a right to be concerned.

"You'll need to return to Sutan next day, Bilternus," said Sharna. "Take several guardsmen with you too, just in case."

"But…" he began, before realising she was better placed to stay. "Fine," he said. "I guess it's leading up to what we anticipated."

"Yes," she agreed. "Let's hope that wiser heads will prevail." Sharna took a long pull of her wine.

A touch on his shoulder brought him out of a light sleep. Bilternus looked up in the dim light of the sleeping hall to see a slim figure bending over him, her scents giving him clear identification of who she was.

"Sencia," he breathed.

"Shh," she said, placing a finger on his mouth. "Come with me and tell me what has happened to Kyel."

She led the way past several snoring men, out of the sleeping hall and down a long corridor. Several turns later they ended up at a dead end where two doors were set in opposite walls. Bilternus followed her into a small room whose only light came from a slit in the wall, a wooden bed on one side and a chair and small table on the other. Sencia reached behind him and closed the door.

As he followed her slim form, her scents caused him to forget any questions he may have had. The hiss of a falling gown, hands pulling off his pants and jerkin, then clasping his bottom as she pulled him against her naked form, made him react without any other thought. He fumbled his way onto the narrow wooden bed before she sat astride him and pushed her small breasts against his face. He tried hard to keep control as she began to move rhythmically against him.

Kyel told me how much he enjoyed being with Sencia, he thought bemusedly as he bit gently on a hard nipple.

Chapter Eight

A low rumble shook the foundations, causing a shower of dust to fall from the ceiling across Sharna's body. She shook her head before reaching out and placing a firm hand on the scent master's broad shoulder next to her.

"Hold still, Tretial," she hissed. "There's little we can do other than allow Brastus to let off some steam. It'll soon be over."

"But why is he so foolish?" Tretial questioned. "Surely, he knows that Jakus is powerful. Why try to raise the Shad's ire by damaging the compound? He'd have to know that there's only several companies here."

"This is but the opening shot in the coming civil war. Brastus is announcing he's returned to lead Sutan, and his only impediment is Jakus."

"So, we just cower in here and take it? Let him and his troops march by, throw scent bolts and do nothing?"

"Oh, Tretial," she laughed over a particularly loud boom and the dimming of light from the narrow windows, "there'll be time enough.

"In fact, I'd like to be in Sutaria when Brastus arrives and confronts his brothers and father, for I have every faith in our master and his power. Now let's wait until the procession has passed, then we can continue our preparations as ordered by Jakus. We have a very busy time ahead."

B ilternus threw the lead of his perac to the stable hand and dashed across the cobbled courtyard towards the side of the palace where Jakus had a private entrance to his rooms. He clattered into the darkened corridor, brushed past two cleaners, and went into the large entry hall.

"Welcome, Bilternus," said Poegna, turning towards him and smoothing the sides of her lilac gown, "I didn't expect to see you so soon."

"Ah, no," Bilternus gasped, "but there's news for Jakus and it was easier for us to ride back than send a scent message."

"Would you like water or something stronger?" she asked, clapping her hands. A young woman appeared through a doorway at the far end of the room. "Fetch scent master Bilternus some water!

"I'll find Jakus, as you'll want to give your report in private?" Poegna walked past Bilternus and through the doorway.

He wandered over to a large table and perused the map on it, taking a moment to recognise it included Sutaria as well as Ean and Rolan. "Always prepared," he murmured as his eyes traced the distances from each country, realising that it was close to scale.

"Ah, thank you," he said as he absently accepted a mug of water from the server. "So"—he took a sip—"the map doesn't include Tenstria—too much sea, I suppose—but it's the first time I've seen all three countries together."

"Bilternus!"

He snapped upright at the authoritative voice.

"So, my brother has arrived. Report!" Jakus, limping slightly, made his way to the side cabinet and poured a glass of wine.

Bilternus hurriedly put down the mug. "Ah, I left last day so haven't all the facts, but we do know that around ten ships, two- and three-masted, were putting into the port as I left. Sharna estimates it is nigh on Brastus' full fleet, so he would have left only a token force in Tenstria."

"Fool!" exclaimed Jakus. "He's exposed our gains in Tenstria to potential loss, so keen is he to defeat me. Not qualities of leadership at all. Continue!"

"That he is preparing for confrontation is obvious. We saw many signs, including negotiations with port authorities and much resupplying of ships and men."

"Again, expected and not of concern," said Jakus. "I am not fool enough to fail to allow for this eventuality. He'll find few friends in Southern Port and even fewer in Sutaria."

"We believe he'll be coming here, to Sutaria, almost immediately," continued Bilternus. "Sharna advises our ships and forces will be at the ready for whatever eventuality."

"Yes"—Jakus absently rubbed his side—"as expected. Sharna is competent and acting on my will. Any sign of ships from Ean, hmm?"

"No, nothing yet. Sharna is keeping in touch with the Harbour Master."

"Early days," Jakus growled. "Now, lad, the time has come for me to check your loyalty. You are proving yourself, but it would be remiss of me to neglect this small matter. Come with me and I will delve into your thoughts." Jakus glanced down at the map next to Bilternus. "Get used to that picture. One day it will be all Sutan." His eyes glittered and his scent aura darkened.

Bilternus gulped, thankful for Xerina's forethought in protecting his mind, and hoped the much-vaunted shadow scent would protect his innermost thoughts from Jakus' probes.

He would never forget the scene in the palace. The vast hall was filled to over-flowing. Guardsmen and sailors from various factions intermingled with many people from Sutan society, servers running around with wooden and ceramic tankards, and platters of food. A hubbub of noise gave a background to the tableau around the large table in the centre.

The clear space left seven imposing figures highlighted, either by shafts of light filtering through cleverly concealed window slits or from the scent auras circling around the group. Bilternus recognised all bar one willowy man, in dark jerkin and trousers, light cloak slung over a shoulder to expose a large knife; he assumed this was Brastus' commander, Strengor. Jakus had Kast, the large, imposing leader of his ground forces and scent masters at his side, while all were overshadowed by Vitaris' enforcer, Dronthis. Bilternus remembered this man virtually killing the young Eanite, Kyel, some years before when they thought he was the threat to Sutan referred to in the Knowing.

Of course, they were only the players. The real force was the family: Vitaris, old and stooped but showing glimpses of his former power, Jakus, slightly twisted from old injuries but tall and predatory all the same, Brastus taking after his grandfather with broad shoulders and an arrogant manner, and Bilternus' father, Faltis. He looked at the thin, stooped man, the only one without a supporter, almost forgotten but there—a presence in the tableau before him. Was it really his father or that false persona inhabiting his body? Bilternus shivered as he waited for the play to begin.

Vitaris raised an arm. The noise died away.

"It has been a time since the ruling family of Sutan was together under one roof with a common purpose. You all"—Vitaris' gaze slowly traversed the throng—"support members of this family, all united with the one goal, to make Sutan great again. To enable us to rule the world. To do this we have to support each other, to cast aside our differences and work towards the common good.

"So," Vitaris continued, straightening, the aura coiling about him in reds and purples slashed by streaks of gold making him appear like the ruler he once was, "the time has come for you all to make a choice, follow the new ruler of Sutan and achieve that greatness. All I can ask is that you choose wisely.

"My sons now appear before you!" He flung his arms out to encompass Faltis, Brastus and Jakus. "It is up to them to convince you who to choose.

"Brastus!"

Brastus immediately pulsed a combination of scents in powerful reds and purples, dark colours flaring up higher into the dimness of the hidden roof of the great hall. He flung his arms wide, emphasising his powerful figure. A man of presence; a leader.

"You will know me. And for those of you who don't, I will tell you why. I've been away, fighting wars for Sutan, expanding our territories, making the name of our country feared. And those exploits have benefitted Sutan and will continue to do so."

As Brastus spoke Bilternus could see the effects of his scent power, a transparent drift of scent filtering across the audience, slowly, surreptitiously infiltrating their scent centres, influencing their perceptions, swaying their feelings towards the benevolence of the man, the future leader. When it reached him, he warded the flow, pushing it away. *Clever,* he thought, *clever.* Even as he perceived Brastus' action he could see that Jakus was reacting, blocking, and diluting the scent influence.

Brastus was concluding, explaining how he, with a wealth of experience and no failures to his exploits, unlike his brother Jakus, was the future leader of Sutan and would take the country to its true pre-eminent position in the known world. Bilternus watched Jakus slide a hand into the pouch at his side and slip something into his mouth. He almost felt sorry for Brastus.

"Faltis!" yelled Vitaris, "you should have a chance to speak."

Faltis started as if he had been asleep, before slowly stretching to a height near that of Jakus. He smiled slyly, showed no sign of scent power, and began to speak in a quiet, clear voice. "I have but one ambition and that is to serve Sutan. To do this I will serve my country's leader both with my considerable skill and the resources I can bring to bear.

"It is not appropriate for me to indicate whom I will back, for my ambition is for the good of our country. Not for me the posturing for position, the mayhem caused by any fighting, I will stand by the leader and give my all to him. You"— he scanned the audience, his eyes glittering with a reddish light—"can be certain of that." He looked back at Vitaris, another's eyes peering from his.

"Thank you for not forgetting me, Father!"

Vitaris frowned, then shook his head and looked at Jakus.

"Jakus!"

Jakus smiled, took a step away from the group and pulsed long ropes of scent high into the air. Dark crimson scents mixed with the deepest of purples sheeted into the air, eliciting a gasp from his audience. He rose slowly until it was clear he was no longer supported by the ground, Bilternus supposing it was achieved through a scent shield of significant power. At the same time Brastus and Strengor stumbled back a few steps, pushed by the same scent shield.

"Contrary to what my brother Brastus has been saying, I have not been idle and failed. Firstly, I have learnt all about Ean and Rolan, our future vassal countries.

"Secondly, and most importantly, the value of scent power.

"I will be a leader who will rule well for the benefit of all!

"This is what I will bring and share with all those who follow me. For I am powerful, I have all I need to provide that same power to those who support me.

I also have the power to destroy those who oppose me.

"Thank you, Father, for the opportunity to speak. I have many plans in place and our future is assured. There are none to stand in our way and I will state that we will soon have conquered the known world. Indeed, we will also dispose of Tenstria, a country which my fearless brother has failed to subdue in many years of fighting.

"Dear brother"—Jakus turned to face Brastus—"I'll look forward to your support in my leadership of Sutan. Should, however, you wish to challenge me, to stop me from leading this magnificent country, then I'll be forced to count you amongst my enemies!

"I think, Father, it is time to dismiss this gathering. There is work to be done."

As Jakus released his scent powers and moved smoothly through the hall with his second-in-command, Kast, Brastus leant closely to Vitaris, talking in a harsh whisper. Faltis stayed nearby, a considered expression on his face.

Bilternus released his breath and headed in a different direction. He felt in need of some wise council, and he knew the best person in the palace for that.

"What is it I haven't been told, Father? What sort of display was that? The power!" Brastus leant even closer, spraying spittle over Vitaris with his harsh words.

"Hold, my son." Vitaris gently pushed Brastus back. "Surely your sources kept you better informed. You must know of Jakus' fixation with the red crystal?"

"I know. The push for Rolan and his attack there. I knew he got supplies of the magnesa, but what I didn't realise was its power, if my brother's display was anything to go on.

"So, I'll ask you, here and now, are you going to support me in my quest to become leader of Sutan? We both question my brother's sanity and know he might lead our country to ruin.

"So, what's it to be?"

"Son, I must be impartial while I still have the strength of rule. It has been tested of late and I know I must bequeath it as wisely as I can." Vitaris pushed a hand across his haggard face. "I'll admit I have leanings to you, as I have misgivings about my other sons, but I cannot be seen to be taking sides."

"Hah!" Faltis moved between the two men. "If you're not certain who you will support, why don't you ask your soothsayer, eh? She's a burden on this country coming up with worthless prophesies that influence everyone. Make her tell you!"

"Xerina!" Brastus pushed his brother back. "You still listen to her, Father?"

"She has proven of value in the past."

"Then let's do it, now, brother dear," said Faltis snidely. "Father?"

"Come, then," said Vitaris. "Let's see what she has to say. Dronthis, Strengor, you may stay with the others to learn what you may."

As the three men walked through to the inner areas of the palace, a slim figure slipped out in the direction of Jakus' rooms. Poegna was certain her Shad would want to hear what she had overheard.

"Settle, Bilternus," said Xerina, a smile creasing her face, "we will be having visitors shortly. Please sit in the corner near the pool. Enjoy for the moment the serenity my rooms bring."

A clatter announced Vitaris, Brastus and Faltis. Xerina rose slowly from her chair at the table in the long, sunlit room and gestured to several seats.

"Welcome, my lords. A pleasure to see you, Brastus, after so long," she said brightly. "I can guess you require some advice?"

"What's he doing here?" growled Brastus, pointing at Bilternus in the corner.

"My son," interrupted Faltis, "this is where you got to?"

"Enough," said Vitaris. "You know, Xerina, what we have come about. What have you discerned? What advice or warnings will you put our way?"

"My Lord," she said, sitting back down, "please excuse me not standing as my old bones are a trial. Please sit and I'll tell you what I have discerned."

The men dropped into their chairs and while Brastus glowered at the old woman, Faltis steepled his hands around his long nose and leant back.

"Begin," said Vitaris.

"For the benefit of Brastus, the warning from many years ago remains. Should Sutan falter, its demise is likely to come from an Eanite. I still can't discern who."

"Still, old woman!" yelled Faltis. "Enough of that old trite. What do you have now that makes your life worth preserving?"

"Patience, my Lord. In the likelihood of a civil war, I see brother fighting brother. I see the influence of the red crystal. I see madness. I see death. I see much war in the future, where the outcome is uncertain."

"Whose death, old woman?" Brastus leant forward. "My brother's? That cripple?"

"If Knowings were that certain we would know of all future events. They can change, depending on whether we act upon them or not. Not all is given." Xerina took a sip from a cup in the table next to her.

"So," said Vitaris, "my role?"

"I think," she replied, "you know it, my Lord. Both you and I are old, near our time."

"Ah." Vitaris slumped in his chair.

"Well, woman?"

"My Lord Brastus, I cannot tell whether your brother or you will prevail, but the red crystal will influence the outcome in ways you may not predict. You need to learn more about it, I would suggest."

"Enough!" Brastus stood, knocking over his chair. "I'll waste no more time here. Coming, Father?"

"I will think on this, Xerina," said Vitaris as he stood. "Come Brastus, Faltis, we will go to my chambers."

They left in a rush, the room suddenly quieter.

"Now, Bilternus, the next while will see much happening. Be certain you are prepared to play your part."

"Whatever it will be, Xerina."

"Yes, young man, whatever it will be."

Chapter Nine

The creature was a picture of dissolution, head supported on ragged arms, bags under its eyes almost as large as its flabby jowls. As if in response to his presence, the eyes opened to sunken pits and the head ponderously rose. A belch-like gasp preceded his words.

"Cer, it's you!" The breath rolled in a sour stink towards Heritis, causing him to step back. "I...I were jest having a drink, is all." The man slowly rose from the table in a dark corner of The Salted Arms tavern, his corpulent body shaking its covering of worn brown jerkin and stained dark trousers.

"Hsst!" Heritis tugged his hood lower while extending a scent barrier to press down on the man's throat. "Not here. Come with me, to the docks. We'll discuss matters there."

He winced as the fat man noisily pushed the stool aside before walking unsteadily amongst the tables along the length of the bar, a small, wizened man industrially cleaning cups watching their progress. They pushed through the double doors and onto the street.

"You're a fool, keeper!" hissed Heritis, forcing the man to a faster pace along the cobbled street. "Now, have you done what I ordered?"

"Cer, I have Cer," the keeper's voice whined. "Though I don't know that I can anymore, not after last time. I can't keep it out of me head. They don't like it. They don't obey anymore. We shoulda have let them all die. We shoulda!"

Heritis grabbed a handful of the reeking jerkin and thrust the man hard against the rough wooden wall of a warehouse. "Enough. You have your orders. Now show me where they are."

The keeper whimpered, ran a dirty arm across his face and edged past the tall figure of Heritis. He led the scent master to a laneway a street back from the Port Saltus docks, then down to a narrow doorway in the wooden facade. A large iron key turned in the lock and he pushed the door open. Immediately a rancid, musty smell emerged. "In. Quickly!" Heritis shoved the keeper in the back and followed the man into the darkened room before pulling the door shut behind him. "We can't let their scent be detected. Too much is riding on this."

A light grew as the keeper lit a lamp and moved forward into the vast dark space.

Heritis recognised the scent well before he heard the characteristic rustling of the bodies of the giant wasp-like creatures kept by the Sutanites as weapons of control. The last time they had been used was in the attack on the Rolanites, where they had been lost in the final assault. But they were fearsome carnivores tracking an enemy by the faintest of scents. The keeper had raised even more of these creatures, which Heritis intended to provide for Jakus' use in the forthcoming war of conquest in Sutan. They would be his entrée to Jakus' side and an influence in the final carving up of territory when the Sutanites ruled the world.

Heritis shook his head at the unhealthy man leading him further into the warehouse. Only the fact that he still had his uses kept him alive.

The keeper lit a second lamp to reveal the large cages holding the hymetta. Six creatures, one per cage, focussed their attention on the intruders. Each stood thigh-high on six thin yellow legs, the faint light glistening off their shiny black carapaces. The yellow mouthparts worked beneath large black eyes as if in anticipation of a meal and wings buzzed, lifting a dust of chitin and noxious droplets into the air. One lifted a long, spindly leg and wiped an ooze of drool from its mouth, causing Heritis to shudder.

"Are they healthy? Are they well fed?"

"Yes Cer, they are, though I've had t' be careful." The keeper looked at his hand. "They'll eat anything, as long as it's meat."

"Good. Make arrangement to get them and their food on board. We leave on the tide."

"But—"

"Do it, man. Failure is not an option." The buzzing of a pair of wings emphasised his words.

The ships were slowly hauled from their berths into the harbour by sailors in tender boats. They rowed hard, pulling the massive weight of the fully laden vessels, each with over fifty guardsmen and sailors keen to help Jakus in his ambitions.

Heritis looked aloft at the sailors setting the three main sails on both masts of each vessel, thankful he had managed to load all he needed in sufficient time to avoid any interference from Jelm and his friends. As soon as he knew Lan was coming to Regulus, he had known time was of the essence and so made the rushed journey to the Port of Saltus to ensure he could leave without hindrance to aid his cousin Jakus' ambitions in Sutan. The hymetta were a surprise, one he knew would please the Shad.

"Cer, we'll soon be able to bring the boats aboard as there is a strong enough flood tide to move the ships."

Heritis looked over at the focused features of Crastus, his captain, and nodded. "Thanks, Captain. What is your reckoning for reaching Southern Port?"

"Reckon around three to four days, Cer," Crastus looked to the west. "It should be relatively smooth. We've prevailing winds and none of the winter storms of course, so it should be a fair reckoning."

"What of the Eanite patrols? Assume they'll be off the harbour. Will they want to check us?"

"Usually don't, Cer," the captain responded gruffly. "They're more concerned with ships arriving than leaving."

"Hmm, I don't think they'll have had time to be on the lookout for us anyway. I'll go below and check my cargo. Inform me if there's anything to report."

The captain nodded towards Heritis' back as he disappeared down the narrow stairs at the foot of the aft deck.

"**R**ancer," Heritis said to the dark, broad-shouldered man entering his cabin, "all is as it should be?"

The former master armsman nodded, lips tight in his weathered face. "Men and cargo secure. Even that fat idiot of yours has stopped moaning."

"Rancer!" Heritis' eyes narrowed above his beak-like nose. "The keeper has his uses, even now. I have no wish to replace him while we have the hymetta. We will see what Jakus wants before acting on that.

"Sit with me." He pointed to the second seat bolted to the floor of the cabin. "Share a glass of this fine malas. This has been an achievement, the result of substantial planning. All the pieces are coming into play and those of us who have kept the faith and supported Jakus will be rewarded when he becomes Shada of the world."

Rancer settled with a grunt, picked up the small glass of spirit Heritis had waiting on the table and took a sip.

"Umm, that's good. One of the best things out of Tenstria. So, we finally leave Ean. It's been a while for both of us, surviving the revolution and living under the enemy's rule until Jakus could shore things up in Sutan." Rancer held the glass up to the light coming through the small cabin window before taking another sip. "What's the news with Brastus? How far are we behind him?"

Heritis leant forward, his scent aura reflecting his anticipation. "Communications have been intermittent, but I'm informed that Brastus should be arriving in Southern Port as we speak, with a large contingent of troops. We are coming in behind them and have hopes that our small force will be overlooked to a large degree."

"So, our troops and our scent masters, plus those stinking creatures in the hold are all part of it? What do you perceive will be our role?"

"Apart from gathering information for Jakus on the situation in Ean and Rolan, we are a back-up force and bring two more ships for Jakus' fleet when he rules Sutan and moves to expand our territories." Heritis picked up his glass and drank.

"There's more, Heritis."

"You always were an astute arms commander, Rancer. Of course there's more. The hymetta can target an enemy using the merest motes of scent and are a potential surprise weapon. We also have sufficient supplies of the red crystal for our scent masters to play their part when needed. I've very quietly built up supplies of magnesa over the last years for when the time comes."

A sudden heeling of the ship sent Rancer's glass sliding towards the side of the table. He snatched it up while holding on to the side of his chair.

"Finish it while I check on our course. By the feel we have left the influence of the land and are on the heading towards Sutan." Heritis stood and opened the door to his cabin. "Oh, can you arrange for the scent masters, Manis, Sinal and Harkule to meet here first thing next day? We need to discuss their deployment within our ranks."

The strong wind pushed his black robe hard against his tall, thin body as he stepped onto the deck.

Heritis investigated the wall of scent from the land billowing up from the rows of wooden piers projecting fishbone-like from a broad stone causeway linking into a mass of warehouses and buildings. Most of the piers were occupied by ships, ranging from two-masted, narrow vessels to squatter two- and three-masted transports. But several subtle flags aided the non-scented in recognising who the ships belonged to.

"Over there!" he said to Crastus, who was peering over the side at the rowing boat towing his ship. "That's where Jakus' ships are berthed." Heritis pointed to one of the piers.

Crastus yelled to the boats towing the two ships towards the docks until they altered course and headed towards the indicated berths.

Heritis continued to watch, his eyes narrowing as he recognised a colourful figure waiting for them amongst the activity around her. People loading or unloading the vessels were everywhere, mainly poorly dressed men in one piece, ochre-coloured clothing tied around the waist.

"Sharna!" he yelled as they approached the pier. "Nice to finally meet up with you." He saw a sailor at the bow throw a length of rope to a person near a bollard. The second caught it and quickly tied the vessel to the pier.

"Pleased to meet you too, Heritis." Her voice was high and welcoming. "Can I come aboard?"

The red-headed woman sprinted up the gangway and headed to where he stood with Crastus on the aft deck. Her scents were swirling with welcome in reds, greens and yellows as she stood nose to nose with Heritis. "Glad to see you. Jakus will be pleased you've finally arrived." She stepped away, nodded to the captain, and turned back to Heritis.

"If you don't mind me saying, you do have the look of the ruling family, other than Brastus. He's much more solid, none of that aristocratic look. Now, what do you require?"

"We have a number of troops to unload and settle. Jakus' compound?" Heritis raised his eyebrows, to which Sharna nodded. "Let me introduce you to my scent masters." He waved a hand at the three men coming along from the bow. "Manis"—the broad, middle-aged man touched her and shared scents, "Sinal"— the slight man did likewise—"and Harkule." The tall, thin-faced man bowed slightly and shared scents. "They are all survivors from the Eanite rebellion and have an interest in seeing the Shada regain his birthright.

"Now, there's a special cargo, one which I don't want anyone to see, and which our scent masters can help protect when it's being taken off ship. Would you have suggestions on how to handle that?"

"Ah, you would have seen a number of scent masters on the wharf already, some of whom work for Brastus—by the way, he has already left for Sutaria with most of his force. You will have noticed his ships on the pier over the other side of the harbour?

"So, my suggestion would be to wait until dark and use covered wagons to transport what you need. If we keep it looking like part of the cargo it should be fine. I assume you mean our, ah, flying weapon?"

"Yes, Sharna, the scent is obvious close up, so we'll need to keep the enemy from getting too near."

"Agreed," Sharna said, bobbing her head. "It's getting towards dusk. If we delay getting them off until after dark, it'll keep them guessing."

"Yes. This is vital. Our Shad has plans."

Chapter Ten

"No, no, no! There's no time for lessons. Too much is happening." Vor looked towards Boidea and growled to emphasise his mistress' statement.

"Don't you growl at me, you fleabag." The large woman shook her fist at the voral. "And Anyar, you shouldn't let your animal do the talking for you."

Anyar fell backwards on the couch and laughed as Vor scrabbled up to lie across her belly. "Sorry, Boidea, but you should're seen your face. You're naughty, Vor." She pushed her hands into the flop of fur around his neck.

"Yes, I'm sure he's adequately chastised," Boidea stood, her hands on her hips. "All right, let's get some cake and talk it over."

The voral jumped off Anyar as if he had heard a magic word, and led them towards the kitchens.

"Food is what you need. You're growing like a weed, maturing into mid-teens now," Boidea shook her head. "I can't explain it. You're being robbed of your childhood, Anyar and it doesn't seem right."

"What will be will be, Boidea," said Anyar through a mouthful of cake. "I have periods when I want to remain a child, then others when the weight of the mountains seems upon me. I can sit there, let it happen and feel right about it. Then I just want to go out and enjoy myself." Boidea was surprised at such introspection in one so young, but old eyes looked out from the fresh face, and Anyar added: "We don't have a choice, my dear friend, really we don't."

The voral growled and rolled over, revealing his belly.

"Hey"—Anyar jabbed the dirty white fur with a leather-shod foot—"you need a bath." She glanced up at Boidea with a twinkle in her eye. "Want to help?"

The group of women, wearing special shifts cleaned to remove their scent influence, moved silently down the dark corridor, with Boidea in the lead, holding up her lamp. Anyar stretched out her hand to grip her mother's, wishing for a moment she could hold Vor's scruff with the other.

"No animals," Boidea had warned when they were heading to the crystal cave. "This is women's business, and we don't need any distractions." Anyar nodded.

"This is an important time," said Xerrita, the buxom scent master, as she pushed a lock of grey hair behind her ear. "We've asked our teachers who use the cave when training our girls to give us space so we can fully introduce you to the woman's scent, the shadow scent. We don't know how much of Alethea's memories are in yours, Anyar, so we must make certain."

"I'm aware of that," she responded, watching their misshapen shadows flicker on the rock ceiling as they walked.

"Don't worry, Anyar, I'm learning too," Cathar said, holding up the second lamp at the rear of the group.

Boidea pushed through the cloth hanging over the entrance and entered the cave. The light was caught by the magnesite crystals and reflected around the walls, giving their forms a bloody cast.

A collective gasp at the magnificence of the display was drawn from the group as they crunched over the gravel-strewn surface to the cushioned benches scattered across the space.

"Leave your lamp by the entrance, Cathar," said Boidea as she set her lamp in an alcove to allow the light to be directed upwards. "Please, everyone, take a seat."

The two sources of light competed, giving their figures double shadows which flickered darkly in the redness as they settled, Sadir with Anyar while Boidea and Xerrita sat opposite, leaving Cathar slightly to one side.

"Are we all comfortable? Anyar?"

"Yes, Boidea," she whispered.

"You're amongst friends, Anyar. We will merely be exploring and expanding on your knowledge, nothing to be concerned about." She smiled, but the shadows gave a harsh cast to her face.

Sadir put her arm around her daughter. "It does look a little eerie, Boidea, but if we all relax, we should be fine." She hugged Anyar to her.

"I'm ready," said Anyar calmly.

"Sadir, why don't you begin?" suggested Boidea.

"Me?" Sadir sat back. "Why me?"

"Your first experience, when you saw the scent, naming it the shadow scent, then your use of it. Each time Anyar was with you. She may recall the same, and at least it will be familiar."

"Hmm, of course I will. At least Cathar will learn more of what happened to me as well." She smiled over her shoulder to the slim form of Cathar sitting quietly.

"It was in happier times. I was in Regulus, in the castle with Regna. We were having drinks out in the courtyard. Targas, my poor Targas, wasn't with us then. We had had Rolan cordial the night before, so I suppose it was a catalyst. I was looking at a solid scent when I noticed a slight shadow surrounding that scent; I had to push at it to get it to separate from the normal one, capturing the shreds of it and bundling it together until it was a ball of the stuff. Even Regna could see it then.

"It was so hard to hold, until something incredible happened. Anyar saw it."

"What, Mother?"

"Even so young you saw and touched it, breaking it apart. You were just a child; you shouldn't have been able to do that."

"Then, when we were trapped in the caves with those horrid wasp-like hymetta Jakus tried to kill us with, it showed its value. I was so desperate when one was about to grab me I just pulled all the scents I could, including the wasp's own stink, there, in the dark, formed it into a ball and threw it at its head. It overwhelmed the wasp in a burst of smell, and it fled."

"Ah," said Xerrita, "it is your *shadow scent*, Sadir. It enables one to better use the scent centres of the brain. Rolan cordial is imbued with a magnesa tang from the containers, the tumblers which are made of the discarded magnesite material from the mining process. It is this which enhances a natural ability which some women have."

"Of course, you've all had experience with it—you too, Anyar," said Boidea. "I hesitate to mention it, but when we were seeking to help Targas in this very place we made significant use of shadow scent to help push into his scent centres. It is a scent which can be used in conjunction with others, and that is what we did."

"Didn't help, though," murmured Sadir.

"I'm sorry, but I doubt if anything could have removed what was troubling Targas. It was beyond our skill."

"He will not be forgotten," Anyar's voice broke sonorously through the dark red atmosphere. "The evil will need to be dealt with."

"Anyar?" Sadir took her daughter's head in her hands. "Anyar."

"Please, Mother." She pushed Sadir's hands away.

"Ah, we must move on," said Boidea.

"So, we recognise that the shadow scent is a duplicate scent not seen or used by many, indeed I don't believe the enemy really knows about it other than there was a counter to their scent attacks in the battle for Mlana Hold.

"While its power is mainly the ability to counter normal scent use, it also has the attributes of encompassing normal scent for protection and offence. You've seen what the best manipulators can do with it. The Mlana, Alethea, was a master at it, culminating with her ability to push her memories into Anyar as she was dying."

"Yes, I learned so much," said Anyar. "I think it's an instinctive thing now."

"Be that as it may, we have to prepare," added Xerrita. "This is the best place to do it, aided by the power of the magnesite, where there'll be no interference. It's our secret weapon for when the inevitable happens. We must prepare."

"Well said, Xerrita," said Boidea, smiling over to Anyar. "I think we should get comfortable and see how far we can aid the new Mlana in her journey.

"Are you ready? Please relax."

Sadir had never experienced what came next. There had been periods in Ean when she had been part of the moon ceremony, where everyone had gathered in the Sanctus cavern, joined in harmony and scent usage, and experienced a sense of oneness, of completeness. Even at the funeral pyre for the dead from the fighting with the Sutanites at Salt Way, where the wraiths of those lost had entered them; so real had it seemed, but this was different.

Boidea and Xerrita began to hum, at the same time visibly releasing scarlet-coloured scent from their mouths into the twinkling lights of the red crystal cave. The resonance of the sound picked up and amplified by the space encouraged her to add her voice to the harmony. She could see Anyar and Cathar doing the same. Soon all had their own drift of scarlet scent rising, joining the thick rope of colour in the red light until it obscured the flashes from the innumerable crystals of the cave walls.

The rope of scarlet became a fog overwhelming them, infiltrating, and making them one. Sadir could feel the presence of the women, the delicate strength of Anyar, the comforting support of Boidea and Xerrita and the freshness of Cathar. But she had little time to wonder as the press of the crystals loomed, filling her vision, and crushing in. But her fear didn't affect her, she felt a completeness from the others' presence and a satisfaction of understanding the knowledge being imparted. She could 'see' the scents around and within her, feel the strength of shadow scent, see how it was a substrate for all scent, an indivisible part that controlled all that came from it.

It became a shield, an armour incapable of being penetrated, of being overwhelmed by the lesser scents. Yet she felt it was not an agent for offence, more one for defence, for protection. Any attempt to use it for an evil purpose would be wrong.

Sadir took a deep, shuddering breath, pushing into her daughter beside her. She could feel the slight body vibrating in synchrony to the vibration of the room. Slowly the sounds died away and she heard Cathar shift nearby.

"By Ean," Sadir said, "I don't know what happened, but I feel I understand so much more. Anyar, are you alright?"

The blanket of scarlet scent dissipated, allowing the reflected light of the lamps to dominate in a myriad twinkling points of red.

"Thank you, Mother. I am well. May our experience aid us in the time to come." The girl stretched and looked at the two Rolanites opposite her. "Can you add more to what we have experienced?"

Boidea glanced at her companion. "Shall I, Xerrita?"

"Please, I'll expand on anything if necessary."

"So, we felt more in-depth areas of scent than we would normally, mainly due to the unusual attributes of this area, the magnesite crystals.

"Essentially, while shadow scent is powerful in its own right, it is the basic scent, a substrate to any other. It more or less controls other scents, so, for example if someone tries to influence or attack you, shadow scent can be a barrier or a wall to that attack. As long as you maintain control, you can shield yourself indefinitely.

"Now you can also use the scent to stop someone. For some reason it is not a weapon as such, unlike the 'scent bolts' we and the enemy use, it is more of a blocking mechanism. It can push, deflect, and even stop an attack. We can use it to stop even the strongest scent master.

"We can disguise, even make ourselves undetectable with it, although normal scent use can achieve similar things. Most of all it can destroy normal scent, but this is an attribute we keep silent on."

"Another point, Boidea," interrupted Xerrita, "is that it is our woman's power. Magnesite, even the tumblers made of its residues, influence this substantially but for some reason no man has ever been really able to use shadow scent."

"A question that's been puzzling me is the magnesa itself," asked Sadir. "Why don't we use that? The enemy does."

"Ah, that's been a rule for as long as I remember," said Boidea. "It is used in small amounts by mystics here in Rolan, but long-term use can be detrimental. We warn anyone who trades for it that it can be addictive, and once someone is addicted, we cannot be sure for their state of mind."

"Why sell it, then?" asked Sadir.

"It is known that we, Rolan, have it. If we refuse to trade it, then we would become a vulnerable target. Unfortunately, it is the lesser of two evils."

Anyar stood bolt upright, drawing everyone's attention. "The enemy can never have this place"—she turned slowly, arms held in a v-shape to encompass the space around her—"for if he does it will mean the destruction of everything we hold dear. He cannot win!

"But we will need it to defeat him, even if we go to him."

Anyar's voice ceased to echo around the cave, and she jerked as if she'd suddenly noticed everyone watching her, puzzlement reflecting in their eyes. "We should leave here now. I believe there will be some news."

She reached out her hand to Sadir. "Come, Mother."

They were met by a gambolling animal as they exited the corridor. Light infiltrating the entrance showed it was late in the day as they moved towards the tables clustered near the cavern entrance.

"I am so pleased to see you!" came a booming voice.

"Jelm!" squealed Anyar and she thudded into the tall, fair-haired man's body.

Jelm clasped the girl in response, then gently pushed her back. "By Ean, Anyar, you've grown and look…much older," he frowned.

"Still got that creature with you too, though he's added a lot of weight since last I saw him." Jelm pushed his foot against Vor's enquiring snout. "Ah…Sadir." He eased away from Anyar and looked at the women coming from the dark corridor at the back of the cavern.

Sadir smiled at the joyful man highlighted against the daylight coming through the cavern entrance, recognising his familiar scents and the greens, yellows and pinks of welcome in his aura. She approached, looked up at his light grey eyes and fell into his scents.

"Ah," he said, "I've missed you. So long since we last met."

"Jelm, yes, I have missed you too. And I'll never forget how you supported me in Ean when we were trying to cure Targas from all that troubled him. Even now, with Targas gone so long ago, I still have fond memories of all you did for me and Anyar.

"But let me introduce you to…"

"Boidea," interrupted Jelm, looking at the large woman standing nearby, "I haven't forgotten you, of course. I was saddened to hear of the Mlana's passing and understand you've taken over the training of Anyar." He smiled at Anyar, who was crouched down with Vor. "So much time… And Cathar? I'm really pleased to see you again—you have matured into a beautiful woman, if you don't mind me saying."

"Please, I'm neglecting your needs," said Boidea. "We'll have refreshments before we hear your news and why you made the arduous trip to Rolan. Xerrita"—she gestured to her companion—"this is Jelm, the administrator of Ean's capital, Nebleth, and a friend. Please join us at the tables and we'll get to know each other."

The tables were set up under the overhang along the extensive opening to the Mlana's Hold cavern where the warmth of several fires created a cosiness to offset the cooling of the day. Already sitting at one of the tables, eating a thick aromatic soup, were people who Sadir knew from her journey from Ean to Rolan years before; the traders Drathner and Telpher, each in the usual Rolanite dark green jerkins and brown trousers, both looking tired.

They scrambled to their feet when they saw Boidea and the others.

"Sit, my friends," she waved them down. "You've had a long journey. Not too hazardous, I trust?"

"No, Boidea," said Drathner as he resumed his seat, "most of the snow has melted and the track is in reasonable repair. Although Jelm here was in a hurry, so we pushed ourselves."

"Ah, I knew I could sense the need in your aura. I assume you have urgent news?"

"Yes, I do," replied Jelm as he sat in between Sadir and Anyar and began filling a bowl from the large pot in the centre of the table. "Important enough that I had to travel back with your trading party to deliver it myself."

Chapter Eleven

Jelm leant back, appreciating the warmth of the fire behind him while mindful of the press of Anyar on one side and Sadir's presence on the other; it felt like he belonged.

"More roast, Jelm?" asked Boidea from across the table, spearing a chunk of meat with a table knife.

"No, I've had plenty," he chuckled, removing an arm from around Anyar to rub his stomach. "I'll have to go on another trek if I keep eating so much. But a refill of the beer would be appreciated."

"Allow me," said Sadir grasping his tankard. "Targas always enjoyed the Rolan beer too." She stood up from the table and walked between the warming fires towards the kitchens.

"I've never realised what a beautiful place you have. Mlana Hold has prime position over the valley, though I'll see more in full daylight. I can't blame Sadir, and you too, Kyel, for staying here."

"All I want is here," said Kyel, his arm around Cathar. "I hope never to go back."

"Yes, it's good to have our friends with us, particularly in view of what's ahead," said Boidea, "and I fear your news will only add to it."

"Yes," added Drathner, pointing with a well-chewed bone, "Jelm and I discussed some of the issues during the journey over the mountains, but it would be good to hear it in context with what you know, Boidea."

"Here we are," announced Sadir brightly, pushing a tray of drinks onto the table. "Beer for you, Jelm, Drathner and Kyel, cordial for Boidea, Xerrita and Cathar, and mead for Anyar."

"I'll have a cordial." Anyar looked up with large eyes.

"But you're only…" Sadir paused as she squeezed into her seat between Jelm and Drathner. "Oh dear… Ah, have mine then." She reached across Jelm with her small glass.

"To safe havens!" said Jelm, lifting his tankard.

They all followed suit as the fires crackled and sparked around them.

Sadir leant closer to the tall, comfortable man as she watched the firelight reflecting in the eyes of her companions across the table. It was a moment that would never be repeated. She knew what Jelm had to say would precipitate their safe world into a maelstrom from which only some would emerge relatively unscathed. War was coming, and it was up to them to ensure it was won.

"Another cordial, Sadir?" asked Cathar, having slipped away from the table to replace the glass now held by Anyar.

"Thank you," said Sadir, glancing towards her daughter, "it seems mine is irretrievably lost."

"Sorry to break up the mood, but I best update you on what I know," announced Jelm. "It all started with a foretelling, or a Knowing, although Regna says it's the first she has experienced." He glanced at Sadir.

"Regna? Have her abilities grown, Jelm?" Sadir asked.

"Yes, and she sends her best wishes. Now, the Knowing… It encompassed Heritis fleeing to Port Saltus and then Regna seeing Sutan. There were many ships in their harbour."

"Southern Port," interjected Kyel.

"Yes, that's right, and we interpreted the ships as being those of Brastus, Jakus' brother, and his rival. And, as we were leaving Sanctus for our journey here, we learnt that Heritis had taken two ships from Ean full of supporters towards Sutan, too.

"The Knowing also drew forth an old woman in a palace in the capital. Regna said she had the look of Alethea…"

"Xerina!"

"Thanks, Kyel. Well, importantly, she told Regna that it was *time to prepare*. Then she warned *beware the enemy within the enemy*—somewhat mysterious, I know.

"So, we believe there's going to be some ructions in Sutan to sort out the leadership, and if they don't kill each other, we'll be targeted next."

"As expected, Jelm," said Boidea. "We've had suspicions, and we believe Xerina is Alethea's sister, captured at a young age and kept in Sutan as an advisor to the rulers. Kyel knew her."

"So pleased to see she is well," said Kyel. "She is certainly on our side and helped me a lot. She knows shadow scent and taught me about it. Any warning she gives should be heeded."

"I know of this *enemy within the enemy*," Anyar said, straightening away from Jelm's side. "He is Septus. He is living in Jakus' brother, Faltis, and he wants me!"

"What!" Jelm swung around to Anyar. "What're you saying? How do you know?"

"It relates to another Knowing, Jelm," interrupted Xerrita. She looked across to Anyar sitting alongside him. "If I may?"

"Please," Anyar murmured.

"Our new Mlana's Knowing directed her to the land of our enemies," Xerrita continued. "Towards the end she saw Jakus and his brother Faltis, then this thing broke through and into the Knowing. The creature we now know as the essence of the dead Septus seems to be able to exist parasitically inside the mind. It was what poor Targas was suffering from, so we're quite familiar with it, and when he passed, this 'essence' jumped into Faltis, Jakus' brother's head as far as we know. Now it has *seen* Anyar in some way and regards her as a target."

"By Ean," Jelm said, rubbing the back of his hand across his forehead, "it seems matters are developing. One of the other things I wanted to make you aware of was that Heritis knows about Anyar. If we had hoped for Anyar's importance to not be recognised by the enemy, it's too late now, especially after what you told me.

"So, the Sutanites are on the move and while we can hope for some delay from their internal battles, we must prepare. The old woman in Regna's Knowing was right. It is time to prepare."

"They come for us," said Anyar in a mature voice. "They want what we have, and we stand in their way."

"Blast!" said Jelm. "I need another beer!"

Vor scrabbled off the bed, his paws pushing roughly into Anya's side. He thumped to the floor, padded to the door, clawed it open before disappearing into the vastness of the Mlana Hold cavern.

Anyar lifted her head and sighed at the noise of the voral going out into the night. "Hmm," she murmured, "as Vor's off doing his business I might as well do some of mine." She grabbed a thick perac-wool gown off the end of the bed, slipped it over her shoulders and got up. Before long she had stoked the fire in her room, taken a sip from a glass of cordial on a bedside table and settled on a small rug on the floor.

She looked up as the door opened, letting in the faint glow of the early dawn, and smiled at the sight of her uncle and mother. "I'm about to try some things with scent. Do you want to sit with me?"

"Don't know whether I want to be on the floor, so I'll take a chair. One for you too, Kyel?"

"Thank you," he said. "Do you mind if we help if you need it?"

"Please," said Anyar. "Now let me begin."

The thick honey scent of mead came easily to her brain, interacted with her smell centre, and allowed the accumulation to pour forth from her mouth and nose.

Anyar held a cloud of it, like a bubble in front of her face, imbued with colours of light brown and gold. She focussed with her newfound knowledge into the cloud until she could see the individual components and their linkages holding the motes together. She found she could target a single mote and push or twist it with her mind.

"Keep going," urged Kyel softly. "Targas taught me to see these, these motes, and sort of weave them to become a sort of cloth. Try it. You'll see."

Anyar held herself in a cross-legged position between her uncle and mother, trying to concentrate while taking vague notice of their whispered comments. She pulled with her mind, joining motes of similar shape and character, twining them together until she had a coarsely woven fabric a handspan in front of her face. Its thinness made it almost transparent but a push with a finger met substantial resistance. Then she wove different portions of the odour into it.

The *cloth* was now visible and more resistant to a push, so she experimented by adding layers until she had a wedge of material the thickness of a finger, but a natural tendency to sink made it difficult to hold.

Anyar gradually relaxed her mental control and allowed the square of *cloth* to settle on the floor, where it remained even after she carefully withdrew her influence.

"Yes, dear Anyar," Sadir murmured, "you certainly have your father's talent."

"Now," added Kyel, "test it."

Despite her weariness, she drew odour bolts from powerful scent memories and drove them into the isolated fabric lying on the floor. And it resisted, the stone floor beneath becoming pitted and scarred before she ceased. There was an unravelling evident along the edge, a fuzzing as the motes began to dissipate. But still it held, not breaking apart.

"So, this is an improvement on the basic skill your father taught both me and your uncle," Sadir said resting a hand on her daughter's shoulder. "Then there's the shadow scent."

"Yes, the shadow scent," echoed Kyel. "Even I can see it, although my tutor was Xerina in Sutan."

"Thank you, Mother, Uncle. I appreciate all you've done. Now I'll need some time alone, with Vor too, so I can work through some things."

"Fine, Anyar," said Sadir, standing up. "Come, Kyel," she added to her brother, "we'll leave Anyar to her work."

"Don't forget to let Vor in, Mother," called the girl from her cross-legged position on the floor.

"Will do, Anyar, will do."

Sadir opened the door leading out into the corridor. The voral dashed past as they left. "I swear that animal is smarter than it looks."

"I'm not sure, Sadir, but I'm happy he's with her," said Kyel. "You never know, but Vor may yet have an important role to play."

Anyar blew a sigh of relief as the door closed, before snapping her fingers to bring the animal under her arm.

"Now Vor," she said, trying not to smile at the earnest expression on the black-snouted face, "we are going to try something. Something we've done before but now I have much more knowledge and may be able to work it into shadow scent, make it more effective somehow."

A long red tongue flopped out of his tooth-filled jaw as he settled his head on his paws.

"Do you remember vanishing when the pria were after us because you were stealing their honey? Do you think you can do it without a threat—I mean, when you want to?"

The voral seemed to wink, black beady eyes focussing on Anyar while nothing happened.

"Hmm." Anyar's nose almost touched his as she thought. "I know." She recalled her terror from when she was younger and chased by the hymetta in the caves under Ean's capital city, Nebleth. Dragging out the terrible odour of those predators was challenging, but she was able to do it. A small waft of the scent drifted from Anyar's mouth.

The voral sprang into high alert and poured a flow of scent from his very pores, shimmering yet translucent. It swiftly covered both so any observer would have seen them vanish.

"Well done, you clever voral!" Anyar said from inside the cover of scent. "I know what you did. Now I'm going to try something else."

She sensed the cover beginning to dissipate and quickly drew scent memories from her smell centre, adding their influence to Vor's shield. Instinctively, the voral bolstered Anyar's efforts and helped maintain the integral structure of the covering shield. An observer would have seen the two figures begin to appear, then disappear again.

Anyar stiffened, her hands clenching with effort as she sorted through the scents bonding the bubble around them. She could see the linkages, small and intricate and recognised the influence of a kind of shadow scent which underlay the normal scent bondings. She inwardly wriggled with excitement as an idea began to develop.

Her ability to examine the scent bonds at such a minute level amazed her, but she didn't hesitate. She dove deeper, pulling apart the tiniest of linkages, examining and rejoining them. It was really on a shadow scent level, but it went even deeper. She was hidden in a bubble of scent, made even stronger by her manipulations, and she was essentially untouchable.

Anyar suddenly wavered for a moment. "Vor, we're too enclosed. We've done so well we're not getting enough air. Help me push it out?"

Whether Vor really helped or not, Anyar felt a flow of outside energy and the bubble expanded with a hiss. Vor sat up.

"No, not yet. We're not finished. Let me bring more air in. Then one more thing to try."

Anyar opened a small gap in one side and the air became cleaner and more breathable. Vor flopped back down with a huff, watching his mistress with a steady gaze.

"Now let me see," she said, looking across to where the constructed piece of scent fabric still lay on the floor. She began to pull at it with scent control, using her new knowledge. A stripe of dark odour edged across to her where she delved into its bonds, deeper and deeper. The motes of scent flew into the air and disappeared; the fabric was gone.

"Hah!"

The voral jumped, banging into the top of the covering bubble, which exploded with a pop.

Anyar burst into a laugh and hugged the voral to her chest. "I think we've done it. I think we've done it."

Vor's snout lifted as he sniffed loudly. Anyar smelt frying food, including her favourite thin strips of cured meat and fungi, then her stomach rumbled.

"Fine, Vor, it's time to eat. I think we've done well enough for now." She stretched up off the floor and turned to follow the voral, who was already at the door.

Chapter Twelve

"Why is Faltis here?" growled Brastus as Vitaris closed the door to his rooms. "I want to speak to you privately."

"Have these, my sons." Vitaris handed a glass of red wine each to Brastus and Faltis. "Now take a moment to relax and we'll discuss things.

"Your brother Jakus is a very powerful man, showing clear ambition to lead Sutan. And I want Sutan to be driven by a competent and formidable leader."

"But…"

"Let me finish, Brastus," said Vitaris calmly, glancing at the amused expression on Faltis' face, half hidden by the glass. "I want both of you to know that it is in Sutan's best interests to be well led and you, Brastus, could be such a one, the new Shada.

"Faltis has already indicated he would support whoever is the Shada but in the interim, he may be able to assist you to counter Jakus. That is why he is here, for he should know what I'm proposing. It is a levelling of the ground, something to allow you and Jakus to either work together or oppose each other on an equal footing.

"I have carefully garnered supplies of the red crystal, enough to give you a chance against your brother. To be truthful, I think you have a more level head on your shoulders than Jakus and, should you understand how to manipulate this scent-enhancing force effectively, you may well become the new ruler. Faltis here also understands how to use this magnesa, and it is in both our interests to make certain you know how to work with it. You should understand there have been issues between Jakus and Faltis which make him more inclined to assist you.

"So, you are helping me to defeat Jakus, one son against another?" asked Brastus, his eyebrows rising into his hairless scalp. "Hard to believe."

"Not *defeat*, but to give you an equal chance. This is logical when you think of what I require," Vitaris responded. "I want Sutan to take its rightful place as ruler of the world. While I have the sentiment of wanting you to lead Sutan to that glory, ultimately it is my country which must triumph, be that by you or Jakus.

"Choose!" Vitaris folded his arms across his chest, his scent aura streaming reds and purples. "Do you want what I have for you?"

"What do you think?" Brastus spat back. "There's no choice! Even if I must work with my weakest brother to do it."

"I appreciate your faith in me, my brother. My resources may be limited but I have substantial knowledge of utilising magnesa, as you will see," murmured Faltis, his eyes glowing redly.

"Kast," Jakus spoke to the captain of his scent masters, "we have little time to prepare for anything Brastus is organising against me. The sooner we are ready to bring the attack to him the better.

"What would be the best location to confront him?" he asked, looking over the map spread over the long table in his rooms. "And remember, this will have to be done to look as if he started it, unless…" Jakus absently reached for a glass of dark wine by his hand.

"No," he said, shaking his head, "a last resort, I think. Now, Kast, your thoughts?"

The large, dark-clad man placed a thick finger on the parchment. "There, Shad, that's where we meet."

"Your reasoning?"

"You know the ground; your forces are mostly here, in Sutaria; and you already know the owner—Poegna." Kast's chuckle rumbled deep in his chest.

"Poegna, my future consort." Jakus gazed intently at the map, recalling that Poegna came from one of the oldest ruling families of Sutan, with estates covering a vast territory. "These lands along the top of her estates, they link through to Faltis' in the west to the Grosten River."

"That's right, Shad," Kast agreed, "and this could be another advantage. The Grosten is wide and shallow with extensive marshlands to the north, a potential trap should we be in the position to drive the enemy towards it."

"A lot would have to go our way if we were forced to use that strategy, Kast." Jakus tapped the map. "But the northern slopes are sufficiently rugged and would allow us to attack through them. As for Poegna, she already has many troops bivouacked on her estates; some of mine too. It would be easy to build up numbers there and surprise my brother.

"But what to do about Faltis?" Jakus took a mouthful from his glass. "His troops may not be as loyal to me as they should be, enough to be a consideration in any conflict. He has been absent from my influence for too long, a factor I must remedy. If I know that scartha he will already be planning something devious against me."

"My Lord?" Poegna called from the doorway, "Young Bilternus has some news."

"Ah Poegna, I was just thinking of you. We have some serious talking to do later."

"My Lord?" she said, her scents showing the yellow of unease and an anxious green.

"Bring Bilternus! Let me hear his news."

Bilternus entered Jakus' rooms and walked towards the two men standing over a map stretched out on the long table. The Shad looked up, his scent aura showing a curious grey rather than darker intent.

"Take a wine," he said, waving towards the jug and glasses on a smaller table, "then join us."

Bilternus quickly poured the rich red liquid into a glass, briefly appreciating the heady aromas before taking a sip and moving to the table.

"Discussing strategies, boy." Jakus pointed towards the outline of the city and its surrounds. "If you had to plan a campaign to counter any forces striving to upset the proper rule, what would you do?"

Bilternus noted the map covered most of Sutan from the steppes in the far north, the Grosten river meandering from those highlands through marshland and harsh country until it bisected the capital and then continued to the ports in the south. "I assume action would necessarily be within a day's ride from Sutaria?"

Jakus nodded.

Kast grunted, "A fair assumption. I can't see south being of sufficient value, too few strategic features. Nor the west." He took another sip of the wine. "The landscape is more rugged to the north. My father's estates incorporate some of this. The ridge running over a substantial distance would be of consideration—any further north or north-west would run into the river; although there may be some strategic advantage to be had there."

"So, easily worked out," Jakus grunted. "My brother's no fool. He'll know too.

"Now"—he swung towards Bilternus—"your father's troops. Are they loyal or sufficiently neutral to be discounted if Brastus moves against me?"

"This I have investigated, my Shad. Most of the men are loyal to the family, me in particular. Although I am merely a youth in some eyes, I have had time to ensure the troops will not be easily drawn to Brastus' cause. I believe most would follow me in preference to my father, Faltis, helped of course by his irrational moments, his injuries from the Rolan campaign."

Jakus held Bilternus' eyes for a long moment before nodding.

"Now, you have news?"

"Yes, my Shad." Bilternus put his glass on the table. "We know that Heritis is nearing Southern Port; two ships we believe, and with significant numbers of troops."

"Good. Good," Jakus' eyes glittered. "And?"

"Sharna reports from detected scents that Heritis carries an additional cargo. Hymetta."

"Hymetta? Jakus straightened with a wince. "So, he succeeded. They have survived."

"We've yet to have confirmation, Uncle."

"No time to waste. Send a message to Sharna to make every effort to conceal their existence from Brastus' spies. Use whatever subterfuge necessary," Jakus' scent aura spiked in flares of red and yellow. "On second thoughts, you will personally ensure the message is received. Take a substantial guard and then escort Heritis and his forces quietly to Poegna's estates. I would have preferred Kast to accompany you, but he is needed here.

"This is your chance to prove your worth." Jakus rubbed his hands together. "I'll prepare a dispatch for you to take with you while you organise your guard.

"Now go! Go!"

Bilternus left his glass on the table and hurried from the room.

Jakus watched the empty doorway for a moment. "I think, Kast, the time is opportune to confront my unreliable ally, Faltis. Too much is riding on his place in this. I need to make sure my brother is not working against me. I need to investigate his devious mind once more.

"We should meet in more suitable accommodation. Get him to my waiting room, after his son has left on my mission. I'd rather not have him in here."

Faltis strode into the well-appointed waiting room, his black robes almost merging with the dark red hangings draping the sandstone walls. Jakus watched him from where he sat on a wide, dark green couch, legs crossed, glass in hand, scent aura a steely grey.

"Ah, my brother, sorry to take you from entertaining your guests. Would you join me? Wine?"

Faltis straightened his thin body and walked to one of the two dark green armchairs facing the longue, pausing at a small table to slowly pour a glass of dark wine while glancing sideways at his brother's subtle scent shield.

"I thought I should come at your request, even though I have business on my estates," his voice hissed softly into the room. "It has been some time since we've had the opportunity, and things are on the move." He sat carefully on the chair and sipped the wine.

"Just so, Faltis." Jakus placed his glass on the small table next to him. "I'm aware of this as well. Too much time has passed since our victory in Rolan, and I fear events have precluded me from rewarding you adequately for the part you played in that campaign."

"I need no reward, brother. I have already indicated I would support Sutan in its future campaigns. And I am still happy to do that," he said, inclining his head to Jakus.

"Ah, yes, I heard your speech in the great hall." Jakus uncrossed his legs and leant forward. "I'm also aware that you have been speaking with Brastus on that future."

"Assuredly, dear brother, would you have it otherwise?"

"Yes, I would, but it may work to my advantage in any case; a spy in the enemy's camp?"

"Ah, I'm not sure if you can call me a spy, Jakus. I must maintain a semblance of neutrality, to work with the new Shada. If I was to openly support either candidate for leader, my effectiveness would be negated in the long run."

"Not if you backed me, for I will be the new Shada." Jakus' scent aura bloomed redly. "But"—he held up a hand to forestall Faltis' response—"I am not going to force you to change your stance, as long as I can ensure your loyalty. Come closer."

"Blast you, Jakus, I don't want you in my mind." Faltis pushed back into the armchair.

"Maybe so," said Jakus, taking a pinch of red crystals from the pouch at his waist and putting it into his mouth, "but it is necessary."

A wall of scent enveloped Faltis, pushing down his instinctive shielding reaction. Slowly his scent shield buckled under Jakus' power and crushed down onto his chest until the barrier evaporated. As the shield failed, Jakus pushed a tendril of odour out of his mouth and up Faltis' nose.

Faltis gasped as the probe wriggled through his sinuses and entered his scent centre, allowing Jakus to sift through scent memories and locate the loyalty area he had reinforced some years before. Faltis allowed himself to appear tractable and accept his brother's invasion, keeping some of the darker portions hidden behind an elastic barrier while letting Jakus link and influence his own odours. He endured Jakus' effort without further reaction.

Jakus suddenly groaned and leant away, his face puzzled, while Faltis slumped in his chair with eyes closed.

Behind the elastic barrier, an entity chortled and rubbed its figurative hands. The moment was so close and so tempting but didn't fit in with his plans. Not yet.

Septus realised that while Jakus, the man he hated with a passion was so open and exposed, he wasn't weak enough. He could not be certain to succeed in any attempt to take over his mind. There would be a time when Jakus would be stretched, would be vulnerable; then he would strike.

Besides, there was work to be done and opportunities to exploit. He needed to keep this body alive and useful. He could influence it to pursue the goals of

Sutanite domination from relative safety. And ultimately, he had another ambition; a young mind of tremendous power was coming his way and he wanted to be able to receive it.

A snigger slipped from Faltis' closed lips.

Chapter Thirteen

"I have a fair area to the west of my main estates where most of your force can bivouac, Brastus," said Faltis as they rode with Strengor, Brastus' commander, and several hundred troops along a wide side road leading towards low hills to the north of Sutaria. The Grosten River, wide and shallow meandered southwards a distance to their left. "It's well defensible and far enough out of the city for movements to be more discreet."

"It'll do," growled Brastus. "Even though Jakus will know I'm here it'll still give me and my scent masters time to experiment with the magnesa. That, according to Vitaris is most important."

"It is, brother, it is," agreed Faltis.

Soon they passed lines of trees marking the boundaries of his estate and approached the extensive brown brick buildings cut into the rocky slope. The surrounding ground was stony and barren, while wooden dormitories and stables flanked a wide, gravelled area to one side.

"You can send the troops to grounds over the ridge. Not too far but enough to show I'm not favouring one brother against the other. Conditions may be rough, but they should be used to it. I'm happy to provide some supplies and animal handling, but it's mostly up to you."

"I'm not without resources," snapped Brastus, swinging down off his perac. "I've had years to get ready for this. Your estates are just a small part of my preparations."

"Assuredly, brother, I am just happy to be of assistance," said Faltis, slinging the reins of his animal to a nearby stable hand. "My scent master, Piltarnis. will be here to aid you with this experiment.

"Now, I have refreshments available. Methra!" he called out. "We have important guests."

"So, this is it, what all the fuss is about?" asked Brastus, running his fingers through the red crystals contained in the small wooden chest held by

Piltarnis. "I've never placed much store in it before. And you say Jakus has a large quantity of this magnesa?"

"Assuredly," Faltis smiled. "Jakus and I carried out an expedition to Rolan and retrieved many such chests. The natives fought hard to stop us, and despite significant losses it was all we could do to get them back to our ships. My"—his face twitched, eyes flashing red—"own role was significant. If I hadn't managed to kill their best fighter, the one and only Targas, we may have not succeeded... not that Jakus appreciates it."

"I did hear of him, a strange scent master indeed, from Tenstria too, where I fought a long campaign for Sutan. Didn't he oust my brother from his comfortable seat in Ean? Didn't he cause some of his injuries and madness of mind?"

"Not all was due to that renegade. Septus himself was attacked by a maddened Jakus, and in defence caused some of your brother's wounds." Faltis felt the push of the *presence* in his mind.

"Septus? I remember him," mused Brastus. "Wasn't he his commander of the scent masters in Ean?"

"Yes"—the word hissed from Faltis' lips—"a truly honourable man abused by Jakus. Never appreciated. Never considered for rewards. A truly...truly great man. A great man who will be rewarded."

"What, Faltis?" Brastus looked up from the chest, eyebrows raised.

"Nothing!" he snapped. "Now do you want some assistance with using the magnesa or not?

"Piltarnis, please prepare to distribute the crystal sparingly."

"It is under my control, my Lord," said the black-robed young man as he placed the chest on a small table. "They will be able to experience its significance with just a few crystals."

Brastus nodded, then gestured to Strengor standing with eleven of his scent masters on the wide surface of the gravelled sparring ground.

Faltis gazed over the group of scent masters around him—five women and seven men, and his arrogant brother wearing his dominant black jerkin and loose trousers. The remainder were clad variedly in greys and browns, their jerkins and trousers making it hard to determine their sex other than by a splash of colour from scarves on several of the women. They had short-cut hair, and the men were clean shaven.

They were all watching him.

Time to perform, he thought, *time to reveal enough to scare them.*

"People, I am going to show you something of this remarkable substance, magnesa. It is a rare crystal and garnered at some cost during an expedition to the country of Rolan. I was part of that expedition and saw how effective the substance is." He gestured to Piltarnis, who tilted the chest until the sunlight reflected a myriad of red sparks off the crystals.

"It requires only a minor amount to enhance your own scent capacities. Imagine how you work with scent, see its intricacies, use it in many ways for both aid and attack." He smiled as if he was talking to children. "Then imagine that ability multiplied, twice, three times, so your control and use of scent is just so much more. That is the advantage of magnesa."

"Is that all it does?" asked Strengor. "We've all heard the stories."

"Certainly, there are many stories, most of them with aspects of truth. A true master of scent can delve even deeper into scent with magnesa's power, investigate the bonds of scent, see how to manipulate them in even more effective and powerful ways. You'll even have heard how Jakus used it to break apart the bonds within other substances such as wood, even stone. This is power."

A small woman near him raised her hand.

Faltis nodded.

"I…I've heard that users can be affected, even driven irrational…?"

"Fair question," Faltis smiled tightly. "Again, there are stories. Overuse or strenuous use can result in reaction headaches. Use over a period can also result in withdrawal symptoms, and, again, there are rumours it can affect the user's mental health."

"So," snapped Brastus, "no guesses for where this is leading. My brother, Jakus?"

"I leave that to your interpretation," Faltis said, spreading his hands. "Now you will try it. Remember, use it sparingly."

S trengor stood behind Brastus and waited as his leader received a small pinch on his little finger, placed it in his mouth and then stepped away.

Strengor's eyes gravitated to the open chest and the glitter of the crystals, his tongue licking his lips. He sucked the several crystals Faltis' scent master had given him off his finger and moved away. He didn't notice Brastus' rigid stance as he concentrated on the impact of the magnesa.

The colours of the day grew richer: trees around the large grounds pushed out obvious coils of scent, dark and thick; the people around him drifted with scent—closer inspection emphasised their auras, making their emotions easier to discern; Brastus, a dark bulk, was enshrouded with dark purple and reds as if he was fighting an internal war, while Faltis was greyer, with flashes of red and purple indicating a hesitancy within him.

He turned away and investigated deeper into the scent, seeing the motes of it, their origin and their makeup. He tried a tentative twist with his mind and saw one scent snag with another until he lost interest.

"Good, Strengor," an oily voice whispered. "Do you think your master will be able to cope?"

"I'm sure he will." He looked into Faltis' reddish eyes. "He is a strong man."

"In that case we better proceed," Faltis said, then raised his voice. "Have you all had a taste? Good, then we better investigate the means of utilising this greater strength, this advantage, and when you'll need it."

Bilternus was over-tired, his seat painful from a day in the saddle and the rapid pace on the first day from Sutaria. He'd been up before dawn for the final push to the port, and as his steed clattered along the wide, Southern Port street at the head of his guard, he could only reflect on how the day must have affected even the most experienced of riders among them. With a sigh he led the group into Jakus' compound and dismounted.

"You tend to the men and animals. I will seek out the fleet commander," Bilternus said to the tall guard behind him. He took the satchel off the woolly back of his perac and went in search of Sharna.

Firstly, he checked the mess hall searching for her distinctive red hair. The large room was partly filled with guardsmen and sailors eating a midday meal, and the waft of scents set his stomach growling. Many of the people in the room were new to him but eventually he saw Sharna sitting next to a tall Jakus look-alike.

He huffed with relief and hurried over.

"My Bilternus!" Sharna exclaimed, her scents welcoming. "What brings you here in such a hurry? Sit and eat." She flung up a hand to signal a server, before shuffling along the bench seat.

"I should introduce you to Heritis." She smiled, nodding to the tall man next to her. "Heritis, meet Bilternus, Faltis' son and an important person in our Shad's plans."

"Hmm," Heritis responded, leaning forward to take in Bilternus' scents, "we're related then. I'm pleased to meet family, finally. Ean is a lonely place without family."

"But weren't you consorted there?" Bilternus asked.

"Yes, but with the fall of Ean things changed. I still had a wish to return to the certainty of Sutanite rule while my consort, Regna, wholly embraced the natives and their cause. Too much for me, I'm afraid."

"Cer?"

Bilternus looked over to the enquiring voice and felt a flush of heat in his face.

"Would you like a meal, young cer?" asked Sencia.

Bilternus nodded while Sharna grinned into her plate.

"You know the young woman?" Heritis asked.

"Mmm, we've met on several occasions. I, ah, have a dispatch from Jakus." He reached into the satchel by his side.

A plate full of sliced roast meat, roasted tubers and lashings of gravy was placed in front of him by Sencia, who raised an eyebrow in question as she backed away. He nodded slightly as Heritis and Sharna scanned the dispatch.

"We leave at dawn next day," Sharna said and then winked. "You'll be ready? Not too tired?"

Bilternus swallowed a half-chewed piece of meat. "My guard and I will be ready."

"Good. And your troops and cargo, Heritis?"

"The sooner the better, Commander," he said.

The long line of troops, more than two hundred strong, including the fifty-odd new arrivals from Ean, headed along the main road leading out of Southern Port. Their attendant mounts bleated and pulled at their leads while trotting beside them. Bilternus could see Sharna and Heritis at the head of the column containing a significant number of scent masters amongst the guardsmen and sailors. Meanwhile he followed at the rear, augmenting his skills of scent control with several magnesa crystals to control and disguise the hymetta scent in the covered wagon.

The road was busy with the arrival of so many ships, their resupply for trade and further voyages, and the movement of people and animals for a range of purposes. Occasional lines of troops moved past towards the port, but a significant number were travelling in their direction.

Neutrality seemed to be the order of the day. It was apparent that different factions were on the move, but carefully discreet scents and neutral clothing kept any potential altercations at bay. So, Bilternus' task was even more vital, to disguise the flying weapon carried from Ean at significant risk by Heritis.

He walked near the keeper of the hymetta, a quiet fat man who kept to himself and whom he remembered from the previous expedition to Rolan years ago. At that time, Kyel had had to deal with him and the hymetta on Jakus' orders, while Bilternus had managed to stay away from the creatures and their minder. Now he was in a similar situation and had an even more important role.

Keeping his concentration on maintaining a scent barrier to lock in the hymettas' musty odours meant little time to observe what was going on around him. Every time a perac, large eyes swivelling in alarm, baulked at pulling the wagon carrying the carnivorous creatures, the keeper would chivvy it along and cause Bilternus to focus harder on his control.

So the day passed, more slowly than he would have liked, and he was more than happy when they reached the Grosten River ford and he could relax his guard.

Rancer, Heritis' arms commander, a heavy weathered-looking man, led his perac over to Bilternus. "Meant to have a chat with you, young man," he said, squinting across the low hills into the setting sun. "This is the first time I've been here, at the ford. Fairly bleak place." He slowly scanned the flat ground until he followed Bilternus' gaze to the river pebbles leading to a wide, deep pool. The growing chatter of the rapids soon drowned out the noise of the animals.

"It is, Rancer," agreed Bilternus, "I've been here a few times. Never a comfortable place to camp but it's fairly central on the way to the capital. Unfortunately, most other travellers feel the same way, so we won't be near the water this night.

"There's a benefit, though," he added. "No scartha."

"Ah, the huge scaly water lizards; I'd like to see one of those."

"Best not," said Bilternus. "They're ferocious. Take peracs and men without a pause."

"Get used to ferocious creatures when you travel with them." He indicated the wagon with a jerk of his head. "Better get the hymetta settled down or the keeper will be asking."

"Yes, I'll go and see him. By the way, Rancer, why did Heritis bring them? They're so few and any good scent defence will stop them. It…seems too much trouble in a way."

"Heritis has his reasons, Bilternus," Rancer answered, "but I suspect that our former Shada requested it and he'd have a purpose in mind, I'd wager. Now I'm off to settle the troops. We'll need to keep a good lookout this night with so many other groups camping nearby."

Jakus, accompanied by Kast and a small detachment of guardsmen, entered Poegna's estate through the white-columned gates of the main road leading out of Sutaria. They rode down a wide, gravelled path shaded by tall trees with olive-green leaves that rustled in the slight breeze.

"Poegna!" he called as he saw the slim woman leaving the large, spreading sandstone house at the end of the drive.

"My Lord, my estates are ready for you," she said, her scents showing welcome with a thread of unease.

"I'm sure they are," Jakus said softly.

They dismounted, walking silently into the house and, the long voyage drawing to a close, only now appreciating the relative warmth of early spring. At the back, the house spread into a wide, covered patio, with spaced white pillars joined by wooden beams allowing light and a breeze to infiltrate. Low polished wood tables held a variety of foodstuffs and beverages.

"Please, my Lord," said Poegna, indicating the tables, "seat yourself and partake of refreshments."

"That I may," responded Jakus, stretching out his legs with a sigh as he sat. He took a skewer of white meat and fruit before seeing a young server standing near the table. "Wine!" he snapped as he ate.

He looked up from the table. "Sit with me, Poegna," he said, patting the seat next to him before accepting a glass of white wine. "All is ready?" he asked as he watched Kast and the guardsmen help themselves at the tables

"Yes, my Lord. We have opened the more remote areas of the estates to accommodate the numbers we already have, and have made arrangement for more troops should, as I suspect, the need arise."

"No surprises there, Poegna. While I have reserve areas available, a significant detachment of my supporting forces from the steppes will be able to block off any route to the north. Festern and his sons have guaranteed this."

"Yes, my Lord," said Poegna, remembering the tall, solidly built leader of the northern steppes region of Sutan, "he is a worthwhile ally."

"Then I expect Heritis with a large portion of troops to be accommodated here. They should be arriving in Southern Port any day now. They will need to be well looked after."

"My Lord," Poegna nodded taking a sip of her wine. "Whatever I can do for you."

"Yes." Jakus looked hard at her. "I think we need to continue these discussions in private. Your sleeping quarters?"

"I would like that." Poegna let her scent aura reflect yellows, oranges and pinks of interest.

"I can detect Bilternus," said Xerina. She was standing in the shade of one of the palace's columns, analysing the skeins of scent drifting through the skies. The strain deepened the wrinkles on her forehead as she used all her skills to separate the tiny motes of scent.

"He's bypassed the city with many others, some foreigners; from Ean, I'm surmising. So, there are newcomers here anxious to avoid being too obvious." She placed a hand on the sandstone column as she sought to understand what her shadow scent was revealing. "A build-up for the inevitable," she said, shaking her head. "But there's more…" She breathed in, long and deeply. "Ah, Heritis, I remember your scents." Xerina breathed in, long and deeply. "Returning after living in Ean for so long. You will know what Ean and Rolan have arrayed against them. You will tell.

"But young Bilternus too, he is becoming strong. He is concealing something, though his will power is lacking. Something is seeping through his control.

"No!" She sank to the cool flagstone floor, her heart fluttering in her chest. "I know you." She recognised an ancient weapon of the Sutanites, one she had thought was extinct.

Xerina sat for a while before getting painfully to her feet. "I must send a message to my people. I must warn them of the situation here, for it will impact on them. Jakus will gain control and Jakus will gain knowledge. I am afraid," she murmured as she hobbled towards her rooms, "Heritis' information will not be good for Ean, for Rolan, and for those who must stand against him."

A tear leaked from her eye as she entered her sanctuary.

Chapter Fourteen

"Cousin!" exclaimed Jakus, his scents spiralling in welcoming reds and violet. "Jakus, I am pleased to finally meet again, to be home," Heritis leant forward and merged scents.

"Refreshments?" Jakus beckoned, and a youth standing near the side tables hurried over with a tray holding wine glasses and a jug. "Well done, Sharna, Bilternus; I trust all remains well in Southern Port?"

"Yes, Shad, the status in the port is stable, no one faction acting against another. I believe all are awaiting the outcome of events in the capital." Sharna took a glass of wine from the proffered tray. "And we had an uneventful trip here, although the way was busy."

"Jakus," said Heritis, glancing towards the broad man near him, "you will recall Rancer, my arms commander?" The man bowed his head before taking a step back from his leader. "Rancer, with the able assistance of Bilternus, has brought the extra forces you requested. The keeper has come through again."

"Ah, another aspect to my strategy. They are safely housed?"

"My Lord, we have converted stables far away from our animals on my estates," said Poegna, from near Jakus' shoulder. "They will be safe there and out of the way. They are not the nicest of creatures."

"Good," Jakus nodded. "Now Heritis and I will leave you. Feel free to partake of food and drink. Poegna will be the host."

Bilternus watched his uncle and Heritis walk into the inner waiting rooms, sorry he couldn't accompany them and hear what would be discussed. He took a meat sausage wrapped in pastry from the table and walked over to where Rancer and Kast were talking.

"Let us sit. My side aches even now from those injuries I took in Ean," Jakus said, pointing Heritis to one of the two armchairs at a small table with a selection of pastries and a wine jug. "Now, what news do you have for me?"

"Jakus, you will be aware I cannot return to Ean as my uneasy alliance with the rebel government is over. I have shown my true allegiance by taking my ships and troops to Sutan. If that wasn't enough, the hymetta will have left their trace. I was able to keep them hidden in Port Saltus while breeding them up, but they are the last. The keeper is old and has almost outlived his usefulness."

"It may be enough," murmured Jakus. "Go on."

"I can fill you in on my domestic arrangements at a later stage but my consort, Regna, is a traitor and supports the Eanites.

"However, more importantly, the Ean and Rolan people are aware of what is happening in Sutan and of our ambitions. They are preparing for the eventuality of invasion."

"This is not a problem, cousin," said Jakus, taking a mouthful of wine. "They would have to be blind and deaf not to know of my plans. My moves to subjugate those countries is next, once the problem of my brother is resolved.

"But back to your insights; you have some news?"

"Yes, it's of the time of your last visit to Ean, to Nebleth. You remember when you tasked me with trapping Sadir, Targas' consort, and releasing the hymetta to feast on her and her brat of a daughter? Well, it was a pity it didn't succeed. If it had, we would have fixed the prophesy in one action."

"Heritis, you're not making sense," growled Jakus.

"Bear with me. It's about that prophesy or foretelling your own soothsayer has raised on a number of occasions."

"Ah, about an Eanite coming to destroy Sutan? Hah! That has been around forever and has caused nothing but trouble; it's just an evil rumour. If it had been Targas, he's dead, we killed him in the attack on Rolan. It's not the Eanite, Kyel; I tested him myself. It can't be either leader of those countries; Lan is too old and Rolan's mystical leader has been dead for some years. So, who else is there?"

"It's the daughter; Targas' brat. Anyar's her name."

"What?" Jakus sprayed out a mouthful of wine. "You must be joking. A child, a female, is going to destroy Sutan? Cousin, have you had too much of the red crystal?"

"Would that I had, Jakus, but I have researched this carefully. This Anyar is safely living in Rolan at Mlana's Hold and has great power. She is mature beyond her years and is even called the new Mlana."

"This would be amusing if I didn't know that you're serious, Heritis. Well, I'll keep it under advisement. And if it is true, one of my first acts as the new Shada of Sutan will be to return our tame soothsayer to her component parts." His aura spiked deep purple and black.

"Food. Drink, Heritis," said Jakus. "We have always got on, you and I, and it is appreciated. Now, if there's nothing else we should hear in private I suggest we move to the planning room and discuss deployment of our troops for the downfall of Brastus, and your part in it."

B rastus toyed over the large map of Sutan in Faltis' planning room with his commander Strengor and several of his stern-faced sub-commanders. Faltis was in the capital, 'keeping out of the way' while his brother used the well-appointed rooms for discussion of troop placement in the forthcoming civil war. Piltarnis, Faltis' black-clad scent master, was standing quietly in the background.

Strengor ran a pointer along the ridgeline to the north of the city. "My observers inform me that Jakus is building up his forces to the east of the city, and to the north. He has had much time to prepare a challenge to the leadership of Sutan and we seem to have similar numbers to oppose him."

"Does the red crystal leave a flavour in your mouth, Commander?" asked Brastus. "I find there is one in mine. It is this flavour that may be to our disadvantage. We may be equal in many ways, but I have relied on my reputation, my constant support for the ambitions of Sutan and my successes overseas—this may not be enough.

"So, how can we defeat Jakus if he uses his skill against us? Faltis' little exhibition is tantalising but too little too late, so we must find another way, and it will not be by force, but by cunning."

"It may not be my place, my Lord," interjected Piltarnis, "but magnesa may indeed prove to be effective. At the very least, I think that Faltis won't mind me saying, we can provide some protection against an overt scent attack."

"Good, good. It may help but still doesn't resolve my dilemma," Brastus responded. "Now, I would appreciate it if you could give us some privacy."

"My Lord." Piltarnis gave a slight bow and stepped back.

"Strengor, we must find a way to isolate my brother, to use our best resources against him where we have a good chance of success. I feel my father is of little help—maybe he thinks Jakus is too powerful, that he will be the new Shada of Sutan. But we must find a way to isolate him."

"Faltis," Strengor said, looking over as Piltarnis left the room, "seems to be neutral. Is he really an ally?"

"Ah, no; he will play both sides, despite what his scent master says. Something,"—Brastus tapped a finger on his lips—"is not right about Faltis. However, we must find an advantage in this campaign."

"This!" Strengor pointed to a narrow ravine bisecting the ridge north to south. "If we can isolate the elite of his army there, it may be possible to overwhelm him, trap him. As it is, we'll have little opportunity."

"It is a quandary, Strengor," mused Brastus, "but there is little time and much to chance. Work on a way to lure him to such a position. I'll have our best scent masters develop a plan even if it must be done with Faltis' connivance, as the training with magnesa makes me understand the difficulties of our position. Without a concerted effort we will not win. But we must chance it for the good of Sutan. We must chance it."

Xerina had dismissed her acolytes and lay on a couch in her favourite room where the pool with its flowers perfumed the air and flickering, twirling lights reflected over the white walls and ceilings. The hum of insects and the slight breezes brought drifts of scent to her nose, allowing her mind to sink into a deep, restful repose.

She knew the urgency of her message, the vital nature of her information, the need to communicate to ensure the future of the known world. She had to get a message to her people, to where her heart lay in Rolan. If all went well then, everything would be returned to a better place; the alternatives were not to be countenanced.

She had to force her own Knowing, her own prophecy against the normal progression of such things; she had to get her knowledge through even if she died to do it. Xerina sunk back on the cushions and delved into shadow scent, deeper than she had ever gone before. She let her mind drift into the intricacies of the scent world and push memories into its web. Where it would float, she had no way of knowing, but she had to try. Maybe, if the world truly was round, the message would drift with the swirls of the air, the scent, and find the poor youngster tasked with the responsibility of saving it by defeating the might of Sutan.

Xerina groaned with the effort of her endeavours as the day slowly slid into night.

Faltis was back at his estates, confident Jakus had dismissed him from consideration in the forthcoming conflict. He had tasked his son, Bilternus, to take a significant portion of the estate's troops away from the area of conflict as an indication of his neutrality in the clash between brothers.

Events had moved swiftly despite Vitaris' efforts at conciliation while Faltis himself had encouraged the forthcoming clash. He had no vested interest in who won, but knew he could influence Brastus if he became the new Shada of Sutan. Jakus was more erratic, yet the history between them was full of humiliation and hurt.

If Faltis closed his eyes and listened, he could feel the *presence* in his mind, the presence of Septus. Usually, the creature was quiet and allowed Faltis to live a normal life, but when it saw an advantage, when it saw a need to intervene, it took it and left Faltis with the consequences. It was this Septus who'd pushed Faltis to take the subservient, yet deadly role. It was Septus who was pushing him to be 'helpful' to Brastus against Jakus, when the result of Jakus' victory could be his death.

What game is Septus playing? he thought, *when he knows the consequences to his host.* Faltis shivered with the word 'host' as he left the house to find his head scent master.

"**P**iltarnis!" he called when he saw the group of black and grey-clothed scent masters in the large open area towards the rear of the accommodation quarters, "where are we with our friends' training?"

"My Lord, Brastus is worrying about the location of the forthcoming conflict, where he can isolate Jakus to most effect and his chances of winning are increased." The young scent master sounded almost jovial.

"Has he determined the site and how he might lure Jakus to it?"

"I believe so, my Lord," Piltarnis said as the group moved towards the gravelled sparring area. "We would like to show you what we consider could be advantageous for Brastus should you wish us to aid his efforts."

Oh, yes! a voice whispered in his mind.

"Do it!"

The scent masters spread out in a rough semi-circle.

"Minimal crystals," Piltarnis ordered, "as this is only for show."

Each of the five scent masters with Piltarnis placed a crystal-covered finger in their mouths and dropped their arms to their sides. They began a slow hum until a visible thickening of the air sheeted in front of them. It grew until it began to bend as if under the weight of gravity, tilting to fall over Faltis' head, cocooning him.

"Speak, my Lord." Piltarnis' voice cracked with strain.

"What?" His voice echoed down the tube of scent.

"Now attempt to break it."

Faltis pushed out a dark scent bolt, smashing it into one side of the scent wall. It reflected, crashing into the ground. He fired another and another with little effect, growing increasingly frustrated.

"Cease!" called Piltarnis, and the scent sheet slowly dissipated.

"Hah!" snapped Faltis. "If I'd taken magnesa I could have destroyed that easily. Why couldn't Jakus?"

"Yes, my Lord, he could, but there were six of us producing the shield, enough strength to deflect an attack and give time for a counter. Should Brastus use our help at a critical time, he might achieve success."

"Yes," Faltis agreed, rubbing his chin as he turned to walk back to his house, "he could. Come with me, Piltarnis, it is time to offer my brother help without appearing to break my neutral stance.

Chapter Fifteen

"Mother, I've had the most disturbing dream," called Anyar, pushing open the door to her rooms in Mlana Hold. She waited while the voral ran past her and into the vast space before shutting the door and hurrying towards the group of women standing nearby.

"Mlana," said the large woman in the group, "was it a Knowing?"

"Come, Anyar," said Sadir, "let's go to the table, have some cooked oats and milk with a little honey, before we hear whatever has happened."

"Apologies, Anyar," said Boidea, "I'm keen to know what occurred but your mother is right, food first."

"Did you say honey, Mother?" Anyar pointed to the whiskered face of Vor peering back from the vast opening to the outside. The first rays of the sun were outlining his body as it slanted into the working space of Mlana Hold.

"I'll swear…"

"Swear what, Sadir?" said a male voice from behind them.

"Jelm, welcome, I was just referring to Anyar's voral. *Honey* is a magic word to him."

"Just as for his mistress, if I remember correctly. She always preferred honey to anything else as a young thing.

"Then it appears I'm just in time," said the tall scent master, "to hear what Anyar has to say, and for the morning meal."

"You're welcome, my almost-uncle, Jelm," laughed Anyar. "I do enjoy my oats with a dribble or two of honey, and what I have to report is for all to hear."

"Food," called Cathar, bringing a steaming tray to the tables located near the ever-burning fires that provided warmth to the vast cavern of Mlana Hold. "Sit yourselves down and I'll go and wake Kyel. He's sleeping in."

"He's your responsibility now, Cathar," called Sadir.

"Not quite, Sadir," she replied, "but thank you for mentioning it."

The food was rich and filling, creamy oats and honey, toasted bread with jam and a stimulating spiced tea; little speaking occurred while they ate.

"Now," said Sadir as the plates were cleared away, "we can hear your news, Anyar, in comfort and contentment,"

"Agreed," said Kyel. "At least I'm awake, thanks to Cathar." He leant back into her and sighed.

"You're too heavy," she said pushing him in the side.

Anyar smiled at their gentle playfulness, until she realised all were waiting for her.

"Come, Vor, settle," she said as the voral draped himself across her feet. Anyar looked at the expectant faces and drew a breath.

"My dream, I think, comes from Xerina in Sutan!" She smiled at Xerrita's twitch since Anyar knew the woman would be interested in news concerning her relative. "It was almost a Knowing but not quite, enough to say that it was. And Xerina was the instigator of my 'dream'."

"Ah," Xerrita smiled.

"Yes, Xerrita," said Anyar. "Alethea's sister, Xerina, has not forgotten us or her homeland. She has exhausted herself to send me this dream. She has used the most intricate attributes of shadow scent to compose and send her message. I know that she has sent it in a way I've never experienced. I wish, just wish I had met her."

"Anyar," said Sadir, her face creased with concern, "take your time as this message is of great import."

"Yes, Mother, I know. Let me do this now." She stood, a slim, pale figure with a scent aura of shimmering colours embracing a power that stilled everyone at the table. "I had a dream from Xerina in which she warned me that Sutan's period of inaction would soon be over. Leadership of their forces is being determined and we must be aware. And should the leader be Jakus, then he believes his enemy is here in Rolan. For as Kyel knows, there is a prophesy an Eanite will destroy Sutan; he believes that Eanite is me. While he can't be certain this is true, Xerina thinks he will act on the warning.

"Apparently Heritis is now in Sutan, having shown his true colours; it is he who will have told Jakus about me. And he has taken with him the wasp-like creatures, those that attacked me and my mother in the caverns below Nebleth, and here at the Hold during their invasion.

"But that is not the worst of it. She confirms what we had determined, the existence of the *presence* inside the Sutanite Faltis. That which infested my father now exists in the Sutanite. We should not forget this thing. Should we do so it will be to our peril."

Anyar slumped and reached to the furry ruff of her companion.

"Anyar," said Kyel, breaking the silence that ensued, "this is amazing news and if anyone could have let you know it would have been Xerina, almost my only friend when I was there in Sutan. She protected me as much as she could from Jakus, Faltis and that damn scartha of a captain, Dronthis. My insides are still sore from his beating even after all this time. It was after that when Xerina taught me about shadow scent and how to protect my true thoughts from interrogation."

"Thank you, Uncle Kyel, she does seem a pleasant person." Anyar stopped and screwed her eyes. "There was something not clear, another presence."

"Not another one!" gasped Sadir.

"No, no, I mean a pleasing presence. She gave me the feel of teaching someone else about shadow scent. She wouldn't have done that if he was an enemy to us."

"A *he?*" asked Kyel.

"Yes, I think so," confirmed Anyar.

"Ah," Kyel nodded, "Bilternus. It must be Bilternus. No one else I can think of."

"Is that all, Mlana?" asked Boidea.

"All I recall."

"Then we must move our preparations for the invasion of Rolan and Ean up a notch," Boidea stated. "Assuming Sutan's leader is Jakus, we can be certain he's fixated on us and our resources."

"Having lived under his regime in Ean for a number of years," said Jelm, "I can say he is not a man to treat lightly, and is ruthless with any who oppose him."

"Anything I can do," Kyel said, looking around the sea of faces, "I will. The last thing I want is to meet up with the Sutanites again."

The voral plunged from the cavern's mouth, darting down the zig-zag pathway amongst boulders and granite walls, over smaller rocks, through narrow clefts, and across broken scree.

"He's so energetic," said Jelm as the group followed him towards the narrow bridge below Mlana Hold. "I have to be much more careful, or I'll break an ankle."

"The path's deliberately this way to make it easily defensible. When the Sutanites attacked we broke the bridge down so they couldn't come at us in a mass," said Boidea, "so it has to stay that way."

"You get used to it, Jelm," added Anyar, looking at him, the green of her dress setting off her light eyes. "Vor and I often run down it."

"Not for me," said Jelm as he scanned the valley before him and assessed its defensive features. The buildings spreading across the slopes were of heavy stone with slate or wooden roofs and arranged to protect defenders from any force coming up the valley. Walls of packed stone angling from the valley sides towards the centre were designed to funnel invaders and make them more vulnerable to the defenders.

"I'll meet you in the hall," called Anyar from the other side of the bridge, Vor by her side.

Drathner, a square-faced man with peppery hair, walked through the sunlit square formed by the buildings, smiling in welcome. "Almost the season to remove your coats," he said, holding his own dark-green jacket across his arm, leaving his brown wool tunic open at the collar, tucked into dark trousers covering his scuffed boots. "Spring is a good time, not as hot and humid as summer."

"We'll go to the hall where the rest are waiting," he said indicating a well-travelled path between two small, solid structures kept for processing pottery and magnesite.

"Is everyone here, Drathner?" asked Boidea as she headed towards the larger building with Sadir and Xerrita, Cathar and Kyel following.

Drathner nodded. "I think most are. They'll be pleased to meet you, Jelm." He pulled open heavy timber doors to reveal several people around a large wooden table.

Anyar was perched on a stool with a solid-looking man next to her. He glanced up as they entered, and rose to his feet. "Welcome to the planning room," he said. "The Mlana and I are here already."

"Xaner, the commander of the Port of Request, meet Jelm, Nebleth city administrator from Ean," said Drathner. "You know everyone else, I suspect?"

"I do," Xaner said, "but let me introduce Telpher, now commander of our city of Nosta's defence." He waved his arm to a broad-shouldered, thin-faced man on the other side of Anyar. "You won't know Jelm.

"And Xennira."

An aged woman rose from the other side of the table. "Sorry, playing with Mlana's voral; very engaging animal. I'm from Nosta, a healer, but I also help in defence co-ordination between Nosta and our port. I'm also the mother of Xerrita," she added, pointing to her daughter, who was standing with Boidea. "Welcome, Jelm."

"So," said Drathner, "let's reintroduce ourselves to our country. Please turn up the lamps, Kyel."

Kyel and Cathar adjusted the wicks of several suspended lanterns to reveal more clearly a relief map of Rolan, moulded from clay and coloured to reflect different portions of the land: higher ground in grey, valleys and plains green to brown, rivers dark and red lines indicating roads or tracks.

"It is the best way to view it, overhead light," said Drathner as they all gathered around the table.

The map began from the mountain range backing the cavern to the north. From there, the course of the river and its tributaries was shown by a depression which deepened and widened as it headed for the southern coast. The limited arable area was shown, Rolan being a land of rugged and imposing mountains.

"Would you like me to provide more details about Rolan before we discuss tactics, Mlana?" asked Drathner.

"If you would," Anyar said while scrutinising the map.

"Fairly obvious are the mountains, making Rolan dependent on mining, timber and crafting more than cropping. We've little cropping or pastureland, and more extreme weather. The main harbour, Requist, is the point of entry to the country; it's where the Rolander River, which starts here at Mlana Hold and goes south past Nosta, exits.

"Our roads mainly follow the river, which means that any enemy will naturally follow the same path, as did the invaders from Sutan some years ago."

"So, once again the Port of Requist is the target, the first point of attack," said Xaner with a weary smile. "But we will be more prepared. Taking the port will not be so easy this time."

"What about this point in the west?" asked Jelm. "It looks like a harbour of sorts."

Drathner placed a thick finger on the coast, due west of Mlana Hold.

"You mean our only other habitation on the coast, Sea Holm? It's isolated, with no roads and no real industry other than fishing, some logging and mining."

"How do people contact each other?"

"By ship. The west coast is rough, subject to storms, with an exposed harbour; there are some safe anchorages, though. There's also a track of sorts that can be used in better weather to get to Mlana Hold and Nosta."

"Ah," said Jelm, tapping his lips, "there may be a possibility here. Can you let me think on it for a while?"

Anyar looked up from the map. "As I haven't really seen the rest of the country, I think it is time to travel and assess our options.

"Jelm, you will accompany me, of course?"

Jelm looked at Anyar, sitting tall with an almost regal air, and felt a pang of regret that this young woman, older than her years, had had such a burden placed on her shoulders. A cloud of light pastel scents rose from her aura with the grey of determination showing her concern.

"I would be happy to accompany you, Anyar. I, like you, want to get a feel for this country and its people. It will also aid with the talk of tactics."

"I'm pleased, Mlana," said Xaner. "Events are moving swiftly, and it is appropriate for you to see what we have done already, and what we will have to do."

"Agreed," said Drathner, "for not only should we be looking at how to counter this Jakus and his ambitions, but we also need to determine how to stop Sutan once and for all."

"My role is clear!" Anyar's voice rose to fill the hall. "But we will need all of us, from Rolan, Ean and even Sutan, to do this. I suggest we commence soon, and also let Ean know of our plans."

"Agreed, Mlana," said Boidea. "Drathner, who can you suggest to lead a small group through the mountain pass? It will be more certain than a scent message."

"I have several competent leaders, so that will not be a problem. Further," said Drathner, looking carefully towards Anyar, "might I suggest that your uncle, Kyel takes our news to Ean? He knows the people and it may be time to re-establish his credentials with our friends there."

Anyar looked at Kyel, eyebrows raised.

"This is a surprise, but I can see where you're coming from," he responded. "It is a good idea, and I can help assess Ean's defences with a good knowledge of what we have here.

"One condition though," Kyel smiled. "Cathar comes with me—that is, if she'd like to."

"Goes without saying," Cathar said, tucking an arm through Kyel's. "I can contribute to the preparations, particularly from the shadow scent aspect, as well as see my homeland again."

"Well," said Boidea, "I can see the value in them going. Anyone have a problem with Drathner's proposal?"

"No," said Jelm, "but I'd like to run a few things past them before they go."

"Agreed then." Anyar gave a sad smile. "I don't want you to go, both of you, but can see the need."

A light, misty rain from the highlands to their right drifted across the stone dwellings and green and brown fields as the party moved through the village below Mlana Hold and out onto the stone-paved road leading down the valley. Almost immediately the road drew near the fast-flowing stream that became the Rolander River. Spray added to the light rain to infiltrate their coats and scarves and make things unpleasant.

Anyar, peering from under the hood of her green jacket, smiled at the bed-raggled form of her voral dodging the small puddles forming on the road, while her perac splashed through them with its wide, splayed feet. Sadir rode next to Anyar, chatting softly with Jelm, the river to his right.

The noise of the river grew as they rode, and at several places sheer cliffs bulged out, narrowing the road, forcing them to go single file.

Soon the road widened, making the journey easier. Anyar switched her mind away from the people and animals around her and quickly sank into her thoughts. They were riding to prepare for a war, to prepare for a future where all would be at stake; a clash where there would be only one winner. So many of her people could be hurt or die just for the ambitions of one man, one race. It was unfair.

She could almost see Xerina, their ally in Sutan, as Kyel had described her, and hoped that they would meet. What would it be like to be a life-long captive so far from home, yet maintain the courage to be true to yourself and your homeland?

If this is the sort of person I'm fighting for, then I have to do all I can. I can't let them down.

"Anyar, love," said Sadir, interrupting her thoughts, "can you see what's ahead?"

The misty rain had lifted, allowing a view of the road traversing a low, flat valley until it disappeared through a pass in the foothills some distance ahead. Clumps of fine-leafed trees grew in the hollows and folds of the foothills while mosses and ferns fought with grasses for space amongst the rocks. As she looked the sun broke through and cast a glow over the scene. Drathner raised his hand and rode off the road, followed by Telpher and Xerrita. Anyar slowed her perac in the rock-strewn area where Drathner was already setting up kindling in an old fireplace.

"Good place to stop," called Boidea cheerily from behind her. "You go and take Vor for a wander, while Sadir and I help make some tea."

Anyar smiled, patted her animal's furry neck, then dismounted before walking to where she had last seen her companion disappearing down a slope to the burble of a stream.

By the time she had avoided being splashed by the saturated voral and led him back to the campsite, the kettle was issuing a stream of steam, and slabs of bread and cheese were being handed around.

"None for Vor," warned Boidea as she handed Anyar a cup of tea and food. "He's foraging."

"He's fat enough, too," she chuckled.

"Now come and sit with me and Xennira, and we'll tell you more about our destination."

Xennira looked at her, crinkling her eyes in the strengthening sun. "You've never been this far?"

"No." Anyar shook her head and took a bite of bread and cheese.

"Well, you're in for a treat. In an hour or so we'll reach the Cascade Falls. They're magnificent, and the scents are spectacular. Your father, Targas, used these falls to delay the enemy, so they have some extra meaning."

"Yes, I remember," said Anyar. "They may yet have value for us."

"Ah," Xennira gulped at the serious voice, "yes, Mlana, yes."

Chapter Sixteen

"This will be too easy," growled Jakus to Kast alongside him at the head of a long column of troops manoeuvring their peracs through the rugged escarpment to the north of Sutaria. "My brother has his forces mainly west of Faltis' estates, no doubt seeking a confrontation to his advantage.

"Heritis," he called over his shoulder, "have your forces reached their location?"

"Rancer is leading my troops across the Grosten River and north towards the marshland as we speak; they will soon be able to block any retreat and provide the other means of attack if necessary. The keeper has Brastus' scent and will wait for instruction."

"I hope I won't have to signal him," Jakus mused, "if I can end this swiftly. We should have little difficulty, with my consort's troops playing their part. A pincer movement will end Brastus' efforts, at the very least force him to concentrate in several areas at the same time."

"Brastus is a seasoned campaigner, Jakus," said Kast, "not easily fooled. Not easily outmanoeuvred."

"I know that!" he spat. "But I don't want to lose any of my forces, be they those headed by Brastus or myself. I'll need all Sutanites available to complete my conquests."

Bilternus didn't know whether to feel upset or relieved. He had been ordered to accompany Heritis' force across the river and essentially act as backup leader in case Brastus tried to retreat south. This was not what he had expected for himself and those loyal troops from his father's estates, but it did keep them from fighting fellow Sutanites. The troops remaining with Faltis on the estates appeared to be neutral, having been advised by the Shada, Vitaris, to not actively take part in the fighting.

Jakus had shrugged this off as of no consequence, although Bilternus realised his father, Faltis, would not remain inactive and would be doing something to his own advantage.

"Boy?"

Bilternus flinched at the querulous voice and saw the keeper's corpulent figure in stained clothed looking at him.

"You referring to me?"

"Yes. My hymetta don't like all the rough treatment. The wagon is hard on them. Can you do something?"

Yes, he thought, *kill them all.* "I'll see how much longer we must go, keeper. It may be possible to settle them soon."

He rode his perac to find Rancer and relayed the keeper's concerns, ensuring that Jakus' 'secret weapon' was looked after.

"I'll try," Rancer agreed, "although the nearer we get to the escarpment the better. It'll not be me who answers to Jakus if this weapon of his is not in range. The marshes aren't far ahead and may be close enough."

"Right," Bilternus sighed, "I'll see what the effective distance is, should they be needed." He turned back towards the wagon.

Brastus and Strengor studied a parchment map on a small table inside their tent as they received reports from returning scouts.

"It appears the movement of Jakus' forces is going much as expected. We know that the largest proportion of his troops is coming through the most rugged part of the escarpment, supported by a secondary force further south. This westwards movement should be countered by my troops and the support of scent masters, enhanced by this magnesa.

"To the south we have a significant force, mostly on the western side of the river. Any attempt at going that way would be made difficult by the marshes, and the northern route is blocked by the Jakus-aligned Steppe people. Looks like we will have our hands full.

"And each of the enemy is countered by us, which could allow a stalemate if that's what I wanted. But"—Brastus stabbed a finger onto the parchment— "that's not what I want. I want Jakus safely tied up with his men in the least desirable situation. Then we can act.

"If I know my brother, he'll react when he sees us open and exposed. If he does, he'll get more than he bargains for. When he extends himself in attack he'll be at his weakest. This is when we strike, and he'll die!"

The sun paused high above the landscape, pushing its heat across the exposed rock and muddied watercourses, causing thick scents to drift. The troops and their animals sat motionless except for swatting the flies they attracted.

Two warring brothers separated by several folds of country, tried to find a means of attack. One, tall and broad, leant forward, seeking the place where he had hope of a victory, a place where he could lure the other to a final showdown.

He knew his chances were slim with such evenly matched forces, but he had to take the chance, had to try.

"Faltis," he said, turning to the man sitting on his perac amid a small group of scent masters, "are you still able to help? Are you still willing to give me this advantage for as long as I need it?"

"I may be many things, Brastus, but I am a man of my word." Faltis emphasised his statement with a grey scent aura showing commitment.

Brastus turned to Strengor. "Ready our scent masters and spear throwers, prepare the trap. Once Jakus moves, we attack."

An angled cleft dividing two ridges of rock left a narrow, flat pathway, giving an ideal way to pass through the escarpment without climbing the steep hillsides. It was there that Brastus headed with his troop of scent masters and guardsmen.

Faltis and his scent masters remained, watching, waiting for their moment.

Observers at strategic locations signalled and various groups began to move. The battle was about to be joined.

Jakus heard the reports and smiled. "The fool, he's leaving himself exposed. Mere weight of arms won't decide this battle. This is the time for my scent mastery to win. He will never know what killed him!

"Come Kast, we move while we have him at his most vulnerable."

"Jakus, is he that foolish, a seasoned veteran like him?"

"Hah! He doesn't know what he faces. Move!"

Jakus took little heed of the small group of scent masters high on the hill as he and his men charged down the gully towards the pass dividing the two ridges.

With a thunderous clash he drove into Brastus' party, scent bolts and spears working in proximity. Though the fighting was furious Jakus found he couldn't force his way through to his brother. The frustration built up until he saw that his men were not winning. Bodies were piling, and still Brastus seemed in control.

"Enough! You all die!" Jakus roared, taking a handful of magnesa from his belt pouch and cramming it into his mouth.

Sheets of purple and black scent power burst from Jakus, rising high into the air, inadvertently sending a signal to Rancer in the west to release the hymetta. Jakus then bent the scent sheets down to smash the people in front of him. But the action was thwarted by a reaction from the scent masters within Brastus' force and Faltis on the hillside. A shimmering, thick wall rose, deflecting Jakus' power and sending the scents scudding harmlessly over their heads.

"It's there! It's there!" screeched the keeper, pointing to the northeast. "The signal!"

Bilternus looked to where the man was pointing, seeing a purple scent plume rising from the hills across the wide river. *Blast,* he thought, *he wants them; they're going to be used.*

The keeper frantically pulled off the wagon's covers and thrust a portion of cloth into the face of each black-and-yellow creature. The hymetta were the length of his torso with bulbous abdomens, powerful winged thoraxes and melon-sized heads. They avidly snatched at the cloth with their powerful jaws.

"Release them!" the keeper screeched to several helpers as he pulled open two of the cage doors. The camp stilled, its people watching the hymetta scan their surroundings with huge black eyes as they clambered to the tops of their cages. They crouched, wings buzzing before they took to the skies.

Bilternus instinctively ducked as the pack circled the camp several times before setting off determinedly to the northeast.

"They have it. They have his scent," the keeper laughed, capering in a fanciful jig. "Nothing will stop them."

No, thought Bilternus, shaking his head. *I pity poor Brastus.*

"Now's our chance, Strengor," screeched Brastus. "Spears!" A group of skilled guardsmen dashed to each side of the rocky walls and hurled a volley of spears at the powerful scent masters, peppering Jakus and his troops despite the personal scent shields. Both sides held their ground.

Kast and a few others fell before Jakus drew a long swath of scent, dark and thick across the battlefield.

"Back," Jakus gasped, pulling his wounded scent master with him. "The blood-cursed scartha. How dare he use my magnesa against me!"

"Regroup," gasped Kast.

"No, we'll not let this go. I have the power. I am the leader of Sutan. We will not retreat."

He dissolved the masking scent to reveal the battlefield covered with bodies while searching for his brother.

"Ah!" Jakus grunted at the sight of the broad figure at the end of the rock-riven pathway, and began to prepare a scent bolt of vast power to penetrate any blocking shield.

A sudden hum made him pause and look skyward. "Hah," he smiled and relaxed, rubbing at his side.

Jakus saw Brastus straighten and turn his head, just as a group of dark shapes dived at him.

Brastus staggered, his scream cut short as his form grew grotesque, bulging with black and yellow bodies. His men slashed at the hymetta, cutting at legs and wings to save their leader, until he fell to the ground. They kept cutting the creatures into pieces with their knives until Brastus' body was clear of them.

Jakus squinted at the headless body of his brother and silently congratulated himself at his foresight. He forgot to take out his anger against the surrendering forces, such was his glee at the effectiveness of his secret weapon.

"Kast," he turned to his grimacing scent master, who was clasping the shaft of a spear sticking out of his shoulder, "negotiate with the losers. Offer them a chance to be true countrymen and support the resurgence of Sutan. I am of a mood to inspect my creatures' handiwork.

"And," he pointed to the rapidly disbanding group on the distant hillside, 'request my brother, Faltis, to attend me. He has some explaining to do."

B ilternus felt no sympathy for the grovelling man holding onto the empty cage door. Anyone who could hold an attachment to such alien beasts had to be addled. He did wonder, however, where they had gone, if they had achieved what Jakus had had in mind for them.

"I suppose we won't have to worry about the hymetta again, Rancer?" he asked.

"No, Bilternus, I suppose we won't," the grizzled arms commander replied. "If they have been used, then the war may have been won before it even really started. I suppose that Brastus is no more and our master, Jakus, will be the new Shada once Vitaris goes."

"Yes," Bilternus agreed. "This may just be the start of Jakus' ambitions. We're in for a lot more yet, I think."

V itaris sat in the great hall waiting, his lined face showing the strain. The outcome of the war between his two sons had not yet been conveyed to him, although he suspected Jakus, with his superior powers, would win the day.

He had no illusions that his ambitious and cruel son would find his attempts to give both leaders some equality acceptable. And he expected Jakus would be determined to punish him.

Vitaris hunched lower in the large chair as if anticipating a blow. He was tired and so past ruling this pitiless land and his quarrelsome sons. All he wanted was peace and anticipated if Jakus had won, he would get that peace.

"My lord, I have news," called his captain, Dronthis, his footsteps echoing loudly. "Jakus has defeated Brastus. He is headed back to the capital."

"So it begins," Vitaris murmured.

Chapter Seventeen

The sun had fallen behind the surrounding mountains by the time the group of travellers from Rolan descended into the forest of tall trees with dark green needle-like leaves covering the lower slopes.

They had made good time on their trek to Ean since leaving early from their overnight camp high in the mountains, and were walking their sure-footed peracs along a narrow trail winding through the jagged boulders and scree in the rugged mountain pass. Here everything appeared to be fighting for survival: the low, gnarled and woody needle-leafed trees rose out of a groundcover of large mosses, while prickly bushes tried to smooth the numerous outcrops of rock.

Kyel glanced at the stern profile of his fair-haired companion as she concentrated on the path. He realised that Cathar had made the reverse journey with his sister Sadir, niece Anyar and Targas some years before in more trying circumstances, a particularly cold winter and a destructive avalanche almost causing the loss of the entire party.

"Not long until we reach Sanctus?" he asked.

"I wouldn't think so." She looked up, a smile lighting her face. "I can't wait to be warm and have hot food. Though I mustn't complain, for travelling in spring has been relatively easy."

"Not like last time?"

"No, thank Ean," she said. "Wait, Undrea is signalling a stop. I'll be glad for a break."

The small party of leader Undrea, Cathar, Kyel and a competent trader, Huthner moved into a wooded clearing on one side of the trail. Their animals immediately gravitated to a pool formed by a small stream running down the slope, thrusting their furry snouts into the cold water.

"Time for tea?" asked Cathar.

"Depends," said Undrea, her face in shadow, "whether you want to reach Sanctus this night. I have done this trip a few times now, and if we travel until a little after dark, we'll make Sanctus: warm, soft beds and good company."

"So, grab a drink of water and keep going?" asked Kyel.

"I'd recommend it," added Huthner, a smile twisting his thin lips. "I think the perac would be right to go for another couple of hours. Our leader is more than capable of following the trail in the dark."

"Thank you for your confidence. So, get some water if our animals have left any, and we'll keep moving." Undrea pulled at the reins, forcing her perac to lift its long-necked head from the pool.

Light winking through the trees and boulders gave the first indication they had reached their destination, then the perac bleated in unison remembering the scents of good stables and sweet hay.

"At last!" Cathar blew a sigh of relief. "I'm on my last legs."

Kyel looked forward to seeing Sanctus. Growing up in the town of Lesslas, a day's travel to the south, had not allowed him time to visit when Ean was under Sutanite control. The rebellion had started in the rebel hideout and Sanctus' secrecy had meant few people visited. His niece had been there with Targas and Sadir on their way through the mountains to Rolan, but at that time he had his own concerns in the distant country of Sutan.

The soft, shuffling gait of the animals quickly moved them down the narrow trail leading towards the numerous granite boulders ringing Sanctus and its surroundings. From there, although it was too dark to see, huge rocks spilled down the hillside and into the valley far below.

"Welcome, travellers!" hailed a tall figure waving a lamp to and fro.

"Lethnal?" shouted Undrea, "I'd recognise that voice anywhere. Greetings from us weary wanderers."

"Lethnal!" exclaimed Cathar. "Oh, Lethnal."

"Cathar and, I believe, Kyel, a pleasure to finally meet you." The tall woman, their lantern illuminating her hooded face, approached them. "And Huthner too. Just the four of you?" She embraced each of them, sharing scents.

"Come," she said, slipping an arm through Cathar's and leading them towards the light spilling from the entrance amongst the boulders. Several acolytes in pale blue robes gathered around in welcome before leading the peracs off.

"They'll be taken to the stables while we relax," said Lethnal leading the travellers through the granite entrance and into Sanctus.

"Wash and refresh yourselves here then we'll brave the throng," she said, pointing to a row of wash basins against a wall of the entry hall.

Kyel held Cathar's hand as they walked into the large common room with its walls of unadorned granite penetrated by narrow window slits, thick wooden supports framing the doors, and floor of smooth rock. The chatter suddenly ceased from the grey-robed scent masters, blue-and-grey-robed acolytes and others occupying the tables.

"Friends," said Lethnal in a loud voice, "meet our arrivals from Rolan. Undrea and Huthner you will know, and maybe Cathar, a former acolyte from here, but although you will have heard of Kyel, an important player in the Revolution, you will not likely have met him."

Scents of welcome filled the air and the chatter resumed, people approaching them with greetings. Kyel could see that Cathar was comfortable with the place and its people, but he was feeling overwhelmed until someone nudged his shoulder and he swung around to see the stocky figure and round face of a person he recognised.

"Kyel, me lad. It's bin a long time since I've seen yer."

"Brin! It's good to see a familiar face!"

"It is thet lad, but you've grown since I saw yer some years ago, 'nd I've gotta look up now. Grown tall 'nd broader, plus I see Cathar 'nd yer are..."

"Yes, Brin, she and I fit well together. So, are you still on the barges?"

"Would thet I were, lad, but circumstances won't allow it. More 'nd more administration 'nd organisation 'nd running Nebleth while Jelm's away in Rolan. Preferred t' remain as leader of th' river people if I'd had me way.

"Yer know what's comin' I s'pose?"

"That's why we're here."

"Well let's stop jawin' 'nd git eatin'," said Brin. "I'll hev yer come t' me table. Lethnal 'nd me want all th' news."

Kyel noticed Undrea and Huthner had disappeared to a table of people wearing the familiar green tunic and trousers of traders and were already in deep conversation.

"They're regulars t' Sanctus," said Brin, "lots t' catch up on.

"Cathar!"

"Brin, lovely to see you!" she exclaimed, sharing scents with the river man.

"Me too. Jest bin speakin' with yer, uh, consort." Brin winked.

"Brin," growled Cathar. "Still the same joker," she added, taking Kyel's hand. "Near as, I suspect, but"—and she lowered her voice to a theatrical whisper—"he hasn't asked me yet."

"Ulp." Kyel's face reddened.

"Enough said," said Brin. "Let's join Lethnal at th' table. Food's already pilin' up."

"Sit, sit," a grey-headed woman said, patting the bench seat next to her. "Eat. Don't let Brin's talking keep you from it."

Cathar slid along the seat next to the Sanctus leader and Kyel followed.

"I'll sit opposite next t' me friend Rasnal," Brin said, placing a gentle hand on the shoulder of a thickset, grey-gowned woman sitting on the bench on the other side of the table. "Move up."

"Don't know if I want to," she smiled from under a mop of brown hair. "But for you I will."

"Please help yourselves." Lethnal waved her hand over the bowls of steaming tubers, sliced meat in gravy and green beans. "There's plenty of bread and butter, too."

"I'll pour th' cider," said Brin, lifting a jug. "You'll all want sum?"

"Eat," said Lethnal. "We're all bursting with curiosity, but food comes first. Oh, I should introduce Rasnal to you, Kyel," she said over a mouthful of buttered bread, 'very important in the scheme of things since she controls our communication, our tina."

"Ah, I know about them," Kyel said as he filled his plate, remembering the giant scent moths that were the focal point of fast communication in Ean.

"I'm pleased to meet up with you, Kyel," said Rasnal solemnly, "they are more important than ever with the running of Ean. We're always sending and receiving messages through the tina."

"That reminds me," said Kyel, "where's Lan? I thought he'd be here."

"Moves between the capital and Regulus," Lethnal replied. "He's needed there more than ever and, quite frankly, didn't feel up to the journey."

"Oh," added Cathar, "we hadn't thought. Our leader is getting on, as Jelm reported. I hope he's well?"

"Frailer than I would like, but full of determination. Down where government happens is the best place for him. From there he can organise things, plus he has plenty of assistance, including a couple of our promising youngsters, Jucial and Eren. It is fortunate you caught us here, as Brin and I are about to lead a large group of people down country, mainly scent-talented and fighters."

"Our news is fortuitous then," said Kyel. "We'll have to head out as soon as we can; next day, I would suggest."

"Agreed," Lethnal nodded, eyes glittering, "first thing then. Rasnal will also send a message after this meal, if agreeable. The tina travel at night, as you're probably aware."

"We'll do that." Kyel took a large gulp of cider. "So, I better tell you our news then."

Kyel and Cathar, each holding a lamp, followed Rasnal down a narrow trail below Sanctus to a wooden ramp bridging a noisy stream. Once across they eased through a dark opening in the rock face to walk across the coarse sand of a large cavern, its walls reflecting their lamplight in tiny sparkles. They accompanied the tina keeper across the space to a series of smaller caves further in.

"You can detect their odour," Rasnal said softly as a slight breeze wafted the musty smell into their faces, before they heard a faint rustle of living creatures from the smallest cave. The lamplight revealed thigh-sized insects on the far wall, wings folded flat across their backs, compound eyes surmounted by feathery antennae with thin legs gripping the rock, their vibrating bodies creating the movement of air.

"Just stand and watch while I place the scent messages on their thorax. We'll send several to make sure they get there, even though they well know the smell of Nebleth's scent tower." She lifted a small strip of soft, flexible cloth. "As you know, we have trained scent masters to interpret scents and their meanings, so, in essence this message will include scents of here, Sanctus; Sutan; urgency; Rolan; your hometown of Lesslas, Kyel, so they'll interpret it relates to you; travellers coming; Jakus and danger; preparation. We have more, too, but this is sufficient explanation."

Rasnal gently stroked the sides of one of the large creatures, slipping the cloth into the fluff of its thorax. "It is secure there; now there's one other thing, the destination scent." She pulled a small tuft of twine from a bottle and touched it to the moth's antennae. Immediately its wings buzzed at a high pitch, and it detached itself from the wall before flying out through the dark entrance to the cave.

"It'll fly through the hole in the roof of the large cavern and should reach Nebleth before dawn," Rasnal said. "Now I'll prepare the next one."

They were ready to retire as Lethnal took them down a short corridor of grey granite walls and ceilings, past openings leading into small bedrooms, before turning into a larger room lit with a small slit window. "This should do you. One large bed to share?" she smiled politely.

Kyel looked to his slim companion, who nodded.

"Now, Cathar, you know where the washrooms are to clean off the dust of your travels? Good. I will rouse you next day, before dawn, I'm afraid." She grinned and left.

"How tired are you, Cathar?" asked Kyel.

"Let's wash first and then we'll see." She reached out and took him by the hand.

The small group of Lethnal, Brin, and Rasnal with Cathar and Kyel, had joined in a communal scent-sharing before leaving ahead of a huge assembly of people and animals on the southward trek to the city of Regulus. The sun was just pinking the horizon far to the east, outlining the vast mountains that formed a north-south barrier to the desert beyond. Before the natural barrier lay extensive plains nourished for millennia by the Great Southern River, itself an ominous dark worm snaking southward.

Heading down the slopes where Sanctus perched among the giant boulders, Kyel felt an inexplicable sadness. One night in the natural fortress explained how his sister and Targas had felt. It was a sanctuary, the place where they had escaped the enemy and learnt to develop their scent abilities. There they had truly found each other.

Last night had done the same for him and Cathar. They had had a curious freedom to explore their feelings for each other, and it had been a night of wonder. From the moment they had come together they had explored each other's bodies, odours of desire making displays of pinks and yellows combined with soft greens and oranges around them.

Waking up with Cathar left him feeling one with her. It was nothing like anything else he'd known, even the experiences with the young woman Sencia, from Sutan, so long ago.

Cathar looked over to him as they rode two abreast and a plume of scents, light yellows, oranges and pinks, rose from her. Kyel returned her smile, echoing her scents of love.

"Enough of thet," grunted Brin, "it's makin' me jealous."

"You're just a grumpy old man," said Rasnal. "I think I might go back to my tina, they're easier to handle."

"Go on with yer, I'm much more fun."

A scrabble amongst the boulders caused Kyel to turn in time to see puffs of lizard alarm scent rising in the air. "Conduvian lizards, Cathar," he said excitedly, "Do you remember me telling you of my friend, Tel, I had when I was younger? Well, those lizards are the same."

Cathar smiled at his excitement. "Long gone now, Kyel."

"Probably, but he was raising a family when I left Lesslas, so at least his descendants would still be there." He sighed and slumped back into the saddle."

"Kyel," called Lethnal, turning to look back from her perac, "as you won't have come this way before you'll see if we turned due south from now and crossed the stream a short ride ahead, we would meet your hometown of Lesslas after about a day or so. Instead, we'll go east until we meet the main road alongside the Great Southern."

"Lethnal, years ago I almost made it to Sanctus, but we were captured by the Sutanites, my friend Luna and I, at the start of the rebellion. Although I was only a teenager, the memories haven't faded."

"Oh, I am sorry to bring that up. I had forgotten that portion of our history and the heroic part you both played."

"Don't worry, Lethnal," said Kyel, "it is good to remind me, and makes me more determined to stop the Sutanites from ever hurting my friends again."

"Oh Kyel." Cathar reached across and took his hand.

Chapter Eighteen

"**F**altis, my dear brother." Jakus, his scent aura a deep purple, sneered at the bedraggled black form who had stepped out from a small group of captured men in front of the victorious Sutanite leader.

"Shada." Faltis bent his head.

Jakus' eyes narrowed at Faltis' acknowledgement of him as leader of Sutan, while he considered how to respond to his brother's role in the battle. Faltis was a turncoat, ready to act in his own interests, yet could he do without him? Was it better to remove him once and for all rather than be forever guarding his back?

"I congratulate you on your victory."

Jakus started. "You dare to interrupt me? Do you realise what I am considering?"

"My Lord," Faltis said, spreading his hands wide, "it is obvious. You are thinking to kill me for my part in the war. But I would urge you to reconsider. As stated in front of our father, I am here only to serve Sutan. Hence, I am loyal to the leader of Sutan, yourself. I am more useful to you alive."

"Faltis!" Jakus growled.

"I am your servant." He knelt on one knee. "You have control of my body and mind. I am willing to submit to your interrogation, brother."

"Enough!" Jakus turned to a bloodied Kast, standing by his side. "Begin the process of returning all troops to Sutaria and ensure those remaining are loyal to Sutan. We will interrogate those who are unsure; my scent masters will weed out any disloyalty."

"Your will, Shad." Kast, favouring his bandaged shoulder, walked to the group of black-and-grey-dressed scent masters on one side.

Jakus looked back to his brother. "I have no wish to dispense with both my brothers in the one day so, against my better judgement you will remain alive, unless you cross me.

"Heritis!" Jakus said, raising his voice.

"Jakus?" Heritis hurried over from a large, open-sided tent erected on a level portion of stony ground near the battlefield where he'd been talking to Poegna.

"Are you able to quickly ascertain whether the leaders of Faltis' men are loyal?" he asked, gesturing at the small group standing several steps behind his brother.

"With your magnesa, assuredly," Heritis grinned. "I'd have no problem then."

"Done."

"Now, Faltis, have them come here. I am interested to see how loyal they are to Sutan."

Faltis bowed before looking over his shoulder. "Piltarnis, my commander and scent master leader will be loyal as will the rest of my people, Shada." He waved him forward. "Strengor, well, he was Brastus' commander. You will have to see for yourself."

Piltarnis bowed to Jakus as he led the rest of the men past to Heritis. Jakus held up his hand, stopping Strengor.

"You I will do myself."

"My Lord?"

"You have lost your long-time commander." Jakus paused, letting his scents thicken. "Are you willing to continue to serve Sutan, to serve me?"

Strengor slipped to one knee and bowed his head. "I am willing to serve."

Jakus pushed tendrils of odour over the man, which manoeuvred their way around Strengor's hasty defence shield until it was criss-crossed with dark lines. Then he tightened the tendrils constricting the shield and forcing it back upon its creator. Strengor's eyes bulged, and his face began to turn blue. His hands ineffectually grabbed at the tightening tendrils, slipping and scratching until his body finally collapsed to the ground. His legs jerked spasmodically, dust rising from his boots until all motion ceased.

"He professed his loyalty, Jakus!" snapped Faltis, still watching Strengor's body.

"He did," puffed Jakus, releasing his scent control, "but he'd been too long with Brastus, too influenced by his ways for me to ever trust him.

"I hope," he gazed intently at Faltis, "I don't have cause to regret my mercy in your case."

Long lines of Sutanites gradually descended on the capital, filling the streets with the noise and disorder of many people, their animals and baggage. Poegna's troops moved slowly to her estates to the east of the city while Heritis took the bulk of Brastus' forces to Faltis' estates for further processing. Jakus' army occupied the fields and accommodation near the palace, readying for progressing the plans of Sutanite conquest now that the civil conflict had been determined.

Bilternus had led the army he co-commanded with Rancer back across the river to meet Heritis on the road to his father's estates, and was pleased to see his relative in a happy mood.

"Ho Rancer, Bilternus," called Heritis, "it seems a while since we last met. Did much happen from where you were stationed, other than the release of the hymetta?"

"We saw the signal, released them, and that's about the extent of it, Heritis," said Rancer. "We left the keeper to make his way back to Southern Port."

"Effective and terrifying weapon," said Heritis, "but I won't be too sad to forget the hymetta. They were destroyed in attacking the target, but they shortened the conflict dramatically. Until then Brastus' forces were putting up a good fight, countering Jakus' scent attack with magnesa-enhanced shields.

"Where they got so much, I wouldn't know," he said, automatically slipping a finger into his belt pouch and taking a red crystal to his mouth. "I've got a taste for it," he smiled apologetically.

"So, Jakus is in Sutaria?" asked Bilternus.

"Yes, with Faltis. I think he will consolidate his power now that Brastus is gone. We must see that there is no resentment from his army, so we'll have a lot to do at your father's estates.

"You'll have to organise it all, young Bilternus," continued Heritis, "since I don't imagine Jakus will release his control on Faltis too readily."

Bilternus eased his heavy tunic top from around his neck as the dust continued to rise from the movement of so many animals and troops on the dirt roads.

"Be glad to get there, clean up," he said. "Expect our supply situation will be tight after billeting so many people."

"I look forward to seeing your estates," said Rancer. "I can see the summers would be hot and dry here but by the looks of those trees ahead you have a good place to get away from all that."

"Yes," said Bilternus. "In fact, I might ride on ahead and help get things organised for our arrival. My father's consort, Methra, is well capable, but with so many arriving it will stress her out."

"Go on, lad," said Heritis, "I've got things to discuss with my commander."

Bilternus was pleased to see Piltarnis in the group released by Jakus arriving through the gates of the estate. He had known the young commander for many years and recalled with pleasure the frequent sparring sessions.

"Piltarnis!" he called as the group neared.

"Bilternus, I am happy to be here," the slight scent master said with a grimace, "I wasn't sure I would be exonerated from supporting Brastus' efforts in the battle."

"Jakus may be somewhat over-reactive when he's angry, but I think he realises he needs all the troops he can for what he's planning. If you can prove you will work for the good of the country, you'll be fine.

113

"If your group could come over to the barracks, we'll get you processed." Bilternus turned and led Piltarnis and the other scent masters to the low line of buildings on the other side of the gravelled assembly area.

"It'll be a mild intrusion of your scent senses with the aid of magnesa. If you've nothing to hide, as I'm sure is the case, then it'll be over in no time. Heritis?"

Bilternus stood to one side as each of Faltis' scent masters walked up to the table and stood in front of the three men sitting there, their auras red and yellow in their nervousness. A group of guardsmen waited at each side, ready to act if there was a negative reaction from the interrogation.

It was quick and effective. A coil of dark scent extruded from the mouth of the interrogator entered the nose of each person standing at the table and infiltrated their brain. If no evidence of deceit was found, they were released and ordered away. Several times the examination was extended but their loyalty to Sutan was still confirmed.

"Doing well, Bilternus," said Heritis, his scents spiralling from the effect of magnesa. "I think these people are only guilty of following their leaders."

"That's good, Heritis. Come into the house when you've finished."

Heritis nodded and looked to the next group of people entering the large rectangular room.

"Getting hot out there, Bilternus; hotter than Ean at this time of the year." Rancer entered the large planning room in the house and took a mug of cold drink from the table. "I think Heritis is nearly finished with his interrogations. We'll end up with a good army to support Jakus when we head back to Ean."

"Try one of the salad and meat wraps Methra has laid out for us and then we'll have a look at the map my father Faltis has. We've used this for planning in the past." Bilternus tapped a large section of parchment spread across a low wooden table.

The two men looked down. "You can see the whole of Sutan. Note how the Grosten River is the larger of the two main rivers going from the Steppes of Stone in the north through Sutaria to Southern Port. To the west is our other port of Sempla, met by the Westforth River, also coming from the north through Hestria, where Jakus and Nefaria lived for a time. I had a pleasant few days in Hestria with the Eanite, Kyel, too."

"Yes, Kyel, I remember him." Rancer scratched a weathered chin. "In Rolan now, I believe?"

"Ah, yes," said Bilternus, looking up from the map. "Maybe we'll meet again, but I hope there's some sort of peace when we do."

"Little chance of that," grunted Rancer.

"Methra!" a high-pitched voice echoed.

"Blast!" Bilternus turned and faced the doorway, arms folded across his chest.

"Bring me food, drink and clean clothing!" The demanding voice was followed by its owner.

"Boy, you're here," stated Faltis. "And you are Rancer, with that lackey, Heritis. Too far away from the action to have suffered any hurt, eh?"

"My Lord." Rancer gave a curt bow.

"Father, are you alright?" asked Bilternus. "What did Jakus do?"

"Jakus? Hah!" Faltis snatched a cup off the small side table, poured red wine and gulped. "Where's that woman?"

"Here, my Lord." Methra, a solid woman with nervous scents appeared carrying a clean black robe and a plate of pastries.

Faltis snatched the clothing, causing the pastries to slide on the plate. She hurriedly put the plate on the small table and refilled Faltis' cup, before slipping back out of the room.

Faltis stripped off his dirty black robe to stand in underclothes, exposing the clear outline of bony ribs while he pulled the new robe over his head.

"Ah Heritis, cousin," he said as the man entered the room. "Come to update me on the forces living on my estates, eh?"

Heritis' eyes narrowed as he watched Faltis stuffing pastries into his mouth, then shook his head. "I, like you, am working for Jakus. We all have the goal of returning Sutan to its former glory, to making our country greater than ever. Let us hope we can both survive to enjoy our victories."

"Bah." Faltis took a gulp of wine before he looked at his son. "Bilternus, come into my study. We must speak."

Bilternus followed his father into the small room off the planning room and waited as Faltis closed the door before turning to face him.

"Father?" he asked, hoping that the face he perceived was his true father, sane and logical. He looked into the red eyes and immediately prepared his scent shields.

"You know," Faltis hissed. "Others suspect, but you know. So, should I kill you now or keep you? No, no." He shook his head. "No value, not yet." His eyes turned inwards as Bilternus watched.

"What to tell you, my 'son'?" Faltis smiled, one side of his mouth releasing a string of drool. "So, you have your suspicions, eh? You know that someone else lives inside your father and is revealed at times? Well, I'll confirm that, to you and you alone. If you tell anyone else, they'll think you're mad, so you'll have to bear this secret hoping your father is still your father.

"Let me say that we are both working to the same end, Faltis and I. His body and you have value to me, so we'll share this burden."

Bilternus' face paled as he watched the stranger in his father and heard the confirmation he never wanted. Should he kill the thing or let it go? He could see the creature watching, knowing what was going on in his mind.

A slow smile spread across its face. "Agreed? Then let's go outside and discuss tactics, my son."

Jakus entered the great hall, a pale Kast by his side, and strode towards his father hunched in the large chair, his captain Dronthis next to him.

"Dismiss the guards, Vitaris," he called as he approached.

Vitaris looked at the strong purple and scarlet scents rippling above his son and then waved his hand. "Dronthis, dismiss my guards and then leave. Whatever happens, make sure you support Sutan and its leader first, and me second. If you seek revenge for what is about to happen, you will have thrown your life away for no purpose."

"Shada?" The large man's forehead creased as he leant towards his commander.

"Dronthis, you and I have had a long association. You have served me well. Now serve my successor. Sutan is on the precipice of becoming the leader of the world and I want you to be there to see it. Do me this one last favour."

"My Lord, my Shada." Dronthis knelt and shared scents with the shrunken old man. Then he stood and strode from the hall, signalling his guards to follow.

"Wise move, Father, to ensure his survival, if I so will it." Jakus watched Vitaris' captain depart, a slight smile on his face.

"You will have heard of the defeat of Brastus?" Jakus tilted his head to one side. "This is despite all the advantages you gave him."

Vitaris looked up tiredly. "Little I can say about that, but I endeavoured to create some balance between you both, to ensure the new leader of Sutan would be worthy of his rank."

"Fool! All this did was cause more Sutanite dead, fewer troops to achieve my plans of conquest. You have interfered too much, too often."

"Remember, Jakus, do not overstretch yourself. Do not become overconfident. And use all your resources wisely." Vitaris' voice trailed off as he saw the strengthening of Jakus' scents, dark and violent.

"Shada," he whispered, bowing his head, and dropping his natural scent barrier.

"Shada!" screeched Jakus as the odours billowed up around him, all his skills amplified by magnesa. An eye-watering tang emanated from the thickening cloud growing higher above the former ruler of Sutan until it descended over the bent man.

Vitaris shuddered as the scents rolled over him, then began to scream, jerking spasmodically as the acids ate into his skin. It was rapid and gruesome, exposing the ribs of Vitaris' back as he slumped onto the table in front of him, rapidly decomposing the man into a bone-filled sludge. The table collapsed into a welter of wood pulp as the acids eroded its structure and fluids oozed across the floor.

"No more, Kast," Jakus huffed to his companion as he relaxed his control and the scents quickly dissipated. "My control. My will. Sutan will rule the world."

"Yes Shada!" his army commander quickly agreed.

S he clutched her throat so hard she began to choke as she shivered in the dark between two columns of the great hall. *I liked him,* she thought. *So many years and now his son, his dangerous son has taken the reins and would lead Sutan into war. More people killed to serve the ambitions of this flawed character. Now I must do what I must do.*

Xerina slipped away from the carnage in the great hall aware she had witnessed the beginnings of the end and only hoped the forces arrayed against this monster would be enough.

Chapter Nineteen

M y goodness!" exclaimed Anyar as they steadied their animals on the road. "Is it a sign? Can we believe that it is?"

"No sign, Mlana," said Xaner, "just a natural phenomenon. Water with sunlight streaming through it, although I'm inclined to believe the rainbow is a sign." He smiled at the young woman with her mouth open in amazement.

The colours of the rainbow drew their eyes and the roar of the water hit their ears. A strong honey aroma wafted through as they observed the beauty of the yellow-hued scent motes assailing their senses.

"The story goes that your father used the Cascade Falls to his advantage with his remarkable control of scent, causing a wall of water to wash down on the pursuing Sutanite army, delaying them and killing many. That tactic allowed the defenders to prepare and eventually drive the army out of our country."

"It certainly is a wonder," said Anyar, "and one we may have to consider. I have still a lot to learn of my father's knowledge."

"Well, you are your father's daughter, same blood. The old Mlana, Alethea, saw much in you," interjected Boidea. "Now, we've a way to go and must keep moving. We'll need to reach Nosta this night."

As they moved through the mist of water, they came over the lip of the pass and saw a wide valley spreading into the distance. Walls of white-flowering trees extending along the drop-off in an east-west line pushed a thick, visible scent into the air, foraging pria darting in and out of the blossoms.

The noise of another stream joining the one they had followed made talking impossible, so they enjoyed the magnificence of the arc of water pouring into the valley while they descended onto the plain.

Anyar observed the panorama before them. The river had broadened and meandered in a silver band, cutting through forests and grassland where outcrops of grey rock made periodic intrusions. Far ahead were signs of cultivation. She manoeuvred her perac to where Xerrita was chatting to Jelm.

"You come from Nosta, Xerrita?"

"Xerrita and Xennira have been telling me about the region and the way Nosta is laid out in a defensive star," said Jelm. "You should hear what they have to say."

Anyar squinted at Jelm for a moment, feeling slightly aggrieved she hadn't been included in the conversation before realising they still thought of her as young, not adult. She smiled at him. "Yes, I should."

"You'll have noticed the lines in the far distance, on the slopes; they're vines. Other crops grown by the farmers are harder to see at this distance. But enough of that. So, the city, Nosta, is set in a star-shaped pattern, with the centre being administration, the main storage facilities, and associated services. It spreads from the centre along the natural depressions where most buildings are residential, but solidly constructed," said Xennira.

"The city sort of melds into the ruggedness of the land with the rock acting as a moderator of the climate and also as a natural defence," she continued.

"So," Jelm said, rubbing at his chin, "if an enemy is coming up from the sea, from Requist, it would have to overcome Nosta before continuing on to Mlana Hold?"

"Yes, and no," said Xennira. "The Sutanites attacked Rolan before they isolated Nosta, so they could target the supplies of magnesa at the Hold. Our strategy then was to force as many of the invaders to remain, blockading the city as we could to give our people more of an advantage at the Hold. Jakus was so fixated on the Hold's magnesa that he probably forgot about its strategic advantage."

"So Nosta's role was to hold out against a large number of the enemy, thereby splitting their forces," said Jelm. "I wouldn't suspect Nosta should have such a passive role in a future attack?"

"No, Jelm," Xennira replied, "not the next time. Jakus will have remembered our strategy."

"And I remember what happened in the attack on the Hold." Anyar's eyes glazed over. "I was young but recall it vividly. My father died there fighting to protect me and my mother. Then Alethea died too, passing the mantle of the new Mlana to me. And, I'll never forget the winged horrors that Jakus sent at us. If it hadn't been for Vor we mightn't be here."

The voral, foraging near her feet, lifted his head and squinted at his mistress.

"Good Vor," Anyar smiled.

"That voral," said Jelm, "I'd swear it understands what we say."

"You have the look of your father about you."

Anyar's mouth opened as she looked at the small, wizened woman sitting next to her, her bright eyes peering from a maze of wrinkles.

"I'm pleased to finally have some moments with you," continued Xennira. "I don't like to spend much time away from Nosta, so am happy to be back."

Anyar, reaching for the tumbler of honeyed juice she'd put down on the table, scanned the room. She noticed her mother chatting to Jelm, while the rest of their party was engaged in eating and talking. Fires roared at each end of the large hall, while servers moved around them offering platters of food and refills of wine, beer or juice.

"I knew your father and feel the strength of him in you," Xennira continued. "There is much about you. Your aura, it's dynamic, almost as if the old Mlana is in you."

Anyar focused her attention on what this old woman was saying.

"Such a domination of grey, the resolve and determination. And what a lovely, almost rainbow-like display of light pastels, oranges, yellows, blues, pinks and greens, showing love, concern and loyalty. My"—Xennira smacked her mouth—"I can only remember one such scent aura in the past. The Mlana has a true successor in you."

"Mother, enough, leave the poor girl alone," interrupted Xerrita. "It's been a long day. Next day will be soon enough to continue the cross examination."

"Daughter, look after this one with all your heart. There's a very hard time ahead and she will need all her friends to get through it." The old woman placed a wrinkled hand on Anyar's head before she withdrew into the darkness of the hall.

"Anyar, my mother is better to take in small doses," said Xerrita with a smile. "Now finish your drink and we'll find our beds. An early start in the morning so you can see the city, eh?"

Anyar snuggled down in a small, warm room off a large dormitory a short distance from the hall in the centre of Nosta. Her companions were mostly outside in single beds, and the snoring made her glad she had her own room. Even so, it took a while for her to get to sleep. The journey had awakened a lot of thoughts: to think that she was following the footsteps of her father when he went to the Port just before the invasion; that, and the unnerving Xennira with her predictions. What did the future hold? Why was so much expected of her? And how was she supposed to save everything?

A laugh burst from her, eliciting a growl from Vor, stretched out alongside her. *Get some sleep*, he seemed to say, although it was a while in this unfamiliar place before she drifted off.

The smell of frying meats woke her, and Vor thumping off the bed in search of an early morning walk made her rise and pull on her trousers and warm jerkin. She followed Vor through the maze of beds and their occupants to a side door. It opened onto a narrow, shaded street. Again, Vor led the way up the street until they reached a grassy space marking the centre of the city. A scatter of benches lit by the morning sun drew her. She sat and absorbed her first morning in Nosta while her companion rummaged in nearby bushes.

A few people were about on various errands. Some smiled, but most went on their way. She could see the whole of the city laid out before her and assessed the way the builders had maximised the natural topography for defence. It was as if a fungus was just emerging from the soil, presenting a hard skin to the world with all its vulnerable parts protected. Long lines of narrow roads emanated from the centre, all capable of being defended if need be. *A truly remarkable city*, she thought.

The drift of scents was purer at this height. The forests around the city sent swathes of odours, differently coloured if she focused: leaves and grasses, wood, stone and soil, lizard and insect interspersed with tangs of moisture dominating, taking more effort to determine fainter more dispersed scents. If she tried, she could see the scented trees from the huge waterfall half a day's ride away, even fainter was the familiarity of Mlana Hold, a scent of home. Her gaze drifted over the city until she noticed a familiar scent aura approaching; she double-blinked to focus.

"Anyar, I tracked you down," called Xennira as she puffed to a stop. "Mind if I sit?"

Anyar shifted sideways on the bench. "Just watching the city, seeing the scents," she murmured, as if to justify herself.

"Good. Good." Xennira held out a small bottle. "Try some of this?"

Anyar took a deep breath. "That's Rolan cordial. Is it good to have it at this time of the day?"

"Good at any time," snorted Xennira, her eyes almost disappearing into her wrinkles. "Straight from the bottle, dear."

Anyar drank and coughed as the liquid ran a fiery path down her throat.

"Leave some for me." Xennira took the bottle back and tipped it up into her mouth.

"Ah." She wiped her lips and replaced the stopper. "So, you ask why the cordial?"

Anyar nodded as she rubbed her running eyes.

"I'm not coming with you on your journey. I am staying here, so I wanted the opportunity to get you alone and add somewhat to your store of knowledge of women's scent."

"My shadow scent?"

"The little time I had with Targas, your father enabled me to view his take on scent, how he managed to do more and better than any before. While he didn't have a woman's sensitivity, he had a system where he saw right into the intricacies of scent, down to the very bits that hold the motes together. And he managed to use these, to bond them and make more powerful ways of using his scent power."

"I know how to do that already!" exclaimed Anyar.

"I thought as much from what my daughter said, but what your father did was even more. He was able to extend his walls of scent by drawing the smallest of bonds together, further and further. I heard that he enveloped a whole castle with soporific scents once, so great was his skill. So, the advantage you have is the cordial. It only works for women, and it will enable you to delve even deeper, maybe extend the wall over a vast distance. Imagine how effective that could be."

Anyar sat still for a moment, vaguely hearing Vor foraging in the bushes nearby. "Yes," she nodded to herself, "it could work. Even now how I *see* scents is heightened, clarified. I could take, say, the smell of Vor, link it with the odours of moisture and push it a long way if I can *see* it."

"So, my dear, you can tell what I'm getting at," said Xennira. "Such a defence could stop the enemy in his tracks. The crystal cave also enhances one's ability, more so, but of course it's not portable like the cordial. The ultimate clash with the enemy would preferably be at Mlana Hold with the crystal cave, but of course that's not possible." Xennira peered closely into Anyar's light eyes. "So, the cordial is the ideal portable scent enhancer, as the fight must be taken to the enemy in the end." She sat back abruptly, shaking her head.

"But I don't want to load too much on your young shoulders. You must be getting hungry?"

A sudden shaking of the bushes attracted her attention and Vor emerged, snuffling through a dirty snout.

"Just mention food and he's there," Anyar laughed. "Shall we go back?"

"Yes, my dear," said Xennira. "I'd be happy if you could escort me."

Xerrita stood at the door to the dormitory and smiled at them. "I hope my mother hasn't been annoying you, Anyar."

"Still a cheeky young thing," Xennira replied. "I think we all deserve a meal."

They walked with Xerrita down to the large hall they had been in the night before and soon ate their way through a good selection of scrambled eggs, cured meats, honeyed cereal and juice. The rest of their party of Boidea, Sadir, Xaner, Jelm, Drathner and Telpher appeared within minutes.

"I hear you went up to the hill this morning, Anyar," said Boidea.

"Once Vor was up, I was," she said. "I could see the whole city from there."

"So, you'll understand the layout somewhat," she said. "I think we may usefully use the day in discussing where Nosta may fit in the event of an attack." Boidea scanned their group.

"Perhaps," she said, turning back to Anyar, "you'll feel like a walk back up the hill? The planning room is situated near there."

Anyar smiled.

They were leading their animals out of the city along the western road, which slowly descended towards the river some distance away. A full day of planning and discussion had been tiring, and after a late night it was a relief to be on the road in the early morning. Xennira was staying to organise the defence of the city and Anyar was sad to leave the old woman behind.

"It is well that you've seen and understand Nosta, Anyar," said Boidea. "It is a jewel in the crown of Rolan: very defensible, capable of holding many troops and withstanding a long siege. I wouldn't anticipate such occurring, but you must know what we have."

"Absolutely, Boidea," said Jelm, "but I'm looking forward to seeing Port Requist, as that's where the Sutanites will arrive. Xaner, what do you think?"

Xaner pulled his animal closer to them. "The port will bear the brunt of any attack, but this time we will be holding on to as much of the city as possible. We allowed the city to fall too easily to Jakus. This time it won't happen."

"Look ahead," called Xerrita, "you can see the granite pillars marking the end of the street. That's our city's first line of defence, Anyar. There are similar pillars on all streets leading away from the centre."

Anyar noted the two stationary guards as they moved between the towering columns. A reinforced metal gate lay against a wall ready to close off the passageway in the event of an attack.

"Solid," said Drathner to Telpher. "We could use something like this to reinforce the entrances into the village and Mlana Hold. We have enough skilled artisans to build it."

"If there's time," his companion replied, "but somehow I doubt it."

They reached an intersection where the party of eight swung onto their animals and turned south to follow a wide, well-used road, the voral trotting almost under the belly of Anyar's perac.

The paved road wound through the valley created by the Rolander River, where rugged hills were covered by tall trees jammed in with thickets of shrubbery and large ferns. The gentle gradient made for a comfortable journey as the sun slowly rose over the eastern hills, giving a false cheerfulness to the party. *Where am I going?* thought Anyar. *Is it going to lead to my death, the death of all my friends and everything I know? It doesn't seem right in this quiet, peaceful place. Is anyone else worried that they're placing their faith in a Knowing, in a youngster, IN ME!* She felt a scream rising and clenched her mouth.

She snatched up her water bottle and took a swallow, shaking her head at her mother's worried gaze.

Chapter Twenty

The Great Southern's inexorable flow paced the travellers along the parallel road and tow path, its broad grey width accumulating more and more barge traffic as the river neared the city of Regulus.

Kyel and Cathar, along with Lethnal, Brin and Rasnal, had spent the night at Main Camp at the confluence of the Great Southern with the Western Wash before continuing at dawn. Lethnal had ensured the administrators of the rest stop were prepared for their following army, due to reach them the next day.

"Barges," Brin said, throwing up an arm as a large, low-slung boat near the centre of the river drifted past. "Far rather be on 'em than this thing," he added, his perac bleating as if in response.

"I'd like to go on a barge," said Kyel. "Never had the chance, I'm afraid."

"No, I s'pose yer didn't, at least not durin' th' war," Brin reflected. "Then yer left, didn't yer?"

"Yes, young and foolish. Thought a Sutanite woman loved me; went after her, all the way to Sutan. But she didn't after all; was too much in love with Jakus. Poor Nefaria."

"She died, didn't she?"

"Yes, Brin. She died. And Jakus didn't care. The damned scartha."

"Scartha? Them's a Sutanite creature?"

"Yes, large scaly lizard. Lives in swamps. Nasty."

"Oh." Brin rubbed a hand through his short grey hair. "In answer t' yer question it'd tek too long t' land a barge 'nd git on, plus we got th' animals."

"Not to worry"—Lethnal leant towards them—"Regulus isn't far now."

They entered the city from the north through gates pushed back against the wooden palisade, last used during the Sutanite rule. On their left the Great Southern slid through the city, neatly bisecting it. Even at this early hour the noise and odours were overwhelming as vendors and stall holders competed for business while guardsmen and workers went about preparing Regulus for defence. Their small group led the animals through the crowd towards the castle overshadowing the city.

Kyel was happy to be with Cathar in this hive of industry. Last time he had been in Regulus he had been sneaking through on his way to the capital Nebleth, further downriver, a despondent youth without friends or hope. Now he had time to appreciate the scents rising around him, ignoring the noxious odours of decaying meats and wastes, and picking through the more subtle odours; under the all-encompassing drift of river odour there were spicy, tantalising scents, the salts, wool and timbers. *Ah yes,* he thought, remembering those from the warehouse region of the city.

Then he picked up a familiar scent he hadn't experienced for so long, here on the steps of the castle. They pushed their way through the thinning crowd to see a slight, grey-clad man supporting himself with a staff, scent aura welcoming with blue-greens, pinks and yellows.

"Lan!" Kyel let go of the reins of his animal and hurried over to meet his old master and friend. "So pleased to see you again." He exchanged scents, feeling pleasure in the old man's greeting.

"So long and many adventures, young Kyel," Lan murmured. "Cathar, too. Too long. Too long." She joined in their scents. "Ah, you're pleased to see me too. And, unless I'm not mistaken you two are more than friends."

"You're still the same old busybody, Lan," laughed Cathar. "Can't keep any-thing from you."

"I'm pleased," said, Lan looking at the rest of the group. "Lethnal, Rasnal, join us. The guard here will take the animals."

As the perac were led away, the five of them moved up the steps towards a tall, dark-haired woman waiting at the entrance to the castle.

"Welcome. Welcome to Regulus," called Regna. "So pleased to see you, Kyel, and Cathar. You've grown a lot since I last saw you."

"Much time has passed, Regna," said Kyel as they touched. "We all have changed."

"Indeed," she said. "Now come inside and we'll continue our welcome in comfort."

"This room has seen many gatherings over the years." Regna nodded to the young server, who quietly slipped a tray of pastries on the low table. "Please let young Heathal know what you would like to drink and then we can relax. I hope it is not too warm with the fire, but it gets chilly in the castle, even though it's the middle of a Spring day."

"You being here, Kyel, means that Jelm is safely in Rolan and involved in the defence preparations," said Lan. "We received messages but it's far better to confirm it face to face.

"Before I go on, I should inform you that Regna is a true patriot of Ean. She governs this city now. Her consort, Heritis, has shown his real colours and sides with the enemy in Sutan.

"Ah, you will not know Jucial or Eren."

Kyel half stood as a young woman in a light blue gown and a youth entered. "No, I don't."

"You're acolytes from Sanctus, aren't you?" said Cathar. "I trained there some years ago."

"You must be Cathar then. I've been told a lot about you. And Kyel too." Jucial sat on one of the two couches aligned along the table.

Eren smiled nervously, his thin face brightening as he sat. "I don't remember you, I'm afraid. I've only been at Sanctus two years, but I have heard of you."

"Jucial is assisting Regna in administration of the city in these troubling times, while Eren is a sort of apprentice to me." Lan took a mug of beer from the server's tray and had a sip. "Mmm, the first of the day. So"—he placed the mug on the table—"a quick rundown of the hierarchy, and then we'll talk. Regna, with Jucial, operates Regulus; Brin and Jelm's offsider, Raitis look after Nebleth and Ginrel, of river people stock, administers Port Saltus. I, with Eren and Lethnal, have a sort of roving role with several other people you may know assisting.

"So, help yourselves," he gestured as plates of meat pies and roast-filled rolls arrived, "and we can talk while we eat."

Kyel bit into a fragrant pie before taking a mouthful of beer and settling into the padded back of the couch. It was time to reflect after a long journey and enjoy the company of people he had not seen for some time. He felt Cathar relaxing beside him and hoped the serious business of eating could have priority for a while.

"We've seen a lot of activity in the city, Lan," said Kyel. "I presume it's readying for the Sutanites?"

"That and enabling us to support the fighters following you. You saw what Sanctus was sending," answered Lan. "Lethnal and Brin were seeing to that force and the emptying of the hinterland for every capable person to face whatever the enemy has planned for us. Should Heritis be returning at the head of an army, then he will have much local knowledge. We must be ready.

"Now, we will be travelling to Nebleth next day to hold discussions on defending the country. Key people from the cities will meet us there."

"Uh huh." Kyel leant forward. "Then we'll see what Ean has planned and how to work in with Rolan. Well, Cathar and I are well equipped to aid you in that."

"So, young man"—Lan's scent aura showed light purples and greens of anticipation—"what have you to tell us?"

"Jelm had some words with us before we left. It is concerning the use of the

Ean fleet, as you might have expected. He's sure that Sea Holm on the west coast of Rolan can be used as a hidden base for the ships if, as we suspect, Jakus is focussed on conquering the country.

"So, depending on the planning meeting's agreement, Ean's fleet, combined with Rolan ships, will have a major role in attacking and overcoming the Sutanites."

"Yes," said Lan, "it is coming together but we know that the Sutanites, headed almost certainly by Jakus, will be very hard to defeat, even with all our combined resources."

"There's none more aware of it than myself, Lan. I travelled with him. I've seen what he can do and how ruthless he is. I'd rather be hiding in the mountains out of harm's way, but he's got to be stopped. I've had enough of his cruelty to me and people I care about, so we must fight him." Kyel felt Cathar's arm twine through his.

"From my perspective," Cathar said, "having spent four years in Rolan and being involved in the battle for Mlana Hold, I've seen how he can be stopped. Even though he had a stronger force than ours, we were able to repel him and drive him out of Rolan."

"Ah, yes, the women's scent," Lethnal added. "It may be the only thing that can defeat him."

"Why I'm here," said Cathar, "other than as a support to Kyel. Because I know the shadow scent. And I know our main weapon, the Mlana. She's grown into a fine and capable young woman."

"Anyar," Kyel said, "my niece."

"I hope I can meet her," added Eren. "She sounds interesting."

"You may yet, my boy," said Lan.

"Kyel, she is an important part of our future, as you know." Cathar gripped his hand. "Now, I've been part of the Mlana's group, training with shadow scent. I know how to use it and link in with what she does. And I will be training those scent-talented of us who can use it." She scanned the room, looking at Lethnal, Regna and Rasnal in particular.

"Me too," Jucial said, raising a hand. "I'm Sanctus-trained."

"My stocks of the Rolan cordial are at your disposal, Cathar," said Regna.

"Thank you," Cathar nodded, "they will usefully augment the supply of cordial tumblers I have with me."

"So," interrupted Lan, "an early start to Nebleth to organise our tactics for confronting our enemy."

"Assume we'll travel by barge, Lan?" asked Brin.

"Absolutely," Lan smiled at the river man, "I like to travel in comfort where I can."

"There yer go, Kyel, a barge trip, jest like yer wanted."

"Looking forward to it, Brin."

"To your quarters, then?" asked Regna. "Heathal"—she turned to the young woman at the door—"can you assist our guests to find their rooms, please?"

Lamps strategically set on the long corridor's walls lit the way for their early start. A flight of steep steps led down to the familiar odour of the Great Southern, so when Kyel accompanied Cathar out onto a stone-paved platform at the bottom of the castle he wasn't surprised to see shadowy barges moored to the bank. The river pushed through the dark space under the castle, rippling along the long sides of the low-slung ships as if eager to start them on their journey.

A blocky figure at the stern of the nearest craft waved them forward.

"Lo, Cynth," called Brin, "Pleased t' see yer. Got sum important people t' move t' Nebleth."

"Welcome, travellers," she called. "Please be aboard, carefully now. We don't want no mishap."

Kyel paused for a moment, recalling the woman from his past—a murky memory.

"C'mon lad, git along. Th' river waits fer no one." Brin pushed them towards the stern of the barge.

"Room fer four in th' stern well; th' others in th' forward cabin," said Cynth.

"Stern for me," said Kyel.

"I'll go with the women, in the bow," said Cathar. "We can usefully spend th' time."

Kyel noticed a young barge woman steadying a plank at the bow as he walked with Brin, Lan and Eren towards the stern. He paused while Cathar, followed by Regna, Lethnal, Jucial and Rasnal boarded at the far end of the long craft, before he stepped over the gunwale and found a space on the bench seat next to Brin.

"Cast off, Tishal," called Cynth to the young woman. "Me daughter," she added before she gestured to Brin, who efficiently untethered the rope holding their stern to the bank.

The barge seemed reluctant to join the river at first, then Kyel noticed a widening gap appearing and the brickwork of the castle receding.

"Hoods up," said Cynth as the barge slowly swept into the murky, rain-filled light of the morning. "Wet ride back 'ere but them's th' joys of bargin'."

The grey water was a handspan below the gunwale and Kyel was tempted to put his hand in to feel the water.

"No lad," said Brin, "yer've forgotten 'bout th' haggar? They're still in these waters."

Kyel pulled his hand back into his lap. "Did for a moment. I'd hoped those blood-sucking worms had died out. But I suppose not."

"Never forget 'em—you too, Eren," said Brin. "They were an important weapon when we defeated the Sutanite army attacking Regulus, a long while ago now. But they're still there, 'nd still deadly."

"First time I've been on a barge." Eren looked around, his short brown hair flicking about. "Not sure about all the water, though."

"Only way t' travel, me lad," said Brin.

"Kyel?"

His head snapped around to where Cynth sat in the centre of the stern holding the large tiller.

"I still hev bad dreams 'bout yer young friend, Luna 'nd how I failed her," the big woman said gruffly. "Tho it's gud t' see how yer've turned out."

"Thanks, Cynth." Kyel coughed to clear his throat at the memory. "None of us were happy with what happened so long ago, which makes it all the more important to make it right now."

"Agreed, young Kyel," Cynth growled. "This time we will. I've a lot t' make up fer."

Kyel looked along the gently sloping deck as the long craft slowly nudged into the waterfront docks not far from the Nebleth tower. The journey had been fast, even if the misty rain had persisted, and they had reached the capital by noon. Heads popped up at the bow at the sudden cessation of movement, and Tishal secured the barge to a large iron ring on the bank.

"We'll all head to the tower conference room. We have much to get through," said Lan as they stood on the pathway leading to the centre of the city.

"Heard they do a gud feed," said Brin. "Be gud t' be dry 'nd well fed."

"Kyel, how was your journey?" Cathar slipped her hand into his. "Oh, you're wet. Nice and dry in the cabin.

"Sorry," she said at his look, "but at least we had a lot of time to work with shadow scent, so it wasn't wasted."

"Good," he said as they entered the tower doors, "but I'm looking forward to being dry again."

They moved into the main hall of the tower and went to the long table, helping themselves to food and drink as more people came in.

"Everyone!" called Lan. "Please sit and let me introduce you to Cathar and Kyel, both of Ean but recently arrived from Rolan. They have news which will help in the coming war with Sutan. I suggest we hear what they have to say and apprise them of our plans.

"From this meeting we will determine what we must do to defeat the Sutanites for, make no mistake, this is the beginning of the end. What we must ensure is that it is us not the enemy who prevails."

Kyel dropped into his chair with a thump.

He lay in the dark of the bedroom high in Nebleth tower listening to the quiet breathing of his companion. Kyel briefly remembered the euphoria of their frantic lovemaking that night before the reality of the situation overcame him.

He would be part of the army that defended the port, prepared to fall back to the capital, and if necessary to Regulus, depending on the tide of battle. They would be fighting against an implacable foe with much knowledge of the layout of the cities and the country, and with powerful scent mastery. He had seen the impact of the red crystal in Jakus' hands and knew their chances of defeating the Sutanites using magnesa were slim.

But their advantage was shadow scent, a scent power unknown to the enemy. He almost gnawed through his cheek with worry knowing that his lover, Cathar, would be leading the other female scent masters into the front line of battle.

Their operations were a tactic to draw off part of the Sutanite army into a perceived easy victory. The harbour would appear to be lightly defended, with most ships having left to support Rolan, and they anticipated Jakus would divide his forces before carrying on to attack his main prize. This splitting of his forces would give a better chance for the defenders of both countries, particularly if Jakus was overconfident and not expecting the power of the Rolanites, even though it was led by an untried and untested young woman. So much rested on Anyar's shoulders and Kyel was determined to do all he could to ease her burden. He had failed to protect a friend a long time ago and he would die before that ever happened again.

He got up to peer through the slit window at the rising sun knowing no further sleep was possible.

Chapter Twenty-One

The smell of the sea was indescribable: a salty tang hiding an intriguing multitude of scents. Anyar was drawn to it in a way she had never felt before. In her short life the largest body of water had been the Great Southern in Ean with its smells of mud, reeds and rot holding many secrets within its murky waters. Intriguing though this was, the sea held much, much more. It was cleaner, as if the odours of the land and man's activities had been diluted, allowing unknown scents to permeate everything: the buildings and clothes, even the people themselves. Fish and shellfish merged with a peculiar smell of seaweed and the odours of land scoured by moving waters. She determined to investigate it further.

Their party had paused at the sight of the plains of Requist, undulating and grass-covered before them as they left the rugged hills. A faint haze drifting below a sky covered with light cloud reflected the smoke of a large city and its inhabitants.

"Might be Spring," commented Xaner, "but my hometown is still cold, and fires are lit early."

"A well spread-out city," said Jelm.

"If it wasn't for the sea and the taverns I wouldn't want to come here," said Telpher. "Drathner and I much rather the mountains: less open space, more solid somehow."

"Mountain men!" scoffed Xaner. "Where do you think we grow that fabulous barley which makes the Rolan beer you guzzle in the taverns? On the coastal plains, of course."

"There is that," agreed Drathner. "We've both travelled a lot, and there's nothing like Rolan beer."

"You men," interrupted Boidea. "Enough talk about drinking, what about moving on? The Mlana's looking a little peaky and I'll be happy to stop travelling for a while."

"Apologies, Boidea," said Xaner, "we'll keep going. Just letting those of you who haven't seen my city before get some understanding of it. Now, we'll be stopping at Lookout Hill this night. If you can see the general confusion of streets and alleys at the rear of the waterfront, then bring your eyes back to where the land rises. The large brick building at the top of the hill is the city's administration area. Being the Commander of the port, I have quarters nearby with a series of rooms to accommodate travellers.

"My partner, Sharia will be ready to put us up, hopefully with a hot meal ready. Should be there before it's too dark."

"Then, shall we?" asked Boidea.

Xaner kicked his heels into his perac's sides, and they began to move down the long slope at a fair pace.

"Again?" Anyar peered through the dimness at Vor scrabbling at the door. "Can't you let me sleep in for once?"

The animal paused before resuming pawing at the door.

"Wait for me!" She emphasised her words with a strong scent push as she got out of her bed and put on clean clothing. Sharia had taken her dirty clothes for washing on their arrival and after a quick meal directed her to a bedroom. Vor had been a hit with Sharia's teenage children and taken their attention, giving her time to assimilate the new surroundings and think on what lay ahead.

She slipped on her boots and eased open the door. "Not so fast," she hissed as Vor hurried along the corridor to the front door. It clicked open and she stood breathing in the unfamiliar scents.

The voral headed up towards a courtyard of trees and bushes while Anyar absorbed her surroundings. The sky was lightening to her left as she gazed across the city assessing the odours of the salt-laden air.

"So new, so strange," she murmured.

She heard the click of the door behind her and detected the scent of Xaner's daughter, Sovira. She was a pleasant redhead only slightly older than herself and had really hit it off with Vor the last night.

"Sorry to startle you," Sovira whispered. "I know you probably want to be on your own, but something woke me, then I heard the door click. Did Vor need to go out?"

"Yes," Anyar nodded, looking towards the obvious rustling in the bushes a short way off. "When he wants to get up, he doesn't leave me much choice."

"If you like I've got a place, a secret place," said Sovira. "Sometimes I go there just before dawn. You can see the sun rising too, and no one knows you're there. Even when they call, they can't find you."

"Yes," agreed Anyar, "I'd like that."

As Sovira walked she grabbed Anyar's hand, startling her. "C'mon, let's go before anyone else comes here. Wouldn't want them to catch us."

Anyar followed Sovira, enjoying the unusual experience of being with a person her own age and not having to think of adult things.

Sovira led Anyar to several logs standing on their ends inside a semi-circle of bushes. "Now sit and be quiet. No one can find us. We can stay here forever if you like."

A crash of branches startled them and a grinning, toothy face peered in.

"Vor!" Anyar admonished him.

"Ooh"—Sovira lifted her feet—"he's scary in the dark,"

"My best friend," said Anyar. "He likes you, too. Now go and play, Vor."

She smiled at Sovira. "I've never had a girl friend before."

"I know about you, Anyar. My Dad has told me you're important, and likely the new Mlana. But you're just a teenager, like me. Why is that?"

"Don't know. Just happened. Somehow the Mlana wanted me, saying the needs of the land must be met. When she died, she came into me, linking me to herself and her knowledge; I guess that could be why I seem to be getting older quicker than normal. Gets a bit hard sometimes. So old now, but I'm so young." She shivered with the knowledge of how responsibility was aging her. "It'd be nice to have a friend my own age...a friend like you."

"Oh," said Sovira, slipping an arm around Anyar. "Yes, let's be friends."

"Anyar!" Sadir's call startled the girls, who'd been sitting shoulder to shoulder watching the sun rising.

"Better go, Sovira."

The girls pushed through the bushes to find Anyar's mother standing nearby.

"Found a friend? Sovira, isn't it?"

"Yes," Sovira said. "I better go, too. Bye, Anyar. Bye, Vor."

Sadir hugged her daughter as they watched her leave.

"Little time to spend with you, but it's nice you've met a friend," Sadir said softly.

"Hmm." Anyar pressed into her mother's warm body.

"Another day of meeting people, discussing tactics and so on. How are you coping, Anyar?"

Anyar remained, absorbing the familiarity of her mother, not speaking for a moment or two. "Sometimes I feel I'm ready for what is to come, other times I feel so small in something so big. It's frightening, Mother."

"That's why we are here, all of us. We don't know what is ahead, we only know we'll be tested, like it or not. And that means all of us. You are not alone. We are going to see it through together. Please, my daughter, don't hold anything back from me. You are mine, and I am yours. I will do all I can to protect you, keep you safe." She squeezed Anyar tightly, enveloping her with light pastel scents of love.

The administration building windows gave unimpeded views of streets and wharves far below, wooden shutters having been opened to light the long, wide room. Anyar leant against one of the brick columns watching Vor sunning himself on the grassy slope, while the room behind her slowly filled with people.

"Anyar," said Sadir, "much as I like being outside, we had better get together with Xaner and his people. I'm thinking too that you'll need to introduce yourself, your powers to them, as the Mlana. You know, I'd prefer you to enjoy your youth like a normal girl. Maybe it's selfishness on my part: I think I'd like to enjoy having a young daughter much more than being the mother of the people's saviour."

Anyar nodded and, almost as a reflex, strengthened her scent shield when she entered the large conference room. She saw her companions mingling with people of Port Requist, with Xaner busy introducing them to a range of strangers, and she straightened her shoulders as he saw her.

"Anyar, Sadir, let me introduce you to some of the city councillors and those who have a role in the city's protection, starting with the Supervisor of Defence, Siliaster." As she nodded at the solid man with greying whiskers and thinning hair, she heard her mother advise Xaner to delay further introductions.

Xaner turned to the milling people, arm held aloft. "It has been suggested we dispense with the pleasantries and instead allow the new Mlana to lead a scent exchange, to better get to know each other."

Boidea reached Anyar's side and touched her shoulder. "Alethea was known for scent-sharing to enable all to give comfort in the belonging. But you would be aware of this," she smiled down at the young woman.

Anyar's eyes widened for a moment, then she squashed down on any betraying scents as a solid body pushed on her leg. She dropped her hand into Vor's ruff and began to hum.

The sound was picked up by those around her and amplified until the room resounded with its vibration. Scudding scents drawn from the outside air mingled with those of the building and people, visibly thickening and swirling in the space around them. The sound grew as they swayed in unison to the rhythm. The darkening scent infiltrated mouths and nostrils filling every part of their being, giving them a sense of togetherness and comfort. They were one; they were united; they would not let their companions down. Everything blurred, then softened, and the hum slowly faded away.

Anyar came to herself with a start as Vor's cold nose pushed into her hand.

"My, but you are strong, Mlana," Siliaster murmured to her. "Alethea left Rolan in good hands."

She spoke with him while Sadir and Boidea talked with others nearby. The room soon hummed with conversation.

Xaner called for the room to quieten.

"I give our welcome to the new Mlana. She and her friends are here because of the impending crisis about to be inflicted on our countries. We are here to plan for the coming invasion of Rolan and Ean by the Sutanites. It will happen, and we must be prepared."

He looked at the long table before him. "For those of you who haven't had time to view this parchment, you will see our country laid out in miniature: the mountains, the valleys, the cities and the coast. We know where the enemy will land. We know where he will attack, and we must be ready. Our forces gather as we speak.

"I'll introduce my friend from Ean: Jelm, administrator of the capital Nebleth and representing Ean on behalf of its leader, Lan."

Jelm moved next to Xaner and strengthened his scent aura, primarily showing the greys of determination and resolve.

"My thanks to your commander," he said, gazing around the room. "As Xaner said, I represent Ean on behalf of Lan. I came to not only warn of the threat from Sutan but also to work with this country to defeat the invader.

"We know the Sutanites will come past Ean's coast on their way to this country, and we are resolved to inflict as much damage to them as we can. But I believe I can safely say Jakus will be targeting magnesa yet again, so he will be focussed here, on Rolan.

"So, we will provide fleet support with our most powerful scent masters working in unison with the Mlana. There are things even Jakus does not know about us, and we must hope that this will give us the edge to destroy the ambitions of this ruthless man once and for all."

"Are you going to reveal your contingency plan, Jelm?" asked Xaner.

"I will. Having assessed the facilities of Rolan, I noticed your other port, Sea Holm."

"Not much of a port is Sea Holm," said Siliaster. "Unprotected in the rugged west coast and few facilities."

"True," Jelm agreed, "but all we need is a haven for the Eanite fleet to wait in when the Sutanites invade. We can then swoop in and harry their ships in port and aid in recovery and pursuit operations."

"That's assuming we're winning," Siliaster added.

"But we have our weapon they don't know much about," Boidea's voice boomed. "Our women's scent, shadow scent, and our new Mlana."

Anyar leant back into the comfort of her mother's body.

The meeting quickly broke into isolated groups discussing various tactics and allocating roles. Anyar heard that Telpher would be co-ordinating scent forces and their location in liaison with Boidea, while Jelm, Xaner and Siliaster would keep the port from falling into enemy hands for as long as possible. Xerrita was the Nosta contact and Drathner was the liaison point for Mlana Hold.

"I'm glad I haven't had too much to do with this," Anyar whispered to her mother. "I believe I'm meant to think through scent issues, how to use it to stop this man and follow it through. Oh, Mother, it all seems staggering."

"Right," Sadir said, putting her arm around her daughter and leading her out of the room. "We're going to see Xaner's partner, Sharia, and get her to take us to see more of Requist. It'll give you time to assimilate all this."

"Glad you could get away from the meetings," said the small vivacious woman. "Things are all so serious and I can't even get Xaner to spend time with me and the children, although they're schooling at the moment, except Sovira." Sharia bent a bright eye towards Anyar. "I believe you've met her already. She seems rather taken with you and your creature. If you find her being too much of a nuisance, let me know."

"No, I like her," said Anyar.

"Now dear, I thought I'd take you to where your father used to go in the brief time he was in the Port. Look out!"

They had entered a wide, busy street near the waterfront with carts and pack animals moving goods in a continuous stream along the thoroughfare, and it was difficult to cross. Workmen were piling barricades of timber and stone at intervals, which made the traffic even more congested.

"Ah!" Sharia pointed ahead of them. "The Sailors Rest, that's what we want." She glanced down disapprovingly at a movement near Anyar's feet. "You should keep that animal under control, dear."

Vor kept his snout almost on Anyar's heels as they manoeuvred their way through the throng, a vague shimmer around his form.

"He's fine," Anyar answered as they came through a relatively quieter section and slipped onto a bench seat outside the wooden structure; several groups of sailors nursed mugs that gave off rich, malty scents.

"You wait here, and I'll get us something to eat and drink. Won't be long," Sharia smiled, and disappeared in through the stained wooden door.

"My, she doesn't draw breath." Sadir hugged Anyar. "Still, it's nice to get out into the sun. Our first real taste of Port Requist."

Anyar twisted her fingers through Vor's ruff as she watched all the activity around her. *This,* she thought, *this is what it's all about. People should be able to live their lives without someone wanting to change it, to impose their own view on others. Yes, that's what it's about.*

Vor grunted, then lifted his head in anticipation as Sharia pushed through the door with a large tray.

"Drinks, food, and a bone for your, er, voral." She plonked the tray on the table. "One way to get him to like me."

Chapter Twenty-Two

"On the move again," said Bilternus, as he rode beside Piltarnis on the dusty road, "this time as part of a massive army. I've never seen so many people and their baggage together at one time. Even when we went to attack Rolan years ago we went with far, far less."

"I was lucky not to have been involved then. Your father left me at the estates, for which I was eternally grateful," Piltarnis squinted behind him through the clouds of dust. "This time I can't get out of it so I might as well appreciate the experience."

"I hope we do, but I doubt it. I know the natives will not let Jakus have his way, so we'll be in for a hard fight. Still, if we have time in Southern Port, we may get a moment or two to enjoy ourselves."

Piltarnis looked at Bilternus, eyebrow raised. "Ah, you have some plans?"

Bilternus remembered a dalliance he had had with the very feminine Sencia and clamped down on his scents before looking at his companion. "I think we'll be too busy to scratch ourselves, unfortunately. Say what you like about Jakus, he's an effective organiser and we'll be expected to do our part."

The exodus from the capital had begun in earnest with all portions of the army proceeding to assembly points in Southern Port and Semplar, Sutan's other port. Jakus' ships, including those won from Brastus, were to take the substantial army to subdue and occupy Rolan and Ean. Over twenty ships from both ports with guardsmen, scent masters with skills augmented by the red crystal and sailors made up the powerful invasion force. Bilternus couldn't help feeling sorry for the enemy, essentially peaceful people about to bear the brunt of Jakus' ambitions.

One of the biggest problems on arrival in Southern Port was the logistics of catering for the force he had taken command of. Fortunately, Sharna had it under control. The energetic redhead had sequestered many areas throughout the city to assemble the supplies and equipment needed, as well as accommodation for the army. Bilternus was happy to leave Piltarnis in charge of bivouacking their people while he headed to the wharf area to report to Sharna.

S harna was in the Harbour Master's office, surrounded by people and frantic activity. She glanced up from a table full of parchments as he entered.

"Ah, a friendly face. Trust you've found your people the place they've been allocated?" She waved him over. "Wait for a moment or two, then we'll go to Jakus' compound. There'll be a tactical meeting there later this day."

Bilternus moved to a corner while she issued orders to a few people who then hurried away. The Harbour Master, a grizzled white-haired man, looked up briefly as Sharna spoke to him. "Please advise the Shada I'm doing all I can. Barring accidents, all ships will soon be fully provisioned and available."

"Come, Bilternus, we'll go while there's a lull." Sharna came over to him, briefly exchanged scents before leading him out of the door and into the busy thoroughfare.

"From the sound of the fighting, I was better off here." She looked over at Bilternus as they dodged and weaved through the traffic of carters and carriers, some pulling carts or leading wide-horned pack beasts through the streets and lanes of the wharf district.

"I'm pleased it's over although I was lucky enough to be away from the fighting, having joined Heritis' forces, led by Rancer."

"Yes, I know of him; he's spent most of his time in Ean, if I recall. I think he will be a competent arms commander." Sharna turned into the main road leading towards Jakus' compound.

Bilternus watched her out of the corner of his eye, seeing the familiar scent aura of greys and pastels indicating purpose and practicality. He took a deep breath, touched her shoulder, and took her off the road to one of the ubiquitous taverns serving beer and wine. "Can we stop for a moment?"

Sharna paused, looking at him quizzically, then nodded. "I don't think the Shada will begrudge us a quick refreshment." They sat on two stools against a long wooden plank table.

Bilternus signalled the barman and observed the crowded thoroughfare while waiting for the beers. When the server had gone, he took a sip, eyeing Sharna over the top of his mug.

"I've a secret," he said in a rush of air, "and I can't tell anyone."

Sharna took a mouthful of beer as her eyebrows rose.

"I mean, it's unbelievable. Anyone hearing me would think I'm addled."

"So?" she asked. "Why here? Why now?"

"We have a long history together and I know you're practical and have the interests of Sutan at heart. And you support its rule, therefore the Shada."

Sharna watched Bilternus closely.

"So, I know something I want to share. It could affect Jakus, but I can't tell him about it."

"What? You want me to tell him instead?"

"No, it's not that. I just want you to be aware, to be on the lookout for it. I'm under a lot of pressure because of this."

"Enough, Bilternus. What is it?"

"It's my father. He's not who he seems."

"Oh." Sharna signalled for another beer. "We'll likely be meeting him with the Shada and others shortly. What is it you want me to look for?"

"Now comes the truly unbelievable part. Do you remember Septus?"

"Yes, of course. He died in the battle for Ean, when the rebels overthrew us, years ago now."

"Well, it seems he didn't. He's still around and lives inside my father's head. Wait!" Bilternus put a hand on Sharna's arm as she started to rise from her stool. "I'm not mad. I know this. He revealed himself to me only days ago."

"Damn, Bilternus, you do stretch our friendship." Sharna wiped the froth off the new beer. "If I didn't know you..."

"So, you see why I can't say anything. I know my father and it's not him, inside him. While it appears to be my father when Septus wants it to be, Faltis is not Faltis."

"Fine, I'll accept that there's something happening, but Septus is a fair stretch," said Sharna, draining her mug. She held it for a moment, as if thinking of ordering another, then banged it onto the table. "So, what do you want me to do?"

"Nothing, just be aware. Septus is there for a reason. He's waiting. So, we'll have to wait too. Be ready for whatever he's planning."

"Bloody scarthas, Bilternus, you really do make difficult things even more difficult," Sharna sighed. "If I didn't know you so well..."

"Sorry Sharna, but I had to tell someone I trust." Bilternus looked down into his beer mug.

"Finish up," said Sharna, patting him on the back. "Let's go and see what the Shada is planning."

The room in the compound was well-appointed, dark red hangings partially covering stone walls, comfortable padded armchairs spaced out with small tables at their arms. A large oval table occupied prime position in the centre of the wooden floor.

The Shada was standing, wine glass in one hand, the other massaging his side, a large parchment occupying the entire surface of the table taking his attention. At his shoulder was his army commander, Kast, with his arm in a sling, together with Heritis, while Faltis was a step back sipping from a glass and watching the group. Crastus and Tibitus, the ship captains, were further away, looking at the parchment and murmuring in low voices.

Jakus glanced their way as they entered and signalled to Sharna to join him, before returning to his study of the parchment.

"Bilternus!" exclaimed Poegna, "Welcome. Come with me. You've met Festern?"

The tall, heavily built man with greying hair stood and nodded. "Pleased to see you, young man. Been a while since I've been here, at the Port."

They exchanged scents as they sat and took a filled bread from the tray proffered by Poegna. "No wine," said Bilternus to the young server who stood by Poegna's side. "Why are you here, Festern? I thought you'd have been with your force at Semplar."

"No, once my people from the northern steppes were on the way to Semplar, I left my sons in charge and headed here to co-ordinate plans with the Shada. I'll rejoin them once we're at sea."

"I assume that's what they're doing?" Bilternus gestured to the table.

"Yes, Jakus is working on the deployment of his fleet; that's why Crastus and Tibitus are there. The parchment is a map of the known world."

"Leave it for a moment," said Poegna as Bilternus made to get up. "Take the opportunity to eat. The Shada will call us when he's ready."

Bilternus sat back and ate before noticing a familiar figure in the opposite corner of the room. "Poegna," he hissed, "that's Dronthis, Vitaris' former captain. What's he doing here? I thought Jakus might have got rid of him."

"Jakus decided that he was too valuable and redirected his loyalties as only my Lord can do."

The big man looked over as if aware they were talking about him and glared.

"Well, if you're sure about that." Bilternus took another bite of his bread.

Bilternus was feeling the effects of the food when Jakus called out, his expansive aura dominated with reds and dull yellows.

"Join us. Familiarise yourselves with my plans for the conquest of Ean and Rolan."

Soon they were standing around the composite map showing the positions of the three countries. Bilternus noticed that Dronthis stood with Kast and Faltis before he turned his attention to the table.

Jakus glanced around the room before grabbing a long, thin stick and tapping the parchment on the far right.

"This map outlines the existing layout of my lands, showing it lying to the southeast of my future dominions of Ean and Rolan. The wastelands and mountainous regions which separate Sutan from Ean and Rolan have kept them relatively free from our expansion plans. That, plus the prevailing winds, even at this time of the year, necessitate a lengthy westerly voyage to reach them.

"But no longer. Sutan is united in its purpose and prepared to bring both of those countries under my rule. I now have the people, the ships and the power to achieve that goal.

"My sea captains, led by Kast, will co-ordinate the movement of my army. Sharna, our fleet commander, assures me our ships are ready to receive our forces. Festern, I've had word your people are in Semplar, so they will be ready to sail once ordered.

"Heritis, my true and loyal friend, will be second to me in command of the army.

"We have organised the disposition of our forces within the vessels so that there are no weak areas. For, be assured, the enemy will put up a fight, so we must be prepared for any eventuality."

He directed his attention to Bilternus, who squared his shoulders and waited. "Ah, the double-crosser's son! Know that no such taint exists on you. You, I have high hopes for now you're in charge of your estate's forces. Continue to show your loyalty and intelligence, and you will achieve more than your father ever did."

"Yes, Shada," Bilternus answered, his attention on Faltis standing near Jakus. A flash of red from his father's eyes reminded him of what lurked within the man.

Jakus' focus was on the map. He dragged his pointer in a long line to the left. "Therefore, we will sail west, the first destination being Ean, and an easy enough conquest considering we know that land well and we have our magnesa.

"Further west we have Rolan, a country never before conquered." He moved the stick higher, to the northwest. "For few would ever want such a mountainous land with so few resources. That is until now. Now I want this land!" He raised his pointer for emphasis. "Our last foray into Rolan achieved much, giving me significant supplies of the red crystal.

"This time we will be even better prepared, a larger force and well trained in magnesa use. I will overcome whatever they can raise against me. The Mlana managed to resist us before, but she is dead, her women and those men who are foolish enough to support her are disorganised. All they can now raise against us is a girl, the supposed new Mlana. No contest.

"I will subjugate that country, take all of their magnesa and enslave the people."

Jakus paused and took a large swallow of wine. Everyone was watching the map as the pointer traced the intended direction of the fleet and ended up at Rolan. Bilternus saw Faltis shifting from leg to leg and wondered if it was him or the creature inside him.

"Brother," Faltis said, breaking the silence, "I have come into some intelligence which I wish to impart to prove my value to your cause."

"What?" Jakus looked up.

"Knowledge of that country and information the natives have tried to keep from you."

"What are you talking about, Faltis?" Jakus' aura darkened.

"Have you heard of the crystal cave?"

"The crystal cave? No." A spasm ran down the side of his face.

"It is rumoured there is a secret in Mlana Hold, a secret they will do anything to keep outsiders from knowing. It's the crystal cave; a cave full of magnesa, so rich that it can give them unheard-of power, allowing them to delve into the intricacies of scent manipulation in ways unknown to us. The power contained in this cave will allow the owner to rule all."

"What?" Jakus' eyes widened. "And you have just decided to tell me this?"

"No brother, no!"

Bilternus saw a crafty creature lurking within his father, luring Jakus with his revelation.

"I was badly injured during the expedition to Rolan. It's only now I've remembered what I overheard during the fight in Mlana Hold. Only now I've managed to make sense of it. For that, I apologise." Faltis bent forward, shoulders slumped.

Jakus glowered as he thought, purple scent aura flickering with stabs of yellow. The room was silent for a long moment.

"It is well I kept you alive then, brother." Jakus peered at the portion of the map featuring Rolan. "An even greater prize than I was anticipating."

Faltis sighed and stepped back from the table.

Bilternus nodded slowly to Sharna's questioning gaze before looking over the assembled group.

He noticed something strange. Their scents were vastly different after Faltis' revelation: Jakus showed a domination of green and yellow in his powerful purplish aura; Heritis' was similar but to a lesser extent, while the rest were more neutral. He quickly clamped down on his own somewhat negative feelings before he glanced at Faltis. If Jakus saw the man's aura now, he would have been extremely wary, for Faltis' aura was shot through with scarlets and light purples, showing anticipation and anger.

When his father saw Bilternus watching, he quickly snapped off his scent display before allowing a slow smile to slide across his twisted face.

Chapter Twenty-Three

Kyel leant into Lan's embrace, feeling an aching sense of loss to the very depths of his soul. If anyone had filled the role of his mentor, it was this man. He had been there when Kyel was re-united with Sadir and Targas following the defeat of the Sutanites. He'd provided support as Kyel had tried to reconcile with the torture and murder of his friend Luna, and willingly aided Targas in training him to be an able scent master and man.

Targas was now dead, having sacrificed his life for his adopted people and leaving Kyel with recriminations of never having said to him what he truly felt. But Lan was still here, loving him without rancour, without judgement for the mistakes of his youth, and now he was leaving.

There was no hiding one's feeling in the true exchange of scents. He knew Lan was leaving Ean out of a sense of duty and doing so willingly. Kyel stepped back. Lan smiled, his lined face lit with an inner light, and placed a hand on Kyel's arm.

"I know how you feel, and I couldn't have put my trust in a more reliable man." Lan scanned the people around him. "Again, I am sorry to leave you, to travel away at this desperate time, but it is necessary. If our plans come to fruition, we'll meet again in happier circumstances."

"Can't believe I'm going too," added Eren. "Only a short while ago I did my first barge trip, now it's the sea. Hope I don't get sick."

"You'll get used to it, Eren. I know I did," said Kyel. "Please give my niece my love when you see her."

"Eren, there is a good reason for you to come, at the very least to support me," added Lan. Now, my friends…" He lifted his arms to clasp the shoulders of Kyel and Lethnal and as Cathar, Brin, Eren and Rasnal linked to them they began to hum. The sound grew, building into a rhythm, forcing odours into the air around them until the sun seemed to dim in response. The scents appeared to flow though the group, bringing a sense of belonging, of oneness to them all.

Slowly the sound faded, leaving a feeling of peace. Kyel saw the light pastels of Lan's scent aura reflecting his sadness and concern and hoped that this wasn't a final farewell.

Lan turned towards Ginrel, the administrator of Port Saltus standing a short distance away, and walked over, his staff rapping on the wooden planking. Eren, tall and slender, walked alongside the scent master, looking back at Kyel with wide eyes before the trio headed towards a two-masted ship with people milling around its wharf side.

Kyel watched Lan, Ginrel and Eren board the ship, wishing the old scent master could have stayed to help them against the Sutanite invaders, even though he saw the sense in his sailing to Rolan with the small Eanite fleet. Lethnal would lead the defenders now, being a capable and powerful scent master with an able backup of responsible and seasoned people. He squeezed Cathar's hand as he realised that he was now one of those seasoned people and would be relied upon to defend his country.

They waited, watching while the gangways were drawn on board and each of the seven ships slowly moved from their berths and into the harbour. The clack of the oars of the small boats towing the two-masted sailing ships came faintly to their ears even as the smell of the Great Southern river's waters merging with the sea rolled across their nostrils.

"Seven ships," mused Brin. "Seven ships, leaving us with only five t' defend against th' might of th' Sutanite fleet. Doesn't seem rite."

"Ah, but necessary, dear Brin," said Lethnal, "for our plan to work. If we don't manage to split the invasion fleet, then it'll all be in vain. But I have a feeling…"

"Me too," he answered, "'nd it's fer food. All this action's makin' me hungry."

"The Salted Arms?" suggested Kyel. "That's where the others will be eating."

"Me favourite place," Brin growled. "Never too earlier fer a beer neither."

"Brin," laughed Cathar. "Shall we?" She pulled at Kyel's arm.

They pushed open the doors of the tavern and walked into a wall of noise, even at this early hour of the day. The large room, lit by long opaque windows, smelt of beer, spirits and spicy fried foods; people were sitting around the small, timeworn tables or at the bar, some eating, some drinking. Mar, a thin wizened woman, looked up from pouring liquid into a mug at the bar as they entered. Her face broke into a grin, and she gestured with her head to a place further into the room.

They threaded through the crowds to find a large table at the back of the room with two of the seats already occupied with familiar faces.

"Ah," asked Cynth, "they've gone then?"

"Yes," Lethnal nodded, "they've left on the tide."

"Time t' fill me belly," suggested Brin, as he squeezed along the back wall.

"Not much room for you, Brin," Rasnal said with a chuckle. "Sure you need to add to your girth?"

"Now I'm hurt," he replied. "Ah, here's Mar."

"At Ginrel's favourite table," she said brightly. "S'pose 'e got off alrite?"

"They did, Mar," said Lethnal. "Now what have you on offer?"

"Th' usual, tho we hev pies this day, meat 'nd onion. "Course we hev toast, breads, eggs, fish 'nd so on. I cud bring a selection. Drinks: teas, beer, wine and milk, fer th' young-un."

"Mar," said Tishal, "I'm no young-un no more."

"Fair 'nough," Mar said, bobbing her head to Cynth's daughter, "not with this war comin'. Whatever yer want then."

They ordered, and when Mar left talk turned to the sailing of the Ean fleet and its destination.

"Lotta our fighters left on them ships," said Brin, "it's goin' t' make our task more difficult."

"We'll be ready," said Lethnal. "We've got time. As we know, if the plan works, we can defend against a smaller Sutanite force."

"Knowing Jakus, he'll see us as weak. He'll not want to spend much time attacking Ean until he's got Rolan defeated," said Kyel. "Though Heritis is a worry."

"Do yer think 'e'll cum back, t' Ean?" asked Cynth, "now 'e's finally left?"

"One thing I learnt about Jakus is that he'll use anyone he can. I bet Heritis will be back."

"Food's here," said Cathar, seeing two servers coming with a pile of steaming plates. "A much nicer topic."

"Thought I'd find you here." A short, round-faced man stopped at their table. "Grefnel, I wondered when we'd run in' t' yer," Brin grinned. "Jest as well we've finished eatin' as yer news don't look gud." He turned to Kyel. "Yer mightn't know Grefnel, lad. He's in charge of th' Port now Ginrel's left."

"Good day," Kyel nodded at the scent master. "Do you know my consort, Cathar?"

"No, but I have heard of you," he said, his face bright. "I know Lethnal and Rasnal too, plus you barge people. Can I sit?"

His polite request didn't really need an answer, but with Brin's gruff, "Well yer make the place look disorg'nised standin'," he took a chair, looked round the table, and spoke. "Beating with fair winds should have them in Rolan in several days or so, but that's not what I want to say. We've had news from a trader in this day. The Sutanite fleet was preparing to sail; can't be long before they're here. Reckon no more than ten days. We had better get moving; lots to do and lots to prepare."

"Too gud t' last," huffed Brin, and pushed at the table.

Lethnal stood. "We should continue this discussion at the administrator's house, Grefnel. That's near the barracks, for those of you who don't know."

"Agreed." Grefnel shook his head as he waited for everyone to stand. "You know, I'm missing Ginrel already, as he's the man for a crisis. Still, he's one of the best scent masters in Port Saltus, and what he doesn't know about shipping isn't worth knowing. I see why Lan took him to command the ships. Doesn't make my job any easier, though.

"You all ready?"

They hurried out of the tavern, noting that the place had cleared as if word had already gotten out of the impending arrival of the Sutanites.

If they had thought the tavern was busy, then the area around the barracks several streets back from the wharfs was chaotic. Squads of guardsmen and soldiers were running off on different missions, streets and alleyways being barricaded with wood and stone, and all buildings heavily fortified. Lethnal had sent word for all squad leaders and scent master co-ordinators to meet at the administrator's house, but that didn't prepare them for the density of people when they arrived.

They moved into a large room inside the headquarters, together with those having most responsibility for the defence of Port Saltus. Lethnal and Grefnel stood in front of a whitewashed wall with a plan of the city and surrounds outlined on its surface. Several wide windows were opened for ventilation as the crowd grew.

Lethnal held up a hand and the room quietened. Kyel slipped his arm around Cathar's waist and waited for the leader to speak.

She briefly outlined the reasoning behind the departure of most of their ships to Rolan and the fact that Lan was sailing to co-ordinate the defence activities of both countries. Whether or not the ploy to divide the Sutanite invasion force worked, the Eanite defenders would still have a fight on their hands, with the Port being the first point of attack. Lethnal took up a long pointer and tapped the diagram of Port Saltus.

"First point of attack. First point of defence. We know it and the enemy knows it, whether it is Heritis leading the assault or not. We must assume that the Port will be the first stage in the plan to take the capital, Nebleth. That is where we will have our main concentration of forces. But we will make it hard for them to gain ground." Her gaze pierced the crowd, and a grey aura of conviction reinforced her authority.

"So, what advantages do we have?"

Kyel listened as a strategy was outlined. The remaining five ships were almost certainly sacrificial victims to the Sutanite attack, but if they could take out an equal number of ships then they would have done their job. The river people would be using their barges to good effect, and the defences by the scent masters were significant aspects in the resistance of the Port; an orderly retreat to Nebleth with many obstacles and much harrying of the enemy would also play a significant part.

It wasn't long before Lethnal dismissed the people, allowing leaders to co-ordinate their people and prepare them for the forthcoming conflict. Once all but a selected few had gone, she ordered the doors to be closed.

A table was set up and seats placed around it to allow those remaining to view the diagram of Port Saltus.

Lethnal sat on the seat closest to the wall so she could use the pointer. Kyel knew all those who joined them, including Grefnel, and was slightly puzzled why no one else had been included in the smaller meeting.

"Welcome all," Lethnal smiled at them, "you might be wondering why you're all here. Simple really, other than your leadership roles, of course. Whatever we decide has a chance of getting back to the enemy. Heritis has many friends here and good information networks. So, we've made no mention of our secret weapon, shadow scent, and any detail of what we may have to do to defeat, or at the very least hold off the enemy." She reached out with her pointer and tapped the docks.

"This will be where the Sutanites attack, as the flow of the Great Southern River is too strong to easily overcome, and the docks are where it's easiest to make landfall."

Cathar raised a hand. "Is this where you anticipate using shadow scent, or would it be tipping our hand?"

"As one of the leaders, Cathar, you would have to be using normal scent interspersed with shadow scent. There will be a lot happening to keep the invaders occupied." She looked for the next raised hand. "Grefnel."

"Thanks, Lethnal," said the small man, looking not at their leader, but at the diagram of the Port. "You can see how the concentration of the Port's facilities are on the western bank; all shipping and most warehousing is there. This is due, of course, to the depth of the port and the sweep of the river. Yet on the eastern, shallower bank, we have some warehousing and many barges—their low draught allows for this."

"So...me?" Brin regarded Grefnel. "Thanks. A few of us, co-ordinated by meself, Cynth 'nd Tishal here will use th' barges in a pincer movement to trap the enemy's vessels against the docks, when the tide is right of course."

"So, how are you going to keep them there?" asked Kyel. "They'd be aware that could happen, especially if Heritis is their leader."

"Back to me, Brin," said Lethnal. "We have a number of strategies which we won't go into now, but if the Sutanite power, augmented by magnesa, is as great as we think it might—and Kyel's experience gives us food for such a thought—then our ultimate weapon is fire."

"Yes," added Brin, "a sacrifice of barges but hopefully not people, if it cums t' it."

"Is it possible the fire could get out of control?" asked Rasnal.

"Yes, especially if th' wind's goin' in th' wrong direction."

"But Port Saltus could burn?"

"A chance we'll have to take," said Lethnal. "After all, if we are fighting for our very survival and it looks like the best way to get an advantage, or at least deprive the enemy of an asset, we will let Port Saltus burn."

Kyel shuddered as his imagination painted horrendous scenes of a conflagration pushing flames and smoke high into the sky and everything burning around him. He immediately stilled his face and released his tightening grip on Cathar, resolving not to predict what might happen when so much uncertainty surrounded him and those he cared for.

Chapter Twenty-Four

The command ship was large, and unlike other ships in the fleet, had three masts—a mainmast, foremast, and mizzenmast—to give it manoeuvrability, and the capacity to carry significant quantities of troops and equipment. Formerly Brastus' command ship, Jakus had been quick to appropriate the vessel, with its well-appointed captain's cabin linked to a meeting room capable of comfortably holding many people. The surrounding officers' cabins were not as cramped as cabins in the two-masted vessels, making it the most desirable of the fleet's ships.

Sailors were already working on the rigging as Bilternus came aboard, bringing his pack with him. The crack of a sail above his head drew his attention skyward at a topsail being unfurled as the wind picked up. The rigging on this big ship was a forest of cobwebs, making him wonder how the men knew what went where.

"You're in luck, Bilternus," called Sharna's cheery voice, "you've got an aft cabin. You only must share with one other, not like those in the forecastle."

"Not the Shada?" he asked before he thought.

"Ha!" laughed Sharna, "nor your father, either. The important people have larger cabins. You're with Dronthis. Expect the Shada wants you to keep an eye on him during the voyage."

Bilternus thought how he would rather have been with Piltarnis and the troops from their estates than here, on the command ship, with a man under suspicion like Dronthis, but he quickly clamped down on his betraying scents.

"Knew you wouldn't be happy, but Dronthis is not all bad. Might even be a good person to have on your side, if you get what I mean."

"Yes, Sharna, thanks. Who else is here?"

"Let me see. Tibitus will captain the flagship, and apart from you and me, the Shada and Faltis, there's Kast and Poegna. Heritis will be on the ship he brought from Ean, with Crastus captaining. They'll co-ordinate the second half of the fleet from there.

"Appreciate the update, Sharna. You know my troop leader, Piltarnis, is on Heritis' ship. It's the two-master further down the wharf." He looked down the row of ships stretching along the wooden wharf like rocks in a sea of ants. "We'll need to communicate during the voyage."

"There'll be opportunities, Bilternus," said Sharna. "At the very least we'll use scent, since the Shada is powerful enough to bend the sea to his will."

Bilternus could see the conviction in Sharna's face as she spoke and felt a trickle of unease down his spine. He realised even those closest to him could not be fully relied upon, and hoped the diminutive woman's blind obedience to Jakus would not prove to be her undoing.

H e was relieved to finally be on board, having endured days of training with the scent masters, led by Jakus and Heritis. The use of magnesa had at first been thrilling, even euphoric, with Jakus driving the scent-talented to work as part of a team to not only thwart any attack by the defenders but to aid in attacking measures. He'd known about the use of acidic scents to eat away living flesh and organic structures such as wood and cloth by pushing blankets of corrosive odours across their targets, but adding resilience to these blankets was different. Jakus seemed fixated on making sure that nothing could disrupt these weapons, concerned by such a use in their past when attacking Rolan.

What made the training worse was the Shada's habit of individually testing people to ensure their understanding of scent usage and control, and to check their loyalty to him. He had seen Dronthis taken away and not return until the following day. Then it had been his turn.

The interrogation room was down a series of dimly lit steps into a windowless room with little residual scent, as if it had been scrubbed free. Two wooden chairs were all that occupied the space but the presence of iron manacles on the wall added an ominous feel. Anyone led down there couldn't help but feel nervous.

Jakus had sat opposite and with little warning inserted a scent tendril through Bilternus' nose and into his smell centre. He strove to keep his thoughts neutral while experiencing a curiously skittering within his brain, knowing that Jakus was testing for any sign of deceit.

He remembered the old soothsayer, Xerina, using women's scent on him to help protect him from revealing any negative thoughts from such an interrogation. The sweat trickling down his neck had seemed to betray him as he waited for the investigation to end.

"Get back to training," grunted Jakus. He limped up the steps favouring his old injuries, leaving Bilternus exhausted on his seat.

B ilternus' introspection was broken by the thump of feet on the deck above his head. He quickly rose from his small bunk to busy himself putting his gear into the small wooden box at the end of the bed. A rap at the door revealed Piltarnis.

"Sorry to come to your cabin but I need to report on our readiness."

"No, that is not a problem, a relief in fact. I had thought it was my roommate."

"I can see you aren't happy about that."

"Dronthis!" Bilternus spat.

"Oh, I think I'd rather be with the troops, then." Piltarnis smiled crookedly. "Easier than being in charge."

"You must be more on your toes, that's for certain. Now, let me check with Sharna and then we can probably use the meeting room while the Shada's not on board.

Bilternus popped his head up to see Sharna on the aft deck in deep discussion with several people. He waved until she saw him.

"What?"

"Need to use the Shada's meeting room. Is that alright?"

"Yes!"

"And do we still sail next day?"

"Expect to sail on the ebb tide, so yes, unless the Shada changes his orders." Sharna smiled before turning back to her discussions.

"We've some quiet time, Piltarnis. Best use it well." Bilternus led him to the meeting room. He turned to face his troop commander and head scent master as the door closed.

"This is something, Bilternus," the young man said, scanning the room. The wooden fittings glowed with polish and lacquer, giving a richness that imbued the atmosphere with a sense of power that would not allow challenge. Thick hangings of a red velvet fell to a plush green carpet which seemed to grab and hold the carved chairs set around a heavy dark table; a parchment map, like that in Jakus' compound was spread across its surface. "Really something," he repeated.

I agree," Bilternus said. "But we haven't long to enjoy it. Let's have a drink as we go over our plans." He glanced at the closed door before pouring two glasses of a rose-coloured wine. "The map," he pointed with his glass.

The parchment, which they had last seen in Jakus' compound, showed the three countries laid out geographically, Ean to the west of Sutan separated by mountains and wastelands, then the mountainous Rolan even further westward. A motif illustrating wind direction showed the prevailing winds they would be countering on their voyage.

"Even though I don't claim to be a sailor, it's obvious we'll be in for a long voyage with all the tacking required."

"That we will," Bilternus agreed. "And I don't know whether we will be taking part in the invasion of Ean or continuing to Rolan. I'm certain the Shada has his plans, but we must be ready to react at a moment's notice.

"So, we are ready? Nothing more we should be concerned about?"

"Yes, Bilternus." Piltarnis then updated him on the deployment of their troops, supplies and equipment as they scanned the intricacies of the map before them.

"Something's worrying you, Piltarnis. Is it anything that will affect us?" Bilternus watched the young man's scent aura fade to light pastels, yet with flickers of bright yellow and red running through it.

Piltarnis put his glass onto the side of the table, snatched a glance to the closed door before speaking.

"The Shada," he shuddered briefly, "took me aside, down into his rooms. He invaded me. No," He held up a hand, "not what you'd expect but deeper. I, uh, felt unclean, as if I had a secret he needed to know. It wasn't right, Bilternus. It wasn't right."

"What did he do? Did he ask you anything at all?"

"It was about your father. He's worried about something to do with Faltis. Though why he'd dig into my memories, I don't know, when he had already ensured my loyalty after the battle. He could're just tested him direct. Anything come out when you went through it?" Piltarnis took his glass and gulped some wine.

"No," said Bilternus, briefly wondering whether he should reveal the protection Xerina had given him. "No, nothing," he reiterated, realising that this was a secret he should keep.

The door opened and Sharna poked her head through. "Thought you'd still be here, Bilternus. The Shada's coming, so it might be good if you, Piltarnis, can head back to your ship, carry out any last-minute things. We sail on the ebb tide next day."

Bilternus put his arm around his commander's shoulders and led him past Sharna and up the stairs. "We'll meet on the docks first thing, then if all is fine the next time we catch up we'll be nearing Ean, I expect."

The young man nodded and hurried down the gangway.

The day started out grey and overcast, a dry dust rolling from the deserts in the northwest. Most had loose strips of cloth tied across their faces, giving them an air of menace as the ships, towed by small rowing tenders, slowly moved into the harbour. The waters, muddied by the outflow of the Grosten River, grew clearer as the tide eased them into their journey. Soon the rows of buildings behind the wharves became indistinct and joined the solemnness of the day.

Bilternus pressed his backside into the railing on the aft deck, keeping an eye on the three black forms in front of him. Faltis, the more skeletal, almost dangled over the rail, looking shoreward as the vessels moved into the harbour; Heritis, more upright stood with Jakus looking towards the sea and the direction of their journey. Without seeing his dark aura, Bilternus knew the Shada would be reflecting on his conquests and his need to crush all those who stood in his way. The man was easy to read from where he stood, and he resolved to keep out of his notice for as long as he could.

Sharna saw Bilternus from the corner of her eye and smiled.

"This is it. We are on our way at last. What an adventure, eh?"

"That's one thing to call it."

"Don't be negative, Bilternus. We will come out of this stronger than ever. A golden era of prosperity awaits us. Let's enjoy it while we can." She placed a warm hand on his shoulder. "Make the best of it. I know I will."

He caught sight of a large figure standing quietly down on the main deck, alone and silent. Dronthis was a hard man to read, but Bilternus knew whatever his concerns were, the former captain to Vitaris would have more. *What a person to share a cabin with,* he thought.

The dust followed them out to sea, making a spectral scene of the ships with their spidery masts and dull wooden hulls. With the small rowing boats and their crew safely on board, the ships were now on their own, rolling in the swells, their pennants fluttering from mainmasts in the light breeze. The vessels gravitated towards the command ship, forming a cluster of ships, eager to unfurl their sails and begin their adventure.

Jakus had disappeared down to the meeting room with Heritis, Kast, Faltis and the captain, Tibitus. Sharna was at the helm with a scent master Bilternus recognised as Tretial, a stalwart man who had been with him during the last expedition to Rolan. Pleased to have another familiar face, he turned to watch as the vessels of the fleet took up station on their ship.

"Fifteen ships here, including us," he murmured, shaking his head, "a lot to bring death to Ean and Rolan."

"Bilternus," called Sharna, "come and meet Tretial. You remember him, of course?"

"Of course," said Bilternus as he approached the helm. "We spent some time together, on the previous trip."

"Good to see you again, Bilternus," said the solid scent master, exchanging scents with him. "Hope we have a good voyage. Last time there were some rough days, if I recall."

"Yes, don't want to go through such weather this time."

"The wind's picking up and when the Shada has finished with Heritis, and he's returned to his ship, we'll sail," said Sharna, looking up towards the rising sun.

"Do we know if we're still meeting the ships from Semplar, Sharna?" asked Bilternus.

"Word is that they've sailed, and we'll rendezvous off the coast in a day or two. That way the full complement of ships will be twenty-one. More than enough for what the Shada plans, I feel." She turned abruptly as a group of people emerged from below decks.

155

Jakus walked with Heritis to the rope ladder leading down to a small boat bobbing alongside talking in quiet tones. Faltis came up the several steps onto the helm deck looking blankly through his son before taking a place on the rails on the port side.

Bilternus mentally shrugged, determined to enjoy the sailing adventure without concerning himself with what others thought.

The clack of oars from the boat taking Heritis to his ship broke through his introspection. He watched the Shada come up the steps and move next to Tibitus, his captain who had had already displaced Sharna from the helm. Jakus followed Heritis' progress until he reached his ship, before he nodded to a sailor standing high on the main mast watch platform.

A flag opened in the strengthening breeze, crimson and strong. Sails unfurled over the ships in response and the fleet began to move away from the coast on its voyage of conquest.

Bilternus shivered and looked at Jakus leaning forward, his face an elated grimace as the command ship juddered at the release of the sails, eager to be on the way.

He wondered what lay in the future for him and those around him. Nothing was certain, other than the reality that many people would die. "Maybe," he murmured, "that would be an easy way out." He set his face and watched the ships transform from ungainly creatures to things of beauty, with sails spread to use the wind.

Chapter Twenty-Five

"**M**lana! Mlana!" She couldn't be sure whether it was the shouting or the thunderous knocking that had woken her. Vor growled, dropped off the bed and raced to the bedroom door.

"What?" she answered, propping herself on her elbows.

"Ean ships have been sighted. Everyone's meeting in the hall."

"I'll be there," she replied and pulled back the covers. Vor looked over and waddled to her, huffing as he went.

"It begins," she whispered to her companion.

Anyar met Sadir at her door, pulling on a similar dark green tunic top to hers, her mother's short brown hair as messy as she felt.

"No time to look our best, eh, Anyar? Always something happening."

"Haven't had time to develop any dress sense, Mother. It's either green, brown or grey; seems no one's worried about how they look."

"No, you really haven't had a proper childhood, I'm afraid. Come on, let's get to the hall."

They hurried down the dark corridor, out of the front door and into the leafy courtyard. Vor dashed into the bushes as they headed to the far side where the administration building was located.

"It seems that voral takes any opportunity, Anyar?"

"He normally won't go out and leave me at night. He's very protective."

"Never know when that may come in useful. Ah, I can smell something cooking. Just as well, as we may be in for another long talking session."

"Come, Vor," called Anyar, holding open the door to the administration building's great conference hall and sampling the complex array of scents dominated by people and food as the voral came bounding up.

"Several strangers here, Mother."

"Maybe, but eat first," said Sadir.

They moved into the crowded room and headed straight to a food-laden table surrounded by people filling their plates.

"Come in, Mlana, Sadir, let me help you through this throng," called Xaner, his solid figure holding a considerable space at the table.

Jelm, standing next to him, saw them. "What would you two like? Honeyed cereal for Anyar, I suspect? Sadir, a meat-filled pancake? Tea? Juice? Toast?"

"All sounds good, Jelm," Sadir laughed as they reached the table. "We'll need something substantial to face the day, I suspect."

Anyar took her plate to a quiet space where Boidea and Xerrita were eating and sat, leaving Sadir and Jelm together.

"Where's Vor?" asked Boidea, searching amongst the sea of feet.

"I wouldn't know," smiled Anyar, looking out of the large window with wide eyes while slipping a large slice of honey-covered toast down by her side.

"You're no good at falsehoods, Mlana. He's a very noisy eater, even in this din," she laughed.

The clanging of a pot caused the talk to die away and Xaner stood. "People, although the food is good and the company convivial, we're not here to socialise. The ships sighted earlier are Ean ships, otherwise there would be much more activity. They are berthing as we speak, and we'll soon have their news.

"Please finish up and we'll recharge the dishes to prepare for the arrival of the Eanite representatives. Siliaster, our supervisor of defence, will bring them to us shortly."

The sun was warming and Anyar felt her head nodding as she sat on the grass, her back against a large stone outside the conference room. She was stroking the voral's coarse coat when he lifted his head and gave a burbling call.

"What?"

The voral stood, shook his shaggy fur, and stared down the hill at a group of people slowly heading their way. She saw her mother break into a run to meet the group, her scent flaring light red, violet and yellow in welcome.

"Ah, they're here. The Eanites." Anyar stood and watched her mother embrace a slight old man dressed in grey, while Vor moved a few steps down towards the oncoming people. She waited in anticipation, recognising a person from when she was a young girl.

"Anyar!" called Sadir. "This is Lan, our oldest friend. You remember him, don't you?"

"Hold, Vor," she murmured, aware of the import of this meeting, "they're coming to us."

Anyar blinked as they approached, focussing on just the one man. All around him blurred, leaving the main figure prominent, like a rock projecting from the water in a fast-flowing stream. She knew he was important to the future, particularly hers.

Another burbling sound from Vor made her focus even more. Her companion was standing on his hind legs, paws resting on the grey man's chest, something she had never seen him do. She stood and waited for Lan to reach her.

"Anyar." His voice was soft as he touched her hands, his scents mingling with hers. The caress of his power gave her a feeling of relief, of not being alone in her future. Here was someone she could truly rely on, who understood her situation. She hugged him while the voral entwined around their legs.

"You have changed, Anyar, out of all recognition." Lan's brown eyes were on the same level as her pale ones. "There is the look of your father in you, although you are much prettier." He chuckled. "I shall enjoy renewing our acquaintance."

"Come, Lan," said Sadir, "there's refreshments in the hall."

"Before I do, I'd like you to meet my travelling companion, Ginrel, administrator of Port Saltus and a river man, as you'll tell by his speech."

"Don't put th' poor girl off me, Lan," laughed the slightly stooped man with a weathered face. "Pleasure t' meet yer. Heard a lot 'bout yer."

Anyar exchanged scents with the man, while eying the youth standing several steps away with Vor busy sniffing his feet.

"You've noticed Eren, an acolyte and my assistant. It's his first time away from Ean."

Anyar waited for the tall youth to approach, an uncertain smile on his thin face. "I'm pleased to meet you." His scents reflected his uncertainty as they intermingled with hers, the greys of determination and loyalty, yet white and pale colours indicating attraction. She lost concentration as she analysed his scents, until Vor nudged her ankle.

"I haven't met you before, Eren, although that's not surprising." She saw Lan smiling out of the corner of her eye. "And I suspect Lan has his reasons for bringing you with him in this dangerous time."

"Do not read too much into this, Anyar," said Lan. "Something felt right about having Eren on this trip, and we will let matters fall as they may. Now, someone was talking about refreshments…"

"I've never seen a tame voral before," said Eren as he and Anyar sat on the grassy slope below the administration building, eating bread slathered with butter and topped with cheese.

"Tame, fine, but don't let him get near your food. But he'll be your friend for life if you give him honey." She grinned at the fixed stare of Vor sitting nearby.

"Anyar," called a voice from the hall behind them, "can I join you? I've got something for Vor."

"Oh, come and meet Eren, just arrived from Ean. Eren, this is my friend Sovira."

The red-headed girl stepped around their legs and sat near the voral, whose eyes immediately focussed on the plate in her hands. She smiled shyly at Eren and began to feed the honeyed bread to Vor.

"Large teeth," commented Eren. "Wouldn't want to be his enemy. Lan mentioned he's already had to fight for you?"

"Yes, he's been a good companion. The way he destroyed those hymetta that attacked us, years ago now, was something to see. He's also special when he uses scent." Anyar squinted as she spoke, noticing the comparative scent auras of her companions. There was a similarity, almost a complementary look about them; where there was a slight deficit in one, it was balanced by the other.

"Hey, do you see Vor's scent? It's shimmering. Why's that?" asked Eren.

Anyar looked closer and watched the blurred outlines of scent around the voral extending out, touching each of them. *Strange,* she thought, there's something happening.

"I can see it too," said Sovira. "Why is it doing that?"

"I don't really know," answered Anyar, looking closer. She squinted harder, looking with her shadow scent abilities, watching the blur of scent building up to a fuzzy grey layer around them.

At that moment she felt a link between the three of them, newly met, from different backgrounds, but a closeness all the same. The voral was triggering something but she didn't know what. Hopefully Boidea or her mother would know.

The introductions were over, and discussions continued regarding the relocation of the Ean ships and portions of the Rolan fleet to Sea Holm. The strategy to counter the Sutanites aimed at dealing the most effective blow to their ships and army. The strength of the Sutanite's scent attack was known, as Kyel had warned them of the effectiveness of war at sea where Jakus' acidic scent walls literally dissolved any organic material it touched. Sea battles with the enemy were not to be contemplated.

Anyar sat in on the discussions with Vor stretched out at her feet while her new friends, Eren and Sovira had headed off to help secure accommodation for Lan and his entourage.

"Sorry Mlana," Xaner looked over and smiled, "you'll not be used to the intricacies of battle planning."

"Nonetheless," added Lan, "Anyar needs to be involved. Much rests on her shoulders." *And Alethea will guide her, too.*

"Granted," said Jelm, "but let's get back to the ships. We're aware that an all-out battle with the enemy is not in our best interests, so how best to use our resources?

"I would suggest we move all the ships out of Requist to Sea Holm before the enemy appears. Keep them there. Add uncertainty in the Sutanite ranks. Make them divide their resources. You agree, don't you, Lan?"

"I don't wish to usurp your role, Xaner and Siliaster, as I am newly arrived. However, as we left recently from Port Saltus, I have some information that may help. We brought most of the Ean fleet with us, leaving merely five ships for defence. These are our oldest and least seaworthy, because they may be sacrificed."

"Ah," interrupted Boidea, "you're seeking to entice the Sutanites into an easy-seeming victory?"

"Yes, but we hope it'll result in Jakus splitting his forces. We believe he has a substantial fleet, and any reduction in it will make it easier to cope with when he reaches Rolan. As Jelm says, moving our ships to Sea Holm, leaving few if any in Requist, will entice Jakus straight into the port."

"But, Lan," said Jelm, "you're hoping Jakus will act with some caution, aren't you, thereby splitting his forces once again?"

"Yes, I am," Lan replied. "An astute leader should hold back on landing his entire force if he sees few ships to counter him. If that happens, then the ground forces opposing us here will be correspondingly reduced."

"A worthwhile aim, Lan," said Xaner, "one of which we heartedly approve."

"Guess it's me role t' stay on th' ships then, if you're happy," said Ginrel. "Our ships together with yer's at Sea Holm?"

"Agreed," Xaner looked at Siliaster, who nodded. "If you want to command the combined fleet from Sea Holm then we'd have no objection. Our Captains are aware of the intricacies of the harbourage and know the coastline."

"We'll need t' work out a system t' let us know when t' move on them haggars t' cause 'em most damage."

"No need, Ginrel," said Xaner. "We've scouts in Nosta and Mlana Hold who know the hidden tracks to Sea Holm, so will send word when the fleet's needed."

Anyar watched them for a while until she was weary yet filled with a sense of foreboding. She nudged Vor on his side, and together they slipped away and up to her quarters.

She pushed open the door and waited for Vor to precede her, but he had disappeared. She shook her head at his unusual behaviour and slipped inside, lying on her bed, letting her mind ponder on all that had happened. Two new friends in a day, the arrival of Lan with his mysterious ways and a compounding memory of Alethea. The old woman hovered in the background of her mind, like an itch waiting to be scratched, always with the puzzle of why she had allowed the Sutanites such easy access to the cache of magnesa stored at Mlana Hold in their previous invasion. Now they were coming back, wanting more, wanting everything.

The Mlana had been a clever leader and had a reason. Anyar had inherited her role and struggled with it, being so young and untried despite absorbing much of the Mlana's essences when she died. *There's a reason, and it has to do with the Sutanite leader, Jakus. Was it to force him to behave impetuously because of the attraction of such a huge prize? Time will tell.*

A scratch at the door broke through her musings and she slipped off the bed to let the voral in. To her surprise, Eren and Sovira were standing outside, puzzlement showing on their faces.

"Sorry," said Sovira, "but your voral is quite determined. He insisted we come here."

Eren shrugged as they followed the animal into Anyar's room.

"All I've got is water, and of course Rolan cordial," said Anyar. "Would you like some?"

She poured three glasses from a tumbler and passed them around.

"Ergh," said Eren as he downed the drink, 'very sweet."

"I like it," smiled Sovira as she sipped hers.

"Why don't we all sit, and you can tell me more about yourselves," suggested Anyar.

They pulled cushions off the bed and two armchairs to make a good pile on the floor.

"This carpet is perac wool," said Eren. "Didn't know you had much of an industry in Rolan."

"We're traders mostly," said Sovira. "Probably comes from Ean in the first place."

"Certainly has the scent about it," Anyar observed as she sat down. "Hey, Vor, don't push."

"Oomph, he's heavy," gasped Eren, as the voral clambered over to lie partially across his and Sovira's legs.

"He's unusually friendly, too," Anyar said, a frown creasing her forehead.

The voral's scent shimmered in the dark room, becoming more pronounced as they watched, and Anyar felt a pull of familiarity at her mind. The translucent scent gradually enveloped them until they were enclosed.

"Be still, everyone," said Anyar, "I think I know what he's trying to do. Please don't panic, but go with whatever happens." She remembered her experiences from before in Mlana Hold and drew on them, bringing forth scent memories, adding their influence to the scent bubble surrounding them.

Like before, she felt her efforts bolstering and strengthening the voral's actions, increasing the integral structure of the scent shield covering them. Dimly aware of the two other presences with them, she delved into the linkages of the scents, entwining and manipulating the bonds, going into the deepest of levels. The shadow scent hovered in the background and came forward eagerly, allowing her to make it stronger, more impenetrable. Her focus didn't allow her to think about the people with her or the reason why Vor had initiated this experience.

The pressure of holding all the bonds together at such a minute level began to tell, and her head throbbed in time with her heartbeat until she felt she had to let it go. Then other presences took over. The pressure lessened, but the strength of the scent shielding didn't. If anything, it grew to be solid, impenetrable. Not only did Vor add his influence but Sovira, and even Eren, did too.

How strange, thought Anyar, *a male feeling shadow scent.* At this time the shielding was impenetrable, nothing able to influence its protection. She basked in the feeling until the air started to foul.

"Oh!" she squeaked and began to pull apart the bonds to allow air to enter. At that moment Vor relaxed and the whole structure began to disintegrate.

"What was that?" gasped Eren.

"I've never done that before," puffed Sovira. "Absolutely amazing."

"I have," said Anyar, seriously. "It was powerful. We could get into the smallest motes of scent and use it."

"Was that women's scent I felt?"

"Yes, Eren, shadow scent. Not many men can experience that. Maybe the cordial helped you?"

"But why us? Why me?"

"Yes, Anyar, why us?" asked Sovira.

"Don't know, and I can't ask Vor, but there's something about the four of us. It was meant to be."

"Oh." Eren looked at the voral and tentatively put his hand on its fur. "I wondered why Lan brought me with him, but I didn't think it was for this."

"It has a meaning," added Anyar. "Whatever it was, it has a meaning. I guess we'll find out."

Chapter Twenty-Six

"You know you're privileged," Dronthis' voice rumbled.

"What?" Bilternus, who'd been deep in sleep, turned his head to look blearily at his companion's large form on the opposite bunk. Dronthis was lying on his side, head propped up on one elbow.

"You're privileged. The Shada's hardly looked at you since we've been on the voyage. Oh, he'll keep a close eye on your father and me, but not you. I can't move without someone tattling on me to our leader."

"What do you expect? I've always been loyal. Always aided Jakus' ambitions, helped where I could, so I can be relied on. You, well, you were my grandfather's right hand, not Jakus', so naturally he's got his eye on you." Bilternus pushed his feet over the side of his bunk and sat up. "What brought this on?"

"I've been thinking." The big man scratched his hairy chest through his gaping undershirt. "I've been alive a while, in a position where I've seen a lot and had to be aware, even advise my master on important matters. So, I can sense when things are not as they seem. And you, Bilternus are not as you seem. You're hiding things."

"So? We all do." Bilternus controlled his scents with an effort.

"I've wondered how, with the Shada's paranoia for seeking out disloyalty, you've managed to keep your secrets."

"Well, if I have secrets, I wouldn't be telling you. You're open to Jakus' interrogation, and anything I told you could easily get to him."

"Ah, so I was right."

"What?"

"You're not as clever as you think, young Bilternus. If the Shada really was suspicious, he would be looking at you more closely. Just as well no one says anything to him."

"Dronthis, what are you getting at?" he sighed. He pulled his dark tunic top on over his undershirt.

"Just that you can rely on me. I'm converted to the Shada's cause, but not all my mind is the Shada's. I'm not happy about the way he handled my former master, and so I could be a friend, if you'd let me."

"A friend?" Bilternus pulled on his leather boots and stood. "Thanks, Dronthis, I'll remember." He opened the door and went through, concerned over his cabin-mate's comments, resolving to be careful to stay out of Jakus' attention.

He climbed the steps to the aft deck where Tibitus, outlined by the first rays of a rising sun, stood at the helm, his weathered face gazing into the billowing sails above his head.

"Captain!"

"Well met, Bilternus," he responded. "Good to see you on deck this early. Been an easy night, though there's a blow coming later this day. You've just missed the commander. She's been with me most of the night and is now meeting with the Shada below."

Bilternus walked to the rails, easily adjusting the slight heeling of the ship to look at the fleet spread out behind them.

"Kept in good order over the night. All accounted for, even those we picked up from Port Semplar. Never been in such a fleet before, led by this beauty, the best ship I've ever sailed on, let alone captained."

"Twenty-one ships in all, eh, Captain?"

"Correct, and here, following us in these mild seas. Pity our enemy, that's all I'll say."

"How long to Ean?"

"Well, depending on weather, several more days." The solid man scratched at his chin. "More long tacks to keep out of sight of land, then we'll sweep into Port Saltus."

Bilternus watched the ships behind them, their white sails making a peaceful sight. He shuddered before turning and heading down to the galley.

The meal of beans and reconstituted meat sat heavily on his stomach as he stood in the large meeting room. Jakus was unrolling a map on the heavy, dark table, but the richness of the wooden fittings, red velvet hangings and plush green carpet did little to distract Bilternus while he waited for the Shada to begin the briefing. Sharna smiled at him as if sensing his slight queasiness when the ship heeled in several shudders.

"Sharna. Kast. Tretial." Jakus' hand flapped over the parchment. "Here. Look at this. Tell me what I'm not seeing." He stepped back as the three of them looked over the map and glanced around the room, spying Bilternus standing with Poegna, Dronthis and Faltis against a wall.

"Ah, Bilternus, you may add your thoughts."

Bilternus pushed a strand of dark hair behind his ear as he came forward to join the others at the table, quickly aware he was seeing a scaled outline of

Ean's Port Saltus. Although he had only spent a few hours in the Port some years earlier, he recognised the structure of the docks and its outlying features.

The port straddled the outlet of the Great Southern River, with most of its infrastructure on its western side since the shallows of the eastern bank limited any commercial activity. Piers extending at right angles from a long wooden wharf along the western bank provided berths for shipping, while behind the wharf were warehouses and the residential and business infrastructure of the city. It was relatively undefended, although any approach would best be made with an ingoing tide to counter the effects of the river's flow.

"Well? Comments?"

"If I may, Shada?" asked Bilternus. "Are we splitting our forces to attack Ean? If so, how many of us are going to be involved in the assault?"

"Planning for eventualities. Depending on our opposition, which Heritis and I will consider in due course. What do you see?"

"Ah, a relatively undefended city easy to capture, which would then allow our forces to move along the river to the capital and beyond."

"So it would seem. Sharna?"

"I echo Bilternus' opinion but must wonder if the enemy would allow an easy surrender of the port. Should they do so it would be relatively simple to push on to the capital. Surely the opposition would not be so facilitating."

"Hmm. Kast?"

"We must be wary, Shada, but remember our enemy will be forewarned and prepared. It will not be easy, even though the port is not structured for defence. I would recommend a mass assault, committing a total force. Obliterate the city, then move on the rest of the country. Do this and we must win."

"Yes, the port is open to us, even with some defence. Heritis and I will consider the best use of our forces and operate accordingly.

"Tibitus, prepare for a rendezvous with Heritis' ship during this day. Time to prepare for the return of Ean to our rule. Ensure supplies of magnesa are available to every scent master. Now leave us.

"Bilternus, Dronthis, stay."

Once the door had closed, Jakus sat in one of the carved wooden chairs and motioned to the two men to do the same.

"Take some wine, Bilternus. You too, Dronthis." He sat watching with a hooded gaze as Dronthis poured out three glasses of a rose-coloured wine and handed them around.

"I am not a vindictive man and don't hold grudges," he began, holding the glass up to the sunlight streaming in through a reinforced glass window, the red-coloured light giving his features an eerie cast. "You, young Bilternus, are not responsible for your father's actions and have acquitted yourself well in my forces. No blame attaches to you.

"Dronthis, I spared your life when most would have expected I shouldn't. You served my father well and I saw value in your years of experience. I have investigated your loyalty and seen you are man worthy of being a Sutanite, and part of the future.

"As a result, you have each been supplied with my most precious resource." Jakus glanced at the belt pouches of the men. "So," he said, draining his glass, "if—*when*—I meet with Heritis, my second-in-command and we decide to split our forces, you two will remain as part of the Ean invasion force."

"Shada?"

"Hmm." Jakus stared at Bilternus, while gesturing to Dronthis to refill his glass.

"I thought we were going to take Ean first, then move on to Rolan? A splitting of our forces may weaken any attack."

"You have not had access to my intelligence, nephew." Jakus took a drink from his refilled glass. "But a fair enough question. No decision has been made but initial reports indicate that little has been done by the Eanites to prepare for my attack, some even fleeing from the port. With our magnesa scent skills and Heritis' local knowledge and preparations, I anticipate the conquest of Ean will be straightforward.

"This is where you will have your chance to prove yourselves, both of you. Led by Heritis, there will be opportunities to show your worth, with rewards aplenty for those who prove true to me.

"Nevertheless, I am still open to committing all our forces to the conquest of Ean but am of a mind to seriously consider the alternative. The Ean opposition is weak, led by an old man, while the leader in Rolan is a girl, untried and supported by an unwarlike people. Our strength is formidable. We are the strongest we've ever been and our scent power overwhelming. And the rewards"—Jakus held the swirling contents of his glass against the light—"the rewards are great.

"Then, there's the crystal cave. With those resources, no one could stop me. Sutan will be the mightiest country in the world, bringing an age of prosperity and stability for generations to come. My legacy to all." He tossed the contents of the glass down his throat with a flourish and sat back in his chair, his magnesa crystals scrunching as his fingers rummaged in his belt pouch.

"Do not fail me, for I don't forgive easily. Now leave."

The great ship, sails furled, tossed in the roughening sea, light from a sinking sun highlighting the dark clouds obliterating the horizon to the south. Within hailing distance bobbed a smaller, two-masted ship, also with furled sails, a rowing boat making slow progress towards them as it battled the waves.

Bilternus stood amidships with Sharna and Dronthis, watching two burly seamen skilfully manipulating the oars while a black-robed figure observed them from the stern. The path the boat was following was smoother than the surrounding water, clear evidence of the use of scent power to flatten the waves. He could see Jakus, with Kast by his side, leaning over the rails on the aft deck, adding his control to facilitate Heritis' approach.

The boat hit with a thump next to a rope ladder hanging over the side of the ship. Several seamen reached down with long poles to help secure the vessel.

"Careful, you fools!" Jakus' strident yell came clearly, his concern for the safe arrival of his second-in-command apparent. "Heritis, welcome."

The wind whipped off his black hood, leaving Heritis' newly shaven head glistening with moisture, his long-boned face set with determination. He grasped the rail and Kast gripped his arm, pulling him through the gap and onto the deck.

"Wel...come, Shada," Heritis gasped. "Glad to be aboard. The weather almost prevented me."

Jakus stepped forward and shared scents. "Come to my cabin. Kast, arrange hot drinks, food."

Bilternus saw the two of them, followed by Kast, disappear down the steps into the ship and felt his anticipation rising for the outcome of their meeting.

A short while later, Kast reappeared and spoke with Tibitus. The captain signalled to his sailors and the top sail on each mast unfurled. A signal flag broke out on the mast, eliciting a responding unfurling of sails on Heritis' ship. Both ships began to move forward as the darkness slowly rolled over them and the wind picked up.

"We're off," said Sharna. "It looks like the Shada has decided to keep Heritis on board, since it appears we're in for a storm."

"Tibitus said as much when I spoke to him earlier," said Bilternus. "I wonder whether this will impact on us."

"Time will tell," said Sharna, touching him on the shoulder. "Now I will leave you. Things to do."

As she left, he caught Dronthis watching him. "Yes, Bilternus, not long now. Though if I put money on it, it'll be you and me with Heritis attacking Ean. No way will the Shada let up on his fabulous crystal cave in Rolan."

Bilternus grunted and left to find a quiet space where he could think over the implications for him and his men in the attack on Ean.

The howl of wind through the rigging, accompanying a violent pitching of the ship, meant everyone but the most essential found places to wait out the storm.

Bilternus pitied those out on deck, particularly Tibitus, the captain. He remembered a similar situation some years before when they had been sailing to attack Rolan. They were a few days out of Sutan when a violent storm hit. He and the Eanite, Kyel, had stayed on deck helping the same captain control the helm and guide the ship safely through to Port Saltus. Yet here he was, in his dark cabin, waiting out the current blow.

"Dronthis!" he snapped to his cabin mate, who was obviously suffering from the erratic pitching of the ship, "I'm going on deck to offer my help. Stay here and be sick, or come. Your choice." He grabbed his waterproof perac-wool coat and opened the door to take a careful course along the short corridor to the steps. He pushed open the doorway, waited as a gush of water washed over his boots, and clambered out onto the aft deck.

Dark figures clustered around the helm, a single protected lamp giving sparse illumination in the scudding wind, and rain pelting the deck.

"Want a hand?" he screamed to the two men holding the helm.

Tibitus' rain-swept figure yelled: "Take over from Kast!"

Bilternus recognised the big man as they exchanged grips on the wooden helm. Immediately the wood kicked into his hands like a live thing, trying to tear out of his grasp.

"Keep it to this angle, into the wind," the captain yelled in his ear. "See the spritsail. Make certain it stays taut."

Bilternus squinted along the deck where the pale triangle of the sail was apparent and opened his mouth to ask for more direction, but Tibitus had stepped back to join a figure near the rail, a dark-clad man looking into the wild storm. The vague light allowed Bilternus to see the fixed expression on Jakus' face, as if the man was daring the storm to do its worst. Then the violent pitching of the ship drew his attention and for a long while took all his effort. Dawn was an age in coming.

Bilternus drifted out of an exhausted sleep, woken by a gentle rocking. He groaned and lifted his head to the smell of cooking. He stood, grabbed his other set of already damp clothes, and staggered past his sleeping companion to the door.

On deck, sailors were unfurling sails and repairing storm damage. He noticed Jakus, Heritis and Sharna on the aft deck so he walked over to join them.

"Bilternus," said Sharna cheerily. "A rough night, eh?"

He nodded with a grunt, combing his hand through his hair.

"Take a while to assemble all the ships," she turned, scanning the horizon. "Not sure if they're all still with us."

"Not going to wait," added Jakus, looking out to sea. "We have a commitment, and they know what's at stake."

"Ean is just over the horizon, ripe for us," agreed Heritis. "And we have decided the attack will begin next day." He turned and looked at Bilternus. "You had better prepare since you will be leading your troops, under my command.

"Meanwhile our Shada has a bigger, more important target, so it will be up to us to secure Ean for Sutan. Time for glory, eh?"

Bilternus walked to the rails and leant over, looking into the flat swell. A fish jumped, then hit the water with a splash to disappear without trace. For some reason it seemed to echo his thinking.

Chapter Twenty-Seven

A dark smudge on the horizon was heralded by a gentle offshore breeze, bringing scents of land and fresh water. Bilternus inhaled to see if he could discern the individual scents and remember anything from his very brief time in Port Saltus years ago.

The dominant odour was the Great Southern River, mud and waterweed masking many others, yet a clear trace of man's activities came through. Unpleasant smells of waste and industry mixed with animal odours, dust and salts, too many to be determined but all giving the distinct sense of Ean.

The entire fleet of twenty-one ships slowly tacked towards the land, troops preparing for their invasion and resistance from the locals. Intelligence reports indicated few ships in the harbour and limited build-up of defences; the size of the opposing forces was expected to be easily countered by the magnesa-enhanced Sutanite scent masters.

Heritis, with Bilternus and Dronthis, had rowed across to his ship. Bilternus was sorry to be leaving the energetic Sharna behind on Jakus' flagship, a person he could relate to and regard as a friend, but he knew Piltarnis and Rancer were on Heritis' ship and needed to meet up with them.

He expected the decision on the size of the invasion force would come once Jakus had determined the strength of their opposition, but now he and Piltarnis could work out the deployment of the Faltis' estate forces he commanded. They would be part of the Eanite invasion and be involved in establishing domination and rule in that country while Jakus was subduing Rolan. He was relieved not to be under the Shada's direct command but knew he would have to acquit himself well, since Heritis and Dronthis would be with him.

Now it was a matter of waiting as the fleet sailed closer to the port, timing their arrival to a late incoming tide.

"I think our troops are as ready as they'll ever be," said Piltarnis, fiddling with the small pouch of magnesa crystals on his belt as they stood by the starboard rail peering at the distant land. "Do you think we'll be going it alone with Heritis"—

he gestured with his head to where the second-in-command stood with Crastus, the ship's captain on the aft deck—"or will the Shada be leading the attack?"

"Unless there's some overwhelming reason, I anticipate we'll be going with Heritis. Jakus wants Rolan. And in my opinion, he won't want to wait for us to defeat Ean."

Piltarnis shrugged his thin shoulders as he continued to watch the approaching land.

"We'll be prepared, lad," came a deep voice. "Heritis is a good commander, knows the territory and is not easily influenced by the lure of the red crystal." Bilternus looked over to Rancer as he gripped the rail with a confident expression on his face.

"You spent a few years in Ean, Rancer. I suppose you know Port Saltus well?"

"Yes, Bilternus, I do. Not too pleased to be fighting the natives but, with any luck they'll surrender to the inevitable." He grimaced as he adjusted his solid body to the sudden push of a wave under the bow. "And I too have the red crystal," he tapped his belt pouch, a wry smile on his face.

The clanging of iron on iron and several highly visible scent plumes warned all in Port Saltus that the long-expected invasion was imminent. A sailor dashed along the streets and burst through the doors of the headquarters of the Port Authority, which doubled as the command centre for the defence.

"They're coming, the whole fleet! They're coming!" he screeched to the room full of people.

"Calm down, said Lethnal, pushing a soothing scent across the agitated man, "and tell us what you know."

Eyes wide, the sailor gulped and took a deep breath. "We could see them. Lots of ships heading to the port. Too many," he said, "Too many."

"Again, how many ships are there?"

"Around twenty. Hard to tell, but a lot. Must be carrying a heap of troops. They'll hit us at high tide, I reckon."

"Sit, man," said Grefnel. "I'm the port commander in Ginrel's absence. Take your time and think it through."

"Yes, Cer… About twenty ships. One of them a three-master. Can carry a lot of troops. More'n that we can't tell."

"Good. Then there's another thing to do. We need to let the captains of our ships in the harbour know they should carry out the plan. I want you to do that."

The sailor nodded and hurried out.

"We better organise our forces, Lethnal," said Grefnel. "Let's hope our early strategy works. If the Sutanites don't fall for it and invade with their whole force, then we're as good as defeated."

"It's but one part in our strategy, Grefnel," said Lethnal. "We best be on the move."

The clamour meant that the city was in action. Like a swarm of ants, the citizenry spread out to their appointed tasks. The threat of the Sutanite fleet looming on the horizon had a palpable impact. Lethnal and Cathar went to a long room at the back of the building to join a few women waiting there. They looked up and Rasnal smiled.

"No guessing what that is all about. We're ready." She swept her hand around the grey- and light-blue-clad women. "We have strategies in place, depending of course on what the Sutanites throw at us. But when should we take the cordial?"

"Too early yet," said Lethnal. "Our brave captains will be sailing away, upriver to the agreed position. With any luck the Sutanites will see what's happening and react accordingly. I don't have the Mlana's capacity for foretelling, but I believe this must be the time to split the invaders. Very few, including you, my friends, know of the deception."

"Be that as it may, we have to be ready. No matter how many we face we must be prepared."

"Still, the question remains, when do we drink the cordial?" Cathar asked, smiling.

"What can you see, Kyel?" asked Grefnel. "This has to be the best place in the port to observe shipping."

"Ships, plenty of them, entering the harbour," Kyel said, leaning on the windowsill of the two-storey administration building. "And ours, heading to be out of sight upriver. From here it looks like they're fleeing, just as we want, making little headway against the flow even aided by the tide. Now," he added, looking back to the lined face of the anxious port administrator, "we'll see if Jakus takes the bait."

"I don't know if I want to see our city destroyed, even if it's strategic," said Grefnel. "I hope our defences will hold against the invaders."

"Watch," said Kyel. "We must see what they do. Will they split up or all come in? Maybe the size of the piers will influence their decision. Be hard to securely tie up twenty odd ships there."

"How are the women going? Are they ready?"

"Every confidence in Cathar and Lethnal," Kyel murmured as he watched the fleet tacking towards them, their shapes clear in the late afternoon. "They are as ready as we are. It all depends on what the Sutanites do."

"You were on the other side, Kyel, when we had that big fight in the port last time they tried to attack us."

"That's well-known, Grefnel. I was caught in with Jakus' attack on the way to

Rolan. Wasn't a good time for me."

"No, I know, but what I was wondering was how the attack was really stopped. I know Lan was here since I was involved in the big scent battle, but it left a lot of damage and now he's back, more powerful, too." Grefnel's eyes were wide in his round face.

"I know you had a part in the battle then, Grefnel. While you'll appreciate that it took everything Lan and his scent masters could do to stop the attack—bit of a stalemate—Jakus was really focussed on Rolan. However, this time he's more powerful, for he's got plenty of magnesa. He's got many more troops, so could easily crush us if he puts his mind to it. But again, Rolan is his focus. And he doesn't really understand what happened to him during the battle for Mlana Hold, how he was driven away. So, we're hoping they won't know about shadow scent and how we could counter whatever force he throws at us."

"I'm aware what we're trying to do but I've never seen shadow scent in action. Is it as effective as we've been told?"

"I've seen it," said Kyel, "and it is effective. But I've also seen Jakus in action, and I really don't want to put it to the test, especially when people I care about are exposed to that monster. No, we must stop him, stop him *now*."

"Hmm, the ships are moving closer. Time to join my men. We had better get a runner to keep lookout," said Grefnel, looking out the window.

"Me too. There's little enough time until they arrive. Tishal should be nearby." Kyel looked down the steep stairs behind them and called out.

Tishal's beaming broad face peered up at him. "Time fer me t' do sumthin'?"

"Need you to watch the fleet. Let us know if they split up, or when anything happens."

"All right." The teenager came pounding up the stairs, her yellow scarf highlighting her dark clothing. "Yer reckon it's abart t' start?"

"Afraid so," added Grefnel, as he and Kyel headed down the stairs. "Keep a close watch."

"**A**re they really that stupid?" Heritis squinted at the distant wharves. "There's little activity there, just the ships scurrying up the river. No shipping tied up to the piers, just a bunch of barges on the eastern shore. I can't believe it. They won't just let us walk into the port, take it over. They won't."

"Lan's up to something, but what?"

"It's not as it seems. Never seen the harbour so empty, or so few barges." Rancer put a hand up to his eyes. "Some people are there. Can see barricades, streets blocked but not much else. What are they playing at?"

"Cer, signal from the flagship," yelled a seaman from a lookout platform high on the main mast.

"What, man?"

"Appears we're to proceed as per orders! Ships limited to those under your command!"

"Signal for repeat of orders," shouted Heritis. "Damn him. Things aren't as they seem and we're effectively taking away two thirds of our forces from the attack. I wish my cousin wasn't so precipitous."

"Cer," called the lookout, "orders repeated! Action confirmed!"

"Well," said Heritis, turning to face Rancer and Bilternus, "it seems it'll be on our shoulders to subdue Ean and hold it in the Shada's name. We must be wary, for I feel we will have a fight on our hands. Crastus," he called to his captain standing at the helm, "signal the fleet under my command to follow our lead. We will head for the wharves and docks. Prepare to approach the port."

Bilternus gripped the rail as the ship changed to the opposite tack, watching the remaining seven ships of the fleet tacking with them. A total of eight ships: the two carrying Heritis' Eanite troops who had travelled back with him from Sutan, and six holding troops from Faltis' and Poegna's estates. Bilternus knew that he and Rancer would be in joint command under Heritis as he watched the flagship, and twelve other ships swing around to run with the wind and back out to sea. He eased himself off the rail and went to speak to his troop commander, Piltarnis, amongst the seamen and guardsmen on the deck.

"They've dun it! They've dun it!" Tishal dashed into the rooms where Cathar and Lethnal were working with the scent masters on their scent defence tactics.

"Slow down. Dun whot?" snapped Cynth at her daughter.

"Th' enemy. They've split, like Kyel wanted me t' see. Sum ships hev gone back t' sea. Sum're still cummin."

"How many are still cummin?" asked Cynth,

"Eight. They's eight still cummin'."

"Tishal. Go and tell Kyel and Grefnel. Now!" said Lethnal. As the girl ran out of the room, she looked at the ashen faces of the crowd of scent masters around her.

"We best be moving to our assigned places. We've not long, and for this to work we must be ready."

The sun was closing on the horizon across the flat plains to the west, making the buildings dark silhouettes to the incoming ships. They were clearly visible to the waiting defenders and appeared ominously lit by the setting sun.

A rattling of rope over wood came echoing across the waters to those alert for the attack. A splash of stone anchors followed, and the great ships stopped, firmly secured near the western banks no more than a short distance from the docks.

The sun finally disappeared behind the far-off mountains of the Great Divide, and everything seemed to settle for a night of waiting.

Chapter Twenty-Eight

The river was a grey swath bisecting the dark and brooding land under a clouded sky. Nothing appeared to move, with the occasional splash of fish and cry of hunting lizards breaking the silence. The group of eight ships was congregated near the western shore, a clear area of water around them. Not a light showed on the ships, or on the land as dawn promised to herald the beginning of hostilities.

The tide had turned, the ripple of water growing in volume, making the sentries on the ships nervous. Strategically located scent masters constantly sampled the air seeking unusual or concerning odours.

Bilternus couldn't rest with the thought of the coming assault and what it entailed. He marvelled at the sleeping troops around him, seemingly unconcerned with the next day. "Damn," he hissed and swung his legs over the side of his bunk. He reached for his boots, trying not to disturb anyone in the large below-deck hold, almost the length of the ship, realising now how lucky he had been to have a shared cabin on the flagship. *Still*, he thought, *at least we don't have animals or worse, hymetta, on board polluting the ship's air.*

He pulled on his dark tunic top and edged towards the steps leading to the deck. There the odours changed remarkably: the river, the land, the city and the distinctive ship smell.

"Ho, the watch?" he called softly. "Anything to report?"

A dark, hooded shape revealed a scent master in a black robe. He recognised the man's Eanite and Sutanite scents as belonging to Heritis' contingent.

Of course, he thought, *he'd be aware of the local odours.*

"Bilternus, my Shad, Heritis is aft if you need him. So far, no areas of concern to report, although the tide is bringing more river debris than I'd normally expect."

"Keep at it," Bilternus acknowledged. "I'll be with Heritis."

He soon found Heritis with Rancer peering over the stern railing into the night. Crastus was standing with them, arms folded.

"You're here, Bilternus. Just in time, I surmise." Heritis pointed eastward out into the river. "What do you make of that?"

Bilternus took position at the rail and opened his senses to the night, trying to ascertain anything different from the normal ambience he had been experiencing. His eyes were virtually useless as the cloud cover had muted any light from the moon or stars, so he concentrated on smell. His hand went to the pouch by his side, took a pinch of crystals and placed them on his tongue.

Immediately the scents around him were heightened. While he could pick out additional scents above the ordinary, an overwhelming salt odour came through in high concentrations.

"I am not familiar with Ean, but isn't the salt scent overly strong, well above what you'd expect from the sea?"

"My thoughts, Bilternus," said Heritis. "Rancer and I were discussing this and have recognised it as the smell of salt-carrying barges. A normal enough odour in port but out here it's suspicious and it's increasing. I think we should put our people on alert.

"Bilternus, rouse the below-decks. Crastus, sound the alarm to our fleet. Rancer, ensure all available lanterns are lit. I think we're under attack." Heritis crammed a handful of magnesa crystal in his mouth and sent a flare of red and yellow scents high into the air.

A row of black, low-slung shapes was revealed swinging broadside toward the anchored fleet. A flicker of illumination came, then increased into a rush of light as flame raced along the gunwales of the barges and began to leap into the air. Small boats were moving away from the barges, figures on board rowing furiously.

The burning barges edged closer.

"Those damn scartha, they're using the tide against us!" screeched Heritis. "We need to drive them off. Scent masters, take magnesa. Join in a blocking wall to stop the barges. We can't let the flame reach our ships."

Bilternus found himself linking with all the scent masters and scent-talented on the ship, too mesmerised by the wall of approaching flame to feel fear. He only knew they had to turn the attack aside or else the invasion would be over before it began.

A real test for Jakus' magnesa if we're to get out of this, he thought when he saw Heritis' signal. Ruddy light reflected off their faces as they produced individual scent blankets to form a barrier around their ship, using the intricacies of the bonds, as revealed by the magnesa, to link the scents and make an impenetrable wall. Slowly they moved its eastern edge outwards, deflecting the flaming barges into the main channel and away from their ship. Each ship's scent-talented added their push to the floating wall of flame, the combined mass of the barges proving hard to repel. Here and there, gaps appeared where individuals failed to fully secure their portions of the scent barrier. Sparks flew through, and the sailors and guardsmen on the ships were kept busy putting out spot fires.

"Keep at it!" exhorted Heritis. "Sink them if you can. We can't let them through."

Sweat poured down the back of Bilternus' tunic as he concentrated, pushing into the scent shield, forcing it against the flaming barges until one slipped below the waters, causing a cheer from some of the watchers.

All too soon, screams overtook the cheering and an orange glow from burning wood and sail lit the sky, turning night into day. Two ships at the outer edge of the anchored flotilla were burning, despite the efforts of the defenders, and another's mainsail was a sheet of flame. Bilternus saw people jumping off the sides and into the water.

Slowly the last of the barges had been pushed away, aided by the outgoing tide, and the ships were out of danger.

"Release the shielding and all hands retrieve swimmers!" the captain's voice rang out.

Bilternus dropped his scent shielding and ran to the railing, while unrestrained embers drifted across the fleet, causing more spot fires on furled sails and woodwork, dividing the defenders' attention.

People first, thought Bilternus as he reached down to clasp a stretching hand and pulled a drenched sailor to safety.

Running feet made him jerk back and avoid the sailors rushing past to pull the burning sails away. He quickly grabbed the end of a spar to help heave it over the side while avoiding the floundering bodies below. As he looked down a swimmer screamed and disappeared below the surface. Bilternus shuddered before rejoining the desperate effort to save the ship.

The glow of dawn competed with the fires to cast a ruddy light from the distant eastern mountains, marking an end to a horrendous night.

"Success, I think," breathed Lethnal as she watched the large glow in the river through the second storey window. "Definitely ships burning. Brave souls, those who steered the barges."

"Me people too. Sick of Sutanites wantin' t' take whot's ours," grunted Cynth. "No shortage of volunteers."

"We've got their overconfidence in deciding to anchor there for the night to thank, but did they think our lack of ships would prevent us from doing anything to them?"

"I found they had a supreme belief in themselves when I lived in Sutan," said Kyel, "though I can't see Jakus falling for that. He must have gone with the remainder of the fleet, otherwise he would're attacked at night. So, it could have been Heritis in command, waiting for daylight."

"Whoever is leading them has been given something to think about," added Lethnal. "Now we must be ready, for I don't believe they'll delay now with the sun rising."

As the tide turned, the ships up-anchored and headed on towards the port. The outnumbered defenders scattered into their planned groups, scent masters and guardsmen waiting behind barricades along the wharf, ready to make the invaders struggle for any foothold. The remaining defenders were spread at strategic places through the city but were concentrated at the guardhouse on the northern side where the road headed upcountry along the Great Southern to the capital, Nebleth.

Kyel walked briskly with Cathar towards the guardhouse. "You sure you and the other women will be safe here? I know shadow scent should protect all of you until we're ready, but I worry."

"I'm more concerned about you, Kyel." Cathar leant forwards and put her arms around his shoulders, sharing scents. "The enemy won't be in a forgiving mood following our attack, and Sutanites are known for being ruthless."

"It'll be fine. We're well organised and should be capable enough, even without shadow scent."

"Remember, they have magnesa so it'll be hard, at least until you can bring them here. Then they won't know what hit them."

"Anyway," Kyel added, "I'm still not happy about using fire as I'll hate seeing the city in flames, but while we're up against it we must use anything we can."

They soon approached the wooden palisade surrounding the two-storey guardhouse where they could see Lethnal and Rasnal in a group of grey- and light-blue-clad women. Lethnal waved and beckoned Cathar in.

Kyel hurried back to join Grefnel and the other defenders at the barricades along the wharf. He'd have liked to catch up with Brin but knew the man would be busy with other defences. His role in firing the city was crucial to their defensive plan.

The five large ships edged up to the piers, small tender boats on their seaward side towing them against the river's pull with the help of the tide. The sides of the overladen ships bristled with troops and scent masters, all eager to make their enemy pay for the loss of three ships and many comrades in the nighttime barge attack. The few defensive scent attacks were easily repelled by the magnesa-enhanced shields, scent bolts bouncing off them, with spears and other missiles relatively ineffective.

Bilternus and Piltarnis had orders to take and hold the southernmost piers of the wharf until Heritis was firmly in control of the northern piers. His troops and scent masters hadn't been on the ships lost during the night attack, and they were able to get onshore in good order. Each had taken their magnesa, and all scent masters were occupied in pressing their scent barriers towards the defenders as they deflected the barrage of scent bolts.

The guardsmen edged towards the long rows of broken and tumbled wood and debris jammed along the large warehouses and in the narrow laneways, their force, aided by scent bolts and spears gradually overcoming the defenders' resistance. Bilternus concentrated, weaving and holding the scent barriers as tightly as he could until they could be close enough for their troops to use their physical weapons.

He was amazed how the red crystal enhanced his ability, and could feel the power driving through his senses as he pressed down on the enemy's scent defences. In the back of his mind, he recalled seeing his uncle, the Shada, ruthlessly driving his powerful scent bolts through men's flesh and felt a similar determination overriding his natural reluctance. A redness overran his brain as he pushed harder in the affray.

Kyel ran between defenders in their strategic groups, keeping them co-ordinated, reinforcing the scent masters' defensive shields. While he assessed the attackers, the size of their force, their tactics and power, he also picked up a significant use of magnesa that made the opposing force more formidable. Alone they could not hope to prevail against such overwhelming odds, but then the enemy didn't know about shadow scent.

Yes, he thought, *that is* our *secret weapon, and it is up to us to use it effectively.*

As he moved he 'tasted' the scents of the opposing force. *Ah,* he nodded to himself, *Heritis is the leader. No Jakus, thank Ean. We should be able to cope with Heritis if things go as planned.* He turned to go but hesitated. A mote of familiar scent had reached him. *Oh, no, Bilternus, what are you doing here?* He grimaced as he ran to meet Brin and his men hidden at the far end of the wharf.

Bilternus, my friend, why are you in this war zone? I can't protect you. You are in the thick of it and will have to suffer the consequences.

He shook his head as he reached Brin's hideout and delivered the order to fire the city, to remove cover and disrupt the attackers' plans.

Cathar and Lethnal watched the action in the city to the south, aware that they would soon be called into action. Their mood was sombre as they saw the first puff of smoke rise into the sky.

"It's happening," said Lethnal. "Now we must prove ourselves. This is the moment for shadow scent to reveal itself and save our countries. People, take your cordial."

Rasnal grinned at the two scent masters and raised her cup. "To the saving of Ean, and all our countries." They drank.

The smoke billowed, pushing huge columns high into a clouded sky. With the smoke came the sounds of a great conflagration as the city burnt. Flames spread on a slight offshore breeze, pushing smoke along the wharves and out to sea.

The defenders left once their position became untenable, rushing through the blockaded streets, heading northwards, dragging a trail of attackers with them. The disorder caused by the flames and smoke made everyone keen to leave the city, and the defenders had little problem in leading their attackers northwards.

"Soon," called Lethnal to the group of women behind her. "Be ready."

The flow of defenders rushing through and past the guardhouse increased. Kyel and Grefnel dashed into the open area inside the palisades.

"Now!" yelled Kyel.

The scent masters formed a wall along the front of the guardhouse, Lethnal and Cathar in the front. She raised an arm, and the air slowly became hazy, insubstantial lines of scent contributing to a barrier in front of them.

A dark swath of people appeared, the black of scent masters, the greys and browns of Sutanites, a scent wall preceding them. Heritis, in the lead, held up an arm.

"This is it!" he yelled. "We have them!"

"No!" called Lethnal, "We have you." With that a translucent wall began to enclose the crowd in front of her. A flaming backdrop outlined the Sutanites, as they used their magnesa-enhanced power to counter the unexpected attack.

The defenders continued to push their power into the scent wall, and it slowly dropped towards the astonished attackers, dismantling the scent bonds, enfolding and smothering many of those in the front line of attackers. Those who didn't fall turned in confusion into the ranks behind them, stumbling to push their way to safety. Some threw spears and scent bolts as they retreated, but disorder overcame training and the army escaped back into the black smoke in a disorganised rabble.

The battle for Ean hung in the balance.

Chapter Twenty-Nine

The defenders at the guardhouse cheered as Heritis and his forces fled. "Quiet!" Lethnal called, raising her arm. "A skirmish has been won. Everything has gone as hoped, so far. But this is a ruthless enemy, unaccustomed to losing. We must follow our plan to leave the city, tend our wounded and dead and make our achievements count."

At her call, everyone readied themselves to leave the city and carry out the next phase of their plan. Stolid peracs, normally used for towing barges upriver, guided their ships back to the western bank where the wounded were quickly placed aboard. The animals then began the arduous towing of the ships northwards to the capital. The scent masters, mingled with the guardsmen and other defenders as they hastened up the main road paralleling the river, trusting that the refugees from Port Saltus, who had left before the fighting, had had time enough to reach Nebleth.

Lethnal, Brin, Grefnel, Cathar and Kyel chivvied the last of the defenders onto the road before they, too, left with their loaded animals, aware they had struck a significant blow against Heritis and the Sutanite invaders. Brin set the guardhouse on fire as they exited, shaking his head at the destruction of another part of his favourite city.

"Cheer up, Brin," said Kyel, "we've achieved a lot, and severely affected their plans. We'll soon be able to turn the Sutanites back, force them to leave and never let them call Ean theirs again."

"'Ope yer rite lad, 'ope yer rite," Brin said, shrugging his broad shoulders before leading his perac onto the road.

"Blasted scartha!" growled Heritis, spittle falling on those near him. "How did they do that? How did they stop us so easily? We had Jakus' magnesa. We had our scent wall overwhelming them. Then it failed. Even the acid scents failed. Didn't eat into the walls or even their flesh. It was stopped before it really began. How?"

Bilternus was in the small group around Shad Heritis and even though he had an idea how it had happened, he kept his silence. If he said it was a special scent power available to women, he wouldn't have survived Heritis' interrogation. Better to go along with him, yet keep his own council.

"What shall we do now, Shad?" asked Rancer. "We had significant losses during the fighting, even though we still outnumber the Eanites. How should we proceed?"

Heritis stared at Rancer for a long moment, scent aura darkening, before he shook his head.

"We continue after the enemy. We can't stop now even though we've had a setback. Our responsibility is to secure Ean for the Shada. That is what we must do."

"Bring everyone together," growled Dronthis, gripping a long dagger at his side. "Attack them on a wide front."

Bilternus looked sideways at Dronthis' outburst, concerned at the man's fervour.

"Done!" exclaimed Heritis. "We can't let them win. You!" he said, looking at Bilternus. "Before you go, make certain there's a skeleton crew on the ships, then order everyone else to the north of the city. The blasted Eanites have taken all the animals, so we march to the enemy on a solid front. We have superior numbers, and we are fighters, not weaklings like our opponents. We must—and will—succeed.

"Move!"

The weather became more inclement, dark with swirls of rain as the Eanites hurried their animals along the highway. Even so, they made a rapid retreat, soon catching the toiling animals towing the ships and the straggling end of the refugee column. Darkness had descended by the time they neared Nebleth. No one was left behind as the final group reached the city's defences. The gates were barred and defended, and people filled the spacious courtyard of the tower, taking time to recover. The ships, masts stepped, offloaded the wounded directly into the city from the docks.

Lethnal led her small group into Nebleth tower and the relative warmth of the large, well-lit hall.

"Regna. Jucial. Welcome!" Lethnal rushed towards two women seated at the head of a long wooden table. "I thought you would be at Regulus."

"Welcome everyone," exclaimed Regna as she and Jucial exchanged scents with Lethnal. "All the fighting is here. This is where the fate of Ean will be decided, and this is where we must all be. We've emptied Regulus and brought all our fighters to Nebleth. I realise we face my former partner and his turncoat army, so we know his ways, but he doesn't know all of ours.

"So please sit, eat, and tell me what has happened. Then we'll work out how to defeat my overconfident Heritis."

Lethnal, Cathar and Kyel quickly filled them in on what had happened with Brin, Cynth, Rasnal, Grefnel and even Tishal adding comments when relevant.

"So, the shadow scent... How effective was it?"

"As well as we could hope for," said Cathar. "The enemy was on a wide front and very aggressive, so it was distracting to concentrate on overcoming their scent attack, especially the nasty acidic elements they were using, but we managed to break it up and push them back. It was the first experience of war for some of our women, too."

"The enemy knew we would resist," said Kyel. "Probably they were also mad at the successful burning of three of their ships. Their scent bolts and spear attacks became overwhelming in several instances. We've damaged them, but just not enough."

"Be that as it may," Regna stood, her scents pluming in scarlet and purple with a deep entwining of grey, "this is where it ends. Either we destroy the enemy, or we send them running back to Sutan. Agreed?"

A gusty wind brought bursts of heavy rain, driving into the faces of the army as it marched five abreast along the northern road. Visibility was limited and they were on edge, anticipating surprise enemy attacks. The impetus of the march had slowed, and those with injuries gravitated to the back of the column.

"Wouldn't mind my perac," murmured Piltarnis from under his black hood as he trudged head down amongst his fellow scent masters and troops from Faltis' estates.

"Wouldn't we all," Bilternus responded, "although it's smart of the enemy to leave us no animals and no barges to carry our supplies."

"What? You're not sympathetic, are you?" Piltarnis looked sideways at him.

"Well look at our situation. Boats destroyed. A lot of injuries. Having to carry our own supplies on our backs. Spread out on the only road, exposed and vulnerable. Even the weather against us. It's hard to not see the strategic advantage to the enemy."

"Blast, Bilternus, you're right, you know. I'm not keen to be fighting for the Shada so far away from home. I left a lovely lady in Southern Port. I wonder what she's doing now, if she even remembers me."

A rattle of rain hit their bodies as if in emphasis.

A small tile-roofed compound appeared out of the gloom, constructed on the high ground away from the river. Logs driven into the ground formed a curve facing away from the water, while the front was a wall of rough-hewn planks broken by a doorway and a small, shuttered window. They saw a group led by

Heritis investigating the structure.

Bilternus held up his arm, signalling his troops to pull up as the crush of people ahead slowed.

"We should move on, see what the Shad's plans are, as I suspect he'll want to use this way station as an overnight bivouac for the army."

"Dark enough already, Bilternus," said Piltarnis. "Reckon only the important people will have shelter, though."

"Yes, pity the poor troops. No choice for us, eh? We'll have to stay with our people."

"Wouldn't have it otherwise, despite this disgusting weather."

"You're to come to the Shad! All scent masters," said a large figure looming up in front of them. "Settle your troops for the night." With that, Dronthis turned and pushed his way back through the stationary army.

"We should go," said Piltarnis.

"A moment. Let our forces prepare to camp. Best they keep together, too." Bilternus and Piltarnis sought out their leaders to let them know to spread out and set up camp before they headed towards the way station.

A fire was already lit in a stone hearth on one side of the commodious interior with a steaming pot over it. It was surprisingly comfortable out of the wind and with the chill off the air. Heritis stood with his arms commander Rancer, his ship's captain Crastus and Dronthis, drinking a hot beverage while looking down at a rough table. A number of black-coated scent masters stood around them.

"You took your time!" Heritis glared, before glancing down again. "This is where I think they'll defend: the gates of Nebleth. See this diagram?" he said, tapping his finger on the parchment. "This is where they'll do it. Plenty of space to spread out.

"So, we'll have to attack on a wide front. We must have maximum scent power—don't stint on the magnesa. We must have all non-scent-talented using weapons. Keep them off their guard. Stop them from focussing on their scent defence." He scratched his chin, searching the faces around him. "Regna and the women with her were up to something when I was here. I wish I knew what."

Heritis shook his head, took a drink. "Any ideas? You're all talented people, you must have some ideas. Bilternus, you look like you're hiding something. What can you add?"

Bilternus felt his heart sink to his stomach while he thought frantically. "Little enough, Shad. They did manage to hold our forces, but all was in disarray with plans hard to follow. I don't know how to do anything better than what is planned.

"I assume we attack early next day?"

"Bah!" Heritis spat on the floor. "We march before dawn to attack Nebleth. We must win this fight. This decisive attack must smash them and the city, too. We must win.

"Prepare those under your command. The scent masters must be united in this, for if we fail then we all fail. No retreat. Forward only, for the glory of Sutan." He spat again and gazed into the fire.

Bilternus and Piltarnis slipped away into the night.

A blutions were quick, with cold rations shared and gear packed for the large army to head up the dark road alongside the vast, grey river. A cold and uncomfortable night broke into a dull morning. The wind had stilled, and the day promised to favour neither side in the coming fight.

Bilternus and Piltarnis had ensured all their people were as well prepared as they could be as they took up their position in the central section of the army. Piltarnis and their scent masters walked in a black-robed group ready to quickly join the remainder of the scent masters when Heritis required it.

The day slowly brightened as a watery sun edged over the mountains to the northeast. The walls encircling Nebleth, the capital of Ean, came into view all too soon and Bilternus' gut tightened, threatening to spill its contents as he saw the dark band of defenders waiting for them on the palisade walls. A roar came from ahead of him as Heritis vented his fury to those who were trying to stop him.

Bilternus would remember little of what happened next.

The army was disciplined, spreading wide and using their resources to best advantage. Spears and scent bolts rained down on both sides as each tried to gain an advantage. The Sutanite army was huge, and the broad band of attackers outnumbered the defenders, breaking through the gates, pushing anyone outside into the dirt. Hand-to-hand fighting was occurring all along the line of attack, youngsters and old men fighting against the prime of Sutan. *No contest*, he thought.

The army pushed closer, through the gateways, pressing into the defenders, inevitably crushing them against the stone and wooden walls. *We're going to win*, Bilternus thought, with a feeling of disappointment. *Despite their courage we're going to win.*

Another roar broke through. He heard Heritis and Dronthis over the hubbub, then he saw it: a grey-blue wall of defenders, women, standing before Heritis, one woman, tall, dark and regal leading them. A visible wall of scent was pushing down on them, tight and dark, ominous in its intent.

Then, as if his eyes were blurring, Bilternus could see grey, smoke-like scent billowing around and over the Sutanite scent wall. Puffs swelled and infiltrated the barrier, breaking and dissipating the bonded scents, smothering those holding the scent wall in place. Bodies fell with little warning. Bilternus took a sudden breath, realising he was seeing the women's scent the old soothsayer in Sutan, Xerina, had shown him. They were using it, and the Sutanites had no real defence.

He was seeing an historic moment, a change in the power and domination of their countries, the potential demise of the Sutanites.

In a sudden rush, a large group ducked to one side and began retreating out of the gateway and down the road. *Heritis,* he thought. *The coward is running, leaving us.*

Bilternus rapidly searched for his command, his people headed by Piltarnis. They were still fighting but were having the worst of it. The battle was lost and all he could do was limit the losses. He sent a huge plume of scent in the air to attract his troops' attention.

"Surrender!" he called, hoping that what his friend Kyel had told him about the character of the Eanites was true.

With Heritis fleeing towards his ships at Port Saltus, the battle for Ean was over. The defenders were the victors and Bilternus had to hope they would be benevolent.

He crouched down, put his head between his knees and took a deep breath. Suddenly he felt a debilitating blow to his back and heard a familiar voice as he slumped to the ground, the feel of steel penetrating his tough vest to pierce his skin.

"Traitor!" screamed Dronthis.

Chapter Thirty

The fleet of thirteen ships tacked in a choppy sea as a grey sheet of rain came with a strong wind from the hidden land to the north. With water running down his lined face under a damp hood, Tibitus had to squint into the gloomy surroundings as he guided the flagship.

"Are you as wet as I feel?" asked Sharna, holding firmly to the rail. "The rain gets into everything."

"Rather up here than below. Here anything can be thrown at you, and you must manage. Makes you part of it, makes you feel alive." Tibitus clamped his jaw tight, as if afraid more words might spill forth.

"Much longer before we reach Rolan?"

"Rolan's off the starboard bow, but well to the north on this tack. Still a day or two out from the port of Request, but it's the Shada's call." Tibitus' gaze strayed up to the top sail on the main mast and he pulled his right arm across on the helm.

"The Shada's down in his cabin. Think he wants some quiet time before discussing strategy," said Sharna. "Poegna's there, too."

"Ah," Tibitus nodded. "Good to be up here without him, then. Leave him to his pleasures if it improves his mood."

"Why, Tibitus, I didn't think you had a bad word to say against Jakus," Sharna said, glancing up at the captain with a smile.

"He's a strong man if you do your job. Only had one main run-in with him, years ago now, and I wouldn't want another."

"Hmm." Sharna straightened and gazed to the ships aligned behind theirs. Four rode the waves within easy signalling distance, another four just discernible through the mists of rain and the remaining four, she knew, would be even further back. "They're lining up well. No sign of any problems, or signals indicating such?"

"All in readiness," Tibitus grunted. "Weather's holding so far, with no indication of worsening. Whenever the Shada decides, we will be ready."

"What the Shada says?" A thin dark shape loomed up onto the aft deck. "Just follow him blindly, no thoughts of your own. Bah!"

"Faltis," said Sharna coolly, "why are you here? Has the Shada finished with you?"

"You," he leant forward until his beaked nose almost touched her forehead, "will need to watch yourself. Things aren't as they seem and I...I"—his eyes seemed to redden—"have needs, too." A skeletal finger extended from a bony hand and pressed the yielding flesh between the swell of her breasts.

Sharna stepped away, her hand reaching for her dagger.

"Bah!" Faltis spat and moved away like a dark shadow in the gloom, to disappear down the steps and through the hatchway.

"Urgh," Sharna pushed back her hood and ran her hands across her face. "What's got into him, the disgusting scartha?" Then she remembered Bilternus warning her how another being inhabited his father Faltis' body, a powerful deranged creature; the long dead Septus. Hard to believe until now when she saw his eyes and felt his hand.

"He'll bear watching, Sharna," Tibitus interrupted her musings. "Pity the Shada didn't dispose of him when he had the opportunity."

Anyar spent as much time in the great conference hall atop Lookout Hill as elsewhere. Here she could keep up with intelligence as it came and went, have some input if required and get a feel for what she would be involved with. Seats were set against the walls where the tables for drinks, food and documents left space, and she had commandeered one near the doors that opened onto the grassy slopes leading down into the town.

Vor often left her side, spending a considerable amount of time following either Eren or Sovira as they came and went. She realised he had his own reasons for keeping links with the three of them, so squashed down any disquiet at his periodic disappearances.

A flurry of activity surrounded her. Word had come in via a fast, small coastal ship that a third of the Sutanite fleet had remained in Ean while the remainder was heading their way. This had been the best result they could have expected. The forces arrayed against them had been diminished, giving them a greater chance of countering Jakus' ambitions.

Anyar worried about her uncle and her friends having to fight the Sutanites in Ean, but she had every confidence in Kyel and the shadow scent power that Cathar and the other women wielded. She could do nothing for them. Her responsibility was the battle for Rolan and all her focus as Mlana had to be on winning the ultimate fight against a ruthless invader. The future was shrouded, uncertain, without a Knowing to give her guidance, but she knew defeating the

Sutanites in Rolan would not be the final conflict with the enemy.

Anyar got wearily to her feet as she saw her mother and Lan headed towards her. She automatically looked for the absent Vor before she was joined by the others.

They headed to the large table where everyone was gathering. Xaner and Siliaster, the Requist defence co-ordinators and Jelm were talking as they arrived. Jelm held out his hand to her.

"We've heard the latest," he said as Anyar came to his side. "The Sutanites are barely a day or so out, and despite the inclement weather at sea we can soon expect their attack.

"Our fleet is safely away and will await our signal before returning here to the port. Timing is crucial and will depend on how things are developing."

"I think we're as ready as we can be," added Xaner. "Ginrel is in command of the fleet at Sea Holm, and we've many defenders throughout the port complexes, so it's better defended than last time the enemy assaulted Requist. Unfortunately, we will have to leave here and travel inland to Nosta and Mlana Hold, but this time we are going to hit them and hit them hard. We will have no compunction in using shadow scent to its best ability."

The discussions and planning carried on for a time before Anyar felt Vor push hard against her legs. She looked up and saw Sovira and Eren outlined against the grey sky in the doorway, so she made a mumbled excuse before leaving.

"What have you been up to?" she asked. "Has Vor been with you?"

They snuck into the back of the hall, grabbed some sandwiches and cider before heading back out to sit against the brick walls under an eave. Vor settled beside them with a humph.

"He's been keeping us together," said Eren, "like he wants us to get to know each other. After our experience of the scent, it appears to be important."

"So, what's the news, Anyar?" asked Sovira.

She quickly outlined what was happening before raising a question that was uppermost on her mind: "Why us? What is our role, now and later?"

"Don't know," said Eren, "but we've gotta be ready. Even," and he reached down to his side, "carry a knife. Can't always rely on scent to defend ourselves." He smiled as he patted his dagger.

"Yes," Anyar nodded thoughtfully, "I have one in my bag, so I should carry it. At any rate we must stick together. Vor is keen on that, and I believe he's right."

It was a dark night. Anyar was kept awake by the continuous hammering and banging echoed from the docks and around the city. Sadir had taken to sharing the large bed with her so Vor was relegated to the middle.

Anyar lay on her back, eyes widening as she noticed a crack opening across the ceiling. It grew wider, exposing wooden beams which broke as she watched, tumbling towards her. She thrust her arms out to ward them off, but the beams fell away as she rose into a dark sky that had no stars, no moon, just a roiling greyness. It took a mere thought before she moved through the clouds and up towards the moon shining down on a carpet of grey wool. She tried to relax into the experience and let herself be carried along.

Soon the clouds gave way to a sticky black rising upwards, staining the moon's golden face. Anyar looked down and saw a city in flames; water reflected the light, showing several ships moving in a darkened harbour. Bodies were strewn in the burning streets, yet a feeling of accomplishment came through. She edged downwards to the light and the flames. Several ships of foreign make listed at the wharf, their furled sails and rigging aflame.

She moved even lower until she fancied she felt the heat. The fires loomed in her vision, then a vast hissing overwhelmed the crackling of the burning city, and a deluge of water crashed onto the flames. Faint screams rose as the water filled her vision.

She echoed the scream.

Vor's furry face looked into hers, as Sadir stroked her hand.

"A Knowing?" her mother whispered.

"Flames. Water," murmured Anyar. "We have to be ready."

Anyar dragged herself to the meeting hall, where large pots of oatmeal steamed; toast, butter, honey, and the redolent smells of crisp meat strips made her mouth water. Vor pushed ahead as he saw Eren and Sovira.

"Go, sit with your friends," whispered Sadir. "I'll bring you some food."

Lan, already seated at a table, patted the chair beside him. "Come here, all of you. I've heard we have some dreams to interpret. I think we all need to hear what happened."

Anyar glanced around a sea of welcoming faces before hearing the welcome sound of a plate sliding across the table towards her. Even Vor's entreating gaze and the need to reveal the Knowing didn't stop her from eating her fill.

"It seems we have an encouraging sign of happenings in Ean," said Lan, running a hand over his bare head.

"I concur," added Boidea, "the Mlana's Knowings could often be that specific. Though the flames and water part?"

"This confirms we'll have to fire Requist?" asked Xaner. "And just when we'd finally repaired all the damage caused last time the invaders came."

"It may be we have no choice," Lan mused. "I suspect the Sutanites, Jakus in fact, will be targeting the magnesa again, with Mlana Hold his objective, so firing Requist seems a significant defensive ploy."

"Flames," murmured Anyar, pushing her hand deeply into Vor's ruff, "are everywhere, but not just for Requist. Water will be important, I believe." She looked around the faces waiting on her next words, then focussed on Eren and Sovira. She pushed her free hand across Sovira's shoulders and took a deep breath.

"We have a part to play too, the four of us. Flames and destruction are in our future. And the cordial plays a part in that future too, even for Eren." She smiled at him.

A shadow darkened the table, and she looked up to see Siliaster's concerned face. "Sorry to interrupt, but sails have been sighted. I think we had better move to our stations."

Everyone scattered, leaving Sadir and Lan with the three youngsters.

"We should stay here," said Sadir. "This is the best place to see the action and be involved where we may. You, Anyar, are too important to risk in the initial attack. If we are required, Boidea will come for us. We have animals and supplies tethered behind our rooms on the north side of Lookout Hill; the track to the main road will be our escape route if needed."

"Mother, I will need to stay as long as possible," said Anyar. "We will be called on to use shadow scent, even with Boidea or Xerrita in charge of the use of it. The enemy is very powerful and determined."

"However, we should wait here for the time being," responded Sadir.

"I think your daughter has spoken," Lan smiled. He looked at Eren and Sovira. "I think you also may be more involved than I'd like, but fate moves in mysterious ways. Let us, my friends, prepare for what the day will bring."

Thirteen ships sailed close-hauled, like an ominous cloud, towards the waiting land ahead. Little could be discerned from that distance, but all were anticipating the coming conflict. Jakus was perched on the prow of the flagship, gazing eagerly at the nearing shore.

Kast stood next to his leader, an immovable bulk in contrast to the fidgeting leader of the invasion force. Jakus' scent aura pushed against the wind, purples and scarlets roiling above his head. On the other side stood Faltis, craning forward, seemingly as excited as the Shada at the forthcoming conflict. Occasionally, he glanced towards Jakus, his aura dark, before returning his gaze to the approaching coastline.

Sharna stood on the aft deck with Tibitus at the helm, watching the figures in the distance. She had prepared all she could for the landings and deployment of their forces, and now could only wait for the ships to dock. A shiver of foreboding ran down her spine as she saw the trio of leaders in the bow. She firmly believed Rolan would not be the easy target Jakus expected, but hoped the Shada would achieve his objective, his desire. Then there was Faltis. What did his presence foreshadow?

For a long moment she wished she was back home in Sutan, not participating in an unprovoked war.

Chapter Thirty-One

A final conference was held in the flagship's meeting room. Jakus almost forgot to favour his limp as excitement stretched his tall, thin figure, clouds of purple and scarlet hovering around his head. He was pointing emphatically at a parchment on the table as his companions in blacks and greys crowded to view the document.

Sharna endeavoured to keep away from Faltis by easing in between Tretial and the bulk of Kast as she came to grips with Requist's layout, and how it related to the country beyond. She knew the plan of the port but wanted to keep up with the Shada's latest thinking. Her role as commander of the fleet would be to ensure effective docking, unloading and protection of the ships. The decision to maximise the numbers of troops by not carrying riding and baggage animals meant fewer issues with unloading.

Once ashore her task would be to fit in with the scent masters, headed by the Shada and Faltis, and guardsmen, led by Kast, with Festern in charge of the troops from the Steppe region of Sutan. Despite her concerns over deployment of their ships and forces, she excitedly listened to Jakus' instructions.

"We've been here before." Jakus began tapping the map of Request with a pointer. "We achieved much but left behind some of the cream of our people, those who were hard to replace."

Sharna saw him glance at the slim figure of Poegna, a silent yet influential scent master standing just behind his shoulder, and realised the Shada would be thinking of Nefaria, who died on the slopes of Rolan's great waterfalls, and who Poegna had replaced in his affections. *That is if he is capable of such an emotion,* she thought.

A rap on the table broke her introspection.

"I have no intention of being caught unawares," Jakus continued. "We have the red crystal in ample supply, so have no excuse. And I understand the Rolanites don't use it in the way we do. However, do not, under any circumstances, underestimate the women. We had some difficulty with them last time, and we need to be ruthless.

"So, we land in one wave, offload immediately, and then march into the warehouses, docks, business districts and residences as planned. I will lead a rapid strike on their headquarters, take it over and co-ordinate our assault from there. A day at most, I believe.

"Then we head north. Mlana Hold is our target, and unless we capture riding animals most of us will have a forced march to achieve our objective. Nosta is the only obstacle in our way, and I will destroy it like Requist. Anything can be rebuilt once we conquer the country.

"But I must have the Hold, for it is where the crystal cave lies."

"Shada!" Tibitus poked his head through the door. "We are nearing the docks. No shipping to speak off and nothing to bar our landing, if I am any judge."

"Sharna!" Jakus focussed his dark gaze on her. "Ensure our fleet is safe as we approach. Carry out your duties."

She nodded and quickly followed Tibitus out the door.

Sharna hung over the bow rail with two experienced seamen, looking into the blue-green water as the flotilla moved towards the long pier projecting out into the harbour.

"Nothing, Commander, just what you'd expect," said a wizened seaman, cocking an eye at her. "Good depth for our draught. So, if there's anything untoward it'd be at the berth."

"Right!" She stood and signalled for a rowing boat to be launched, before looking back to the helm where Tibitus stood.

Behind him she could see the spread of the fleet, aligned in four groups of three. Their few open sails outlined against a grey horizon gave them little forward motion as they waited for a signal from the flagship. The splash of the small boat's launch drew her attention, and she watched the sailors pull hard on the oars as they rowed shoreward.

She walked back to Tibitus as she waited for the boat to reach the pier.

"Can't reckon it'd be this easy," said the captain.

"Likely not, but I won't take any chances."

A frantic waving from the sailors at the pier caught her attention, the signal saying that the pier had been sabotaged and was not suitable for landing.

"Thought as much," sighed Tibitus. "Guess we'll have to berth along the shore. Reports indicate deep water to the shoreline."

"Agreed," confirmed Sharna. "It'll make us more of a target, but to be expected. Signal the fleet for a cautious towed approach. We'll go in first."

She nodded to Tibitus and went below to inform Jakus.

A nyar watched the toy-like ships approach the shore, even smaller boats pulling them into their anchorage. *So far away*, she thought, *yet so deadly.*

"That's the enemy, then," said Eren, standing with Anyar and Sovira. "Only thirteen? Don't look much of a threat."

"Be careful what you say, young Eren," said Sadir, as she brought drinks for the three of them. "All too soon there'll be fighting, and in that fighting people will be hurt and people will die."

"Sorry," gulped Eren, pulling at the neck of his tunic in the dark Rolan greens, "but I'm nervous. This is so new."

"Me too," added Sovira, leaning up against him, her face pale. "I remember when they came last time but we were kept far away when it happened. Not this time, though."

"I apologise for my words," said Sadir, "but we need to be prepared. I can't imagine the Sutanites will be gentle. There're a few hours of daylight, so I suspect there'll be fighting right into the night. We must be ready to retreat if things turn against us, as it must be looking at the size of their fleet."

"Aren't we prepared for that?" he asked.

"Yes, we are," replied Sadir. "I forget you were not at the briefing. Some of what we do will come later but, for the time being, there'll be lots of smoke and fire with the fighting. I suspect we'll be on the road before nightfall."

"We must stay here for as long as possible, Mother. I am certain," said Anyar. "Now, please go and help Lan and the others. I want no one left here in the hall. The enemy must be allowed easy access."

"Oh, Anyar." Sadir grasped her daughter to her chest. "I know this is what you want, but why can't we stay?" She looked into her daughter's implacable eyes and sighed. "Look after her and yourselves, you two, and Vor. Remember, when you leave, go to Sovira's house. Your mother, Sharia, will be leading a group and waiting there with your animals." Sadir released her daughter, put a hand to her mouth and hurried down the hill to where the scent master women were assembling.

"Now, my dear, dear friends," said Anyar, turning to her two companions standing pale-faced in similar green tunic tops and brown trousers, "we're dressed for what's to come and we're here, placed here because we 'need' to be." She gripped their hands and pushed a calming scent across their faces, smiling into their eyes. "Come, let's take our cordial and prepare."

As they sipped their drinks, Anyar surveyed the meeting hall with its brick columns, from the open windows set in the seaward-facing brick wall to the long wooden table dominating the centre of the large wide room. Smaller tables were set against the far wall. Her eyes narrowed as she saw a solid table set near the door in the back corner. A glance to the heavy beams supporting the tiled roof made her nod.

"I think we'll use that table, against the wall. It's enough for the four of us."

"What?" asked Eren, letting go of Anyar's hand to scrub at his short brown hair.

"This is what I'm planning. It is necessary and we'll come to no harm, at least that's what I foresee."

"I don't like this, Anyar," said Sovira.

"We will not be in significant danger, you'll see," she answered. "I've promised your mother. Besides, we've got Vor."

The long, solid animal looked up through his shaggy fur and grinned, sharp canine teeth exposed.

The fleet was lined up along the wooden-boarded wharf area that stretched along the shoreline, each ship secured to bollards. They presented a long line, vulnerable to seaward attack. Sharna had ordered two two-masters to offload their troops into a multitude of rowing boats and then to return to sea to patrol.

She was restless as she watched the unloading of the troops of guardsmen and scent masters. The dock area was clear—no people, no defenders—which was worrying. She knew they wouldn't just let the Sutanites take over, but what were they planning?

In her gut she felt that the fleet was the target, but no enemy vessels remained in the harbour. The two ships on patrol were a safety measure, but was it enough? A black and grey spread of troops on the docks quickly formed into blocks with their designated leaders.

Jakus, with obvious scent shields, stood with Poegna, Faltis and Kast, pointing towards the buildings that stretched in a staggered fashion up the slopes of Lookout Hill. She could see a large brick building perched on the summit and remembered the Shada mentioning that as a command point. No doubt the enemy was doing just the same, so it was a significant target.

Sharna took a last look along the line of ships, picked up the backpack containing her supplies, and pulled it over her black-clad shoulders. She regretted covering her favoured clothing but left the black hood down, exposing her signature red hair as she moved to the gangway linking the flagship to the shore. She had to leave the safety of the ships in the hands of the captains and seamen and meet up with Tretial to lead her own group. Her target was defined, and the Shada expected everyone to do their part.

Sharna looked along the crowded wharf remembering a similar scene some years ago, only this time they had a significantly larger force and more power. *The magnesa gives us that*, she thought as she reached into her pouch and withdrew a pinch of the red crystals. As they dissolved in her mouth the power pushed into her brain and crowded away her anxiety, *Yes,* she thought, *this is worthwhile.*

She took her place next to Tretial, at the head of her troops of over a few hundred guardsmen with scent master support and prepared to move into the western section of the port's warehouse district.

Jakus lifted his arm and pushed a huge scent plume into the air, deep purple with flashes of yellow crackling like lightning.

They surged forward. The Sutanite invasion of Rolan had begun.

Immediately they entered the maze of streets and buildings surrounding the waterfront, the intent of the defenders was revealed. All avenues were blocked with firmly constructed barricades, forcing the invaders to push out with their scent shields to protect their troops trying to remove the obstruction. A flurry of scent bolts and spears, adding to the confusion, delayed the Sutanites' move through the city.

Jakus had taught his commanders how to best utilise the scent attack, with acid-based scents to eat into any organic material and reinforced individual bonds to make them almost unstoppable by any scent defence.

Slowly, their efforts made an impact and the invaders moved forward, rooting out and killing any defenders caught or left behind.

Sharna maintained her strong, scent-bonded shields easily, the magnesa coursing through her veins making her feel invulnerable as she urged her troops forward through the narrow streets bracketed by one- and two-storey buildings, the powerful wall erected by her scent masters overwhelming almost everything in their path.

She and Tretial came out of the narrow street into a broad thoroughfare and stopped, their troops spreading out behind them. Facing them was a group of women, dressed in the greens and browns of the Rolanite defenders, backed up by a force of a hundred or so spear-carrying men. It took her a moment to think before she and her scent masters pushed out their acidic scent blanket, not caring in the magnesa-induced euphoria what it would do to the people before her.

And it failed. Like oil on water, the scent wall thinned and dissipated as it met a grey fog emanating from the women, boiling up from them in an unanticipated attack. The acidic scent then fell to the ground in a corrosive slurry, eating into the boots of the attackers.

Sharna's mouth dropped open at this, even as she remembered the Shada speaking of some unusual power the Rolanite women had.

A flurry of spears broke through the defunct scent wall, hitting into the astonished attackers. Sharna instinctively pulled up her personal shield, barely stopping a spear from slicing through into her chest. Instead of finding her heart, the spearpoint merely nicked her skin, but the shock of it almost prevented her from seeing what happened next.

"Fire, Sharna!" yelled Tretial.

The opposing Rolanite force had rapidly retreated, and puffs of smoke were rising all around them, flames shooting upward.

"Withdraw!" yelled Sharna, anxiety shrilling her voice. "Regroup near the wharves." She and Tretial hurried their people back along the way they had come. A tenth of their force had been lost in that one confrontation and while she dreaded breaking the news to the Shada, she had to inform him of the unusual scent defence.

"They're coming!" yelped Eren as he stood in the open window space looking down the long slope to the wharf. He pointed to a dark mass of Sutanites heading up the hill.

"I knew he would come," murmured Anyar. "That is the enemy's leader, together with his creature, the one I have 'seen'. Now I will view him, up close, for the first time." She straightened and looked at her friends.

"We must prepare."

They closed and barred the shutters on all the windows and hurried to their table against the wall, scrambling onto a thick perac-wool blanket set under it. Sovira and Eren settled together against the wall; Anyar and Vor on the outside, knees, hands and fur touching. She blew out calming scents as they waited, listening, hearts pounding. A clamour rose as the invaders drew closer.

"Now," said Anyar, "we do what we did before. Same as before. I know you are scared but remember we have each other, and Vor. Nothing can harm us if we do as we must.

"Complete concentration. Do not be distracted."

Vor growled, then a translucent shimmer covered his body; Sovira gulped and Eren fidgeted as Anyar felt a familiar pull on her mind. She could see a translucent scent slowly enveloping them in the gloom of the large room and began to push into the bonds of the scent at its deepest level, seeing the beginnings of shadow scent from her strongest scent memories come forth. It grew, linking at the smallest of levels, impossible for anything to penetrate, and yet they could see through it. She pushed at the envelope of scent extending it to fit securely within the box-like confines of the table legs.

The pressure caused her head to throb until she realised that four pulses took part: four hearts, four minds, adding support and strength.

"We have it," she encouraged. "Don't let go of each other, no matter what happens."

The shutters crashed open, and light flooded into the room. Dark figures poured in.

Sovira whimpered.

"Hold," Anyar whispered, squinting towards the people thudding across the wooden floorboards. Tall and dark, they came like a tide, filling the hall, scouring the rooms leading off the large space. She focused on them, seeing powerful scent masters, mainly men, although one female stood out by her poised demeanour and a pale colour showing through her black robe. *But she's still an enemy,* she thought and closed her mind to the consequences of what she planned.

"No-one here!" screeched a voice and she recognised the leader of the Sutanites, Jakus, from her Knowings. "Search. Kill anyone you find!"

Sovira whimpered again and Vor purred softly to her, adding comfort.

Then Anyar saw the 'other', the black-clad skeletal man, pause, his booted feet near the table they hid under, the strength of his magnesa-enhanced scent investigation touching, wriggling along their invisible shadow scent barrier, seeking entrance.

"Someone's here, Jakus!" he yelled, his voice strident.

"Where, Faltis?" snapped Jakus. "They've all fled. Bring my people in. We have a command centre to set up. Poegna, the maps!" The woman Anyar had noticed pulled out a wad of documents from a backpack and spread them out on the central table.

Anyar held her friend's hands, trying to keep them calm, while endeavouring to see and learn all she could of the men trying to destroy her country. Faltis wandered around peering into every corner of the hall, eyes flickering redly.

Time passed while they watched the large, black-clad group around the main table discussing tactics, working on their maps. Their energetic leader, Jakus, repeatedly crashed his hand onto the map, demanding intelligence to aid them to reach Mlana Hold and the crystal cave without delay.

Anyar sank back on her haunches as she heard the man's fixation aided by the high-pitched tones of Faltis, his unnerving offsider.

The atmosphere in their hideout grew staler, causing Anyar to reluctantly open a small hole at the far end to draw in fresh air.

Faltis lifted his head and sniffed. "There it is! Someone is here. I told you." His voice rose shrilly as if another was talking. "We have spies in our midst."

He stood abruptly, his chair crashing over, peering towards their hiding place, red eyes flashing.

Anyar, realising that the creature who had spied on her in a Knowing was in this man and could perceive them, had to act.

"Now!" she whispered, drawing on their combined strength to push out with the shadow scent barrier in an overwhelming thrust. The pressure exploded into the building, causing walls to collapse outwards and bring wooden roof beams and rubble crashing down on those inside.

Anyar pulled the scent barrier back in tight, shielding them from the impacts.

D arkness fell.

Chapter Thirty-Two

Sadir lifted her head as a thunder-like rumble filled the darkening sky from the summit of Lookout Hill.

"Anyar!" she gasped.

"Yes," confirmed Lan, "she has carried out what she intended. Now Sadir, we must let her complete her task. Do not concern yourself, as the Mlana is moving in her. Our role is to send the remainder of the invaders back to the sea before we leave the city."

"But?" Sadir jerked aside as a gust of breeze brought embers swirling near their group of scent masters.

"We must finish this!" called Boidea. "They are on the run, and we've got to keep pushing them back, to the docks. Come!"

Green- and brown-clad Rolanites wielding shadow scent followed the last of the Sutanites down the main thoroughfare, only desisting as the flames and smoke grew too thick. Bodies lay strewn across the cobbled roads like flotsam; black and brown interspersed with the occasional green.

Another swirl of defenders came from the burning houses lining the lower slopes of eastern side of Lookout Hill, Xaner in the lead.

"Hate to see my city going up in flames but it's necessary; some of my people have been lost, but we've had an impact," puffed Xaner. "How have Siliaster and Jelm gone? Did the shadow scent work for them too? Have we managed to contain the Sutanites to the docks?"

"Unsure, but our ploy seems to be achieving its aim," answered Lan. "Jelm's yet to report in, although the city on the western side of the Hill is on fire. Siliaster's group has already continued through to the Nosta road. They've pushed the invaders back to the wharves; our tactics were effective. Jelm knows to meet us on the Nosta road if delayed. We have to all leave by evening.

"You came near the upper slopes of Lookout Hill. Did you see what happened?" Sadir asked, grabbing his arm.

"It's gone. The administration building's gone, just rubble. Don't know how, but a whole lot of Sutanites were there when it blew up."

"Oh!" Sadir cried. "Anyar's there. Your daughter, too!"

"What? How? She should be safe, not there!" Xaner turned and began hurrying back up the hill.

"Wait, Xaner!" called Lan. "It's all planned. The Mlana's in charge and your daughter is with her. She will be alright. Your consort, Sharia, is waiting with a small patrol to bring them to the rendezvous point."

Xaner stopped, looking back at Lan half obscured by the swirls of smoke. "You're sure?"

"I am," Lan's aura burst of greys and pastel colours emphasised his words. "Now we must be heading to the road. All we've done is given the enemy a setback, a tweak to his tail. We must be on the move." He took Sadir's hand and gave a comforting squeeze, before leading the crowd of defenders through the walls of flames engulfing buildings on each side of the main thoroughfare.

Xaner hesitated, casting a fearful glance through the gloom to the changed skyline of Lookout Hill before leading his contingent after Lan.

The large mass of defenders, carrying their wounded, hurried down the road to the western suburbs of the city where hundreds of animals were saddled and waiting. Behind them the flames of the city lit the evening sky, effectively holding the enemy to the docks and blocking their progress inland.

The placement of their lair under the table near the back door of the hall was well chosen. The tabletop, reinforced by the shadow scent barrier, prevented the rubble from crushing them, although Anyar realised they couldn't keep the weight of the collapsed room off for long.

"Hold!" she whispered. "We've all done well, but a little longer."

The rubble creaked and groaned as she edged the scent barrier towards the space where the door had once stood. Bricks crunched out of the way as they wriggled along the remnants of the back wall and out into the dark space of the doorway. The crunch of a gravel path meant they were through, and Anyar slowly disengaged them from the scent shield.

Sounds assailed their ears, timber shifting and groaning. Anyar realised the people inside the demolished building were injured, maybe dying, but all she could think about was getting her group to safety.

"Follow me," gasped Sovira, grabbing Anyar's hand and pulling her onto the grass of the park on top of Lookout Hill. Eren, gripping the back of Anyar's tunic, followed them into a black night filled with flickering light.

Even as smoke filled their nostrils and she realised what the light sky meant, Vor growled. They halted as a dark shape loomed up in front of them.

Anyar breathed in, readying a powerful scent bolt to release at the menacing figure until Vor's growl changed to a delighted *whuff*.

"Anyar?" hissed a familiar voice.

"Jelm!" she exclaimed and hurried forward into his wide arms, with Sovira and Eren grappling him from either side.

They hugged in a tight group for a long moment, Vor pushing in and out of their legs emitting low whuffs. A strong scent cloud rose over them and Anyar had never felt as safe as this strong man made her feel.

"You've all been though the wars, even though you're just youngsters," he said, hugging them tighter. "Covered with dust and smelling like a building has collapsed on you. Are you hurt? Is everything alright?"

"Jelm," said Anyar. Her voice, muffled by his shoulder, deepened, became more mature, and she continued: "We've done what we had to do. Seen the enemy, learnt his plans and dealt him a blow."

"Certainly, there seems to be little left of the administration building. You sure you're not hurt?"

"Jelm, Anyar, can we get moving?" whispered Eren. "There were heaps of Sutanites in the building when we were there. They'll be coming soon so we must get away."

"Well said, Eren. Sovira, you haven't spoken. Are you hurt?"

"I...I don't know. There's nothing left, nothing." She rubbed a sleeve across her eyes. "This is where I've always played; our home is just over there, though it's burning. I don't know..."

"Come on," Jelm said, pulling her into his side. "Let's get to the animals. A small group of us are waiting there to help you to the meeting point. Your mother is there too. Now that we've pushed the enemy back, she will need to know you're safe. Your efforts here will have dealt the Sutanites a significant blow."

A rumble of bricks crashing through the night from the ruined building made them hurry, Vor growling as he led them across the grassy hilltop.

Jakus expanded his scent shield, thrusting bricks and debris high into the air with an explosive bang. *What happened?* His brain refused to comprehend. *Faltis? What did he see? What did he do?*

Groaning drew his attention, and he forced out a crackling burst of scent power to illuminate the room, highlighting a tumble of beams thrown haphazardly over the brick rubble and debris of the great hall. Some of his people, black robes dust-covered, were moving slowly, rising to sitting positions, bemused by what had happened. More of concern was the number of his scent masters who had not been prepared, their lifeless bodies entwined with the rubble scattered through the room.

He glanced to his side where his companion, Poegna, had been at the moment of the explosion. She lay on the floor in a splash of lilac and black, the side of the large table across her legs, a wooden beam across her head, which was leaking red onto the floor.

"Told you!" a voice shrilled in his ear. "Scent masters of unbelievable power, here, in this room. Look what they've done."

Jakus curbed his instinctive reaction to blast Faltis as he bent down to touch Poegna's body. *She is dead and they killed her.* Another consort lost to this scum. *Ah, they'll pay. Yes, they'll pay.*

"Get everyone outside!" he yelled. "Faltis, the maps. Retrieve the maps!"

"She's dead. Face half gone. Lost another one, eh?"

Jakus felt a wave of ire rising, darkness covering his vision. He swung his gaze to Faltis, preparing a killing blast, when he saw something that stopped him, his habitual cunning taking over. Faltis was watching him, expectant, deliberately goading him, eyes gleaming redly. *What is this,* he thought, *enemies from within as well?* He took a deep, calming breath. "Just find the maps, Faltis, then we'll meet at the docks." He brushed dust from his robe as he stood and went to organise the rescue effort.

A nyar's head slumped, and she slipped sideways until the strapping stopped her. The perac took another step and she swayed back upright.

"Doze for a while, Anyar. You need to get some rest after what you've been through. I'll keep a watch on you."

She half-smiled in her stupor, comfortable her mother was with her on the trek from the Requist plains. The mass exodus of defenders from the port city had gone as well as could be expected and they were now plodding up the inland road alongside the Rolander River. Locals who knew the road well led the defenders past the tighter corners and the prepared pitfalls to reach comparative safety of the city of Nosta.

The enemy would not be long in following, but they had the advantages of riding and travelling at night on a familiar roadway. The Sutanites were stuck in Requist until daybreak and, without animals, it would take some time before they could organise a pursuit.

Catching up with Lan, Sadir, Boidea, Xerrita and Xaner, Anyar quickly shared what she, Sovira and Eren had found out about the enemy's plans and Jakus' fixation on the Mlana Hold and the crystal cave.

A fter withdrawing from Requist, they were hastening along the inland road so the locals could make the road as impassable to the enemy as possible.

Anyar felt relaxed and comfortable in her situation, not concerned with what had gone on before. Finally she had had a chance to interact with the enemy, get to know them, feel what she had to do, and to feel the weight of knowledge that Alethea, the grand old lady she had known for such a short time, had left in her on her death. She now believed she knew what being a Mlana, the spiritual head of Rolan, meant.

And with her two friends, her first real friends, plus Vor, the future seemed more secure.

"What are you smiling for, Anyar?" Sadir's voice carried over the soft shuffle of the animals' feet around her.

"Hmm, just happy being here," Anyar answered drowsily.

The alarm call of lizards woke her from the repetitive movement of her perac, sun splashing on the side of her face. She straightened and saw a mass of activity around her. They had stopped in a large clearing where a brook ran down under the road and towards the place, some distance away, where it would meet the Rolander River. Fires were already alight, and the delicious smell of frying came to her nose.

"Off you get." A strong pair of arms lifted her and placed her on the ground.

"Ow!" she yelped as a cramp gripped her thigh.

"Sorry, Anyar, did I hurt you?"

"No, Jelm, I'm just stiff from all that riding." Anyar rubbed her thigh until the cramp eased. "Is everyone here? Vor, Eren, Sovira?"

"Vor's over there," Sadir pointed, "near where the food's being prepared. Eren's with Lan and Sovira's with her mother and father. Now let's go to the brook. Time to wash up. Women are allocated that side, where there's some privacy with plenty of bushes."

"Uh huh." Anyar kept rubbing at her thigh as she walked. "Hope the water's not too cold."

"This time of the year, after a cold winter, we'll just have to brave it, as we definitely need a clean-up."

They had built a large fire, and after a brief meal washed down with strong tea, they gathered to discuss tactics. Again, Anyar explained what she had learned from the enemy and the potential results of the explosion. Vor lay across her feet, warming his belly by the fire while Eren and Sovira bracketed her.

"A moment for those of us injured or fallen defending our way of life against a ruthless invader." Lan looked across at Anyar and began to hum.

She joined hands with Eren and Sovira, feeling Vor on her feet and began to follow Lan's lead. As the sound grew, everyone in the clearing joined in until over three hundred people were swaying with the energy. Scudding scents came in from around them, from the verdant greenery, the animals, even the creatures hidden in the undergrowth, until the air thickened and swirled in a dark haze. Soon a secondary shadowy scent added substance as it infiltrated their mouths and nostrils, giving them a sense of togetherness and purpose. They were united until death in their fight against the invader and would not let their companions or the land down. A slight breeze pushed in, blurring then softening the scents, and the hum slowly faded away.

"Now, Nosta and what we must do." Lan nodded to Boidea, then looked around the expectant faces and the planning began.

They met in the flagship's meeting room, the smell of blood and smoke thick in the air. Jakus sat, hunched over the ragged parchments spread across the dusty table, a decanter of wine and glasses in its centre.

Sharna sat next to Tretial near the end of the table, as far away from the Shada as possible, realising his mood. She hoped he would be rational, not apportion blame, but of late his moods were unpredictable and the red crystal only emphasised them. The loss of Poegna hung over the room. She was a woman Sharna liked well enough but had felt sorry for her situation as the Shada's newest consort. Kast was his usual stolid self, blocking Jakus from the spasmodically twitching Faltis. On the other side a bedraggled Festern sat, an elbow on the table, toying with a half-drunk glass of red wine.

Jakus reached over, grabbed a glass off the table, filled it from the decanter and drank deeply.

He slammed the glass down and glared at the assembled group.

"We had a minor setback. The scartha were able to bite us, and we let them. How? What did they do that we didn't anticipate, didn't suspect?

"Did they use a new kind of defence, a scent we couldn't penetrate, one the women use? We had warnings about it, yet at the first encounter we falter, we lose troops, we withdraw. Not good enough." He gulped down the rest of the wine and held out the glass. Kast refilled it with a steady hand.

"We had a small setback, but we have learnt. The burning is over. The enemy has done our job for us, and the city is destroyed. Now we move on. No mercy. The crystal cave waits for me. Get your troops ready." He gazed around the table. "Now go!"

Sharna stood with Tretial, relieved she had not been targeted by Jakus, and began to move out of the room.

"Hold, Sharna!" said Jakus. "Tretial, you will take charge of the Commander's troops. She will have other duties."

Sharna stood there, her heart in her mouth as everyone else left. The door closed behind them.

Jakus looked at her. "You and I will be working together more closely, from now on." A slow smile crept across his lined face. "You will know that I lost my consort, Poegna. She needs to be replaced."

Sharna gulped, blood draining from her face. "Yes, my Shada," she replied woodenly.

Chapter Thirty-Three

More riding, resulting in a sore rear and chaffed thighs, meant Anyar was too involved with the aches of her body to notice the granite pillars of Nosta emerging from the gloom. The push from Requist to Nosta had meant a hard day's journey, even with the early morning stop. Moving so many over such a distance had been onerous. Some of the slower people, including the wounded, were still a distance behind them, but scouts had ensured the leaders that the Sutanites had not yet emerged from the smoke of the burning city.

"We'll head straight to the dormitory," said Xerrita, moving up between Anyar and Sadir. "You remember that, don't you, just off the food hall in the centre of Nosta?"

"Oh!" Anyar yawned. "Sorry, yes, I do. Food too." She looked down to her companion trotting by her side. He twisted his head up at her and grinned toothily.

"A good night's sleep and then next day we'll be planning, no doubt."

They continued through the granite pillars and along the paved streets leading into the centre of the city. Anyar saw the sides of the protecting rock in which Nosta was built rising above her head.

Before long, crowds of people had emerged from the buildings alongside the road to help with the animals and the wounded. A sense of comradeship and defiance came with it, and Anyar felt like she was coming home to a vast family.

The large doors of the food hall burst open to greet them with warm atmosphere and cooking smells. Wholesome food soon filled them and Anyar caught up with Eren and Sovira, noting they were holding hands while they walked into the large open dormitory. She smiled to herself, pleased for the two of them, while they found cots to sleep on, soon settling onto narrow beds near each other. Anyar didn't know whether there was any further planning or discussion on the invasion that night as the trials of the day soon caught up with her.

Anyar was pulled out of a deep, dreamless sleep by the touch of a wet nose and sharp teeth gently gripping and pulling on her hand.

"What?" she mumbled. "Go away, Vor, I'm still asleep."

The voral thumped off the bed and in quick fashion had roused Sovira and Eren by the time Anyar had shrugged on her tunic top and bottoms. Slipping on sandals, she stood and waited while her friends complied with Vor's demands.

Knowing the animal was on a mission of some sort, the three of them followed him in a daze through the lines of sleeping people.

They exited through a small door into a narrow street under a waning moon. The road angled upwards into the centre of the city, and they quietly followed Vor higher, until he turned abruptly and scurried onto a grassy space. Isolated benches set on the ground were placed to catch the rising sun, and Anyar recognised being there before, on the way to Requist. It was there she had met Xerrita and had the layout of Nosta explained.

A faint glow on the eastern horizon showed the coming dawn, and so she huddled with her friends on a bench waiting for light to reveal the city, while Vor rummaged in bushes nearby.

"What is Vor up to?" asked Eren, slipping an arm around Sovira's waist. "Couldn't we have seen this in the daytime?"

As if he had heard the mention of his name, the voral came dashing over and sat before them, his tongue hanging from his mouth. Anyar drew a breath to admonish him when she noticed his gaze wasn't on them but over their shoulders.

"Look!" gasped Sovira, turning around. "A lady."

"Alethea," Anyar murmured, "you've come back."

A glow enveloped the four of them. It could have been the moon or the early rays of the sun, but Anyar understood and relaxed into the Knowing. She drifted off her seat, looking down, seeing a tableau of the four of them all watching a glowing light.

"Anyar," whispered Alethea, gazing into her eyes, "you have your people, you have your friends with whom to meet the enemy. You have all you need. You will defeat the enemy on this soil, but you also need to defeat him on another ground.

"Keep your friends true. Keep your faith, for the fate of everyone depends on this."

"Alethea," Anyar whispered. "If you're here, can't you help me? Can't you stay and help me? I can't do this without you."

"You are strong, and a Mlana to lead Rolan and the world. When the final decision needs to be made, I know you will decide rightly."

"What?" Anyar covered her eyes, face ashen.

"Oh, she's gone," said Eren.

Anyar dropped her hands. The beams of the rising sun lit her face as the enormity of her responsibility hit her.

"Alethea," she sighed.

They stayed in the park as the sun rose and highlighted the star-shaped pattern of the city, spreading out from the centre along natural depressions; long, narrow roads snaked out from here, the area's topography providing rocky cover over its vulnerable parts.

The drift of scents from the surrounding forests was pure and let her recognise much of the environment. She instinctively began to identify what she was breathing, when she recognised a particular scent and remembered a story from her father's time in Rolan. It rang so true she wondered if Alethea had wanted her to remember, to understand what it meant.

The scent of the Cascade Falls with their blanket of aromatic trees came clearly from over half a day's ride away, and she knew then what she had to do. With her compassion locked firmly within her breast, she stood and headed her friends down the slope to the great hall. She had to discuss a plan for the defence of Rolan.

A black stain spread from the smouldering remains of Requist, merging at the main thoroughfare leading out of the city, Jakus at its head. Despite the best attempts of the defenders, they had found a few perac still in the city, which allowed the Shada and his entourage to ride rather than march with the remainder of the invasion force.

Sharna sat mounted at Jakus' right hand, for once not her optimistic, effervescent self; the previous night had seen to that, as the Shada had released his pent-up energies on her, giving her real empathy for what the deceased Poegna had suffered. She could see her troops, now led by Tretial on the left-hand side of the clearing, Festern's Steppe contingent on her right, while they led from the middle of the remaining Sutan force. The large force of guardsmen and scent masters hung on the Shada's scent-enhanced words, his arm raised in a dramatic fashion.

"My fellow countrymen, we are now poised to take control of this place, this Rolan. Together we will march to Nosta, and Mlana Hold. Together we will gain this country and the magical supplies of the crystal cave. With it we will conquer not only this country, but Ean and beyond. Those of you who are with me this day will benefit from our conquest. You will be remembered as being the start of the Sutanite dynasty, the era of peace throughout the known world. And you will be victorious.

"Remember what you have learnt, what you have been taught, and you will be able to overcome anything the enemy brings against you.

"Now, we march to Nosta. Next day we will destroy that city, and then we will gain Mlana Hold.

"Come with me, my people. Make me, and yourselves, proud." Jakus slumped to his saddle and nodded to Kast, who sat stoically on his animal next to him.

Kast ordered the troops to move, and the mass of black-and-grey uniformed troops began to march up the road and into the hills above the smouldering remains of Request.

Bolstered by a substantial meal and small sips of the revitalising Rolan cordial, Anyar sat with her friends at a table set in the meeting room to one side of the kitchens. She smiled, feeling the empathy of the people around her. Lan, as usual, caught her eye, projecting comfort. It was he who had the closest connection with the previous Mlana, Alethea, and who understood why she had come to the youngsters early that morning. Sadir, Boidea, Jelm, Xerrita and, Xerrina were there as well, joined by Telpher and Drathner, who had come through from Mlana Hold.

Anyar smiled briefly at the joined hands of Eren and Sovira before she explained the Knowing that had come to her. They swiftly understood the final battle would not be at Mlana Hold, nor would it be at Nosta. While the city would be another sacrifice to the rapacious drive of the Sutanites, the final and deciding battle would be at the Cascade Falls.

"So, we must do another Request. We must drag the enemy into Nosta and destroy as many as we can. Those who can be spared from the defence will continue to Mlana Hold or to where the Mlana needs them. Agreed?" Lan looked around the circle.

"Anyar needs to be protected, needs to be helped," said Sadir, "I don't want her to be involved in more deaths. It's not right. She's only a youngster."

"Mother," Anyar's voice projected across the space, "I was young. Now I'm the Mlana with the responsibilities that entails. Already I have been exposed to the worst the enemy brings. If we want him to leave, flee this country and never again be a threat, then we must do this. My real reluctance is involving my friends"—she lifted Eren's and Sovira's hands—"but that too must be."

Sadir looked helplessly to Jelm, who placed an arm across her shoulders and pulled her to him.

The city was actively organising defences against the imminent arrival of the enemy. Anyar was divorced from the preparations of Nosta's defence, preparing to go further inland, to the Cascade Falls.

"I'll control the scent masters," said Boidea. "I've always been at the right hand of the Mlana, and I need to be now. Never more so than now." Her broad face took on a peculiar twist and she pulled Anyar into her arms. "You, my

Mlana, are the one, and I'll protect you with every fibre in my body. I'll make certain the wishes of you and…and Alethea are respected. I'll lead our scent masters with the most powerful demonstration of shadow scent this Jakus has ever seen. We will beat him."

Anyar eased herself away from the large woman and smiled. "Thank you, Boidea. We must get to the Falls with those scent masters who can be spared, leaving now even though dusk is falling. Jakus will not be far away and, once he's finished with Nosta, he will continue to Mlana Hold. We must be ready." She bowed her head.

Sadir quickly took her in her arms. "My daughter, you really don't have to do this. Our shadow scent will prevail. We will beat him. You need to stay safe."

"Oh, Mother, you know we must go, follow the plan," Anyar entreated. "I'm sorry."

Gently, she released Sadir and stepped away, drifting, it seemed, from the safe harbour of her mother's love and towards the battle.

"**A**nother trap? Pathetic!" screeched Jakus. "They'll never stop us."

"They are doing well," hissed Faltis, bending over from his position on a perac. "For people who have never fought a real war, they are doing well."

Jakus ignored Faltis as he stood in his stirrups to see where a large portion of the hillside had collapsed across the road, taking a patrol of twenty men with it. "Fix it and move on. We must reach the city by nightfall!"

Sharna watched the antics of Jakus as the Sutanites moved up the road towards Nosta. Many traps had been triggered as they headed inland, causing disruptions to their advance. Jakus had been downplaying any attack, pushing his army to the limit as he attempted to reach Nosta, the second of his targets in the conquest of Rolan.

The road turned eastwards. In the distance loomed the granite pillars marking the entrance to Nosta, pale in the dark night. Jakus had been there before and had no empathy for the city. Last time, he'd left Nosta to his besieging troops so he could spare most of his army and their reinforcements to fight for the magnesa supplies at Mlana Hold. This time, he had decided not to leave this festering sore behind him; this time he would destroy Nosta.

The main body of his troops followed the Nosta road, ready for whatever the enemy could throw at them. Jakus led, with Festern and his Steppe contingent. "Time," he said, "for my allies to prove their worth. Destroy Nosta, burn every part of it. Let it sink into the black hole it came from, never to cause me a problem again."

Darkness didn't stop Jakus from advancing and trying his best to smash the city. Acid scent walls moved with him, eating away at the wood and organic structures of the city. Continual attacks from the defenders hit his forces as they moved into the centre of the city. Jakus concentrated on the bones of the city, firing scent bolts at the igneous rock composing the plateau into which the city had melded itself. Walls shook and crumbled, buildings fell.

Barrier scents against defender response worked for the most part, but shadow scent countered the Sutanite barrier and enabled strikes against the enemy. Fire took hold and soon turned night into day. Each side took tremendous losses until dawn revealed a devastation of epic proportions, making it certain that Nosta, with its collapsed buildings and roadways and a pall of rising smoke, would not be an influential force in the future. The Sutanites had achieved their aim of breaking the city.

Jakus squinted into the rising sun, a sharp smile on his face. "Sharna, I have won. And I still have over half my forces, more than enough to destroy what's left of this country. Now we have only to capture the crystal cave and I will rule all."

He looked at Sharna, not noticing her gaze was focussed on a skeletal black figure over his shoulder. Faltis stood there, red eyes focussed on Jakus' back.

"Yes, my Shada," she responded.

Three scouts on fast peracs slipped away from the ruined city and took a barely discernible path westward. The track followed a tributary of the Rolander River through rough, almost impenetrable country to the settlement of Sea Holm.

Chapter Thirty-Four

She breathed in the array of scents, enjoying the strong honey smell rolling down from the huge flowering trees perched high along the escarpment, the roar of the vast waterfalls a distant rumble.

A sudden movement, accompanied by a loud splash, caused the perac to rear and paw at the air. "Ahh!" Anyar screeched as she slid over the back of her saddle onto its woolly rump.

"Hold!" called Boidea, automatically producing calming scents to drift over the animal while snaking out an arm to grab the reins.

"I'm alright," said Anyar, slipping off her ride and standing on the gravel road.

"Look at Vor! He's under the water." Sovira had her hand to her mouth as she watched the long, sinuous shape of the voral slipping through the bubble-filled waters of the large pool extending along the left-hand side of the road. Eren quickly joined them to watch the antics of the voral as he sought his prey in the deep waters of the pool. A sudden rush out of the depths showed Vor holding a pinkish worm writhing in his jaws. He flicked the animal into the air, then snapped it in half, gobbling both halves down with relish.

"That's a haggar, Boidea," said Eren. "Didn't know you had them in Rolan."

"Here too, Eren, though not as much of a problem as in Ean. Vor's very good at dispatching the horrid creatures, isn't he?"

"I have nightmares about them, Boidea," added Sadir. "Targas and I had several run-ins with them, years ago."

"You want to get to the top of the Falls, Anyar?" interrupted Lan.

"Uh huh," answered Anyar, rubbing her sore bottom.

"A quick stop first won't hurt, since we've been travelling all night," said Sadir firmly. "I could do with tea and a bite of food, at least."

They proficiently set up a campfire on the ashes of a previous fire. Rocks scattered over the level surface made suitable seats for their large party to settle as they reflected on their purpose, and on those they had left behind in their precipitous journey from Nosta.

Anyar was pleased she had friends with her. As well as her mother, Boidea, Lan and Jelm, she was happy to have the competent scent masters, Sharia and Xerrita, in their group. Her plan involved an extensive and intricate use of shadow scent and the more users of that power, the better. A hot mug of tea was placed in her hand and a slab of day-old bread with cheese filling in the other.

She nodded her thanks as she watched Eren and Sovira sitting against each other, with the backdrop of the spray of water tumbling from high up on the escarpment. A beam of light from the sun high in the east reflected through the droplets, creating a rainbow behind them. Her eyes glazed over, and she knew she couldn't involve her two new friends in the next stage of the battle. Their role would come later, in another country, not here. What was to come would not be for their untried sensibilities.

Anyar looked over to her mother, who was speaking with Lan and Jelm, and attracted her attention.

"It is time to talk," she mouthed.

Boidea was watching and nodded to a place where several boulders rose high off the ground. "Come behind these," she suggested, "then we won't have to shout above the noise of the Falls. I also think it's time to try a little Rolan cordial to help our deliberations."

Anyar stood, looking back to Eren and Sovira as they started to rise. "Please stay," she said, before walking to boulders with Boidea and Sharia. "The next part I'm planning had best not include your daughter and Eren," she said to Sovira's mother, "It'll not be pleasant."

"I…I'm grateful," Sharia responded. "Sovira's had a rough time already."

"I assume it's to do with harnessing the waterfall?" asked Boidea, as they met with Sadir, Xerrita, Lan and Jelm.

Sadir patted a flat boulder and handed her daughter a small cup as she sat. Anyar took a sip of the cordial, appreciating its strength before she spoke.

"You're right, Boidea, it's the waterfall. My vision included water, as well as fire and destruction. I'm sure we must use it to confront our enemy."

"You're aware that your father, Targas, used it effectively against the Sutanites when they last invaded," said Sadir. "Jakus was leading them, so will be wary of this place."

"Yes, Mother, I am. So, we will have to be clever about it. My Father didn't have shadow scent and the advantages it gives us. We will have to use it to defeat them."

"Then let us hear your plan, Anyar," said Lan, his aura light purples and greens in anticipation. "Alethea would be proud of you, very proud."

Anyar took a deep breath and allowed her plan to rise in her thoughts, aware of the shadowy figure in her mind's eye.

"Mother, remember what my Father taught you about the bonding of scents, how he used minute links to pull together a vast cloud of soporific odours with which to infiltrate and take sleep to the inhabitants of Regulus castle?"

"I was there too, Anyar," said Lan, "on the barges with the Resistance as they floated down to Regulus. We all helped to hold the scent bonds with Targas, although he was the prime manipulator in the attack."

Sadir nodded, "I won't ever forget it."

"So, you're aware. We just need to make everyone here understand my plan. Shadow scent will form a prime part of it, but male scent masters will be heavily involved too." Anyar looked around the intent group.

"In fact, the answer's in the air around us, the fine mist from the Falls, even this far away, and the ability of shadow scent to form an impenetrable blanket to block and stop other scents.

"My Father could develop a vast swath of scent to float on the water. I plan to use the air itself to support the water, bring it over the Sutanites and drop it on them. It is ambitious, but we have enough women of skill for it to be attempted."

"Yes, but the enemy has the incredible power of their magnesa-enhanced shields," said Lan. "I've seen what even a few of them can do. Won't they just deflect our attack?"

"Not all our attack will be shadow scent-based, Lan," answered Anyar. "This is why we need to be at the top of the Falls to do it. Here, at that place, we have much in the way of rocks and trees for it to be the second attack for our male scent masters to provide. Two attacks from two sources should be enough to stop them." She looked around her friends and smiled, hope and anticipation showing in her scents.

"**N**ot happy about leaving more of our troops behind," grumbled Kast. "Together with those in Requist, we have less than half of our original force. Don't trust them Rolanites."

"You're right, Kast. Never trust the enemy. But they've tried their best and look where we are. Everything behind is destroyed, and only the Mlana's nest is ahead. What matter a few more or less if we win in the end?" Jakus pushed his face into his commander's. "We are so near the prize I can almost taste it." He turned to look at Faltis, riding in the group near him at the forefront of their marching army. "Faltis, tell me again. Tell me what awaits us."

Faltis watched the road ahead for a moment before turning to Jakus, eyes red in the rising sun. "A place filled with blood. Sparkling, glittering power. That is what *she* hides from us."

"What?" Kast looked at his Shada. "Is…he…ah…?"

"No," said Jakus, "he's not mad, if that's what you're saying, just overcome with the magnitude of the prize waiting for me.

"Sharna," he said, glancing back, "get the army moving. Leave any who can't keep up. We have a long march ahead of us."

Sharna moved her perac to the black and grey trail of troops still turning from the Nosta road onto the Mlana Hold Road and held a quick discussion with Festern and Tretial to carry out the Shada's wishes. The night had passed in a blur, her body weary from the fighting and from her new position as Jakus' consort. Even surreptitious imbibing of magnesa didn't give her the euphoria it once had.

Another battle, *and for what?* she thought, but her mind refused to supply the answer.

"**M**lana!"
A large group was waiting where the road came over the lip of the escarpment. Anyar recognised Drathner and Telpher, who had gone on ahead and pushed out a welcoming scent of light reds, yellows and violet.

"So pleased to see friendly faces," said Boidea. "We are in need of such succour."

Soon everyone dismounted and joined in mutual scent sharing and welcome, before moving off to one side where animals and baggage were stored, and a meal was waiting.

"We haven't much time," murmured Anyar, as she took a hot drink.

"Agreed," said Lan. "I never expected to return to this part of Rolan. It has been many years since I was here, when Alethea and I were young." He paused in the throng of people, eyes bright. "But enough of that, let us bring the Mlana Hold defenders up to date and then work out what we need to do."

"Drathner," called Boidea, "have everyone assemble and we will explain how we plan to stop the enemy at the Falls and prevent them reaching the Hold."

Anyar saw Sovira and Eren standing to one side, looking a little lost in the flurry of activity, so she walked over.

"Why aren't we helping," asked Eren, "if this is where you expect to stop the Sutanites?"

"Yes, Anyar, why?" asked Sovira, holding Eren's hand.

"Not much time to talk, but believe me when I say I'll need you later, not now. I…I have the Mlana in me. I know what I must do, but you I want to spare at this stage. You will have your time."

"Anyar?" called Boidea. "The scent masters are ready. We're all ready. We need to prepare."

"Just wait here, in each other's company," Anyar whispered. "Stay safe. C'mon, Vor." She moved across to the large group poised on the top of the long rocky ridge where water tumbled in a huge roar to the valley below, the spray reflecting the light in a myriad of colours.

They heard the distant rumble of the falls as they marched up the road towards Mlana Hold.

"I remember this place," Jakus said, slipping off his animal. "Unpleasant memories." He gripped Sharna by the waist. "You remember it too, don't you? Where that scartha, Targas, ambushed us. Some of us died here. Then he paid for what he did. He did! Didn't he, Faltis, my brother?"

His skeletally thin brother grimaced, a toothy smile across his face. "Oh, yes, I remember Targas. His body and his mind were mine." He leant towards Jakus' shoulder.

"Get back!" snapped Jakus, thrusting his arm towards Faltis. "I help direct our troops. We must be ready. We are not to be caught again. This time we will march up the road on a broad front, maximum scent shields, angled to disperse anything they throw at us. Once we're out of the valley the crystal cave is ours.

"Remember, no prisoners. I want them all dead!" he screeched, as the army began to form in solid blocks headed by scent masters.

The wind rose, bringing a drift of fine water droplets over the army while the roar of the Falls smothered the noise of their advance.

The sun, angling from the west, produced long shadows while the mists of water droplets blurred the view to the south and hid the approaching menace.

Around the large group on the road at the top of the Falls was a heap of jagged rocks and many of the magnificent trees sacrificed to provide the stack of material for the second wave of the attack."

Boidea had the women in a wide circle, not far from the piles of wood and rock. They looked focused, knowing they would have to work in unison to follow the lead of the Mlana. Boidea and Sadir would be providing their strength to bolster Anyar as she directed the attack. Nothing like this had ever been done. Never had shadow scent been used on such an extensive scale as a supportive base to hold a vast weight of water. Everyone was apprehensive, despite Anyar's calm assurances; at times she seemed a true leader of her people, but at other times an unversed youth.

Lan stood back with Drathner and Telpher. Their role was to co-ordinate the second wave, to use their power to force the rubble down on the Sutanites as they reacted to the shadow scent attack. This was the best chance to drive the Sutanites back to their ships and to stop their immediate threat.

Signals from lookouts far to the west and east revealed the time for action was imminent. Lan noticed the women passing around tumblers of Rolan cordial for a final scent-enhancing drink as they prepared. He nodded at the preparations before turning his gaze to the people gathered around him.

"It is time, my friends."

The scent of the Falls brought horrific memories to Sharna, now marching in the lead group of Sutanites. She remembered a wall of muddy water rushing down the road, her companions injured and dying, their lives shattered. All this built into an overwhelming fear at what they were doing. She longed to call out, stop their inexorable, doomed progress, but her mouth refused to obey her thoughts, refused to call out to the Shada to try to convince him.

She could see him ahead of her, Kast on one side, Faltis on the other in the forefront of their army, an unholy trio if there ever was one, knowing that she couldn't change their destiny.

Festern and Tretial were nearby, heading up long phalanxes of troops, scent masters interspersed amongst the guardsmen to provide scent shield cover. Jakus had demanded all the scent proficient to maximize their intake of the red crystal for this portion of the journey. They were powerful, invincible, and ready for anything the enemy could throw at them.

The road was wide enough for three to four columns of troops with the roadside occasionally enabling a wider spread, but they were vulnerable and exposed despite the Shada's overwhelming belief in his superiority. Sharna took a few more crystals of magnesa, forced her strength into the scent shield and exhorted her contingent to follow Jakus' lead.

The sun was soon to slip behind the western mountains when the Sutanite march neared the Falls and the site of their previous disaster. Jakus didn't pause their progress, just signalled a stiffening of shields and to be ready for any enemy attack.

Anyar's concentration caused painful stabbings in her head as she sought to maintain control on the water suspended in the air. Like filling an enormous bladder, the river's water rushed in, spreading horizontally above the Falls in front of the Rolan defenders. It only took moments until she realised the enormity of what was happening. The weight of the vast volume of water pulled at the shadow scent envelope and forced it down, needing rapid shoring of attachments with the other less-solid scents around them: air, soil, vegetation, even the honey scents were pulled in to add solidarity.

This had never been done and, if it wasn't for Anyar's belief in the mystical Alethea, the power of shadow scent and the women supporting her, the plan would have failed. No more than a few seconds had passed as the downward pull of the water's weight was converted into an outward push and the pressure on

Anyar grew astronomically.

"More time, more time," she muttered through gritted teeth. The seconds passed until her head felt like it was being pulled apart.

"Enough!" she screamed and released her control. The cloud of water dropped into the valley in an instant, soon followed by an audible thump, the backlash of the release collapsing all the women scent masters to the ground. Anyar vaguely heard Lan ordering the follow-up rock and timber avalanche as she slumped in exhaustion.

It began with a darkening of the light, as if the sun had prematurely dropped behind the western mountains. A wedge of thick clouds pushed out from the escarpment against the slight breeze coming from the south.

Sharna held up an arm, slowing her contingent's march while strengthening her shields even more. "'Ware!" she called.

The progression of the army halted. Jakus glared back at Sharna.

"What!"

"Look, my Lord!" she pointed at the heavy black cloud approaching them against the wind.

"Hold!" screeched Jakus, pushing up his arms and strengthening his scent shields.

The deluge of water thundered down in a massive dump to crash and splash over the strong shields held by the Sutanites. Those to the forefront of the army were protected by the enhanced scent shields, but the torrents of water pushed through the columns of troops and followers behind, driving them into the river or against the rocky countryside.

"Is that the best you can do!" screeched Jakus. "Is that all?"

A rumble followed his words and a roiling mass of rock and wood tumbled down the roadway, smashing into the scent shields, pushing their weight onto the already weakened scent barriers. Jumping from one form of defence to another stressed the capabilities of the Sutanite scent masters, causing breaks in their resistance.

But the head of the army, with its phalanx of the most experienced scent masters, still remained firm. Strong and resilient, it held against all aspects of the attack, the water rushing past, and the rocks and timber plummeting down the slope. Jakus was supreme, confident in his power, confident in his right to rule.

Sharna lifted her head at a break in the onslaught to see the magnificence of the Shada, overcoming all that was thrown at him, resilient, unbeatable.

So, we win, she thought, *my life as Jakus' plaything continues.* Yet even as she thought this and saw the power of the Shada of Sutan, a strange thing happened. While Jakus was focused on defying all the Rolanite defenders could throw at him, a skeletal form moved behind the Shada. She saw Jakus shudder as Faltis' head touched his, his body jerking, arms outstretched, his focus broken.

Without Jakus' concentration as keystone of the scent shields, the remaining scent masters lost their focus and the waters broke through, bringing rocks and timbers roiling past in a rush. Black-and-grey bodies tumbled around her while she held her shields with all her might.

Night fell quickly and the water receded, before Sharna was able to release her shields and go in search of any survivors.

Even though she knew the war was lost.

Chapter Thirty-Five

"Uh!" groaned Jakus, as he awkwardly lifted himself from the mud, mind spinning from the enormity of what had happened. His eyes blurred as he took in the scene of devastation, black-and-grey twisted bodies lying in muddy, rubble-filled pools all around him, dead before they could even fight.

Movement nearby caused him to focus over a blinding headache and see several scent masters endeavouring to stand. More moved further afield as the grey of the dusk slowly closed in on his vision.

"Kast? Sharna, Festern?" he yelled. People began moving towards him. He recognised his scent masters and forced words gratingly from his lips.

"Find how many are alive and get them moving. Those blood-cursed scartha have delivered us a cowardly blow. We must fall back, regroup."

"My Lord," said a bloodied Kast, "half of our army has been lost despite our scent protection, even your...brother, Faltis. But we have enough troops to protect our backs if we move now, during the night."

"So Faltis is dead. No loss," he snapped, his head jerking in a sudden spasm. "Leave him where he fell, the traitor."

"Traitor, my Shada?"

"Traitor, who failed me when I needed him!" He glared at his army commander, eyes glowing redly in the gloom. "Now go, pass the order to move. Leave the dead and wounded, for we travel light."

Jakus squinted through the dusk and grunted when he spotted the slight figure of Sharna.

"Come here!" He limped out of the sticky mud to grip her sodden shoulder. "You can help me, my Sharna, my consort.

"Yes," his voice shrilled, "you can help me. The Shada needs all the support he can get."

"My Lord," asked Sharna as she attempted to wriggle away from his grasping hand as it slid over her shoulder towards her breast. "Are you alright?"

"Never better," he sniggered. "Never better."

The early morning sun lit the eroded road as the Rolan defenders descended into a destroyed land, bodies lying everywhere like so much flotsam on the muddied countryside below the Falls. The river still tumbled in a joyous sound as it fell to meet the valley floor and continue its journey to the coast, never concerned about the death of so many by its waters.

A spreadeagled black form lying amongst many was recognised.

"Ah, this is one of the ruling Sutanites," said Boidea, "Just a man, now compost in the land of life. What was it all about? What did it achieve?"

"Anyar, don't come down here. Don't look at all these dead people. It's not right," added Sadir.

"Mother, it's my responsibility," said Anyar, looking at the deflated body. "You can't hide me away from this. And"—she bent forward to almost touch the thin skull-like face,— "it's not him. He's gotten away. It's not over."

"What?" asked Sadir. "What do you mean?"

"Anyar will explain in good time, Sadir," said Lan. "Meanwhile we must organise burial parties and a pursuit of the remnants of the Sutanite army. For I believe Jakus has escaped, and unless he is stopped this war will continue."

"Lan, Boidea, what will he do now?" asked Anyar. "Will he go back to Nosta or to Requist? If he has been as damaged as we hope, then maybe he'll attempt to leave Rolan?"

"I think he'll find that difficult, Anyar," interrupted Jelm. "Ginrel will see to it."

"You'll recall we left the fleet at Sea Holm," said Lan. "By now they will have received word to bring the ships back to Requist and attack the Sutanite fleet. Should Jakus get back to the port then his transport will be decimated."

"No, Lan," Anyar said, shaking her head, "we haven't the resources to defeat them here in Rolan. Some must be allowed to escape and flee these shores. We'll then pursue them with the resources of Rolan and Ean to finish what they started. This is what I know we must do."

"Ah," Lan said, looking around the small group of people, "I believe you may be right. I spoke more in hope than understanding."

"True," added Boidea, "there will be remnants of the attackers at both Nosta and Requist, too many for us to easily defeat. All we can do is pursue them, drive them to the port with as little loss as possible. We've denied them our supplies of magnesa and driven them away with many casualties. Now is the time to send them out of Rolan."

"We're ready to move, Boidea," called Drathner. "Supplies and animals are where the road was unaffected from the deluge, if we could make our way there. And Mlana, we are bringing all the supplies of our cordial from the Hold as you required."

Anyar closed her eyes, feeling the rightness of bringing quantities of the scent-enhancing cordial with them on their journey, and nodded to the tall Rolanite. She looked over the mass of people picking their way down the ruined road through the slush before turning, a muddied Vor at her feet. The familiar figures of Eren and Sovira with Sharia hurried by, eyes averted from the bodies lying amongst the rubble.

"Come, Mother, let us join our friends," she said, pulling at Sadir.

A gale from the northwest carried sleet in its winds, rattling the sails, causing all but the most able-bodied to find shelter as they skated alongside the rugged and inhospitable coastline to the East. Local knowledge was vital to avoid the tongues of land creeping far out into the sea to seek victims for their hidden rocks.

Ginrel blessed the waterproofing in the thick perac-wool hooded coats that prevented much of the ice from reaching his skin as he added his weight to the tiller to help the taciturn Rolanite captain, Terner, guide the flagship in their desperate sail from Sea Holm to Requist.

Word had come from the besieged Nosta to return to the port and attack the enemy shipping there. Time was of the essence for, if the enemy was stopped on its drive inland, then their means of escape, their fleet, was now at its most vulnerable.

Ginrel had gotten to know a few of these hard-bitten sailors and scent masters while they waited for word in Sea Holm, enough to understand they were as keen to defeat the enemy as he was and would push themselves and their ships to the limit to do so.

A hard two-day sailing had brought them within sight of the entrance to the bay, and there the seven Eanite and six Rolan ships rendezvoused in large swells to co-ordinate their attack on the enemy's fleet.

"Not as easy as we first thought," Terner spat with the wind over the rail. "Seems they've got a coupl'a two-masters patrolling. We might look to be equal, but I wouldn't like to reckon on it. There's a three-master there too, almost twice the size of ours."

"No choice," said Ginrel. "We've gotta git 'em. Hafta stop 'em gettin' away."

"We'll do our best, but we've few scent masters and I've heard the enemy is good at what they do. Still, we've got weapons, fire, and manoeuvrability to give us a chance. The wind's as good as it's going to be. Shall we?"

"Let's signal th' fleet t' attack," agreed Ginrel. "We owe 'em plenty."

U sing the nor'wester to their advantage, the fleet tacked down the western side of the bay and then almost due east, running in a long line at the two patrolling ships. The invading Sutanite vessels didn't stand a chance with the wind against them, and the Rolan fleet coming at a sharp angle forced them to flee. In no time at all, both ships were beached, with fire greedily consuming their superstructures.

The fleet then swung around to parallel the stranded Sutanite ships and send flaming projectiles and scent bolts at them. Despite the strong winds, they were countered by solid scent shields and attempts to project acidic blankets of scents at their ships. This was where the superior Sutanite scent masters, with their magnesa-enhanced power, made a difference.

Slowly the enemy managed to damage some of the defenders' ships, reducing their effectiveness, until a tactical withdrawal was signalled. The Rolan flagship led the remainder of the fleet to the head of the bay, where they could blockade any attempt by the enemy to put to sea.

"Looks like we damaged them somewhat," said Terner, "though would we'd done more."

"Enough," agreed Ginrel. "By me reckonin' we destroyed or incapacitated six of their ships. Now if we wait 'ere we kin carry out repairs 'nd block any of them from leavin'."

"Depends tho if th' Mlana wants us t' do thet."

"Best send a boat to meet up with our people. Find out what's happened and get word," said Terner.

"Agreed," said Ginrel. "Now, hev yer got any of thet Rolan beer? I think we deserve a drop."

Sharna had never felt so dirty, both inside and out after a long trek with their decimated force of mud-covered companions, all on foot. Only Jakus rode, with the remainder of the appropriated animals used for baggage.

They had proceeded as fast as they were able along the road to Nosta, collected all those Sutanite troops blocking the city and then to Requist. Jakus, strangely ignoring his obsession with finding the crystal cave, was fixated on returning to the port city and joining the remainder of the invasion force.

Sharna had little time for thought, little time to think on her responsibilities as commander of a section of the troops, or co-ordination of the fleet. Jakus' focus wasn't on order and conquest; it had changed. When he wasn't mumbling to himself or abstractly looking around his people Jakus was interested in *her*.

As soon as they stopped on the road, he had a tent erected and called Sharna in. She realised something wasn't right. If she was upset by Jakus' indifference to anything but his own needs before, now he had changed. His touch was different, unclean, as if some ravening creature just wanted her body for his own, as if he was trying to get inside her head.

But she couldn't tell anyone, even Kast, who had his own issues. She recalled her converstion with Bilternus, so long ago in Sutan, and wished he were here. Was it true? Was there someone else living inside Jakus? She shivered and fervently wished to be clean.

Smoke billowed into the sky as they came into sight of Requist, not from the remains of the city still burning but from the shore where the ships were berthed.

"What!" screeched Jakus. "What has happened to my ships? Faster! We must get to my ships!" The long, weary army broke into a foot-shuffling rhythm to follow the irate Jakus down into the city.

They made it without incident, learning that the Rolanites had a fleet blockading their ships and in doing so, had destroyed a significant proportion of the Sutanite vessels.

"We must sail!" yelled Jakus, jumping off his beast and limping towards the flagship. "No time to waste. We have enough ships to carry all of those left." He turned away, seeming to fold into himself even though physically nothing had changed. "Better planning would're been good, not letting the enemy get such an advantage. Pah, Jakus, but you were a fool!" He looked up, waved a hand at Kast and another nearby. "Get everyone on board! We have enough power to deal with anything the enemy ships can try to do to us."

As he hobbled away favouring his old leg injury, Sharna wondered whether anyone else was concerned about the mental state of their Shada. Would anyone query him; wonder why the invasion force had suddenly lost its purpose? She watched the army filtering onto the ships with barely a murmur, even Kast and Festern saying nothing, just accepting the Shada's orders.

Sharna shrugged mentally, and briefly thought of Bilternus and the Ean campaign. At least he was far away from this defeat. *Will I ever see him again?* she wondered. *Did they suffer as we have?* Her thoughts suddenly blanked off as she saw Tibitus, her friend and captain of the flagship waiting at the gangway, an uncertain smile on his face.

He placed a consoling hand on her shoulder as she followed the Shada onto the ship, giving her a small measure of hope that she would have an ally in the time ahead. She gave a brief smile in return as she passed him.

They had rested at the top of the long slope leading into Requist, watching the last of the dark line of the enemy entering the city. A rider had met them to tell them of the effectiveness of the strike by the Rolan fleet on the Sutanite ships. It was quickly decided to tell their fleet to withdraw, not engage the enemy, and let them escape.

"Things are moving in a desired direction, Anyar," said Lan. "Your thoughts of meeting the enemy on his own ground are gathering momentum."

"Yes." Anyar crouched to rest a hand on Vor's ruff as they watched the activity around the remaining ships along the shoreline. "They will never return to Rolan. It is us who must pursue them."

"I think we can head to the city, find what the enemy has left. Although, with our planning I doubt we'll have much of a problem, eh Xaner?" said Boidea.

"Take more than a few Sutanites to outwit us," he responded. "And I think we all need time to recoup before we proceed with the next stage of our campaign."

"Come, Sovira and Eren," said Anyar, "let's find our special place in the park. Leave the others to organise things."

She held out her hands to her friends and together they urged their animals down the road.

Chapter Thirty-Six

Ginrel's fingers clawed Terner's shoulder as they watched the distant Sutanite ships heeling in the strong winds, sailing east, away from Rolan and towards Ean and their haven of Sutan.

"Th' damn haggars, gittin' away with murder," he spat through gritted teeth. "Why couldn't we attack, finish 'em off?"

"We haven't come out of this without damage, Ginrel. And our advantage is gone. Our orders are now to disengage and come into harbour, so we best follow them," said the captain, having a nearby sailor put up signal flags to the fleet. "Now, we'll head into port.

"Just hope they've repaired the pier."

"What blood-cursed reason is that scartha doing here!" screeched Jakus, his outstretched arm shaking. "Why isn't he in Ean, readying it for my rule?"

The space on the aft deck around the furious Shada had cleared, no one wanting to go near him with his rage showing in the black and purple scent clouds enveloping his body. He capered on the spot, gesticulating towards the fleet of ships on an interception course only a few hours out from Requist.

"And," Jakus paused, "only five ships? Heritis has only five ships? He had eight of my ships for the assault on Ean, against no opposition. How did he lose three?" He swung around to Tibitis at the helm. "Signal him to heave to. Come to me!" he snapped. "He better have a reason for his failure."

The three-masted flagship, sails luffing into the wind, rolled in the large swells as they waited for Heritis' ship to launch a boat in the difficult conditions, the darkening sky as the sun dropped to the far west making it even more difficult. Jakus' obvious rage had diminished as he organised Sharna, Tretial and Kast to assist him with expanding a blanket of scents to dampen the waves to make it easier for Heritis to make the hazardous journey between the Sutanite ships.

"Take your magnesa!" Jakus ordered as he saw the rowing boat hit the water and two sailors, then two black-robed figures, clamber aboard. "Follow my lead!"

Sharna felt rather than saw Jakus pull scents from the surrounds and link them in a familiar way, using the bonds to tighten and suppress the waves beneath it. As they joined in, Jakus pushed the blanket across the large distance to where the small boat was beginning its journey towards them. She knew that, despite his anger at Heritis he needed the man, his second-in-command.

Her mind was still pounding with the realisation that beneath the Shada's exterior there lived an alien, a secret being not showing itself. Sharna dreaded the time she would have to spend in the cabin with the man. There she would not be protected by the company of those around her. There, she would be finally confronted by whatever Jakus had become.

"'Ware the ship," called one of the sailors as the boat thumped into the flag-ship's side next to a rope ladder.

One of the men held fast to the ladder, the other to a long pole extended by one of the ship's crew, while Heritis pulled himself on board. She was surprised to see the large figure of Dronthis following, as if he was the Sutanite scent master's right hand.

"My meeting room, now!" Jakus ordered with a measured calm before turning to Sharna. "You and Kast come with us.

"Tibitis, signal the fleet to resume its course. Ean is our destination."

Sharna noticed the surprised look on the captain's face as she followed the others down into the ship.

The plush green carpet deadened the sounds of the outside sea and wind as the five of them entered the meeting room; the dark wood table bolted to its centre with carved chairs set around it was bare.

Jakus sat at the head of the table and looked at the cabinet against one wall. "Wine, I think," he looked at Sharna, "to help my mood while I hear your excuses."

"I think we both need an update, Jakus," said Heritis as he sat. "We both have had some trouble with the opposition, by the look of it. Your limp hasn't got any better too."

Sharna noticed Jakus' eyes drawing together over his thin face and a considerable thickening of his aura as she placed a glass in front of him.

"I'll have one too," said Heritis, seemingly unconcerned with the effect of his words on the Shada. "It has been a rough few days."

Sharna snapped a quick look at Jakus, before hurrying to the cabinet and pouring four more glasses of wine. She took one to each of Heritis, Kast and Dronthis before sitting at the table to nurse her own.

"I noticed you ordered the captain to take the fleet to Ean," said Heritis.

"Wouldn't you want my report before making that decision?"

Sharna closed her eyes, waiting for Jakus to explode with Heritis' challenge, but nothing happened. She noticed Jakus staring at him, eyes reflecting redly.

"Remember where you came from. Remember what we both lost. Work out what is most important to Sutan, to me." Jakus flung out his glass, red droplets scattering across the dark wood of the table. "We've both had setbacks, that is plain, but I clearly made a mistake when I sent you to secure Ean on your own. Now I will rectify that mistake."

Heritis' scent aura strengthened, flickers of yellow through its purple and scarlet.

"Ha! You'd like that, wouldn't you?" Jakus laughed. "But that would be foolish. You've already learnt from your mistake and unfortunately, I still need you. I've lost my brother, Faltis, neglected creature that he was, and you're all I have left. Support me and you'll be rewarded. Fail, and you will be dispensed with, and believe me, I would know.

"We will go to Ean, retake it, crush any resistance, and I will rule." He thumped his elbows on the table and leant forward. "That is now my priority!

"Now, let me hear your excuses. Let me hear what you've lost. Let me hear how a depleted people could send an undefeatable army running, for we will learn from your mistakes and turn Sutan's fortunes around."

Heritis leant forward to meet Jakus' eyes. "Agreed, we have a lot to compare and rectify, particularly why our scent power cannot cope with the scent the women wield. For, unless I miss my guess, we both have suffered under their power and must both cope with it to defeat the rabble."

"First then, your losses. Then tell me who we still have!" Jakus growled.

Sharna waited in the Shada's well-appointed cabin. She had listened to the report from Heritis with increasing horror, worst of all the cost of her friend, Bilternus and most of his men, including Piltarnis. Dronthis gleefully described Bilternus' surrender of his troops in the face of overwhelming scent power, and how he had killed the traitor before they retreated. Her depression deepened.

The loss of around half of the total Sutanite invasion force, plus nine ships, should have been enough to send the army back to their Sutan, to re-supply and regroup, but Jakus didn't agree. For some reason he didn't seem to regard the losses as a setback: he had just changed his focus, his target. Even the crystal cave and the supplies of magnesa didn't seem to drive him. Now it was Ean that he wanted to conquer.

Heritis hadn't questioned it, probably relieved to have escaped so lightly from a major defeat, so now the focus of the Sutanites had changed.

As Sharna waited for the Shada to walk through the door and demand that she serve him, she thought she knew the reason but dreaded the answer.

Would the Shada remain Shada Jakus, the leader of Sutan, or would there be someone else within him? Bilternus' concerns, raised with her long ago in Sutan about the long-dead Septus, were coming true, and there was nothing she could do about it.

Jakus sat alone at the meeting table, his body adjusting to the long swells as the flagship led the fleet through the seas on its way to Ean. He was trying to come to terms with the weird thoughts and feelings roiling in his head. One moment he was in complete control, the next he was an outsider sitting as an observer, feeling his mouth and body working.

Ever since the battle at Cascade Falls his reality had changed, his body had not been his own. At times he felt a redness passing through his thoughts, a hysterical need to let it out, at other times he felt normal.

So why am I going to Ean? Why don't I want the crystal cave? he thought. *I can't control what I want, what I've wanted all my life. I can't control it!* Jakus felt like screaming, but his mouth refused to open and let him have that relief.

His body shifted and he stood, even as a shrill voice echoed through his mind. *"I won, Jakus. You let me die, but I've won. You will die, but I will live. I will rule. I will rule all. Just one more stands in my way, and her body is young and fresh. In her I will live forever, and I will be supreme.*

"Now," it chortled, *"I have your woman, your Sharna, waiting for me."*

He didn't remember his body leaving the meeting room without him in control until he saw the frightened eyes of the red-headed woman in his cabin.

A cheering crowd gathered at the pier, welcoming the Rolanite ships as they were slowly manoeuvred into their berths by the tender boats after the wind had finally abated. Despite the welcome, the backdrop of the burnt and ruined city provided a dampening effect on their celebrations. A significant portion of the city had been destroyed in the brief Sutanite invasion with the most dominant feature, the Administration building on the summit of Lookout Hill a mere pile of rubble, testament to the power of the Mlana.

The Mlana was surrounded by a number of people, but Ginrel particularly noted the two taller youngsters on each side of her, one being the budding scent master he had travelled with from Ean and the other the daughter of the city administrator. At their feet, like a large, dirty-brown rug, was her pet voral, gaze fixed on the unloading ships. *There's something about them,* he thought as he leapt off the side of the ship onto the solid wood planking, *almost as if there's a glow around them; something special. And the Mlana seems a lot older than her tender years.*

He shook the thought from his mind and hurried down the pier to greet Lan and Eren, then Jelm, Sadir and Anyar. The nimbus of scent auras, light red, yellow and violets surrounded them all as they expressed their joy and renewed their bonds of friendship. Soon they moved away to allow the unloading to continue while he and the other ship captains were updated on the state of the war.

The constant banging of hammers, the noises of carts and equipment, came clearly to those in the hastily erected building, one street back from the wharf. The canvas roof overhead flapped in the light breeze as people sat on anything they could find while they talked through the next stage of the proceedings.

They found that over half the invasion force had been destroyed, with far fewer defenders being lost. The deluge at Cascade Falls had been catastrophic for the enemy yet resulted in no losses for Rolan. Most significant of all had been the death of Jakus' brother, Faltis.

Further, news from Ean had revealed another defeat for the Sutanites, causing them to retreat from that country, too. The capture of a significant number of the Sutanite troops meant that the enemy was vastly depleted, both in men and ships. Time was ripe for defeating them, once and for all.

One brother, Jakus, was all that was left of the ruling family. They understood that to kill him would take away Sutan's desire for conquest and should bring peace to all countries.

"Mlana," asked Lan, "is this in keeping with your visions? Do we follow Jakus, take our forces to wherever we can confront him?"

Anyar seemed to shrink at the direct question, realising she had the power to determine the direction they took. Did they want peace for the time being, or peace forever? To have peace forever was the much harder option, involving more hardships, more deaths, but the timing was right, and all her Knowings had led her to this point. Her aura expanded, high and dark, scarlets and purples of anger filling in a background of determined and controlling grey. Her stature grew until she was the most dominant being in the room.

"Do we have a choice? We owe future generations the opportunity to live in peace and harmony by removing the blight that is upon us. We must take the fight to the enemy while he is hurt. We must prepare to follow his retreat as soon as we are able, and cast him down."

A low hum began, each person adding to it until the air vibrated, outside noises faded and thickened scent flew. Everyone swayed in unison, feeling a oneness, a sense of purpose, a belief in doing what was needed, what was right. No answer was required as they grew stronger in their unity, the scents filling them.

Chapter Thirty-Seven

Ships were made ready for sailing, including the temporary repair of two of the abandoned Sutanite ships. All vessels were provisioned to cover those taking the several days' voyage to Ean and beyond to Sutan. Word had already been sent by fast coastal pinnace to Ean about the fleet soon arriving in Port Saltus, to garner support for an attack on the enemy in Sutan.

Anyar crouched at the rail on the deck of the flagship looking to the rolling swells at the mouth of the bay, her hands firmly screwed into Vor's ruff. "You will be alright, Vor. It's only water. You like water."

The voral pulled away to gaze at the group of people coming along the pier. He huffed as he saw Sovira with her father and mother arriving at the gangway, then looked enquiringly at his mistress.

"It's up to them, Vor," she whispered. "But Sovira has to be with me and Eren, as much as none of us wants to go to sea."

Soon Xaner, then Sovira hugged Sharia at the gangway before her mother looked up at Anyar. "Does she have to go?"

Anyar smiled sadly to her.

"No, I know," Sharia answered herself. "Now, please be careful. Stay safe," she said to Sovira, before turning to walk back along the pier with Xaner.

Anyar welcomed her friend on board. "That's all of us, Sovira," said Anyar. "Do you want to come down and see the room we've got? It's small but it's solid, lots of stuff packed away in all sorts of places."

"I...I don't know," Sovira said, waving at her mother, already heading along the pier to her siblings waiting at the wharf. She sighed and stood taller. "Let's. Eren's down there? Bet he's taken the best bed."

"No, he's bunking with Lan and Jelm," said Anyar. "My mother and Boidea are with us."

"Oh," Sovira responded, looking out to the rough seas at the head of the bay, before putting her hand on the voral. "How's Vor going to go, at sea and all?"

"He'll cope. Imagine trying to leave him." Anyar smiled, putting out her hand to her friend. "Now let's go and I'll show you your bunk."

Boidea watched Anyar and Sovira go below, followed by Vor, before her gaze swung back to the bags being loaded on board. She nodded to Xerrita, who was supervising the movement of a very important cargo onto the flagship. "Almost all done, Xerrita?" she called.

"Just these last bags of cordial tumblers, Boidea, then we're finished."

"Good, I'll make certain they are safely stowed, then meet you in the galley. Ginrel says we must set sail, and all this exercise has given me a powerful hunger."

Becoming accustomed to the pitching of the ship, aided by a scent balm for sea sickness, a small group huddled together in the bowels of the vessel, the dark only broken by light coming through the hatches. Anyar sat next to Eren holding his hand, the other on Vor's solid back, while Sovira had Eren's other hand.

"Good time to be together, out of the hustle above," whispered Anyar as she leant on a sack behind her.

"Yes," whispered Sovira. "Despite being at sea and away from my family, it's an adventure, too."

"Still can't really see why we need all these bottles," said Eren. "They're really lumpy to lean on, too. Besides how I am part of this, and me a male using cordial?"

"Well, I…I like having you with me," said Sovira. "I don't know how to do this, be part of it without you all. I mean…"—she looked over to Anyar—"you're different. You're chosen but me and Eren are not, despite all that's happened."

"Oh, I so glad to have friends here but, more seriously we have at least one more event and I will need you to be with me when we are tested."

Vor lifted his head and growled, the sound coming over the creaking of the timbers and the gurgle of the water alongside the hull.

Anyar pulled the animal's head up and kissed him on the snout. "To tell you the truth, I don't know what it's about either. All these Knowings that must be worked out, interpreted, have led us to where we are now. But if it wasn't for Vor, and you two, I'd be lost. Me, the leader of the people; me, just a young woman. So, I need my friends, for we have a part to play in making all safe for our future.

"Please, if you concentrate now, you can feel the power in the cordial around you, feel the workings of shadow scent within you.

"That's what it's about. That's what'll get us through. For the moment, though, just relax with me." She bent forward, took their hands, and they enjoyed the subtle play of scents in the comfortable darkness, the sway of the ship almost hypnotic.

"Kyel, they're coming, my love!" Cathar squealed as she dashed into the room. "They're finally coming, as we heard from the dispatch. Oh, I'm looking forward to seeing my friends, hearing what's happened."

She plumped onto Kyel's lap and flung her arms around his neck.

"Hah, I love your excitement," he laughed, rubbing his bristly face against hers. "Do we know yet how many ships there are? I suspect it's too far out yet to confirm that it's the Rolan fleet?"

"Who else could it be?" she asked. "We've had the report from Rolan about what happened, and that the enemy's fleeing."

"I suppose you're right." He stood and walked with Cathar to the second-floor window to look out through the morning haze, across the wide channel into the harbour. "And there's so much to tell them and so much to find out. All I know is that this is the time of history, a time to remember, to tell our grandchildren about. For this is when we are going to stop the Sutanites forever, and I can't wait."

"Grandchildren?" Cathar focussed on Kyel's brown eyes. "Are you intending to become a father?"

"Cathar!" Kyel hugged her to him. "There's time enough for that when the enemy is defeated." He smiled to lighten the mood. "Come, let's check in with Grefnel."

They took one last look out into the harbour for the reported sails before heading down the stairs of the second-story observation post in the Port Saltus administration building.

"Grefnel's not here. He'll be in The Salted Arms if he's any sense. That's where Bilternus will be, too. He's finally come right after that cowardly wound that Dronthis gave him. I've horrible memories of that man, too.

"Bilternus and Piltarnis have just come from Nebleth after being released from the hospice. There's a lot of repair work for the prisoners here and they insisted on coming to help."

"Has Regna come as well? She was helping him recover, wasn't she?" asked Kyel. "She's furious with her ex-consort, Heritis, for what happened."

"No, she's stayed in Nebleth," said Cathar. "As for Heritis, she's had to put up with him all these years, then to have him returning to Ean to take over in the name of that Jakus? Huh!

"And he wasn't very nice to you before, when you met him?"

"No. He was too smooth. Strange things seemed to happen when he was around, too. Anyway, let's get moving."

They exited the administration building and headed along the rubble-filled streets, avoiding the many carts where Sutanite prisoners were working to remove burnt timbers and rubbish from demolished buildings.

They reached The Salted Arms and pushed through the doors into the tavern to see the diminutive figure of Mar behind the long bar cleaning mugs. She smiled and, with a tilt of her head, indicated the back of the large room.

They noticed the short, round harbour master talking to the lanky figure of Bilternus, wrapped in white bandages, several Eanite scent masters and Piltarnis sitting with them at the table.

Grefnel swung around as they entered. "Yes, I've heard ships have been sighted. Just going down to the wharf to confirm their identity and prepare for their arrival."

"It is the Rolan fleet, though?" asked Kyel.

"Don't know who else it could be; the damn sea mist makes it too hard to be certain." Grefnel took a last swig from his beer mug. "I'll let you know as soon as we find out."

They took the vacated seats and ordered drinks from Mar as the harbour master left the tavern.

"Well," Kyel said, looking at Bilternus' tired face, "it's good to see you again, and finally looking healthier. So, things are moving on, particularly with the Rolan fleet coming. This is where you really must show your true colours, the time when we have to decide the future we have spoken about.

"You too, Piltarnis." His gaze swung to the young Sutanite scent master, who coloured slightly and bent his head.

"Agreed Kyel," said the former enemy. "If this is the predicted turn of events you spoke of, then we will support you. You have shown great compassion for the invaders of your lands, and with our surrender we have agreed to help in the defeat of those elements causing Sutan to be such aggressors. We do not want our country in the hands of a madman."

"Knock off the flowery speech, Piltarnis," said Biltarnis, wincing as he leant forward. "Kyel, let's see what your allies want and we'll help in any way we can. Jakus needs to be defeated, and we'll help that happen. Besides, I have a score to settle with the coward, Dronthis."

"As do I," added Kyel, "as do I."

"I better get back to our men. There's so much to do in repairing the damage to the city." Piltarnis nodded and headed out of the building.

"Your beers, young Cers," said Mar as she deposited a tray full of mugs on the table.

The doors to the tavern crashed inwards.

"Everyone! We're bein' attacked. Th' enemy's back; lots of 'em," Tishal screamed before she ran back out.

"Damn and blast!" yelped Kyel, standing up, causing the beers to spill across the table. "It can't be the Rolan fleet after all. We've been too complacent. We need to call everyone together to defend the city and send word to the capital. "Come on, Bilternus, let's see what your words are worth now."

The mass exodus from the tavern joined the rush of people into the streets as they prepared for the surprise enemy invasion.

A hurried gathering of Eanites decided to evacuate Port Saltus in the face of the invasion of the overwhelming Sutanite force. The entire population, including prisoners, were on the move northwards, taking anything that could aid the enemy, despite having to abandon their moored ships.

Once the evacuation orders had been given Kyel, Cathar, Lethnal, Cynth, Tishal, Brin and Bilternus met in the meeting room of the administration building to decide on strategies for dealing with the unanticipated turn of events.

Recognising that the Sutanite forces had recombined and were targeting Ean rather than Rolan meant that defence had to be concentrated where they had an advantage, at the capital, Nebleth. Also drawing the Sutanite army away from the port meant the Rolan fleet wouldn't sail into Port Saltus and be confronted by the full force of the enemy.

Fortunately, everyone was efficiently evacuating Port Saltus, as many things were transportable and most of the population had only recently returned to the damaged city.

The Sutanite fleet came into the port in a dark flood, overwhelming everything in its path. An aura of menace hung over the ships, some showing signs of damage and hurried repair as they swept down the main channel on an incoming tide, targeting the five Eanite ships tied to the piers.

The few remaining sailors and crew scrambled over the sides of the berthed ships and ran for the safety of the broken and burnt buildings stretching along the wharf's side.

"Destroy them!" ordered Jakus from the aft deck of the lead ship. "Make them pay!" Aided by the power of the red crystal, the phalanx of scent masters on the deck pushed out a wave of acid scent towards the stationary vessels as the captain skilfully swung the flagship past their sterns. The odour wall drifted like fog across the berthed ships as the scent masters concentrated their power. It ebbed and flowed, biting into some vessels more than others as the fleet sailed on unopposed, each ship adding its component of scent attack.

Jakus looked back, eyes gleaming redly as he waited for the effect of the attack. "Too little!" he screeched to Tibitis. "We need to do another run at them."

"Sorry, Shada," the captain replied, "the tide's too strong; wind's against us."

Jakus didn't reply as he watched the masts, spars and furled sails slowly eroding and breaking apart, rattling down like rust particles onto the decks of the vessels.

The lapping waves met the disintegrating gunwales of the ships and began pouring over the decks.

"Hah! I've done it. Their puny ships are useless. Tibitis, get the tender boats to take us in to a berth. We need to press home our advantage and make the damned scartha pay."

No one countered the Sutanite fleet as the twelve ships lowered their rowboats to manoeuvre to the spare berths along the piers.

A small group stood amongst the rushes and sedges on the bank of the Great Southern looking anxiously south to the distant piers of the city where the enemy were disembarking. A sea mist made the ships appear ghostly, masts rising towards a darkening sky as if supporting the grey clouds pressing down on the rippling waters of the ebb tide.

A small boat with a stepped mast lay camouflaged amongst the vegetation. Kyel carefully helped a grey-clad man down to where the solid river man and young woman stood on the deck to receive him.

"This is your chance," Kyel hissed. "Tell them what's happened. Convince them to follow the plan; your knowledge of the enemy is invaluable. Remember, Brin and Tishal will help you. They know how to sail and get you out of the harbour to the fleet, and Brin's a real strategist."

"Got a way wid words, Kyel, ain't yer?" Brin smiled as he helped Bilternus settle into the boat. "Nah, sit there, mind yer wound 'nd don't git in th' way, while Tishal 'nd I git us past them damn haggars."

"Thank you Kyel, my friend," grunted Bilternus as he shifted on the bench seat.

"Don't forget to use the messengers when you need to," warned Kyel, pointing to the small carrier case in the bottom of the boat. "Rasnal left them with us for just such an emergency."

"Be careful. Me daughter's neva bin t' sea," said the large woman on the bank, stretching out a hand towards the boat as it began to edge out into the flow of the river.

"Don't worry, Cynth, yer daughter's fully capable 'nd she has a very important role." Brin pointed to a carrier case at Tishal's feet. "Them tina will 'ome in on Nebleth tower when we're able t' send a message. Knowledge is what'll defeat th' enemy."

Tishal, with one hand on an oar, raised an arm in farewell to her mother.

"We'll angle upstream t' cross th' river, let th' tide pull us t' th' other side. They'll neva see us goin' past 'em, 'specially in th' dark," said Brin.

"Go with good speed," called Lethnal. "A lot is riding on this."

"Go yerselves now. Yer've more t' trouble abart than us," called the river man.

The group hurried off to join the exodus of Port Saltus defenders along the river road as the small sea-going boat slipped away from the bank, to be rapidly lost in the greyness of the river.

Chapter Thirty-Eight

Heritis looked to Jakus and shook his head. "Jakus—er, Shada—what are your orders?"

"Easy enough. To do what you failed to do. Leave a small, reliable contingent to seek out any vermin left in this miserable city and secure the ships, then march on Nebleth." Jakus looked into the northern evening sky to where scattered stars were making an appearance through the sea mist. "It was there I had my greatest triumph, had a good life and had my enemies under control.

"No, we need to reconquer Ean, and wipe out those who dare to stop us," he snarled. "So"—he swung his red-eyed gaze back to Heritis riding one of several perac they had been able to secure—"are you up to the task? Will you be able to act when you're confronted by your turncoat consort? Kill her at my command? Hmm?"

Heritis' face froze, and he slowly nodded to the Sutanite leader. "Yes, my Shada."

"Good." Jakus stood in his stirrups and gazed over the large, black-clad army all around him, relieved to be suddenly in full control of his body. "This time," he said quietly to Heritis, "we will be prepared. We know what awaits us and we will not be taken unawares." He glanced behind to where Sharna, eyes blank, sat on her animal.

"Consort!" he snapped, "remind me of your belief that the enemy women can use scent in different ways, how they managed to thwart our might, both here and in Rolan."

"Shada"—Sharna forced her perac forward after a long moment—"it is as you suggest. Something the women do changes scent, an underlying aspect to it that can supplant what we do, cause our scent attack to…fail."

"Why can't I see it then?" His aura grew dark.

"I really don't know but I think it's because you're not a…uh…woman." She closed her eyes and shrunk back.

"Bah!" He hawked and spat on the ground. "Then we kill the women we find!

"Dronthis"—Jakus looked over his shoulder to the bulk of the taciturn Sutanite on the other side of Sharna, before jerking his head towards Heritis—"I rely on you to keep our priorities straight. Can you do this?"

"Yes, my Shada," Dronthis grunted.

"We move at pace! Be prepared and above all, keep your positions!" Jakus bellowed as he led the army along the dimly marked, paved road out of the city and into the night.

Darkness had fallen in the city, the surroundings only lit by occasional smouldering coals and small signal fires strategically placed along the wharf. There was no rest for the contingent guarding the ships and the port against possible surprise attacks from defenders creeping from their boltholes amongst the rubble.

Jakus had left strict instructions to his captains, Crastus and Tibitis, to keep watch on the harbour mouth, and left his most reliable people, men from the northern steppes of Sutan, to carry out his wishes. Festern, their leader, liaised with the ship captains as he searched the city. One ship patrolled the harbour in the dark in case of any surprise attack from the sea.

Anyar lifted her head from her pillow. Vor, a log along her side, lifted his head and growled.

"Pish, Vor, we've got to get up anyway. Too much sleeping's not good for anyone."

"Speak for yourself, daughter; it's early and I need my rest." Sadir's sleep-tousled head rose from the bunk next to Anyar.

"Anyar," came Sovira's drowsy voice, "why are we stopping?"

"Something's up," she replied. "Where's Boidea?"

"On deck, if I don't miss my guess," said Sadir. "She needs to be on top of things."

A thumping, echoing on the side of the ship, forced them to hurry to join the flow of people climbing the few steps to the deck. The sun had risen on rolling seas, silhouetting figures climbing over the side of the gunwale. Ginrel pulled a stocky man onto the deck and clasped him in a strong hug.

Anyar paused at the main mast, feeling the comforting wood as she assessed the man's scents. He was familiar, yet she couldn't remember him, but definitely a river man with strength and purpose.

Her assessment was interrupted by the arrival of another stranger, thinner, with a squarish jaw and distinctive nose. The young man had a recognisable scent about him reminiscent of the enemy, yet he held himself awkwardly, and the accompanying smell of blood told her he was injured.

A stocky young river woman came up the rope ladder behind him, her scents also unfamiliar. Vor pressed tightly to Anyar's legs, watching the proceedings, alert but unconcerned.

"Go straight to the captain's cabin," said Lan as he clasped the river man to him. "Brin and his companions have urgent news."

Lan saw Anyar standing at the mast, Sovira and Eren with her. He smiled tightly. "We need to hear what has caused our friends to risk this hazardous journey. Join us in the cabin."

The captain's cabin was a crush, people sitting on the bunk, on small chairs, and leaning against the wall; the strangers occupied the centre of the room, the injured man sitting.

Vor had pushed through and was investigating the man's feet.

"What is that?" he asked nervously, his dark eyes flicking up and catching sight of Anyar as she moved into the room.

Her chuckle of amusement caught him by surprise. "Sorry, it's just seeing your face when you saw Vor."

"Oh, so, it's a pet, albeit a large one? Ah, forgive me, my name's Bilternus and I'm here to help you defeat my uncle."

The room fell silent except for the snuffling of the voral.

The revelation that the Sutanite fleets had reformed and were attacking Ean caused a rapid re-assessment of their plans. The Rolan fleet held station just out of sight of Port Saltus while a battle plan was formed.

It was decided to bring the attack on Jakus' forces from the rear while they were engaged in travelling inland to besiege the capital. While the shadow scent defence had been effective on both Heritis' and Jakus' armies as an unknown factor, now the enemy was forewarned. This time, though, the entire force of shadow scent manipulators could be deployed. This battle might prove to be the tipping point in the war.

Their advantage was in knowing what they were up against, and in keeping Jakus unaware of the army behind him. The stage was set for a great battle and a final conflict.

The decision made, the fleet was to set sail for Port Saltus with the aim of hitting the harbour on the incoming tide, mid-morning.

Anyar learned more about the stranger and how he was a friend of Kyel's from the old days.

The fighting against the people of Nebleth was a turning point for Bilternus. The uncalled-for viciousness of the Sutanite leaders and their demands sat badly with him. He had lost many of his own people, and to what end? The subjugation of other countries who despised them? The surrender of his forces at Nebleth allowed Bilternus to reflect on what would be best for his country. His agreement to help stop the Jakus-led attacks would give him a chance to contribute to changing the future and bringing Sutan back to peaceful ways.

When the discussions had concluded, Anyar saw Bilternus watching her, his scents showing the greys and pastels of enquiry. She nodded to him and indicated the door. He lifted himself off the chair, favouring his side, and came over to her.

"Come to the cabin I'm sharing," she said. "You and I should talk."

Vor pushed through into the small room and climbed onto the bunk. Anyar sat next to him and Bilternus made himself comfortable on Sovira's bed. He smiled at her raised eyebrows and spread his hands.

"I've heard a lot about you, Anyar. When Kyel and I first met he talked about his family, especially you, although I thought you were much younger."

"I was," she answered. "What do you want to tell me?"

"Xerina. Do you know of her?"

Anyar nodded.

"She taught Kyel, and later me, about shadow scent."

"I had heard," said Anyar. "My uncle recognised you in one of my Knowings."

"Ah, Knowings…" Bilternus breathed out. "Xerina spoke of those, particularly about one that had drastic implications for Sutan and the coming of an Eanite who would destroy Sutan; it caused Jakus and my father no end of concern."

"Oh, your father was Faltis? You haven't heard, then?"

"No, what?"

"He died, so sorry," she reached over and patted his hand.

"No!" Bilternus coughed out. "No, I'm not." He straightened with a wince. "It wasn't him, you see, it wasn't him. It was an evil Sutanite called Septus. He had taken my father over somehow. So, it ends. The evil is gone. Septus is dead."

"Oh, Bilternus." Anyar's scent bled soft colours of concern. "You don't know. You really don't know. Septus is not dead. I believe he now lives in Jakus, controlling and leading him."

"What?" Bilternus thumped his fist on his knee with a wince, "Still alive? How? Blood-cursed scarthas. Then how do we get rid of that damn parasite? How?" He sat in silence until Vor jumped off the bunk and leant his head on the young man's knee. He dropped his hand to the voral's ruff and stroked him for a while.

"That explains it," he said, suddenly looking into Anyar's eyes. "That's why he's attacking Ean and not Rolan again. Septus wasn't focussed on magnesa like Jakus, so he wouldn't necessarily want to go back to Rolan; that was Jakus' fixation. Septus wants Ean, it seems, and he has a need to rule all. We have to stop him."

Anyar took both of Bilternus' hands in hers. "Yes, this is what we must do. We must stop this evil from destroying our countries, and it appears our meeting is more than just fortuitous."

The sun was an orange globe hanging in a bright blue sky, driving off the remnants of sea mist. A strong wind sent the Eanite ships scudding purpose-fully across the ocean to attack the Sutanite fleet and destroy it. Anyar and her friends stood at the bow of the flagship, enjoying the whip of wind across their faces, trying not to think of the battle that awaited them.

A ship hove into view, masts unfurled, rising and falling on the rolling waves. A shout from the crows nest alerted all on deck. The Sutanite captain must have been surprised at the approaching, vast armada, the wind at their backs, for there was a clear attempt to come about, to meet the opposing force, but the manoeuvre merely caused the vessel to lose way and be exposed to the might of the force bearing down upon it.

The fleet continued into the harbour in an aggressive push to take their attack to the docked ships while the enemy was relatively off guard. The Sutanites's weak, unprepared scent defence failed dismally. Each ship of the fleet sailed along the shoreline attacking the enemy vessels with scent bolts, spears and burning projectiles, forcing many of the defenders to escape to the wharf area.

The onshore contingent of Sutanites quickly absorbed the fleeing sailors and scent masters, bulking up their force against the attack from the fleet. They spread across the wharf area utilising the damaged buildings and other structures to form a significant defensive barrier. It soon became apparent that the force from Rolan would be hard pressed to overcome this resistance.

Anyar had been forced by her many protectors to take a position behind the forefront as part of a back-up group. While she couldn't see much, it didn't stop the sounds and smells of the action coming through. The crashing, yelling and frantic activity around her made it hard to remain in her position and focus on what she had to do. The screaming from a sailor as he ran past pulling at his acid-riven face snapped her focus and made her more determined. She strengthened her scent shields and moved to the rail.

Her first sight of Port Saltus revealed a long strip of wooden wharf interspersed with piers projecting at right angles into the confluence of the river and the sea. The piers were substantially blocked by wrecked and sunken ships, both Eanite and Sutanite vessels. Such was the lack of space that many ships of the fleet had to tie up against those damaged vessels instead of at the piers.

Their flagship slid into position alongside the huge Sutanite three-master now resting at a slight angle against its berth. The damage from the attack had been enough to leave two of its three masts lying across the deck in a welter of sail, rope and wood.

But Anyar had little time to observe her surroundings as the attackers were facing a well-structured defence. Sailors and scent masters swarmed over the gunwales of the listing Sutanite ship, fighting enemy sailors with their spears, knives and scent bolts. A spear from above hit a scent master in the shoulder before he retaliated by blasting a scent bolt into the air. A dark form fell from rigging with a scream. The Rolan attack was brief and ferocious, quickly overwhelming the remaining enemy sailors and making the ship theirs.

Around one hundred Sutanites had formed a substantial barrier along the first line of buildings and in the alleyways, reinforced by scent walls of significant power. Backing the enemy scent masters and their scent bolt attack was a large contingent of troops hurling spears and catapulting rubble at the attackers. They were well protected, having learnt from the previous battles, and kept targeting the ships and attackers with a barrage of strengthened acidic scent bolts.

The defensive scent barriers couldn't protect all aboard the ships. Many fell, and a Rolanite fighter stumbled past holding his shattered shoulder before his calves hit the gunwale and he tumbled backwards, screaming, into the murky waters below.

Lan, Ginrel and Boidea were kept busy organising the disembarkation of their animals and supplies, and the protection of their ships as the battle for Port Saltus became a stalemate.

With dusk falling they held a hasty council of war trying to determine how they could quickly overcome the enemy before continuing to the main fight, the battle for Nebleth, and Ean.

"Hard to use shadow scent," said Boidea. "They are cunning in the way they have structured themselves, and it's difficult to counter their scent use."

"Cud git around behind 'em," suggested Brin. "Their line doesn't extend too far along th' river."

"No," said Lan, "their role is to delay us while Jakus attacks our cities. We must stop them, and quickly."

"Could I suggest something?" a young voice interrupted them.

"Eren, lad," said Ginrel, "I doubt thet yer wud be aware of th' intricacies of battle."

"No," said Lan, "let's hear him out."

"In Rolan, when we had to destroy the building in the port, we built the strongest scent shield I've ever seen. Not only was it strong, but the enemy couldn't see us. What about that? Anyar?"

She was crouched down, one hand on Vor's shoulder as she thought. "Yes, could be done, Eren, but if they know we're there, what we're doing mightn't be enough. If several of us could just manage to get down there"—she looked pointedly at two of her friends—"we could get a few of our scent masters through and behind them…"

"What about the danger?" asked Sadir.

"Mother, it's what I do. What I'm good at," said Anyar. "With Eren, Sovira, Vor and myself we can produce a very strong shield, enough to get through their defences together with some shadow scent users, if,"—she looked at the anxious faces around her—"there's sufficient distraction."

"A good thought," agreed Jelm. "I'm very familiar with this place, along with Ginrel, Brin and Lan. If we can't find a way to distract the defenders, then we're not worthy of fighting for Ean."

"Anyar," said Xerrita, standing behind Sadir, "is it a good time to take our cordial, then?"

Anyar nodded at the buxom, grey-haired woman.

"So," said Boidea, "Let's go to it."

Chapter Thirty-Nine

Fires were set along sections of the wharf, lighting up the walls and piles of rubble and timber where the defenders were firmly entrenched. Attackers surged against the enemy blockades causing a swift reaction, in some cases scent barriers being broken by scent masters using shadow scent, but mostly the positions remained unassailable.

Dark areas where the light didn't quite reach were also filled with the enemy, but the lack of fighting kept them quiet and on edge. In one such alleyway, where piles of rubble reached out towards the bulk of a smashed ship, Anya and her friends crouched down; behind them was their strongest group of shadow scent users, led by Sadir, Boidea, and Xerrita.

"Stay back while we build up a structure," ordered Anyar. "It'll take a few moments. Then we'll have a little time to make our way to their scent barrier."

"We'll be ready to create another distraction," said Jelm, standing with a group of men nearby, "keeping their eyes diverted."

Anyar nodded and then offered cups of cordial to Eren and Sovira. "Come, drink, prepare. Remember how we did it in Requist. This is what we're here for, to do it again. I'll try to extend the shield behind us to get us all through the barrier. You'll have to let me hold it, as we'll be dismantling their scent structure at the same time."

"That man won't be there, will he?" asked Sovira.

"Oh, the one who could 'see' us? No, he won't be. Bilternus said so."

"What?" asked Eren. "How would he know?"

"Long story," said Anyar. "Simply that he'll be with the rest of the army and attacking Nebleth."

"I thought he was dead, too?"

"Eren, concentrate." Vor shifted across their legs as Anyar gripped their hands and breathed out, drifting a calming scent across them.

Soon a rippling in the darkness began as a translucent scent emerged, scents drawn from their deepest scent memories linked into a blanket, enveloping them.

Then the aspects of shadow scent became apparent as first Anyar, then Sovira and finally Eren saw the fuzziness around the edges of the bonds. Vor's strength added an impetus, a push which aided Anyar to guide their efforts to link the minute elements, the bonds, into a strong, virtually impenetrable blanket of scent, rigid and controllable.

A slight murmur behind them reminded Anyar to extend the blanket back to envelop the scent masters crouched with them, making all within invisible to the outside. The larger it grew, the more pressure it put on the four of them manipulating it, the shield pulsing in time with their heart beats.

"Quick!" she hissed. "We move."

Like an elongated box, they edged out of the shadows towards the alleyway and the scent barrier before them. A crackle of scent bolts and the thunk of weapons arose on one side as they shifted forwards.

Anyar guided them into the darkness, feeling the structures in front of her, tightening and manipulating their scent bonds to move on, all the while hoping that an observant scent master didn't spot them. Despite their careful approach, bricks and rubble blocking their path had to be pushed noisily aside. However, the nearby conflict served to obscure their approach, making the defenders uncertain as to what was happening.

The main scent barrier was finally reached, taut and quivering as the Sutanite scent masters kept their focus, despite the nearby attacks. Anyar manipulated eddies of shadow scent against the barrier, slipping amongst the scent bonds, destabilising it. Then it unravelled in an instant, leaving the defenders vulnerable to the assault from the Jelm-led attackers. Anyar and her group slipped through in the confusion, behind the defenders and into a narrow street parallel to the wharf area. With a quick glance, she collapsed the structure in a quiet, shadowed area and, keeping Sovira and Eren behind her, aided the group of women to use the shadow scent to destabilise the enemy's remaining scent-defensive structures.

Night closed early for the enemy in Port Saltus, as one by one the scent barriers withered away, leaving the Sutanites vulnerable. Once their position became hopeless, their leader, Festern, ordered the surrender.

"Ah, Jakus' memories." He sat with his back to the fire, arm around Sharna. "This is one of the way stations. He stayed here many times, even fought off an attack here."

"My Lord?" Sharna turned to face Jakus, stepping back with one foot to put distance between them.

"The one chance to be alone on the whole of this campaign." He looked across the rough walls of the small building separating the two of them from his troops, bivouacking around the way station on the northern road.

Septus watched the pretty red-head's face crinkle in confusion through Jakus' eyes.

He didn't understand why he'd remained alive and in control of another body, but it showed how much of a scent master he was. It had begun when he was dying in the Great Southern River, being sucked out by the parasitic haggar that dwelled there. In the pain of being eaten alive he had flung out his being, all the scent stores of his long life, and linked with a reciprocal mind, one he knew intimately.

It took time to make sense of his situation, to understand he still lived and in such a way. The long inner fights that he'd had with Targas' powerful presence had steeled him for this day. He had left the man to die in an instant when the opportunity arose during the battle at Mlana Hold in Rolan, to live in Faltis, all the while developing his skills, his power, waiting for the opportunity to achieve his ultimate goal, to be the supreme ruler.

His opportunity came at the time when Jakus, the Shada of Sutan, was most stressed, most tested, then he sprang, leaping into the man's mind, overtaking his body, his memories, and his personality. Though Jakus had fought against his *presence*, Septus was firmly in control and had dictated the course of the war from that moment.

He huffed before taking a large swig of a fine red wine direct from the bottle and clasped Jakus' consort to his side. Using this new—though not perfect—body would suit him for a time but he needed one more step to achieve his ambition, and the time was coming. A young body and a powerful mind would soon be his.

"Sharna"—he leered at the woman's pale face—"shut the door. We attack next day but this night, this night I have needs."

A long watch on the palisades kept everyone on edge. Regna stood with Lethnal, Cathar and Rasnal in hurried conference as the night darkened, the light from a thin crescent moon giving little illumination to the scene. Kyel stood by Piltarnis and Grefnel.

"I trust they can organise the shadow scent defence when Jakus comes," said Kyel, "since I think it won't be as easy this time."

"No, he will have learnt," said Piltarnis. "We didn't expect your shadow scent to be so effective. We had an inkling that your females had an extra scent capability, but nothing like that. So yes, the Shada will be ready."

"Also, from what I can see he has a larger army than we've had to face before," added Grefnel. "There were a lot of ships, which made short work of the five vessels we had there. Shouldn't have been so complacent, I suppose. Still, no use worrying now, even with the excuse that the wind and tides were against us when they attacked."

"Maybe it might work against them too, that is if Brin and Bilternus made it to the fleet from Rolan," mused Kyel.

"Yes, it might," said Grefnel, nodding into the dark. "Now all we have to worry about is what's out there."

"I would rather be here, helping," added Piltarnis, "but I best keep to the terms of our surrender and stay with my people out of the fighting."

"That's appropriate, Piltarnis," Kyel answered. "I know you are a man of your word, but others don't, so it's best. I'll send word if you are needed."

"**K**ast, you will take charge of the main part of the army; Dronthis, you will support Heritis to lead the remainder. Tretial, you will, as an accomplished scent master, have the bonus of accompanying me on a separate mission. Our forces need to spread out in our approach to Nebleth. No one will fail, no one will be beaten down by this unknown power the women have, for we will be in overwhelming numbers on a wide front. And Heritis, this time you will not fail. This time you will please me, get into the city, and wipe out all who stand in your way. We will not be merciful, so my cousin, remember, no mercy to *anyone!*

"Further," the Shada continued, "there is more than one way into Nebleth, more than one way to defeat them. While we no longer have our weapon, the hymetta, to deploy, we do know of the vast caves beneath the city. We will use these to get around the enemy.

"This is what I and a select group will be doing. For this to succeed we need to break through the walls and distract the enemy. While you attack on all fronts, other things will be happening. Use magnesa rigorously, for this is it. Defeat the vermin here, in their home, then no one will ever be able to resist us."

The Shada made his commandeered perac rear and bleat loudly as he dug sharp heels into its flanks. He raised an arm into the air, then pointed to the distant city.

The army spread out from the river and into the fields in a broad band and began a slow march to the city in the wan light of an early morning sun filtering through high clouds on the still day.

A small rearguard spread across the road, digging into the soft ground of the riverbanks and surrounds. Mindful of the enemy fleet in Rolan, the Shada was leaving nothing to chance in his push for the conquest of Nebleth and Ean.

The whirr of wings in the dawn air slipped by the most astute of the Shada's observers as several message-carrying tina, kept safely by Tishal during the assault on Port Saltus, flew overhead, drawn to the familiar scents of Nebleth.

Rasnal, the most astute interpreter of scents transported by the large moths, waited in the tower and quickly interpreted their messages.

A wave of hope spread through the defenders, even as the black line of the enemy approached the city, with the expectation that the attackers would soon be sandwiched between both allied forces. The battle was crucial, for whoever won would be in prime position to determine the future.

Slight mists rose in the early morning air as the Great Southern flowed with its usual majesty, clear of the usual craft that plied its waters. Jakus was familiar with the river and its trade, in particular the barges that carried salt and other goods between Nebleth and the port. He had been quick to snare two of the craft abandoned by their owners alongside the bank and, with the few animals he had acquired, towed them in the wake of his army on their northward progress towards Nebleth.

Having entrusted the operations of his forces to Kast and Heritis, he and a small group of scent masters and competent guardsmen boarded the barges and followed the river away to the right of his forces. Their ploy as barge people was weak at best, but once the battle was joined there was every hope that what they were about wouldn't be noticed.

Sharna, again in her role as a commander, was given a trusted role in the second of the two barges. Her skill with scent control enabled her to help disguise the barge, blurring the outlines, making them shabbier, non-threatening, merely river people trying to avoid the warring armies with a late cargo from downriver.

Sharna sat cramped in the stern of the barge as two perac pulled the vessel along the tow path by the river, watching the mass of Sutanites marching along the road and approaches far to her left towards the palisades and the south gates of Nebleth. She wasn't sure what she wanted to happen, still in shock from her night with the Shada and her realisation that he was Septus, not Jakus. At best she was a realist, making certain she'd survive the coming conflict, but she had no idea what she could do about the man himself. She missed the youthful chatter and camaraderie of Bilternus, and his knowledge of the man who had inhabited his father, Faltis, for so long.

She still hoped Bilternus was alive and a prisoner, despite Dronthis' glee in recounting stabbing the 'traitor' when he surrendered during the failed Heritis-led attack on Nebleth.

A roar resounded as the army reached the city walls.

Chapter Forty

K yel held Cathar to him as he watched the Sutanite army approach, spread across the road and fields. In the harsh glare of the sun now rising above the eastern mountains, the wavering line of black-and-grey troops seemed to pose no threat. As he scoured the assemblage for weaknesses, anything that might help them in their defence, he noticed two components: the straighter lines of troops marching along the road, and the outlying group trudging through the scrub on the side away from the river. Each was led by a powerful group of scent masters. The leader of the first group was obviously Kast, Jakus' right-hand man. The other, apparently in charge of the second group of the army moving through the scrub, would surely be Heritis, supported by a man he had hoped was dead: Dronthis.

Kyel's free hand instinctively felt his ribs, remembering how he had been abused by Dronthis in the dungeons of the Sutaria palace a long while ago.

"Cathar, I better let you join Regna's group, as you will be in the forefront of the attack. They're close, coming on two fronts. We haven't long now."

"Be safe, love." Cathar squeezed his hand. "Remember, our people are coming. All we must do is hold out for the day." They exchanged scents before she hurried along the walkway at the back of the palisade to join the group of women at the gate, led by Regna and Cynth. Further to the west, Kyel could see Lethnal and Rasnal organising the other shadow scent users.

"Hmm." He paused as he turned to slip through the spear-carrying guardsmen around him to join the male scent masters providing defensive shields against the attackers. Far off, against the light reflecting from the bronze-coloured river waters, were two barges slowly pulling against the current, soon to enter the first of the wharves on Nebleth's shoreline. He knew that the area was well defended but was puzzled at a pair of trading barges travelling at this most dangerous time.

"They're coming!" came a panicked voice, breaking through his thoughts and making him hasten to join his group defending the city walls.

A thin line of guardsmen and several scent masters protected the city's water-front and the vessels secured there. People were coming and going in a disorganised haste, and it was into this panic that the two barges slowly slid. The animals headed towards known food and water stops while the harried wharf master, backed up by a trio of armed men, rushed to the barges to ascertain their identity and purpose.

"There's a war on!" he shouted to the hooded figures in the stern. "You shouldn't be here! Keep moving upriver, away from this area. It must be kept clear."

A cloaked figure leapt off the bow and began securing a tether to a bollard behind the master's back.

"Hey! Stop!" shouted the wharf master, swinging about to see what was happening.

A scent bolt of tremendous power smashed into his unprotected back, catapulting him into his men. The barge hatches opened and black-cloaked, grey-tunicked men jumped onto the wharf to make quick work of the defenders with scent bolts and knives.

"Leave the barges!" yelled Jakus into the brief lull of the fighting. "You two"—he pointed to Tretial and another scent master—"keep anyone from following for as long as possible, then join me. The rest of you, follow."

"Sharna!" He held out a hand and she joined him as they clattered along the rough cobbles of the warehouse district, before turning up an alleyway between two wooden buildings.

"Hah!" he puffed out as he bent over near a bare stone wall at the end of the narrow alley and rubbed his leg. "This...my new body...isn't as fit as I'd like. Still, there's time..." His voice trailed off as he inspected a small, stone-coloured door set into the wall.

"Ah, Jakus' memories are useful." He exuded a dark, sinuous scent spike from his mouth and inserted it into a small hole beneath the latch. "Got it," he said, and pushed open the small door.

A nauseous odour drifted out as he beckoned to the people behind him. "Light torches; come through. No time to waste!"

Bearing flaming torches, the column of scent masters and guardsmen pushed past Jakus and Sharna into a long dark corridor. The moment the last had gone in, Jakus shoved his companion through and followed, slamming the door shut and blasting the rock ceiling with a scent bolt. A rush of rubble blocked the opening.

"No fear of a rear attack. Move forward!" he ordered.

"I recognise the smell. Is this where you kept those creatures, the hymetta?"

Sharna's curiosity overcame her concern at her situation.

"Yes, we had good use for them in the past. Pity they're all gone. Maybe, when all this is done, we'll breed them again." Jakus' voice echoed eerily against the sound of his people descending into the dark caves below the city. "Keep moving!" he ordered, "we have a distance to go before we get to the hymetta caves and the way up into the tower. Those damn scartha will be in for a deadly surprise."

Cathar had little recollection of the next while, so engrossed was she in developing and supporting the shadow scent barriers to counter and disassemble the scent attacks of the enemy. The noise of the enemy attack, with the screams and cries of the wounded and dying, resonated in her head as she concentrated. Defended by the weapons of the guardsmen and male scent masters, she worked assiduously in concert with her compatriots. Fortified by liberal draughts of Rolan cordial, they countered every scent attack, breaking down the acidic nature of the blankets the enemy attempted to float across them and returning the noxious blankets back to their senders.

Eventually, the pressure of so many of the enemy on such a wide front began to take its toll. The gates fell with a crash, enabling a swarm of Sutanites to enter the city and begin to overwhelm the defenders.

The sun was high in the late Spring sky, heating up the fighting and adding misery to the combatants. The surges of the enemy had pushed the defenders back, blocking the roadways leading to the tower.

Cathar could see where Kyel and his group were countering the enemy scent masters even against their magnesa-enhanced attacks and hoped their use of shadow scent was helping to keep the fighting away from those she loved. A screech suddenly shattered into her awareness as a black knot of the enemy loomed up on the small group of women. Fighting intensified, with Regna heroically leading the way with her significant command of shadow scent. They held their ground even as their supporting defenders fell to the spears and scent bolts of the enemy.

A familiar face suddenly broke through the wedge of black-covered attackers. Heritis, Regna's former consort, loomed up in front of them, face contorted in her effort to demolish their scent shields. Regna's concentration faltered, causing a ripple through their defence. *Damn,* Cathar thought, *it can't end here. I don't want to die and leave my love, just when I've found him.*

"Traitor!" screeched Heritis. "Traitor to me and to our country. You've left me no choice!" With an enormous effort cording his neck, he reached his scent power forward in a spear-like wedge, pushing into Regna's scent shield, forcing the point closer and closer to her neck.

Cathar couldn't assist as she was helping to maintain the shadow scent shield, keeping apart from those fighting with the enemy leader. She didn't see what happened next due to her intense concentration.

At the crucial moment, when scent shields were flattening against each other, and the might of the enemy's attack was certain to prevail, Regna stepped through their scent barrier and grabbed her former partner tightly to her body.

A shimmer appeared as odours intertwined around the couple, shadow scent working against magnesa-enhanced power, her intricate understanding of scent manipulation allowing her to delve deeply into the structures and bonds of the scent. Time seemed to stand still, fighting forgotten as the battle between former consorts, now enemies, took place.

It was as if a second couple merged with the first, like a paler shadow of their bodies, slowly taking root, becoming more solid, bolder until it tried to take the place of their physical substance. Then, in an instant, a silent explosion occurred and they disappeared. A vast inflow of dusty air whipped into their space, blasting a million motes into the atmosphere.

Heritis and Regna had ceased to exist.

K yel reacted quickly in the lull that followed. He saw that the shock of this unprecedented event had caused the fighting to falter, the enemy losing one of their leaders. He dashed forward towards a shocked Cathar.

"Fall back, to the tower!" he called and began to push the stunned defenders along the street, away from the gates. He hesitated as he saw Dronthis, slack-jawed standing behind the empty space that had held Heritis only moments before, but the opportunity to attack him quickly passed as he hurried Cathar and the other women scent masters down the street.

He looked into the sky at the westering sun and hoped that relief was not too far away, for if not, all was lost.

A line of perac carrying supplies and the all-important tumblers of cordial slowed the pace of the Rolanite army along the northern road to Nebleth. They were aware of the need to hurry but the pace of any army is always determined by its slowest components, and they needed to be fully prepared for what they were to face in the capital.

Anyar was grateful that she no longer had responsibility for her two friends; their part had been played and they remained safe in Port Saltus while she rode her perac towards a final confrontation, her faithful Vor matching her pace on the paved road. Her mind kept fluctuating, going from relaxing into the perac's gait to slipping into a kind of Knowing. Momentous events were on the move and would culminate in this place. She knew she had a major role at the finish of it all, and then she would be alone. This was the moment her whole short life had been preparing for. This was the end of things as they knew it. Her friends would keep her safe, enable her to play the part she had to play, and she had to let destiny take its course.

The city was a dark smudge on the horizon, and they could see movement around its walls. As she watched, a void came in the drift of scents that filled the air around her, a ruction in the fabric of the world. Death of two powerful scent masters in an unfathomable way had happened, and it signalled that everything was on a precipice. They needed to hurry.

The pace stepped up.

"**D**amn scartha!" screeched Jakus. "Hold the torch closer."

He stood in a long, well-crafted corridor at the top of a slope leading out of the deepest part of the caves where noxious smells of death, blood and wastes thickened the air. Behind him waited an apprehensive group of Sutanite scent masters. Sharna, grateful for the comfort of Tretial's presence, watched as Jakus stared into the space before them.

"How are we to get through here? My memories tell me this was clear right through to the dungeons and the stairs leading to the tower. The scartha have blocked it." He swung around to glare at his companions. "Well, get to it. Clear the rubble. We need to get through to the stairs, or my plan fails. You all have skills to remove the blockage."

Jakus stepped back, watching as the scent masters began to break up the rock with well-placed scent bolts, others coming in to remove the broken-up rock.

Sharna found herself relegated to the back of the corridor wondering what was happening on the outside, how the fighting was going, whether Jakus' ploy to come in behind the defenders and connect with his forces would work. There was no way of knowing what was occurring, trapped in the bowels of the tower.

Eventually, a way was made through the piles of rubble and to the door leading out of the dungeons to the stairs. This door, too, was blocked and reinforced by metal, resisting the efforts of the scent masters.

Jakus shoved his men aside and bent low. Sharna saw a thick blackness emerge from his mouth and stick to the door. Soon, over the laboured breathing of those waiting in the thickening air of the corridor, there came the sound of something tinkling against the stone floor, and she was surprised to see a steady patter of iron particles falling from the door. She'd known he was powerful but hadn't realised this man—this *creature*—could exude such a corrosive, acidic mix from his scent memories. Sharna realised that the power of this man, this creature, was incredible.

They waited as the door eroded away, until Jakus impatiently kicked at it with a booted foot, smashing it to pieces.

"Now!" he screeched, the sound echoing to the furthest depths of the caves. "We win. Through here is our opportunity to wipe out the enemy from behind and win Ean for Sutan."

The attack force pushed up the stairs, out of the darkness and into the dimly lit corridors.

Chapter Forty-One

"What just happened?" Sadir turned to her daughter as they approached the distant walls of Nebleth.

"I don't know," Anyar replied. "All I know is that it was momentous, a loss of scent power into the fabric of our world. I don't know how it happened, but it suggests an inkling of what may be."

"Anyar, you are more mysterious every day. I do hope I don't lose my daughter over this."

"Be that as it may, Sadir," interrupted Boidea, "but the ways of the Mlana are unfathomable in themselves, and we are living it right now. I have full faith in what is happening."

"Well, I'm happy for you," grumbled Sadir. "Let's just get this fighting over with as soon as possible.

"Gripping times, eh?" Boidea muttered, as the Rolan army moved closer to the fighting.

"I'm home." The creature that had been Jakus spread out his arms and slowly whirled in a black parody of a dance in the large bedroom on the third floor of the Nebleth tower. "This was the Shada's room many years ago, where one could stand on the balcony, observe the ants below and be content to rule such a weak people. All was the Shada's.

"But Jakus wanted more. Not satisfied with what he had, he tried to defeat the rebellion, defeat the outsider with special powers. And failed, bringing me down with him. Where is he now, hmm, Sharia?

"I have Jakus crushed under my thumb, trying to get out. Yet when I leave him, when I move into my final host, he will die. He doesn't believe me. I can hear him inside my head trying to be heard, to get away, but if he leaves, he will die. The false Shada will die.

"All is mine." His uneasy troops scattered throughout the large room, watched as the man they knew as the Shada moved across the floor, arms outstretched. "The time is coming, and everything will be mine.

"Now we wait. Use the balcony to spy on them until they come to us. We'll destroy them utterly. Then I will seek her out, find the great Mlana, take her body for my own and cast her essence to the four winds. I will rule forever! Hah!"

"**H**old!" called Kyel as he stood next to Cathar in the entranceway to the Nebleth tower courtyard. "Make a stand. If we hold, gain time, we can win. Get ready to close the gates!"

People were coming from every direction; guardsmen providing a front rank of steel spears to confront the enemy, scent masters lining up behind and the grey-cloaked shadow scent users forming a thin line after them. Anyone else who could be spared was involved in taking the wounded into the tower and preparing barricades behind the low palisade surrounding the structure. There was no time for much else as the enemy swarmed into the city and headed towards the towering structure marking the centre.

"Lethnal!" Cathar hissed. "What happened with Regna and Heritis? How was it possible?""

"Our friend made the ultimate sacrifice to keep us, her adopted people, safe. Regna was more powerful than we knew and used shadow scent in an unheard-of way. Maybe our Rolanite friends will know? In the interim, we must do as Kyel says. Defend the tower with all that we have. Hold on until our friends reach us. They won't be far away."

"I'll leave you, love," said Kyel, "and join with Grefnel and the other scent masters. Keep well back when you deploy shadow scent. I don't want to lose you."

"Be safe!" Cathar flung out an arm towards him as he hurried away.

The gates to the low palisade surrounding the tower were closing, despite several stragglers trying to come in. The attacking Sutanites roared loudly, jetting clouds of a dark scent to unsettle the defenders. Kyel and Grefnel stood on a low platform to co-ordinate the defence and keep a watch on the approaching army.

The quiet inside the palisade contrasted with the attackers' racket, each defender quietly determined to sell their life as dearly as possible with the example of Regna fresh in their minds.

It was soon apparent that the enemy was divided into two fronts, the first led by the solid and commanding Kast and the other by Dronthis. Kyel's brow narrowed when he saw the familiar figure, realising that he must have taken over as leader on Heritis' death.

"Where's Jakus?" he hissed. "Where's he got to?"

"Not a clue," Grefnel replied. "No time to worry. They're on us." He signalled to his command and a solid scent wall rose in front of them even as an attacker's acidic scent blanket dropped over the palisade.

"Spears!" Grefnel screeched, and wave after wave of missiles flew over the wall, some making it through the defensive shields of the enemy.

Kyel added his might and experience to the scent defence, utilising his knowledge of the bonding aspects of scent, helping push back against the enemy's scent attack even as parts of the wooden palisade began to crumple from the acids eating into them.

He sighed with relief as he recognised shadow scent drifting over them, protecting them and disassembling the enemy's scent barriers and acidic attack. All the while, people were dying as scent bolts and missiles got through.

With a sudden crash the walls collapsed, and battle was joined face to face. Kyel saw a scent-shielded Dronthis push towards him, a determined expression on his face and a dagger clenched in his fist.

He had no doubt what was on the big man's mind, and his insides clenched in fear as he prepared to meet his old enemy, determined not to let him get past to those he loved.

Anyar, where are you? he thought as he fired a scent bolt at Dronthis and readied his own dagger.

The rapid approach of the Rolan forces remained undetected by the enemy as they rode their animals to exhaustion. They swamped the rearguard left by Jakus at the approach to the city, before swarming across the rubble of the Nebleth walls, skirting bodies and pockets of fighting with urgency, knowing they had to reach the besieged defenders as soon as they could. The women scent masters were fully primed to use their shadow scent in a most emphatic way, having learnt from their fighting at the Cascade Falls. Anyar was confident the enemy wouldn't be able to counter a full out shadow scent attack.

They had spread out in a long line, male scent masters and troops on each end and a solid group of shadow scent users in the middle; Lan and Ginrel were on one side and Jelm, Brin with Bilternus on the other, Anyar having argued that the Sutanite be allowed to join in the attack. She was determined to lead her women from the front, with her mother, Boidea and Xerrita supporting her. This was her role and she fell into it without thinking. Pulses of Rolan cordial coursed through her veins while the previous Mlana filled her mind with her comforting presence.

Her destiny was here. *Now.*

"**W**hen do we move, Shada?" asked Sharna as they sat eating rations in the third-floor room. The group of Sutanites, food forgotten, looked up to hear his response.

"Want to be killing, do we?" Jakus ripped off a piece of dried meat and chewed noisily. "When my army drives the enemy into the tower, then we move. We come down behind them and trap them. Not long now." He shouted towards one of the windows, where a man stood, back to him: "Tretial! What do you see? Is it time?"

"Shada, they're being driven back," said the man at the window. Our army's almost at the tower. But," Tretial's voice came urgently from the balcony, "there's another army out there!"

"What!" Jakus hurried out to join him. "You fool. Why didn't you warn me?" He slashed a scent-enhanced hand across his scent master's face, ripping a red gash. "The damn scartha have crept up on us.

"Now!" he screeched, ignoring the bleeding scent master. "We go now. Take them from behind." He dashed to the door and led his troops into the dark corridor.

The walls of the tower provided a solid backing behind Kyel as the overwhelming Sutanite force pressed forward. Already most of the defenders had slipped through and headed up the stairs to the great hall while the efforts of the shadow scent workers protected them.

Kyel was one of the last to ease through the doorway as he sought to keep back the onslaught led by an intent Dronthis. By now the forces had converged, Kast and Dronthis joining in a massive assault on the tower, with only the stone walls and sturdy wooden doors to prevent them.

Cathar and Lethnal applied shadow scent to reinforce the doors, easing a thick barrier over its surface to help disassemble the scent attacks of the enemy. Several guardsmen protected them while they worked, others pushing sturdy metal poles in the wall sockets to provide an additional barrier.

Then it began, a rhythmic thudding on the door's surface.

"What is it?" Cathar asked.

"Axes," growled a sweaty guardsman. "They've axes. Be through it in no time."

"Back!" urged Lethnal. "Up the stairs. Fight them all the way."

"You women go up," said Kyel from the side where a large room led off from the entrance. "We'll be able to attack from here, close-in fighting."

"But you'll be trapped!" yelped Cathar.

"No. There are stairs at the back of this room, which is where Jakus and Septus used to process their victims in the old days. We'll be able to delay them, then escape to you."

"Oh," said Cathar, putting a hand to her mouth, "you're sure?"

"Yes!" urged Kyel. "Now go. Anyar's army will be here soon."

The strikes of the axes booming in the enclosed space added impetus to the defenders' pace as they rushed up the stairs.

"Now we wait," said Kyel glumly to the guardsmen and scent masters with him. "We wait."

Nebleth tower loomed high above the clutter of the city, its bulk lit by the rays of the setting sun. The holes of the scent collection chamber at its summit looked like black, pitiless eyes gazing over the melee of the creatures below it. It had seen much over its existence and here was yet another incident to disturb it.

Anyar shrugged off the feeling to concentrate on her role. She was now in the second line of attack, letting her larger and more experienced companions precede her. They snuffed out smaller pockets of the enemy as they moved through the battered city The defenders had fought a brave rearguard action but had been defeated. They were aware that the tower was the focus for the enemy. It was there they would meet the bulk of the Sutanite army, and there they must prevail.

They trod through the bodies and debris, their long line now bunched as they approached the tower.

The noise and black mass of the enemy confronted them as they came to the broken gates and smashed walls.

"Prepare!" yelled Boidea as the enemy turned from their attack on the tower to face them. "Full force."

The scent masters attacked with scent bolts and defensive barriers, troops throwing spears into the shadowy bulk of the enemy. The Sutanites fought with a fury that suggested they realised a powerful force faced them and for a few moments it was a stalemate, no one giving ground.

"With me!" ordered Anyar. She felt the comforting presence of Vor against her legs as she delved into the depths of her being, remembering the intricacies of her scent control, where scent was broken down into the minutest elements. She joined all the vagaries of scent memories with those around her, linking, binding, feeling the input of her fellow shadow scent users, their pulses beating in time with hers. The shadow scent emerged, joining the scent barrier and growing until it was a powerful force. Then she pushed it forward.

It impacted the enemy's scent barriers, absorbing their structure, twisting within, and dismantling their scent control. Scent bolts came hissing through the dissolving structure, hitting the barrier, absorbed in moments. Anyar felt the presence of Vor's unique talent providing an additional layer of protection as she pressed forward, driving the enemy to the walls of the tower.

She pushed all the worries, the deaths and injuries out of her mind as she strove to press the powerful scent blanket down on the enemy. She heard the screams of wounded and dying enemy but hardened her heart against it.

Again! Kyle thought, as yet another black-garbed guardsman approached, teeth bared and spear clenched in his fists. Kyel pushed out with all the scent control he could muster, thrusting the man away with the flick of a solid scent bolt, smashing him into a wall. He was waiting for bigger prey to appear in the doorway. He was waiting for Dronthis.

The fighting had been continuous once the great doors were breached, and the enemy flooded in. More combatants were injured by spears and knives than scent bolts as the Sutanites entered the tower. Groups of Eanite scent masters blocking the stairs and the doorway fought a last-ditch battle to prevent the enemy's ingress.

He saw Dronthis enter the room, instantly recalling the torture that this large Sutanite had inflicted on him. The man smiled in recognition, raised his cudgel then licked a dribble of blood off the dagger he held in the other hand. Kyel backed away through the dimly lit room, maintaining his scent protection while keeping his own knife before him.

This is it! he thought as they came together. *Sorry, Cathar.*

A piercing scream from above caused everyone to halt momentarily. "They're behind us! They've got in behind us!"

As Kyel realised that *they* would be Jakus, using his intimate knowledge to enter the tower through the caves, Dronthis slashed down with his dagger. Kyel belatedly lifted his own weapon to counter the Sutanite's furious assault.

Chapter Forty-Two

"Fall back!" yelled Lethnal when the flickering light from the wall sconces revealed black-clad Sutanites descending the stairs and entering the large, second-floor room. She pushed out a hasty scent barrier towards the invaders as the enemy flooded in, firing scent bolts and throwing spears. Cathar, Rasnal and Cynth joined with her, reinforcing their scent barrier with shadow scent in reaction to the pressure of the magnesa-enhanced acidic scents.

"Yer blasted haggars," called Cynth. "I'm certain thet's Jakus leadin' 'em. They've got 'round us, no mistake."

"Too late to worry about how they're here, we've got to stop them, or they'll crush us between them. There can't be too many, surely?" Lethnal queried the evidence of her eyes as she flung scent bolts at them.

"They're coming from below, up the stairs!" called a voice. "Hard to hold them!"

"Kyel?" said Cathar. "Kyel!"

Kyel felt, rather than heard, his partner's desperate cry from the room above while he struggled to hold off Dronthis' descending dagger, the man's foul breath gusting into his face as he fought; the tip of the blade slowly twisting towards his chest.

The Sutanite was huge, rotting teeth clenched, and was confident of defeating the younger, slighter man as the struggling pair pressed up against a wall, ignoring the fighting around them. Eyes bulging with effort, Kyel sought for a last vestige of strength to overcome his enemy.

"I almost killed you before," Dronthis hissed. "Now I'll fix my mistake."

The blade began to pierce Kyel's skin.

A sudden gust of wind swept the room, causing the flaming torches of the few wall sconces to flicker, rapid movement and rising voices around them distracting the large Sutanite.

Kyel took his chance, slipping his dagger through Dronthis' guard and into the soft skin under his throat. The Sutanite reacted and forced downwards with his weapon almost breaking Kyel's arm, pushing the point into his flesh. Kyel thrust upwards with all his might as the enemy's blade entered his chest.

A rush of Sutanites to the door took no notice of the two men crumpling to the floor.

She viewed the scene as if she were high above, the sun now a mere glimmer far to the west, stars already sprinkling the purpling sky over the disturbed city. She could see the tower standing tall above the dark moving masses at its feet, cries faintly reaching her ears before she swiftly returned to her situation.

The stench of humanity entered her nostrils; cries of pain and effort assaulted her ears, her body bumped and pressed by the fighting around her. In all that mayhem she felt the push of her constant companion hard against her thighs, her fingers reflexively gripping the coarse fur of his neck as she continued concentrating.

They had pushed forward, the men linked in with the women, each reinforcing and amplifying their scent attack on the enemy now pressed against the stone walls of the Nebleth tower. Anyar could feel her friends around her, the individual personalities of her mother, Lan, Jelm, Boidea, Xerrita, Brin, Ginrel and others, all working for the common cause, all putting in a stupendous effort to defeat the enemy. Then there was Bilternus; his aura was pure, not an enemy. *Ah,* she had an incidental thought, *he's a future leader.*

Blast, Anyar mentally shook herself, *first things first.* She looked at the numbers of the enemy before her and focussed. *We must win. We will win. Our friends are in there fighting for their lives. Concentrate.*

The Rolanite scent wall advanced, despite the best efforts of the enemy's barriers, scent bolts and acidic scent attack. They had no counter to the shadow scent. Every time they sought to break through, their scent structures were broken apart, fraying into individual odour motes, dissipating into the air.

A surge of Sutanites emerged from the tower to push into the attackers, their impetus briefly forcing the Rolanite army back. Soon the power of shadow scent, enhanced with the cordial, overcame the enemy.

Anyar sighed with exhaustion when a large, black-clad Sutanite leader shouted for a halt. "Hold! I am Kast, army commander. I call for an end to hostilities. I will meet with the Mlana and discuss terms."

"Hold!" repeated Boidea.

The fighting rapidly stopped, the noise of battle fading, broken only by the cries of the wounded and dying.

Anyar looked at her companions when Boidea leant towards her. "Mlana, I suggest you let me take your place, talk with the enemy leader, see what they will agree to."

"No. You will come with me," she said firmly. "Mother, Lethnal, Lan, we will all meet with this Kast. We have little time. Not all fighting has ceased, and I fear the enemy is still active within the tower."

A cleared space in front of the gates into the tower allowed Kast, with two supporting scent masters, to come together with Anyar and her four companions.

The large Sutanite glanced apprehensively at the voral, before acknowledging them. "We are in a difficult situation, and I call upon your humanity to allow us to take our injured and depart in peace." He looked directly into the eyes of the imposing Boidea. "Can you guarantee us this?"

"It is not up to me," she replied. "It is to the Mlana you must address your request."

Kast's eyes widened as he saw Boidea deferring to the diminutive young woman in the centre of the group.

"This? So, this is the Mlana?" Kast spluttered. "A mere youngster."

"Kast!" said Anyar, firmly. "You require a pledge from us. But first you must order your people to cease fighting. We have friends inside in need. Do this!" Anyar drew her strength to her pushing out with a rush of her scent aura, causing it to flare in a powerful cascade of greys and browns, with purple dominating.

Kast's face turned ashen, and he immediately called over his shoulder. "Is there any sign of the Shada? Has fighting ceased within the tower?" He turned back to face Anyar. "I will ascertain what I can, Mlana."

"Be quick. I will not be merciful if my friends are in danger."

They waited for a brief interval until a Sutanite dashed out of the tower door and whispered to Kast.

"Ah, there's been some fighting, but it has ceased. The Shada has disappeared, can't be found."

"Quickly," said Lan, "we need to enter, see what the situation is. Jakus is the key to all this. He must be found. He must be stopped."

Cathar was concentrating so hard on scent shielding against the Sutanites moving down on their thin defensive line that she hardly noticed a sudden lack of pressure from behind them. More defenders quickly joined their ranks as the enemy pushing up from the bottom stairs broke off and headed back down. The additional support aided them against Jakus' attack, helping them slow his aggressive assault.

Cathar noticed the battle taking its toll, thinning the numbers around the dynamic, black-cloaked leader. *We have a hope here,* she thought even as the scarlet and purple coils of scent surrounding the man's head and shoulders darkened with his extraordinary use of magnesa-enhanced power.

A slim figure, red hair showing above a black cloak, cried out in pain and slumped to the floor. This distracted their leader, and he snapped a look around the large hall. She saw him hesitate as if noticing how his numbers had thinned and the rearward attack had faltered.

"Back. Fall back!" his voice rang through the room.

"Push! Push harder!" Lethnal's higher voice responded. "Don't let them get away!"

Cathar added the last dregs of her strength to the shadow scent in the defenders' scent shielding as she and her companions shuffled forward to drive the few remaining enemy back up the stairs and into the top floor of the tower.

Anyar hardly noticed the surrender procedures of the Sutanites, allowing others to take over. Her concerns were for those still fighting in the tower, not only her friends but her vicious enemy, the man they called the Shada.

Vor swelled in size, the fibres of his shaggy coat standing on end, mouth in a toothy snarl as Anyar, hand on his ruff, entered the tower. She blocked off the sight of bodies, the smells of blood, offal and the refuse of battle, secure in her cocoon of scent shielding. A large group, along with her mother, Boidea and Lan flanking her, went through the smashed doorway and into the space before the stairs. She noticed the room leading off to the side and hesitated, sifting the odours for anything familiar.

"Kyel!" yelped Sadir. "He's in there." She pushed past and into the room, Cynth and Jelm accompanying her.

Anyar called her attention back, lifting her arm and pointing upwards. "As harsh as it seems to leave them," she said, "we need to go up there." Lan and Boidea nodded grimly, and with Bilternus and Brin began picking their way up the body-strewn stairs.

"Anyar!" called Cathar as she saw her enter the large second-floor hall, "thank Ean you're here. Lan! Boidea!"

They manoeuvred through the people milling around, some tending the wounded, others helping move the dead to reach their friends.

They took a moment to share scents, their warmth, their love, their relief, yet through it all Anyar couldn't prevent a sense of urgency slipping through.

"Time for a true welcoming later," said Lan. "We have more pressing matters."

"Yes!" stated Lethnal, pointing at the stair leading up to the third floor. "Jakus. He's escaped through there!"

"Kyel?" asked Cathar. "He's not with you? Where is he? Oh!" She pressed her hand to her mouth as she hurried away to descend the stairs.

"We've no time," said Anyar grimly, twisting her hand in Vor's ruff. "We must follow Jakus. Stop him. Now!"

"Right!" Lan affirmed and began to lead the group to the upper stairs.

"No!" Anyar lifted her hand. "Not you. Just me!"

"Mlana!" said Boidea.

"Just me!"

"Oh," Boidea said quietly, and placed a hand on Anyar's shoulder. "This is the time, Mlana?"

"Yes, this is the time," she replied and took a gulp of cordial from her belt pouch before weaving through the bodies lying on the floor. Anyar paused, seeing Bilternus nearby. "I believe your friend needs you." She nodded towards a slight body huddled on the floor, red hair just showing over a black cloak, before walking onwards with Vor.

For the first time in many years, Septus felt alone. He had lost all his support, even his Sharna, to the enemy, and now his only companion was Jakus. Yet even he was no friend, just a conduit for his life. Now he knew the full impact that the women's special scent had even over magnesa-enhanced scent control and had suffered the consequences.

His gaze flicked over the edge of the parapet to the dark city below sparsely lit with burning fires of rubbish and flaming torches. A chill breeze drifted over the narrow walkway leading to the scent chamber above him and he shivered as he remembered when he had fallen from there fighting Targas, the now-dead hero of the past Eanite rebellion.

Then, as now, he had been fleeing for his life. But this time there was hope if he used all his cunning, guile, and new-found powers.

"Pah!" he blasted a breath into the air. "The brat, Targas' spawn, will come to me. Then I will overwhelm her, take her body, and be the supreme ruler." He reached into his pouch of magnesa, took a handful of the red crystals and crammed it into his mouth.

Septus moved up the walkway, in full control of Jakus' body, to wait, like a huge black spider, against the doorway to the collection chamber.

Anyar paused at the top of the stairs assessing the scents ahead of her. Vor huffed as he sifted the odours, but seemed content, so Anyar moved along the corridor and past the bedrooms until she came to a doorway leading to the outside. This was the way to the scent-collection chamber, and the way Septus had gone.

Vor growled. Anyar took a step through into the darkening evening, knowing it was the most momentous step of her short life. She felt the presence of Alethea, the previous Mlana, backed up by others, generations of Mlanas, and knew she wasn't alone.

Even as she slipped through the door, climbed the few stairs, and began to move along the narrow walkway, her mind returned to the incredible event earlier that day: the deaths of Regna and Heritis, and what it signified. It was a sign, and it scared her.

She clamped down on her fears and focussed on the ominous building summiting the tower and the blackness of its doorway.

Vor's growl became constant the nearer they came to the tower. Anyar put extra strength into the scent barrier around both, linking in with her companion's unusual power, her body tense with anticipation.

Vor suddenly yapped furiously as a black, skeletal figure loomed out of the doorway. With a tremendous heave he pulled loose from Anyar's hand and leapt forward.

"Argh!" snapped Septus, flicking a concentrated burst of scent power at the charging animal, hitting him with enough force to send the animal skidding towards the parapet. Vor scrabbled furiously, claws scratching on the stone as his body teetered on the edge.

Anyar couldn't react quickly enough to prevent Septus adding another push of power to send the voral plummeting into the darkness.

Her mind screamed with disbelief and rage as Septus turned with a sardonic smile on his face.

"Meant something to you, did it? Just an animal." He stood, legs spread as if inviting her to attack him. Anya fought against her wish to do just that.

She felt the push of Alethea dampening her emotions, allowing her to do one of the hardest things on her life, to forget Vor's sacrifice and focus on the evil before her.

Before she knew it the black figure was on her, feeding long fingers into her scent barriers, his weight substantially more than hers. They wobbled together on the narrow pathway as she felt the spidery tentacles of his scent power digging into her. Somehow, he had gotten around her scent control and was seeking to invade her mind.

She recalled the warnings from Kyel and Bilternus, but even they didn't know what it was like: the raping of a mind with the thin cries of Jakus, Faltis and, even more faintly, her father, Targas, adding a background clamour to the invasion.

A kernel of her resisted, tightening her hold on her mind and her body, even as they fought an outwardly silent battle. She remained curiously detached while she fought, remembering her shadow scent training, and using the minute aspects of the scents to target and negate Septus' incredible strength. She had never experienced such scent power, where someone could demolish another person's scent memories and their whole being to take over and subsume their personalities.

Slowly she felt she was succumbing to this horrendous creature's attack, the loss of her friends and her faithful companion impacting on her ability to fight. Then the momentous event when two powerful scent masters were destroyed in a cataclysmic explosion rose in her mind.

Yes, she thought, *if that is what I must do, then I will.*

Each push from Septus was countered by her; each twist was reacted to; each strong scent was countered by a corresponding unravelling of that scent. The fight continued until the creation of shadow scent was almost continuous, depleting her, draining her strength. Anyar felt herself slipping into the long vortex of power loss, Septus alongside her. Soon she could feel him shoving her away as he realised the danger. She stayed locked to him, holding on, letting the shadow scent unravel all the scents around them, continuous and unstoppable. She was a mere mote floating in a sea of odours, waiting for the inevitable explosion.

If she died, he would die too.

Her world whitened, mind spiralling higher, and Anyar forgot where she was as she followed a burst of energy into the depth of a Knowing. A fleeting dissipation of darkness left her feeling pure and content.

Anyar relaxed at the moment of release.

Chapter Forty-Three

Sadir rushed up the stairs with Jelm at her side, and into the hall. People throughout the room were helping the wounded, moving bodies and debris. She focussed on a group at the bottom of the stairs leading to the third floor.

"Where's Anyar? Where's my daughter? Why aren't you with her?" she demanded, staring accusingly at Boidea and Lan.

Boidea glanced up the stairs, before holding up her hands to halt the approaching couple.

"She's up there. The Mlana's up there. We can't interfere."

"What! She's my daughter." Sadir tried to push past.

"No, Sadir," said Lan. "As much as it pains me, there are events bigger than us happening. We must wait, not distract the Mlana from what she must do."

"Jelm?" Sadir swung back into his arms. "Help me."

It began as a sibilant inrush of air, hissing through the large room, drawing up the stairs, rushing through the tower and into the night. Sadir saw a mass of odours full of the shadowy secondary scents flowing past, twisting in a glutinous, insubstantial mass.

She felt the tug on her body and her brain as the scents left her, dragged by the enormous pull from above. Cries from her companions came faintly as she struggled with the feeling. They were all frozen, standing, fighting this massive unravelling of scent from their beings. Something momentous was happening, and her daughter was at the centre of it.

Even as she held onto Jelm while he suffered in the same way, she saw a large brown shape tear through the motionless people, bumping them aside in its haste to dash up the stairs. It snapped her out of her introspection.

"Anyar!" she called and pushed after the voral.

She noticed the stars around her, huge balls of energy as she floated wraith-like in the heavens. It mattered little as she drifted, content in her state, nothing impinging, time of no consequence.

Slowly she became aware of others in her consciousness, gentle, loving voices whispering, encouraging. She chose to ignore them until they became more insistent and irritating, turning her thoughts from her contemplation of being. In the confusion of words, she recognised a voice which caused her to focus, that of a wise person she once knew.

Alethea, she remembered. Her thoughts came tumbling back, bringing with them awareness. She remembered more: the significant events that had brought her to this point, the people who relied upon her, her home. Her thoughts coalesced into a fleshy envelope. She felt her body, insubstantial at first, then solid, cold. And a pulling at her mind, familiar yet demanding, bringing her towards it.

Something pushed into her hand, cold and wet, coarse fur under her fingers. She smiled as she slumped over the solid, warm body of the voral, there on the freezing stone on the heights of the tower.

Home.

Blood pulsing through her warm body, lying in a soft bed, a long solid shape pressing against her legs. Sounds came to her, the murmurs of people, the feel of a hand smoothing her forehead. She tried to draw in scents, but none came.

Anyar reluctantly opened her eyes.

"She's awake!" called the owner of the hand stroking her brow. "My daughter's awake."

"Mother?" her voice croaked.

"Mlana, you're alive."

"Hmm, it seems that I am, Boidea." Anyar tried to shift herself up in the large bed, but a low growl forestalled her.

"Vor!" she exclaimed, driving a hand into the voral's fur. "You're here. How?"

Vor gave a toothy grin and dropped his head back on the bed.

Pillows piled beneath her head gave her a view around a large bed chamber, a room she had been in years before. She smiled up at Jelm, the owner of the room, belatedly noticing his arm around her mother's waist.

Sadir lifted her daughter's head and held a cup to her mouth.

"Mmm, thank you. My mouth was very dry."

"No wonder, with all you've been through," said Lan. "Shall we talk about it, or do you want to rest?"

"Just let me know how things are; my uncle and my friends?"

"Well, Kyel and Cathar are in another room. He was injured but should recover."

"Ah," she sighed.

"Many good people were lost in this campaign, including Regna, but the fighting has ceased, and the enemy rounded up. The disappearance of Jakus aided that. We were unable to find him, Anyar. Only you and the voral were on the walkway. No Jakus."

"No, I don't suppose there was," she murmured, then looked at the enquiring eyes around her.

"I thank Regna for that. Jakus—or should I say *Septus*—fought me on the walkway. He pushed Vor over the edge, then attacked me.

"Septus was fully in possession of Jakus' body, as some of you realise. It was him that I fought. His power was unbelievable for a creature that had taken over many before him; even my father."

Sadir gasped.

"Then he wanted me; my body," Anyar looked solemnly around the room. "And he almost managed it."

"But how could he, Mlana? You are the Mlana, the most powerful person ever," said Boidea. "How could he, without shadow scent, do that?"

"We'll never know," she continued. "Something to do with the strength he drew on in his death throes, and magnesa; the scent power of that creature was phenomenal.

"So, he was overwhelming me, even with all my shadow scent working for me. It was then I realised what Regna had done to Heritis. That's what worked."

"I think I know," said Boidea. "That would explain what's happened to the scents. If you haven't noticed, our scent power is down now, not working. You destroyed his scent with shadow scent, just like Regna. But…"

"Yes, Boidea. I didn't die, although I thought I could." Anyar smiled into her mother's horrified face. "In the depths of our fight I reached into the very essence of shadow scent, continuously countering everything Septus threw at me. Regna did the same to Heritis, unravelling his scent, his very essence, but unfortunately, she overreached her abilities, and they destroyed each other.

"Me? I had to reach into the world of scent, not realising just how powerful Septus was. I started a chain reaction which I couldn't, and wouldn't, stop. All the strength and power of scent magic from our world drained into us. It was too much for us to survive."

"So, my Anyar," murmured Sadir, "how are you here? With me?"

"I think my advantage was those who had gone before; the Mlanas. They were there, with me, in my fight. They protected me from annihilation. That's all I can imagine."

"I've been thinking," said Lethnal, "about what you said and the distinct lack of scent power here, in Nebleth. It seems like a chain reaction has led to an unravelling of scent, impacting on all, even the Sutanites. While there are hints of it remaining with the healers and other 'good' people, just how far afield it has gone, who can say?

"Scent power, in whatever form it returns to us, is certainly something worth cherishing for the future."

"Mmm." Anyar yawned and smiled. Vor lifted his head and growled at those around the bed as Anyar's eyes closed.

They stood in a busy city, the restoration work of Port Saltus aided substantially by the many Sutanites around them, all dressed in the earthen colours of the citizenry. Black cloaks, a symbol of the hated Sutanite scent masters, had been burnt with the bodies of the dead in the funeral pyres of Nebleth and the port city. Those who did not commit to the change were kept isolated until a decision about their future could be made.

Ships were being raised and repaired, and the air was full of promise under the blue sky of early summer.

"Once again we are here to say goodbye," said Lan to the group of people around him. "But this time, we say goodbye with the promise of a prosperous future.

"Anyar—or should I say *Mlana?*" Lan bowed to the diminutive young woman with the ever-present voral at her side.

Anyar smiled at Lan. "My words are not really needed. We are entering a new age where all lands will be friends and trading partners, headed by responsible people. It has taken much hardship and many lives to get to this point, but we have achieved it.

"We wish you well in your voyage to Sutan, Lan, and hope that you find Xerina in good health; she was a true friend in a hostile country when all was dark around her."

"I feel I know her already," Lan nodded.

"Now, to you, Bilternus. You will return to Sutan and take on your role as leader. Your people have suffered for too long under harsh rulers. Help them. There will be many who will not like the change, so find good people to support you. May you and Sharna be benevolent leaders of Sutan, to bring it to a time of peace after so much turmoil. You will have many people of similar mind with you, plus the guidance of a very wise man, as much as we'll miss him."

Bilternus, his hand clasped in Sharna's, came forward, and they hugged each other. "All I can say is that we'll do our best and hope to have much contact over the coming years—that is, if you can spare the time from all your duties."

"I've many capable friends," Anyar replied, spreading her arms to encompass the teary-eyed Lethnal, her mother and Jelm, Kyel and Cathar, and Boidea.

A shout from Ginrel at the huge, three-masted Sutanite flagship caused them to hug each other again, which only emphasised the continuing absence of scent from their make-up.

"Doesn't seem right, not having our scents working," murmured Lethnal as she watched Lan walk towards the ships with Bilternus and Sharna.

"An acceptable consequence," said Anyar. "Think of what could're been and what we've gained. Besides, there are hints that scent magic may regain some of its loss, but this time it will be in good hands."

"Mlana," said Boidea, "when are you thinking of returning to Rolan?"

"Soon, Boidea," she replied. "Enough of our people have already left to fulfil my role for the time being. In the meantime, I want to enjoy the country of my birth. To travel, see what my father saw, and spend time with my uncle, my mother and their friends."

She saw Eren and Sovira approaching the group from a side street already cleared of the debris of the battles and smiled when she spotted their clasped hands. "And, Boidea, to enjoy some of my lost childhood with my friends."

Anyar, with Vor bounding by her side, walked to meet them.